Hidden in a Whisper

Other Five Star Titles
by Tracie Peterson:

Entangled
A Shelter of Hope

Hidden in a Whisper

Westward Chronicles 2

Tracie Peterson

Five Star • Waterville, Maine

Five Star Christian Fiction Series.

Published in 2002 in conjunction with
Bethany House Publishers.

The text of this edition is unabridged.

Set in 11 pt. Plantin by Al Chase.

Printed in the United States on permanent paper.

Library of Congress Cataloging-in-Publication Data

Peterson, Tracie.
    Hidden in a whisper / by Tracie Peterson.
        p. cm.
    ISBN 0-7862-3678-7 (hc : alk. paper)
    1. Women pioneers—Fiction.   2. New Mexico—Fiction.
    3. Waitresses—Fiction.   I. Title.
    PS3566.E7717 H53 2002
    813'.54—dc21   2001053226

To Ramona
With thanks for the years of friendship—
for walking through dark valleys with me—
for celebrating in the sun.
You are truly a gift from God.

Prologue

Chicago, February 1885

Inevitable. Her mother had said it was inevitable.

Rachel Taylor stared at her gloved hands and tried to imagine what she would say when Braeden made his appearance at the park gazebo. They had met here every Sunday afternoon for the past two months, defying the cold, bitter winds that blew off Lake Michigan. Defying the gossip that surrounded any lady who met a man unaccompanied.

But today would be the last time they would meet.

Her mother had said it was inevitable that a dashingly handsome man of means such as Braeden Parker would find himself attracted to women of more physical beauty and social standing than Rachel could boast. And so it had happened—at least according to the women who boarded in her mother's house. The esteemed Mr. Parker was seen to have been in the company of a rather wealthy and beautiful blond socialite. Not only in her company, but in her arms—maybe even her bed, as some suggested.

It hardly seemed to matter that Braeden also inhabited Rachel's heart and would for as long as she lived. But fate seemed cruel and God rather distant on the matter.

Rachel considered herself plain and at times even unpleasant with her curly auburn hair and green eyes, but Braeden had pledged to her his love and showered her with words of admiration and praise. He had likened her ruddy

7

complexion to the blush of a rose. Her green eyes, he had said, were like twin emeralds burning with the fire of adventure and love of life. He saw in her the epitome of perfection. At least that was what he had told her.

Rachel rose and walked to the gazebo railing. Pieces of white paint were chipping away, evidence that the winter had been unduly harsh. Life was unduly harsh, she decided.

She sighed, trying to pretend that this wasn't the most difficult day of her life. Her head ached with a dull pounding that seemed to permeate her every thought. The pulsating beat was driving her mad. *Fool! Fool! Fool!* It seemed to beat in a driving rhythm. Rubbing her temple with gloved fingers, Rachel closed her eyes, hoping, even praying that when she opened them again she would find it was nothing more than a nightmare.

But opening her eyes revealed the culmination of her pain. Even now she could see Braeden making his way down the cobblestone path. He whistled a tune and it carried on the chilly, damp breeze, reaching Rachel's ear as a painful reminder of what she was about to lose.

It seemed destiny had mapped for her a future that did not include her beloved Braeden.

He waved from the distant walk, then grabbed hold of his bowler just as the wind caught hold of the edge. He smiled as though all was right with the world. Perhaps he had hoped she would never find out about his secret—certainly he had never figured on her putting an end to their romance. But then, ending their romance had been the furthest thing from Rachel's mind as well.

Only a year ago Rachel lost her father, a rail yard worker, in a tragic accident. Crushed between two freight cars, he had died within moments of the impact, love for his wife and daughter the final things he had spoken of. Rachel still found it difficult to believe he was gone. He had doted upon her as his precious little princess, and Rachel had found herself rather accustomed to his spoiling.

Her mother, now widowed and forced to turn her home into a boardinghouse, busied herself with her friends, listening to one tale of woe or another, encouraging news from the neighborhood, and reveling in the information. Always given to seeking out the latest tidbits on the community, the boardinghouse made this lifestyle even more productive, and Elvira Taylor always knew what was happening well before anyone else. That's why Rachel couldn't doubt her now. As much as it grieved her, Rachel knew her mother was seldom wrong when it came to telling tales on other folks. She didn't share this latest information with Rachel to be mean or malicious; in her mind she was simply looking out for her only daughter. Her hope was to keep a young and vulnerable Rachel from falling in love with a man who would only use her and then discard her for someone else.

Her mother believed there was nothing wrong with sharing the news of one person's mishap or another's triumph. The neighborhood was her personal domain, and everything that took place was of the utmost importance. It didn't matter that the preacher spoke out against gossip on Sunday mornings. As far as Elvira Taylor was concerned, it was her civic duty to know the lives of her neighbors. After her husband's death, this duty only became more prominent and essential. Her mother clung to her friends while Rachel had turned to Braeden for comfort. But no more.

Braeden had nearly crossed the park, and Rachel turned her attention back to the water of Lake Michigan—fearful that if she did otherwise, she might betray her misery.

God help me, she prayed. At twenty-one, the last thing she wanted was to turn down the prospect of marriage to the man she loved. But at twenty-one she was also old enough to understand that emotions counted for very little when it came to committing your life to another person. Her mother constantly reminded her of her gullible nature—her willingness to believe the best about everyone. Rachel had thought it was Christian charity that allowed for this, but her mother said it was immaturity and lack of life experience. She supposed, given the most recent events of her life, that this fact was well proven.

"You must be half frozen," Braeden said, ascending the steps to the gazebo. "I shall have to warm you up."

She could hear the teasing in his voice without even turning to greet him. She bit her lip for courage. What should she say? How could she explain? Once she turned to face him, he would see the redness of her eyes and guess that she had been crying.

As if understanding something was wrong, Braeden's voice changed. "Rachel? What is it?" He turned her gently to face him and his voice became more pleading. "Has something happened? Is it your mother?"

Rachel shook her head and forced herself to meet his gaze. Her heart seemed to shatter. She had thought it already broken, but it wasn't until just now, seeing him face-to-face, that she knew her heart was completely destroyed. She would never love again.

"Then what is it?" he asked, the compassion evident in his voice.

Rachel studied him for a moment in silence. She wanted to memorize everything about him—his blue eyes, fringes of golden hair at the base of his bowler. She wanted to remember the squareness of his jaw, the prominent nose, and thick blond moustache. She wanted to take these things with her—to hide them in her heart for those long, lonely nights when the memories came to haunt her and her conscience taunted her that perhaps she had not made the right choice.

"I'm afraid this is good-bye," she said, her voice barely a whisper. Funny, she thought. In a whisper of hearsay her future had been destroyed. Now in a whisper she would bid her love farewell.

His expression changed from compassion to confusion. "What are you saying?"

"I'm saying that I cannot marry you."

"Am I entitled to a reason?" he asked gently yet urgently.

Rachel shook her head. "I believe you know the reason, and speaking of it would only give me pain."

Braeden's brows raised. "No, I don't know the reason, and as much as I am loath to cause you pain, I must know what divides us."

Rachel turned back to the railing. "I have been given some information."

"Do you mean gossip?" he questioned sarcastically. He pulled her around and forced her to look at him. "What has your mother told you this time?"

"Leave her out of this!" Rachel demanded.

"Why? Is she not the reason you are breaking our engagement?"

"We are not yet formally engaged."

"We are enough so that our hearts are one. Or so I thought."

"I thought so too," Rachel said, her voice quivering. She was desperately close to tears. "Apparently you have different plans. Would you have kept your other friend on as a mistress once we were married? Or would I have suffered the fate of mistress while you married her?"

"I have no idea what you are speaking of," Braeden replied.

11

"You were seen with another woman. A lovely blond-haired woman of means."

Braeden shook his head in confusion. "I don't know what you're talking about."

"Oh?" Rachel replied, moving away from him and pulling her cloak tight. "You were seen in her arms at the Tourey Hotel as you made your way up the stairs to . . ." Her voice broke off.

"What?" Braeden paused, as if trying to remember the scene. "You can't believe for one moment—"

"I didn't want to believe," Rachel interjected. "But my mother's best friend saw you with her own eyes. She was at Tourey with a group of women from the church to meet the choir director and his wife. They all saw you, Braeden."

"It isn't what you think. It's nothing more than a misunderstanding. I swear to you." He came to her and reached out to take hold of her.

"There have been other times," Rachel replied. "It isn't the first time someone has come to me about you being in the company of other women."

"Of course I've been in the company of other women. I move about in many circles of friends, family, and business acquaintances. How can I help but be in the company of women?"

"You know it is more than that."

"No, I don't. Why don't you explain it to me."

Rachel twisted away. "I know I'm not a wealthy woman, nor am I beautiful and endowed with elegance and graceful charm. But I am a woman of my word, and I expect to be treated with honesty. If you had found another woman more suitable to your interests, you could have simply told me. I would have been hurt, but not like I am now."

Braeden's expression changed yet again, and this time

Rachel recognized the anger in his eyes. "You would believe those ninny-headed women who live to tell tales and spread all matter of story over me?"

"My mother wouldn't lie to me," Rachel protested.

"Your mother wasn't there, according to you. She simply took the observation of her friend."

"You weren't at the Tourey Hotel last Friday?" she asked, seriously considering that he might be telling the truth.

Braeden's face paled. "I was there, but it was on business." He sounded guilty to Rachel, even as he spoke the words.

"You are a prosperous accountant," Rachel said softly. "You are handsome and easily hold the attention of most any woman who comes into your presence. I do not blame you for finding someone more beautiful, more fitting to your status." Tears filled her eyes as she moved toward the steps of the gazebo. "But I do blame you for the deceit."

"And I blame you for destroying our love with mistrust!" Braeden declared. "How dare you come to me on a matter of such grave importance and base your entire decision on nothing more than the words of hearsay! Love requires trust. Have you not learned that in your twenty-one years?"

"I've learned a great deal in my twenty-one years," Rachel replied sarcastically. "My father was a good teacher, even if my mother tended toward gossip, as you are so good to point out. Perhaps the most important thing my father taught me was that men often deceive innocent young women in order to get something that should never have been theirs to begin with."

"Are you accusing me of less than proper behavior?" Braeden questioned.

Rachel quickly walked down the stairs and started up the cobblestone walkway. Braeden was at her side before she had taken five full steps. He grabbed hold of her arm and turned her to face him.

"Answer me," he said, his face only inches from her own. "Has my behavior not spoken for itself? I have treated you with nothing but gentleness and respect. I didn't even kiss you until you agreed to become my wife."

Rachel trembled from his touch. She was so under his power that it became imperative to get away from him before she changed her mind and agreed to believe him over her mother. "You stole that kiss, along with my heart," she murmured. "But you'll get no other part of me. Now leave me to go in peace."

He dropped his hold. "Then go," he said, his voice edged with pain and regret. "Go and listen to your stories and lies and let them keep you warm on a cold winter's night. Let them speak to your heart when you are lonely and sad."

Rachel said nothing more. She pushed up the walkway, praying he would not come after her. If only he had denied being at the Tourey, she might have believed it a case of mistaken identity. But he hadn't denied it, and something in that helped her to believe that she was justified in ending their engagement.

A light snow began to fall as the sun was swallowed up by heavy gray clouds. Tomorrow she would board a train for Topeka, Kansas. She would accept the position offered her by a friend of the family, becoming a trainee for the Harvey Company restaurants along the Santa Fe Railroad. And she would forget that Chicago and Braeden Parker ever existed.

Chapter 1

August 1891
Morita, New Mexico Territory

Rachel stared at the gathering of twenty-five black-and-white-clad Harvey Girls and smiled. In six years of service she had reached what many considered the unobtainable position of house manager for the Harvey House Restaurant at Casa Grande Resort. It hadn't been that long since she'd sat where these frightened, fresh-faced girls now sat. She could remember her early days of training in Topeka, Kansas, as if it were yesterday. Standards and decorum, Harvey rules and regulations . . . all of these were drilled and enforced until she could recite them in her sleep. And now it was her job to instruct others.

"If everyone will quiet down," she said rather sternly, "we will begin."

Those who weren't already seated made their way to one of the empty dining room chairs as a hush embraced the room.

"My name is Miss Taylor, and I am the manager of this Harvey House dining room. Casa Grande, as you probably already know, will have its grand opening in three weeks, and we need to be ready." Rachel moved around the room, inspecting the girls.

"All of you have had training in Topeka, and most of you have worked at least six months or more elsewhere on the line. There are a couple of less-experienced girls joining us, however, and I want to make it clear that these employees are no less valuable in my eyes and should be treated with the same respect afforded someone who has been with the company for years." The girls nodded and continued to watch Rachel with expressions that betrayed their curiosity and excitement.

Rachel enjoyed getting to know her girls in a collective group, as well as interacting with them one at a time on a more personal level. People reacted differently depending on the audience, and Rachel had learned to recognize troublemakers and those who would refuse to take the job seriously by watching them respond in a group setting.

"In a few moments," Rachel continued, "you will each be issued a numbered badge. The badges will be used to identify your employment status in this particular Harvey resort. The initial issuance will be based on your time served in Fred Harvey's company. However, as you progress and perform at levels of extreme competence, you will work your way up and take a higher number."

"Who decides if your work merits a higher position?" a petite blond-haired girl questioned.

"I will," Rachel replied, recognizing Ivy Brooks, the niece of the town's matriarch, Esmeralda Needlemeier. Ivy had already shown herself to be a troublemaker of sorts. She had complained about the uniform, argued about not being allowed to fashion her hair in a more appealing style, and generally made everyone around her disgruntled. Rachel tried to have compassion on the girl, for she was an orphan. Life had dealt her a heavy blow, and Rachel knew full well how that could harden a person's heart. Nevertheless, Ivy would have to comply with the rules, just like everyone else. It was imperative for the running of Mr. Harvey's restaurants.

"Miss Brooks, you will come to realize that everything that has to do with you and your position here will pass through my review. Very soon I will appoint a head waitress who will be your immediate supervisor in matters taking place on the dining room floor. She will also help me to determine who might qualify for a step up in the ranks."

"And who will that be?" Ivy challenged.

"I've not yet decided," Rachel countered, steadily losing her patience. At twenty-seven, Rachel found herself rather intolerant of sassy teenagers. Ivy was barely eighteen and had been allowed to accelerate her training in Topeka and take a coveted position at Casa Grande only because her aunt owned the town and had sold Fred Harvey and the Santa Fe Railroad the land on which the resort had been built. The old woman was to be esteemed and coddled at every turn because of some undone business dealings with the Santa Fe. Ivy knew this and counted on it, but Rachel was undaunted. She would fire the presumptuous teen without remorse or outside influence if she refused to pull her weight. This issue was clearly addressed in one of her many meetings with Esmeralda Needlemeier.

"Miss Taylor?" a dark-headed girl spoke up.

"Yes, Miss Whitehurst?" Rachel questioned, trying hard to keep the correct name with the right girl.

"What type of things will merit a promotion? And, if you go up a number or two, what happens to the girl whose number you take? Will she assume your number?"

Rachel again came to stand directly in front of the girls. "Each girl will be judged according to her service, attitude, and even her reputation and actions away from the dining room. Your ranking will be determined by your actions. If the girl wearing the number four badge does her job but conducts herself in an improper manner off duty, she will no doubt slide down several notches and others will rise to take her place. And if the girl at number twenty performs in an exemplary manner, while those above her merely squeak by doing what little they can, she will be promoted and they will lose their standing.

"Mr. Harvey is very concerned that we represent ourselves in the utmost of propriety. You are hired here and paid the generous sum of nearly twenty dollars a month and given your clothing, room, and board. And you will generally receive tips from the patrons you service. Your laundry will be collected and done for you, and you will be given one day a week to do with as you please. At the end of your contract, you will receive a pass to go anywhere the Santa Fe Railroad can take you and given time to visit your family or friends.

"In return, Mr. Harvey asks that every customer who comes to dine at Casa Grande, or any other Harvey House for that matter, be treated with the utmost respect and consideration. He demands complete attention be given the rules he has set up, and the design of training for service must be strictly followed."

She watched each of the young women carefully as she continued to explain their duties. "You will report to your station in the dining room by five o'clock each morning. You will be properly attired in your uniform, your hair neatly contained in a hairnet, and your face void of any powder or paint to enhance your beauty. If I have reason to believe you are wearing cosmetics upon your face, I will not hesitate to take a wet towel to your face and confirm my suspicions. You will then be sent back to your room to repair yourself, and you will be issued demerits for your behavior. It is this type of thing, a blatant disregard for the rules, which will see you lose your standing."

In spite of how she tried, Rachel couldn't help but refocus her attention on Ivy Brooks. "No one will be given special favor for any reason other than meriting it for themselves through their work. If I find that you have done a good job on your assigned tasks, you will continue to be valued as an employee. If I find that you have done an excellent job, I will so note and merit your performance. If you should perform in a manner that goes far above and beyond those tasks for which you are responsible, your actions will also be noted and remembered for consideration during such times when promotions are available or bonuses of extra time off are issued."

She then explained Fred Harvey's concept of treating each customer as though they were in the finest restaurant in New York City instead of a small resort in a New Mexico town. Several of the girls asked questions regarding the resort and the hours of the dining room, and as Rachel concluded her talk and began handing out the numbered badges, she answered their concerns. She noted the frown on Ivy's face as she issued her the number twenty-five.

"To begin with, we will assign your work based on hotel occupation. If the resort is full, we will need to maintain a larger staff and therefore your shift may well run twelve hours. If the hotel is less than half full, you will probably be assigned to work one of two shifts. The first shift lasting from five o'clock in the morning until one o'clock, the second shift running from noon until nine that evening. If there should be a special party or festivity such as a dance or a banquet, then you will be assigned according to need. Now, I'd like everyone to go to your stations and acquaint yourself with the duties at each place. I have assigned you based on your experience. After this, we will do a run-down on serving procedures and hotel etiquette."

Rachel gave an inaudible sigh of relief as most of the girls went quietly to their proper stations. Some would be responsible for serving drinks, others for taking orders for meals, and there would be linens to care for and silver to polish, along with a dozen other jobs both great and small. It was no easy feat to run a restaurant to Fred Harvey's demands. Of course, the biggest responsibility given the girls would be their service of the customers. There was additional kitchen staff to help with the odd jobs, but the art of greeting, serving, and seeing to the needs of the resort visitors would fall upon the shoulders of these soberly dressed young women.

Rachel watched them silently for a few moments. Her memories took her back to her arrival in Topeka and the training she'd endured to become a Harvey Girl. The training had been rigorous and demanding, but the work was very satisfying, and Rachel always made wonderful tips in addition to her regular pay. She often found herself the envy of other girls in her house because the regular customers went out of their way to wait for Rachel's service, and the visiting customers always seemed to tip more generously at her tables than at any other. To Rachel, it was nothing more than taking an interest in their needs. She listened to them talk, as much as time would permit. And given the fact that they served four-course meals in thirty minutes or less, it didn't allow for much in the way of idle conversation. Casa Grande, however, would be different. There would be more of an atmosphere of relaxation, although there would be the occasional rush to catch a train. Most of the train traffic would wait until Albuquerque before putting their customers through the paces of the routine Harvey service, but Casa Grande was a resort for relaxation and restoration. Rachel shook her head at this thought, knowing that personally it would probably not afford her either pleasure.

But I took this job on knowing it would be a challenge. I am the first woman to be allowed to manage the restaurant of a resort hotel, and as such, I must keep my wits about me and show them they've not been mistaken to take such a risk with me.

Rachel knew the hardest part wouldn't be keeping up with the job. The hardest part would be the long, lonely nights of isolation. Ever since her first promotion to head waitress, Rachel had known the pain of being separated from the crowd. She made friends easily, but as the waitress in charge, she often had to rebuke those friends. This in turn inevitably created hard feelings and conflicts. There were exceptions and a few friends had remained, but Rachel had never known it to be enough. She knew the emptiness of a life unfulfilled. A life lacking what she most desired—a husband and family. Refusing to let her emotions get carried away, Rachel refocused her attention on the girls. There were some very promising young women in her group, and she had little doubt that the affairs of the dining room would run smoothly in no time at all.

After allowing the girls to acquaint themselves with their duties, Rachel put them into teams, with one of the more experienced girls heading up each group. They practiced being customers and servers in order that they might have an understanding of the days to come.

With the girls duly occupied, Rachel made her way into the kitchen and found Reginald Worthington reorganizing his new kitchen. A refined gentleman in his forties, Worthington cut a striking figure in the sterile kitchen. Rachel had thought him a handsome man upon the occasion of their introduction, and seeing him now only confirmed her assessment. His brown hair, parted down the middle and slicked back with tonic water, was no less orderly than his kitchen, and his eyes, dark brown and quite appealing, seemed to take in everything around him in a manner that suggested he might well be taking inventory.

"Ah, Mr. Worthington," Rachel announced with a smile, "I'd like to introduce you to the girls when you have a chance."

The tall, slender Englishman glanced up from where he sorted through his knives and returned her smile. "Miss Taylor, I would be delighted."

He put the knives away in exacting order while Rachel watched him in fascination. He knew precisely where he wanted each instrument and assigned it a proper place in no less detail than Rachel had used to assign her girls.

"Well, then," he said, coming from around the massive preparation table. "Let us be about our business."

Rachel nodded. "The girls, as you know, will report to the head waitress and ultimately to me. Should you have trouble with any of them, I would appreciate it if you would bring the issue to me rather than try to deal with it yourself. As chef, you will have a free hand with the kitchen staff, but the girls are strictly my responsibility."

Worthington laughed. "And happy is the man who knows his place."

"I beg your pardon?" Rachel questioned before opening the door to the dining room.

"I'm very glad they are your responsibility," he replied soberly. "I would no more know how to deal with their tears and tempers than I would know how to construct a building. Women are a peculiarity to me, and save a quiet relationship with my dearly departed mother, I am at quite a loss to determine exactly how to conduct myself with them."

Rachel nodded. "I wouldn't worry overmuch about it. We often feel the same way about men."

"Do tell," Worthington replied, his thin moustache quivering ever so slightly at the tips as a hint of a smile played upon his lips. "I can't imagine you suffering from that feeling."

Rachel looked away, not willing for him to see that the same words that amused him caused her to feel a sharp pang of regret and pain. "I assure you, Mr. Worthington, the enigma regarding men and women is mutually acknowledged and endured."

She moved through the swinging kitchen doors into the dining room, where her girls were still working amicably together.

"Ladies!" she called, and all heads turned to her. "I would like to introduce the chef for Casa Grande. This is Mr. Worthington. He comes to us from a very prestigious New York hotel at the insistence of the Santa Fe management. His culinary skills are highly regarded, and he will no doubt bring to Casa Grande a flavor of the European continent as he has trained in Paris, Milan, Madrid, and his own native London. You will heed his instruction regarding the serving and preparation of food; however, should any problems arise regarding your conduct, Mr. Worthington will not hesitate to bring the matter to my attention."

"I'm delighted to make your acquaintance," the Englishman said, his accent clearly marking his origins. "I shall endeavor to better know each of you as our duties require."

Rachel thanked Worthington, then turned to address her girls as he returned to the kitchen. "I believe it is necessary to restate something for your benefit as well as for mine. There is to be absolutely no fraternizing of Harvey Girls with male staff members. You are under contract to Mr. Harvey, and in being so, you agree to refrain from marrying before your contract is up. Those of you who have been with the Harvey system for longer than the initial contract realize the importance of these rules. They are for your own good," Rachel told them, but her mind was taken back to a time when she had been young and in love. Who could have possibly convinced her that such rules were wise and necessary?

It was hard to convince the heart that some matters were

better left unexplored. She would, if she could, advise each and every woman before her to avoid romantic entanglements at all costs. Nothing was quite as hard on the spirit as realizing that the only dream you had dared to allow yourself would never come true. And, as far as Rachel was concerned, nothing lasted longer or hurt more than a broken heart. Which was the case with Braeden Parker. Even the mention of his name—the single thought of his smile—caused Rachel to tear up, even as she was just now. Coughing, she excused herself and appointed Gwen Carson, a young woman she'd trained several years earlier in Topeka and the one to whom she'd given the number one badge, to take over supervising the girls in their duties.

Back in the silence of her office, Rachel took several deep breaths and forced her emotions to reorder themselves to their proper places. She would not allow Braeden's memory to destroy her happiness. She couldn't. He was in the past and that was where he would stay. No matter the cost.

Chapter 2

Two days later, as the girls finished cleaning the dining room after practicing a supper service on area railroad men and hotel staff, Ivy Brooks watched as Rachel took Gwen Carson aside to discuss some matter in private.

This has to stop, Ivy thought. *It's bad enough Gwen gets the number one badge while I have twenty-five. I won't be able to stand it if Miss Taylor assigns head waitress to her as well.*

She finished washing down the last table in her assigned area, then turned to see what her newest follower, Faith Bradford, was doing. Faith, a short, skinny nineteen-year-old whose immaturity irritated Ivy, stood listening to two of the other more experienced Harvey Girls explain their way of clearing a table. Faith, being the rather mindless twit that she was, would be the perfect victim to Ivy's plots and schemes. Manipulating such a creature would hardly be a challenge at all, but then, it was better that way. Faith would do as she was told without question, and Ivy would never have to worry about informing Faith of her comings and goings, especially when those activities kept her out past the ten-o'clock curfew.

Ivy smiled to herself. *I might be the most inexperienced Harvey Girl on staff at Casa Grande, but if I have my way, it soon won't matter.*

When Rachel finished with Gwen, she made another

boring speech about the details of Fred Harvey's beloved system. Ivy found the entire matter unimportant. Her only reason for demanding that her aunt Esmeralda allow her to work as a Harvey waitress was in order to set herself up to acquire a wealthy eastern husband. The railroad restaurants owned by Harvey were, as she had noted in the local paper, notorious for bringing couples together. Ivy would have seen this as an answer to prayer—if she'd been the type to issue such requests. A husband would be the answer to all of her problems. He would be rich enough to see her kept in a fashionable style, with all the comforts she could possibly desire, and he would live somewhere other than Morita, New Mexico. These were the most important requisites for the man she would marry.

Rachel concluded with some sort of nonsense about the Harvey Girls keeping themselves spotless at all times. As if a person working in and around food and sloppy diners could be responsible for such a matter. She further enraged Ivy by instructing that should their uniforms become stained or spotted, they were to immediately retire to their bedrooms and quickly change their clothes. The idea was ludicrous, but Ivy kept her mouth closed on the matter. She wanted and intended to have the head waitress job in spite of her inexperience. She might be new to the system, but her aunt was wealthy and influential, and Ivy intended to use that to her benefit. Already she'd penned her aunt a letter and sent it by way of one of the hotel maids. Esmeralda might have stupid notions about making Morita into some sort of desert oasis, but Ivy knew she was capable of even more impossible feats and intended to enlist her aunt's help in the matter. Until then, Ivy planned to bide her time, doing what she could to ease her discomfort while plotting to change the Harvey system.

When Rachel dismissed them with high praise for a job well done, Ivy grabbed hold of Faith's arm and fairly dragged her back to their room.

"We need to talk," she told Faith, and the easily influenced girl simply nodded her head enthusiastically and followed after her new mentor.

Once inside the small bedroom, Ivy began stripping off the hated white apron and black skirt and shirtwaist. "I am embarrassed to have to be seen this way," she said, unbuttoning her skirt. "I believe Mr. Harvey to be unusually cruel to dress us as nuns in a church."

"At least we don't have to pay for the uniforms," Faith offered in a singsong voice. She plopped down on her bed and smiled.

Ivy cut her with a glance. She knew the power of a look and had spent many an hour crafting her expressions to be just right. "You fool. It certainly doesn't excuse the fact that I must go about looking ridiculous while handsome men of influence and fortune make their way about the resort grounds."

"I don't understand," Faith replied, her tone more modest and sober.

Ivy pulled the net from her hair and unpinned her thick blond hair. Shaking it out, she reached for her hairbrush and began to stroke through the lengthy mane. "I couldn't care less about Mr. Harvey or his rules and his resort," she explained. "I'm simply here to get a husband of means and to leave this sad excuse for a town behind me."

"Oh," stated Faith as though such an idea made no sense whatsoever. The puzzled look on her face made Ivy frown.

"Why did you come to this job, Faith?"

The girl brightened a bit. "Because my family thought it would do me good."

"And has it?" Ivy asked, halting her brush long enough to consider Faith's response.

The girl shrugged. "I don't know."

Ivy wondered if the girl had a single thought in her head that hadn't been previously placed there by someone else.

"Well, I wouldn't count on it doing you much good, unless you're looking for a husband. I certainly don't intend to wait on people and serve meals the rest of my life, and frankly, polishing silver is something the servants will do when I have a home of my own." She resumed her brushing, stroking the cornsilk-colored hair until it crackled. "And I will never again wear black and white, at least not in this capacity."

She put the brush down and finished undressing until she stood in nothing but her lace-edged chemise, silk corset, and drawers. Positioning her hands on her tiny waist, Ivy gave a twirl.

"I won't grow old in this town. I won't be an ugly spinster and boss other girls around like Miss Taylor does. *I* shall have a beautiful mansion in St. Louis or Chicago and fifty servants to wait on me hand and foot."

Faith giggled. "And beautiful clothes of taffeta and silk."

Ivy stopped and smiled. "Yes, and jewels and lavish finery enough to make all of my friends green with envy. But first I have to find a proper husband, and I must have a position of merit at this resort."

"A position of merit?" Faith asked, reaching up to take her own hairnet off.

"Yes. I want to be the head waitress, and with my aunt's help, I will be just that."

"But Miss Taylor said—"

"I don't much care what Miss Taylor said," Ivy retorted. "She may believe that plain little mouse Gwendolyn Carson

28

is entitled to the position by right of her three years with the Harvey Company, but I shall see how she reacts when my aunt Esmeralda instructs her to give the position to me. My aunt is a powerful woman, and she will see things my way."

"How exciting!" Faith declared. "When will you talk to her?"

"As soon as we manage to set up a little bit of a complication in the life of Gwendolyn Carson," Ivy said, going to the closet to thumb through her regular clothes. She chose a pale pink dressing gown and slipped into it without saying another word.

She would devise a plan—a plan that would put Gwen on poor terms with those around her. But how? Ivy mused over the problem for several minutes before coming up with a plan.

"Of course," she said with a smile. "Faith, I shall need your help."

"My help?" the girl questioned, a stunned look on her face.

Ivy rolled her eyes. "Yes. Your help. We need to make Gwen look bad, and I have the perfect solution. She will steal your hairbrush."

"*My* hairbrush? But it's right here in my drawer," Faith said, getting up to open the drawer of her tiny dresser. She reached in and held it up for Ivy to see.

"Yes, I know it is," Ivy replied in irritation. "But we shall hide it among Gwen's things, then declare it missing. When Miss Taylor searches the rooms, she will find it, and Gwen will no longer be quite so favored." Ivy knit her brows together as she continued to consider this. "Of course, that might not be enough. We might have to do this several times. Maybe we could find something really valuable and hide it in

Gwen's room. Maybe some jewelry from one of the guests."

Faith's expression revealed her confusion. "Steal from the guests?"

"If we need to," Ivy replied, finishing up the buttons on her gown. "Look, give me your brush and I'll sneak across the hall and hide it under Gwen's pillow."

"But it's my only brush," Faith protested.

"You shall have it back before an hour's time," Ivy countered, snatching the thing from her roommate's hand. "You'll see. Just go along with me in this, and I'll remember you fondly when I'm the head waitress."

Faith smiled. "Truly?"

"Absolutely," Ivy replied. "You shall be second only to me."

"Oh, how wonderful!"

Ivy smiled. "Yes," she murmured.

Going to the door, Ivy opened it just a crack and listened. Faith watched her and looked about to speak, but Ivy put her finger to her lips. She couldn't believe how dim-witted the girl really was. But then, a smart girl might not have agreed so willingly to Ivy's schemes. Sometimes a person simply had to utilize whatever was at hand in order to accomplish what they desired.

"Oh bother!" Ivy said, leaning back against the wall. "Gwen and several other girls are talking at the other end of the hall."

With their room positioned at one end of the hall and Gwen's room directly across from theirs, Ivy had only worried about the fact that Rachel's office and suite were positioned between the two rooms capping the hallway that served as one of two entrances into the Harvey Girls' dormitory. Now, with the girls gathered to chat at the other end, Ivy knew she would have no chance to slip into the hallway without being seen.

She tried to think about what she should do, but anger was overrunning rational thought. She simply had to put herself into a position of control. Her entire life had been mastered by others, but no more. The past might stand as witness to her previous mistakes—even regrets—but she wouldn't allow it to rule over her. She had made mistakes, but then, everyone did. No, she wouldn't remember the past or bathe herself in sorrows from her losses. She had suffered enough at the hands of those around her. First by her aunt deciding to stay in Morita to find a way to make the town prosper, then at the hands of the Harvey establishment and their personnel.

She peeked again and, seeing things basically the same, sighed and started to close the door.

"Why not just give the thing a quiet shove?" Faith asked. "Just nudge it into the hall and maybe Gwen will pick it up."

Ivy stared at the slightly older girl. "That's a positively brilliant idea."

Faith's face lit up. "Truly! Do you think so?"

Ivy nodded and opened the door enough to slide the hairbrush across the highly polished hall floor. "Perfect!" she exclaimed in a hushed whisper. She waited to see if anyone down the hall noticed her action and when nothing was said, she breathed a sigh of relief. "Now we wait a few moments and see if Gwen picks up the brush when she comes to her room. And if she does, then you must kick up a storm and holler your head off about your missing brush. Make it look good, or Miss Taylor will never believe you."

Faith, still standing on her laurels of having thought up the idea of sliding the brush into the hall, nodded enthusiastically. "I'll do it."

Ivy grinned. This was going to be simple. She narrowed the door opening to a crack and waited.

In a few moments, Gwen appeared outside her room. At first Ivy didn't think she would see the brush in the dimly lit hall, but then, just before she opened her door, Gwen glanced down and noticed the object lying at her feet.

She reached down and picked it up and while she stood observing it, Ivy clued Faith to begin her rantings.

"My brush! My brush!" Faith squealed.

Ivy threw open the door and loudly protested that someone had stolen Faith's hairbrush. The commotion instantly brought Rachel and several of the other Harvey Girls to see what was going on. Gwen stood speechless in the midst of the ruckus, almost as if the suddenness of it all had stunned her.

"What is going on?" Rachel questioned.

"Someone has stolen Faith's hairbrush," Ivy announced.

"Stolen it?" asked Rachel.

"Yes. It was in her drawer here in our room and now it is missing. In order for it to be so, someone would have had to have taken it."

Gwen held up the brush. "Is this it? I just found it here in the hallway."

Ivy scowled and Faith expressed glee. "Yes!" Faith exclaimed. "That's it!"

"Why do you have it?" Ivy asked suspiciously.

"As I said, I just found it here on the floor when I came to my room."

"That makes no sense," Ivy said, hands on hips. "I believe you took it."

"But I didn't!" Gwen protested.

"Now, wait just a minute," Rachel interceded. "There is no sense in accusing someone falsely."

"How can it be falsely?" Ivy asked. "She's holding the object in her hands."

"Yes, but she said it was found on the floor. Isn't it possible that Faith simply dropped it?"

"In the hall?" Ivy's voice held a tone of complete disbelief. "Why in the world would Faith carry her brush to the hall?"

"Well, given that the bathroom is at the end of the hall, perhaps she carried it with her when she took her bath this morning," Rachel offered. The other girls nodded, as this seemed quite reasonable.

"You'll have to be more careful in the future," Rachel told Faith as Gwen handed her the brush. "Now everyone go on about your business and leave off with this nonsense about stealing. We are a family here, and families do not steal from one another. If I should find it to be otherwise, that person would be immediately discharged."

The girls went back to their separate quarters, and Ivy smiled to herself as she closed her bedroom door. She had set the stage and placed Gwen at the center. Now she would simply have to look for other ways to draw attention to her dishonest actions. . . . Perhaps another theft.

"Perhaps a rather large theft," Ivy murmured softly. "One that can't be chalked off to a misplacement on the way to the bathroom."

Chapter 3

The Harvey dining room for Casa Grande bore an air of elegance and refinement that rather startled the senses. Of course, all of Casa Grande was that way. From the artfully crafted brick exterior, complete with sun porches that faced masterfully landscaped gardens, to the rich walnut wood floors and chandelier-lit interiors, Casa Grande was something created from the ancient imaginations of European architects and designers. There was an air of Spanish flavor to the styling of the archways and porches, a presence of French palaces in the lobby and ballroom, and a homey warmth of English manor houses in the fire-warmed library.

For the dining room, Fred Harvey insisted on the very best furnishings. There were elegant sideboards and dining room chairs along with numerous oak tables that could easily seat ten people, sometimes more. The tablecloths were of the finest Irish linen, as were the napkins, which were nearly four times the size that would be found at any other restaurant. The dishes were china, the place settings silver, and the goblets were crystal. But Casa Grande was nothing special in this area. Fred Harvey insisted that his dining rooms bear the same charm and warmth of welcome no matter where they were located along the line.

Charmed completely by this elegance, Rachel enjoyed walking through Casa Grande whenever time allowed. The lobby itself declared an opulent wealth that dazzled the eye. No expense had been spared—from the marble colonnades and tiling to the brass fixtures on the walls and cappings on the marble stair railings. There were oriental rugs on the cream-colored floors with rich, dark walnut furniture upholstered in a golden raw silk. Blended with the red and gold accents of the carpet and furniture, heavy brocade draperies complemented the enormous floor-to-ceiling windows. Rachel knew from experience that the scene transported the person who walked through the doors of Casa Grande from a quaint, dusty village to a wealthy resort.

In spite of the grand opening still being a couple of weeks off, Casa Grande was, even now, aflutter with activity as the girls worked to feed breakfast to a bevy of railroad workers. Rachel felt pleased, in general, with the way things had progressed. She had heard that it might be difficult to pull together a staff of twenty-five girls, especially given that they were experienced in working elsewhere along the line and might expect to do things their own way. The uniform training and regulatory operations of each dining room along the Santa Fe made it easier, however. Every girl knew what was expected of her under the Harvey rules, and because of this, Rachel felt confident that the transition would be fairly simple.

Now if she could just eliminate the pesky problems that seemed to frustrate her efforts. Problems like Ivy Brooks's insistence to stir up strife and problems like . . .

"Miss Taylor!" an elderly voice boomed out, causing all heads to turn toward the main entry doors.

Rachel sighed. Problems like Esmeralda Needlemeier.

Crossing the dining room, Rachel smiled. "Good morning, Mrs. Needlemeier. What may I do for you today?"

"I have come to observe your operations," the older

woman replied, tapping her cane on the hardwood floor.

"We are nearly finished with the morning meal. It was only a trial run for the railroad staff, but if you would like to partake of breakfast, I could check with the chef."

"Mercy, no!" the woman exclaimed. "I've already taken my morning meal. I've merely come to watch you work and to speak to my niece."

"Very well," Rachel replied. "You may take any seat you like."

She watched the elderly woman move across the room to position herself in one of the far corners. Sitting very primly on the edge of the oak dining room chair, Esmeralda Needlemeier observed the room with a critical eye.

Rachel tried to be unaffected by her presence, but the icy blue of Esmeralda's eyes chilled her. The old woman was difficult at best to relate to, but she was nearly impossible to understand. Rachel had tried to extend a warm welcome on many occasions, but inevitably Esmeralda held her at arm's length. *No,* Rachel smiled to herself, *she keeps me at a far greater distance than an arm's length.*

Jeffery O'Donnell, stationmaster for the Santa Fe in Morita and a very dear friend from Rachel's past, had told her that the old woman was key to the success of Casa Grande. She owned most of the land upon which the town surrounding the resort sat, and she appeared to be highly esteemed by the board of directors for the Santa Fe Railroad—especially given that additional negotiations were still in the works. Jeffery had explained that the Santa Fe was dependent upon her good graces since she owned the passageway from the depot to the resort. She also owned the omnibus company that would transport passengers along that same passage.

Rachel thought it rather amusing that one tiny old woman

could cause the mighty Santa Fe Railroad to come to its knees. She glanced up and found Esmeralda frowning in her scrutiny of the operations. She was dressed in black bombazine from the tip of her high-collared jacket to the hem of her skirt. Her snowy white hair had been pulled back in a tight bun, its severity only altered by the application of a rigid black felt hat and veil. Her widow's weeds were reverent attire in the memory of her dearly departed Hezekiah, or so Rachel had been told.

Jeffery explained to Rachel that if they should harbor any ill feelings at all, it should be toward that stately gentleman. Having never sired a child, the man turned his attention instead to siring a town. Morita was that town, and in spite of being located along the Santa Fe Railroad, its close proximity to Albuquerque seemed to keep it from becoming a major stopping place. It was only after Hezekiah Needlemeier's death that Esmeralda took up the issue and went to work to bolster the fledgling town.

When the last of the railroad workers left the dining room, Esmeralda called once again for Rachel.

"What are those girls doing?" she questioned.

Rachel turned to see Gwen and two of the other girls stripping the tablecloths from the tables. "They're taking away the soiled cloths and will wipe down the tables and put on new ones."

"Seems wasteful," Esmeralda declared.

Rachel smiled. "Mr. Harvey says that each guest is to arrive to a freshly set table. The Irish linen tablecloths are to be in pristine order."

"I should speak to this Mr. Harvey about his waste. I have seen the portions of food served by this organization, and it is clearly in excess. Why, one of the steaks took up an entire plate! The man can't make a profit that way."

"I don't believe Mr. Harvey is overly worried about making a profit, Mrs. Needlemeier."

"Ivy! Ivy, come here at once," Esmeralda called out upon seeing her niece. She didn't seem to care about the disruption, nor did she apparently worry about leaving off with her previous conversation.

Ivy approached and kissed her aunt on the cheek. "Why, Aunt Esmeralda, what a surprise!"

Rachel watched their reaction to each other before deciding to slip away and see to the remaining work. Esmeralda, however, would have nothing to do with that.

"I have not finished speaking with you, Miss Taylor," she stated firmly.

"I apologize," Rachel replied. "It's just that I do have responsibilities here and it affords me little time to stand about in discussion." She wanted to make it clear to the old woman that she might have bullied the Santa Fe Railroad into submission, but she wouldn't find it quite so easy to control Rachel Taylor.

"I want to speak to you about my niece. I find it abominable that she should live here in such small quarters. In my home, she has a suite of rooms at her disposal and would no doubt be far more comfortable there."

"No doubt," Rachel countered. "However, I find it is good for the spirit of the group if they live and work together. There are areas along the Santa Fe where some girls live at home while working for Mr. Harvey, but because Ivy is the only one who comes from this area, I thought it might make her feel isolated to suggest such an arrangement. Together, they come to better understand what it is to be a family, and Fred Harvey wants them to act like sisters."

"Poppycock!" the woman replied, tapping her cane on the floor. "My niece is not a farmhand, nor is she a soldier. There seems little to be gained by forcing her to bed herself down as one."

Rachel saw Ivy smile smugly at this declaration. She wondered if the girl had put her aunt up to the task of insisting Ivy be allowed to move back to the Needlemeier mansion. On the other hand, Rachel thought, it just might solve a great many problems. If Ivy were housed elsewhere and merely availed herself for work as her schedule demanded, perhaps she would have less influence over the others.

"Mrs. Needlemeier, I completely agree with your thoughts that the girls are neither farmhands nor soldiers. They are quality workers for Mr. Harvey's dining rooms, and they are expertly trained to act in accordance with his wishes." She smiled at Ivy, feeling the girl's disdain radiate from her dark blue eyes.

"But I see no harm in allowing Ivy to move back home. She would, of course, have to maintain her duties and adhere to the schedule in the strictest manner, but I see no other problem. After all, your estate adjoins the resort gardens, and it is merely a short walk across the footbridge. I see no reason to force Ivy to remain here." Rachel turned her attention completely to Ivy and added, "If that is what she wants."

"No doubt," Ivy whispered none too quietly, "I would be made to suffer for a decision such as that. Perhaps Miss Taylor says it would meet with her approval, but I seriously doubt it does."

Rachel clenched her teeth and refused to be goaded by the younger girl. Ivy maintained a pose of angelic indifference, while Esmeralda considered her words.

"I would not have you treat my niece with hostility."

"I wouldn't dream of it," Rachel countered. "And I would seriously reprimand any girl who would try. As I told my girls when they first arrived, Ivy is not to be treated any differently,

39

neither because of her inexperience with the Harvey system nor because she is your niece. Partiality would only lead to conflict."

Esmeralda seemed to consider this for a moment before nodding. "Yes. Yes, you are correct. Ivy, I believe it would cause a threat of conflict between you and the other workers. However, you may always resign your position. You don't have to work here, and you know it better than anyone."

Ivy frowned, seeming to sense that the tables were starting to turn against her. Rachel smiled pleasantly and leaned closer to Esmeralda. "I'll leave the decision to you and Ivy. After all, we want our girls happy. Now, if you'll excuse me, I must see to my work."

Rachel took herself away from the ordeal, a smile still playing on her lips as she walked into the solid form of Jeffery O'Donnell.

"Jeffery!" she exclaimed, then glanced around her. "I mean, Mr. O'Donnell. Please excuse me, I wasn't paying attention."

Jeffery laughed. "It's quite all right, Miss Taylor." He emphasized her title and gave her a wink. They had been on very informal terms in Topeka, and would be again in moments of privacy, but for now they carried the formalities for the sake of the organization.

Rachel smiled. "How is your wife?"

"Bearing up as well as she can. These first few months are said to be the most trying."

Rachel nodded, a twinge of jealousy coursing through her heart. Simone O'Donnell had become a dear friend during her training in Topeka as a Harvey Girl. Her marriage to Jeffery and their move to Morita had seemed to coincide nicely with Rachel's promotion to house manager for the resort's restaurant. She had even intended for Simone to be her head waitress. That is, until Simone had become pregnant shortly after their wedding. Jeffery wouldn't hear of her working in her condition.

"So what brings you here today?" Rachel questioned.

"I have brought the new hotel manager. You two will work closely together to control every aspect of this resort, so I want you to get to know the man well. You should both have a clear understanding of each other's jobs and responsibilities."

"I see," Rachel replied, looking behind Jeffery but seeing no one. "And where is he?"

"He'll be right along," Jeffery replied, turning to look outside the dining room doors. "Looks like he's been stopped by Mr. Smith, one of the top men from the Santa Fe offices in Topeka. He happens to be here to see to some of the details of the grand opening. He had several things to share with our new hotel manager. Ah, here he comes now."

Rachel couldn't yet see the man, but she immediately smoothed down the lines of her black serge skirt. *No sense in making a bad impression,* she thought. She looked down to make certain she had no food stains upon her clothes and, feeling confident of her appearance, raised her gaze to meet that of the new hotel manager.

"Braeden." She whispered the name almost reverently, but the shock sent a ripple through her body that nearly knocked her backward. Their eyes met, and Rachel found it impossible to draw breath.

"Do you know Mr. Parker?" Jeffery questioned, turning back in surprise.

Her heart felt as though it had come to a complete stop. For all of her pretenses that the past held no power over her, seeing Braeden Parker standing before her now quickly dispelled that hope.

"I . . . I . . ." She could only stammer. There were no words.

She lost herself in his gaze. He appeared unaffected. Calm, self-assured, not at all surprised by her appearance. His tanned face was more handsome than she'd allowed herself to remember, and when he smiled in greeting, his thick blond moustache moved ever so slightly at the corners.

"Miss Taylor, it's so nice to see you again."

Chapter 4

Rachel felt immediately put off by the smug expression on Braeden's face. She tensed and looked at Jeffery, as if expecting some form of explanation.

"I had no idea you two knew each other," Jeffery said, grinning from ear to ear.

Braeden chuckled, breaking the spell for Rachel. Emotions and longings from the past blended with fears and worries. Why was he here? What could it mean?

"Well, I imagine this will make things much simpler," Jeffery added.

"Don't count on it," Rachel muttered, crossing her arms against her breasts. Her reaction caused everyone in the room to immediately take note. Seeing Braeden here, his countenance suggesting that he knew he'd find her here, as well, caused a spark of anger to ignite within her. She clung to it in hope of ignoring the longing stirred deep within her.

"No," Braeden said matter-of-factly. "As I recall, nothing with Miss Taylor is ever simple."

"Perhaps that was due to the company I kept," Rachel countered. Her anger gave her strength. She refused to back down, even as the Harvey Girls gathered a little closer. "Mr. Parker has proved difficult to work with in the past. I'm uncertain as to why you would bring him on for something as important as Casa Grande."

Jeffery's confusion was evident in his expression. "Mr. Parker came with the highest of references. His reputation in Chicago precedes him."

"That's putting it mildly," Rachel said sarcastically. "Though I'm certain there are plenty from that wonderful city to vouch for his, shall we say, many talents. It seems to me that people were always willing to share news of Mr. Parker."

Braeden, too, stood his ground. "Yes, indeed, Miss Taylor. And it seemed not to matter much whether those opinions were stated out of fact or fiction."

Rachel smiled a tight, fixed smile. "Ultimately we are judged by the fruit which we bear," she stated.

By this time even Esmeralda had gotten to her feet to edge her way closer to the trio. Rachel glanced up to see all gazes turned toward them. Jeffery apparently saw this, too, for he reached out and took hold of Rachel's elbow.

"I would like for us to adjourn to your office, Miss Taylor. There is much to be discussed regarding the resort and the grand opening."

Rachel nodded. "That would be perfectly acceptable, Mr. O'Donnell. Allow me to meet you both there. I need to see to my girls and make certain they know their duties."

Jeffery dropped his hold. "Very well. Mr. Parker and I will meet you in your office."

Rachel refused to look at the men as they departed. Instead, she went immediately to Gwen. "You shall be in charge, Miss Carson. I will expect each station to be spotless when I return."

Gwen nodded and her gaze seemed to express sympathy. Perhaps she had some instinctive idea what Rachel was about to face.

"Ladies, I will expect you to give Miss Carson your utmost

44

respect and attention. I will be inspecting your stations upon the conclusion of my meeting."

With that, she left them to talk amongst themselves about what they'd just witnessed. She hated being the subject of gossip and speculation. Hadn't she suffered enough from the suppositions of others?

She thought to follow Jeffery and Braeden's path by exiting the dining room into the lobby, then changed her mind. Her office actually contained three doors. One entrance from the lobby, one exiting door into her private living quarters, and one door that entered in from the dormitory hall. It was the latter that she chose to make her entrance. It afforded her a few more moments of calming distance. Plus, she reasoned that Jeffery and Braeden would be expecting her to appear from the lobby entrance. She smiled, thinking that this arrangement would allow her the upper hand. She would keep Braeden off-center by taking unexpected actions, and in doing so, she would safeguard herself against his plans—whatever they might be.

She hurried through the kitchen, ignoring Reginald Worthington as she passed. He appeared somewhat concerned, as if someone might have explained the scene to him, but she refused to stop and tell him of her situation. Reginald was just one more Harvey employee as far as she was concerned. They'd certainly not had enough time to become the kind of friends who shared confidences.

She entered the parlor and closed the door behind her, leaning against it heavily for a moment. Seeing Braeden had robbed her of all strength.

Dear Lord, she prayed, *why in the world has he come back into my life?* She looked to the ceiling, as if expecting God to be there smiling down. For as long as she could remember, she'd looked upward in anticipation of some visible sign of

God. And for just as long, she'd not received anything to bless her sight . . . but much to bless her heart.

"Weren't things difficult enough here?" she questioned aloud. "I don't know how to deal with this. The man is to be my partner here at the hotel. How in the world am I suppose to manage this?"

She tried to regulate her breathing before pushing on toward the hallway. She stared down the long, well-lit corridor at her closed office door. The glow from electric lights, a real novelty in rural New Mexico and a feature that was bound to attract eastern visitors for the sense of convenience, reflected on the polished wood floors. They seemed to beckon Rachel forward. He was there. Just beyond that closed door sat the object of her longing and affection. Her heart ached at the thought.

"I can do this," she told herself. "It's been six years, and everything is settled between us. I can simply deal with this as a business arrangement."

But in her heart she understood the irony of her statement. Who was she trying to fool? If she couldn't be honest with herself, then she might as well pack up her things and leave now.

She still loved him. That had never changed.

The tightness in her chest seemed to increase. How could she look into his eyes again and not tell him everything? How could she sit there calmly discussing Casa Grande affairs and not beg him to understand that she had never stopped caring for him—that every day her thoughts somehow always found their way back to him?

She reached out for the handle of her office door and bit her lip. Six years. It should have been enough time to prepare her for this moment. But somehow it had failed miserably, and Rachel knew that if it had been twenty years instead of six, she'd still feel the same way.

She opened the door without any announcement or regard for where Jeffery and Braeden had positioned themselves. She refused to even look at the men until she had taken a seat at her desk.

"Gentlemen," she said, finally glancing up to where they had risen to their feet. "Shall we continue?"

Jeffery nodded and closed the lobby door, while Braeden took his seat. He looked at her as though he wished he could say something. Rachel thought it might be her imagination, but she would have sworn his expression was almost apologetic. The look softened her resolve.

"I'm sorry, Mr. O'Donnell," she began, deciding that directing her apology to Jeffery would be easier than dealing with Braeden. "Your actions took me by surprise. I realize that's no excuse, however—"

"Rachel," Jeffery said rather sternly, "would you please explain what's going on here? Apparently you both know each other well enough to share a feeling of animosity, and I would very much like to know what it's all about. Mr. Parker refuses to speak on the matter, suggesting that I consult you."

Rachel bowed her head. "It isn't important, Jeffery. I assure you it won't affect the affairs of Casa Grande. It simply startled me." She looked back up, giving Jeffery a pleading glance. At least she hoped her expression appeared pleading, for she sincerely wanted him to drop this subject.

To her absolute horror, Braeden seemed to take up a protective response. "Miss Taylor was once a dear friend. We were unable to keep up correspondence with one another and had no idea where the other had taken themselves off to. I do apologize for my part in this."

Jeffery studied them both for a moment, as if trying to decide whether to pursue the matter or leave it be. He ran a hand back through his brown hair, pursed his lips together for a moment, then nodded. "Very well." He took his seat and waited for a moment before continuing. "Since you two know each other, I suppose we can do away with the formalities of detailed introductions. Mr. Parker came to us highly recommended by another railroad company in Chicago, and with his accounting background, I believe he will be the perfect man to run the hotel portion of this resort."

Rachel nodded, forcing herself to listen and say nothing. She felt almost sick to her stomach and wondered if she'd end up making a scene before it was all said and done. She glanced quickly at the door to her living quarters, grateful that she'd remembered to close it this morning before heading out to oversee the dining room progress.

"Casa Grande, as you know, is only one of two resorts of this type. The other, located near Las Vegas, has been hindered by many problems, including the fact that the place has burned down twice. Some folks believe it to be cursed, but of course we don't hold with that theory. Financially speaking, we believe it to be simply based on logical conclusions. Namely, there is very little to entice a person to stay more than one night in Las Vegas, unless they are there to take advantage of the curative waters and hospital facilities available. So while the place does quite well for itself at times, we hoped for better.

"Casa Grande, however, is positioned closer to Santa Fe and Albuquerque. Also, the scenery is more enchanting with the mountains in the background, and our own hot springs and baths offer the same advantage and curative features."

"I understand that nearly every type of diversion is offered here for the entertainment of our guests," Braeden interjected.

Rachel heard the rich timbre of his voice and immediately

felt light-headed. *This is ridiculous,* she told herself. *I'm not a schoolgirl, all swooney and silly.* But it did little good to argue with her heart.

"Casa Grande will offer it all. Later, during our tour of the grounds, you will see for yourself," Jeffery replied. "But for now, let me tell you some of what you can expect. We have a theatre room with seating for two hundred. This will be available for concerts, operas, plays, or even lectures. There is a ballroom more grand and glorious than any New York has ever seen. The chandeliers were shipped from Tiffany's, and the decor will enchant even the most hardened heart."

Rachel thought this a rather poignant expression. Against her will she glanced at Braeden and felt a small amount of relief to find his gaze fixed upon Jeffery.

"There are also sun porches and gardens," Jeffery continued. "You will find because of Mrs. Needlemeier's meticulous attention that the gardens on the east side are as much an oasis as any desert could boast."

"Mrs. Needlemeier?" Braeden questioned.

"She was the elderly woman in the dining room," Jeffery replied. "The one who maneuvered herself closer in order to better understand your reunion with Rachel."

Rachel felt the wind catch in her throat. Why couldn't this meeting just be over with so that she could go to her room and rest? She desperately needed to think about all that had happened, but Jeffery didn't seem at all concerned.

Braeden was smiling and nodding, while it was all she could do to remain seated. "I do recall her. Done up in widow's garb and armed with that silver-headed cane."

Jeffery laughed. "Yes, armed is a good way to think of it. The woman is fanatical about this town and about issuing her opinion. Nevertheless, she has maintained a lovely ten-acre garden and is graciously allowing us to share it for the benefit

49

of our guests. Her mansion adjoins the gardens on the other side."

"I see."

"The hot springs and bathing pools and houses are to the north of the hotel. There are separate facilities for men and women, as well as a lovely common pool for all to enjoy. The resort maintains very conservative bathing apparel for the guests, and as a staff member, you are also welcome to enjoy this refreshment when duty does not require you to be elsewhere. Besides this, we have stables for riding, croquet, lawn bowling, badminton, and a bandstand where musicians will perform periodically throughout the day and evening hours. Indoors we have a wonderful library with writing desks and quiet nooks for those who would rather remain inside, and as you were already told, we are fortunate enough to have electricity. The powerhouse is just across the front drive, positioned at the base of Morita Falls."

"I must say, I'm impressed," Braeden said, considering all he'd been told. "And how many rooms are available for hotel guests?"

"At this point, seventy. There are ways to allow for additional rooms, but for now this seems sufficient." Jeffery passed his gaze to Rachel. "As you've already been told, Miss Taylor is house manager over the Harvey House Restaurant. She has absolute charge of twenty-five girls, most of whom you saw there in the dining room. She also has final authority over the kitchen staff, including the chef. She will be responsible for ordering all food items and arranging with the local citizens to provide what Fred Harvey does not ship in."

"She was always very capable," Braeden stated matter-of-factly.

"She has proven so for the Santa Fe as well," Jeffery confirmed. "Rachel has been a longtime favorite of mine. She was responsible for training other Harvey Girls during her time in Topeka and has worked her way up the ranks over the last—" he paused and looked at Rachel. "What has it been? Five . . . six years?"

"Six." The word came from Braeden before Rachel could even open her mouth.

She could only nod.

"Well, for what it's worth," Jeffery continued, "it is hoped Casa Grande will offer the Santa Fe a bit of salvation from its economic woes. Kansas farmers suffered a horrible crop last year, and that, along with poor investments, has brought problems upon the railroad. Casa Grande is seen as a true oasis for the line, as well as for its passengers. And with Mrs. Needlemeier's enthusiastic support and promotion, we perceive the possibility of something very, very big here."

"And my duties will be to oversee the hotel portion of the resort, while Miss Taylor operates the restaurant and other food services for the guests?"

Rachel felt her mouth grow increasingly dry. She twisted her hands together in her lap, grateful that the desktop hid them from view.

"That's exactly right. You will have a hotel staff," Jeffery replied. "Many of the staff are native to the area. They were chosen because they had good reputations with Mrs. Needlemeier or other impeccable references. Positions that could not be filled with local people were advertised back East, and people were brought in from elsewhere. Your head housekeeper, in fact, was hired from Kansas City. You'll have a chance to get together with your staff later tomorrow. I'll give you a brief tour of the grounds today—show you where your office and living quarters are—then tomorrow we will arrange for your job to begin in earnest."

Braeden shifted in his seat and looked quite seriously at

Jeffery. "What might we expect from the grand opening? I understand it will be mostly dignitaries and Santa Fe board officials."

Jeffery smiled. "Rumors do fly when you're about new business. But to answer your question, yes. The grand opening will be in just under two weeks, and there are all manner of activities planned for the celebration. Besides the band hired to perform here full time, there will be two other musical ensembles on the train to Morita. Miss Lucretia Collins, the renowned opera singer, will perform opening night, and a grand ball of such enormous proportions that even my head tends to spin a bit at the thought, is to be held on the third night. Both you and Miss Taylor will find yourselves very busy, and working together will be of the utmost importance. I want to know that I can count on you both to organize and maintain this resort in perfect order."

"I assure you, on my account," Braeden began, "that your trust will not be misplaced."

Trust. Rachel cringed inwardly at the word. Was Braeden trying to twist the knife that was already firmly implanted in her heart? Trust had been the reason for the demise of their love. Trust was now the issue that would stand between them to help create a new relationship—or divide them hopelessly.

A knock sounded on the door before Rachel could speak her answer. Jeffery got to his feet and opened it to find a young messenger.

"Mr. O'Donnell, you're needed back at the depot as soon as possible," the boy relayed.

Jeffery turned to Rachel. "Would you be so kind as to show Mr. Parker the grounds and the living quarters and office we've secured for him?"

Rachel wanted to refuse, saying that she'd have no part in it. She feared being left alone with Braeden, yet she could find no reasonable excuse for denying Jeffrey's request.

"Of course," she managed to say without sounding totally dumbfounded.

"Wonderful!" Jeffery exclaimed with a broad smile. "It will help me a great deal if you will see to this matter." He bid Braeden good-day with the promise that he would see him early the next morning, and then he was gone. Thoughtfully, he had closed the door behind him, leaving Rachel once again feeling completely trapped.

Allowing her eyes to meet Braeden's, Rachel was at a loss as to what to do or say. So with a deep breath, she said the only thing she could think of.

"What in the world are you doing in Morita?"

Chapter 5

Braeden knew the situation was extremely trying for Rachel. After all, he was suffering on his own account and he had known she was here. Of course, he could hardly tell her that. It wasn't like he accepted the job because of her, for he'd already applied and been chosen for the position before being told that Rachel Taylor was a part of Casa Grande's staff. He could have bowed out at that point, but his heart bid him to stay.

His mind raced with the possibilities of what he could say to put her at ease. She looked quite angry and frightened, but even more so, she looked beautiful. He had often thought of her, wondering where she was and if she had married.

"I'm here to do a job," he finally said, realizing he couldn't very well go on studying her indefinitely.

Rachel pushed back a wispy auburn curl and squared her shoulders. "Did you know I was here?"

Braeden nearly choked. The very thing that he had sworn he'd keep secret he would now have to lie about or admit. "Why do you ask?"

Rachel shrugged. "I suppose I am curious. It hardly seems logical to accept that fate has thrown us together."

"What about God?"

"What about Him?"

Braeden shifted slightly. "I think it's possible that He brought us together for a reason."

Rachel tensed. "Yes, I suppose it is possible. The Bible is full of stories where people were tested."

Braeden couldn't help but laugh. "So you believe working with me is a test?"

"Without a doubt."

Seeing they were getting nowhere, Braeden tried another approach. "I tried to find out where you'd gone, but your mother wouldn't divulge the information."

"She was following my instructions," Rachel countered. Her green eyes narrowed ever so slightly. "I told her there was no purpose in you knowing my whereabouts. I had no desire for deceit and lies to follow me into my new life."

Braeden couldn't help but react. "I'm surprised she managed to keep the information to herself." He felt his anger mounting. In his thirty-six years of life, he'd never found a woman who affected him more than Rachel. Be it in anger or love, Braeden knew her to consume him. "So did you ever marry?" he asked, his voice tinged with sarcasm.

"No." Rachel spoke the word simply, as if daring him to pry for a more detailed answer.

"Couldn't find a man perfect enough to meet your standards?" Braeden questioned, regretting the words the minute they were out of his mouth. *I didn't have to say that,* he chided himself. *I can't let my anger get the best of me.* He looked into her green eyes and saw her wince.

"I suppose not," she finally answered. "And what of you? Did you ever marry that woman whom you were dallying with?"

Braeden clenched his teeth together. He angered at her insistence that he had somehow wronged her by being unfaithful. He had a perfectly logical explanation for his actions that day, but up until now, no one had even asked him for such an answer. And being the stubborn, prideful man he was, Braeden wasn't about to offer it.

"I've never married."

For several moments neither one spoke. Rachel appeared completely drained of energy, Braeden thought. Her normally rosy cheeks were pale and her eyes averted meeting his, as if the action might cause her too much pain. He hated seeing her like this, and for the first time since realizing that the Rachel Taylor of Casa Grande was *his* Rachel Taylor, Braeden wondered at the sanity of accepting the position. After all, he would be working with Rachel on a daily basis. And not only that, but they would be housed under the same roof and live their lives in a tiny little town where neither one could avoid the other.

He eased back in his chair and wondered what to do next. He glanced up at her as she studied her lap. The anger and sarcasm that tainted their words was getting them nowhere. He would have to swallow his pride and find a way to make this arrangement less consuming.

But consuming was the only word for it. She had consumed his thoughts and dreams for the last six years, and now that he was here, sitting not two feet away, Braeden longed to take her in his arms. She hadn't changed much, he decided. Her ruddy complexion and auburn hair stood out in contrast against her high-collared white blouse. She had fashioned her hair in a popular style of the day, with the bulk of her dark red curls pulled back and rolled into a knot atop her head. Wisps of hair curled down gently, softening the effect and framing her face. She was just as lovely and enchanting as Braeden had remembered.

"It seems we are in a bit of a fix here," Braeden said softly.

"I suppose that's putting it mildly," Rachel said, folding her hands on top of the desk.

"Look, I don't want to spend the next months snapping at

each other and creating scenes."

"I have no intention of creating a scene with you, Mr. Parker," Rachel said stiffly. She pushed back her shoulders and lifted her chin ever so slightly.

"I think the folks in the dining room would tell it another way."

Rachel narrowed her eyes once again. "I was shocked by your sudden appearance. I feel my actions were justified."

"You've always felt your actions were justified."

"I try to base my actions on the facts at hand."

"We're playing games here, Rachel," he said, leaning toward her. He hadn't intended to use her first name, but it had come out without hesitation, as if their separation had never occurred.

"I'm not playing at anything, Mr. Parker."

"Don't!" he said, getting to his feet. "Don't try to pretend with me. I know you too well."

"You don't know me at all!" Rachel retorted and jumped to her feet. "If you knew me as you suppose you do, you would understand why I've reacted the way I have today."

"As well as how you reacted six years ago?" Braeden questioned, putting his hands on her desk. Leaning forward, ever closer to those wonderful red lips, he pressed his point home. "You acted out of mistrust then . . . just as you are now."

"I have no reason to trust you," she said rather lamely. Her bravado was fading as fast as it had come.

He thought she looked rather lost and vulnerable. Like a child who had turned down the wrong street and found himself separated from all that was familiar. He wanted to comfort her—wanted to tell her that the past didn't matter. But pride stood in his way. He would not yield on this matter. He could not.

"I have never lied to you," he said simply. "Trust is earned through actions, that much we agree upon. My actions were never out of line, but your trust was fleeting and given only on whim."

"You're wrong about that," she replied, her voice barely a whisper. "My . . ." She halted awkwardly.

Braeden wanted her to continue. In fact, his desire was so great that he felt something akin to rage when she refused. He had never been able to justify himself to her—had never been allowed to explain his actions at the hotel the day her mother's friends had witnessed him there. And he had never, ever gotten over her walking away from him. Ending their engagement. Destroying his dreams.

"I suppose it might be better if we saved this for another day," he said, trying hard to keep his temper under control. "Mr. O'Donnell expects you to tour me around the grounds, and it might be wise to do that before the sun sets and we have to go about in lantern light."

Rachel took her cue from him and drew a deep breath. "I have to take care of my girls and tend to their needs first. If I had my way about it, I wouldn't have to deal with you at all."

"Well, that is too bad," Braeden replied, "because you do have to *deal* with me. I'm not going anywhere. Casa Grande is a fine resort in a beautiful location. I intend to be here for as long as there is a job available for me. At thirty-six, I have a good number of years to look forward to life and employment, and just because you intend to treat me poorly is no reason for me to retire my position. Unlike you, I'm not the type to run away."

He watched Rachel's hands ball into fists. She kept her hands tightly at her side, but her gaze never left his face. "I do what I must to survive," she stated, then moved toward the door. "I would like for you to wait by the fireplace in the front lobby. I will see to my girls, and then I will show you where things are."

He reluctantly followed her into the lobby. He didn't like the fact that he was so angry. Neither did he like that she was upset with him. He had known she would be surprised to see him, but he had rather hoped that she would put the past behind them and give him another chance. He had never stopped caring for her or desperately wondering where she was. And now that he knew, he was hard-pressed to decide exactly how to handle it. Should he go back to Chicago and make her life less miserable? Or should he stay and hope for a miracle?

"Wait here," she told him.

"Yes, ma'am," he said with a stiff little bow.

She stopped in midstep and looked at him with a frown. "You needn't be so tiresome."

"Perhaps you would rather I had called you Rachel?" he asked, a bit of a grin forming on his lips. She was just so incredibly beautiful, and he loved that she was so obviously affected by his appearance in her life. Perhaps behind her anger he would find tolerance . . . and eventually love.

"No," she replied, and he saw the pain flash across her expression. "Miss Taylor will do."

He took a hesitant step forward and extended his hand as if to ease her sorrow. "Please understand—" he began.

She backed away, shaking her head. "I have work to do. Wait here and I'll come back to show you the grounds."

He watched her go, feeling a conflict within his soul. On one hand, he questioned his own sanity in coming to Casa Grande. On the other hand, he wondered quite seriously how he had lived the past six years without Rachel at his side. The future promised to be more than he'd bargained for, yet for the life of him, Braeden couldn't force himself to simply turn and walk away before it was too late.

"It's already too late," he whispered, knowing that his appearance here at Casa Grande had changed everything for both of them.

Rachel moved through the dining room, instructing her charges in a methodical, mechanical manner. She could scarcely draw breath, much less think rationally. He was here—and he was staying! She had often wondered what she would do if he reappeared in her life. She had pictured herself happily married with children at her side, meeting him on the street in passing. She would have loved for him to have seen her happy and content without him in her life.

Shaking her head, she knew that wasn't true. A tear came to her eye as she walked into the kitchen. Without thought to who might see her, Rachel paused, leaning heavily against the immaculate counter top. Somehow, she had to get a tight rein on her emotions.

"Miss Taylor, are you all right?" Reginald Worthington's soft British accent broke through her overwhelming misery.

"I'm perfectly fine, Mr. Worthington."

"I say," he continued, as if buying into her reply. "Would it be possible for us to work on a first-name basis? I realize it implies an intimacy and closeness that you might otherwise not feel, but I would rather enjoy the refreshing simplicity. It seems most folks out here in the West are less inclined to use such titles."

Rachel looked up and found his compassionate gaze fixed upon her. She wasn't sure at that moment that she could have denied him anything. He appeared so completely concerned for her well-being that it seemed only natural to grant him this request.

"Why, yes. We generally do business in a less formal

manner in the Harvey House. Of course, when customers are present . . ."

"I will address you quite properly in sight of others. I simply hoped that in private we might form a friendship. If I've overstepped my bounds, then forgive me."

Rachel offered him a brief smile. "No, Reginald—"

"Please, call me Reg," he interrupted. "Reginald still seems too formal."

"Very well," she replied. "I don't believe you have done anything out of line. You asked my permission for less formality; you didn't impose it as a demand. I appreciate that very much."

"I would like for us to be friends," he said softly.

"It does make for smoother operations," Rachel answered, feeling her anger and emotional state lessen. "I would be honored to be your friend."

He shook his head and boldly took hold of her hand. "No, the honor would be all mine. I would happily do anything I could to ease your burden."

Rachel felt strange standing there in the kitchen while Reg held her hand. Fred Harvey had strict rules about any Harvey staff members dating, and while Reg was asking for nothing more than friendship, she couldn't help but wonder what else he might expect.

"You seemed quite distressed when you arrived here moments ago," Reg stated. "I wonder if there is something else I might assist you with?"

Rachel shook her head. "It's just that there is so much to do in preparation for the grand opening. Now Mr. O'Donnell brings me the new hotel manager, and I'm supposed to show him around the grounds and help him become familiar with his new surroundings." *But unfortunately,* she thought, *he's only managing to become more familiar with me.*

61

"I could show him around," Reg offered. "I have everything under control here."

Rachel brightened. "You wouldn't mind?"

"Not at all," he said, giving her hand a squeeze before letting go. "I would consider it a privilege to relieve you of this added burden."

"It would help me a great deal," she answered, her mind focused on how Braeden would take this form of rejection. She smiled. "Yes, I believe I would like it very much. He's waiting now in the lobby. Come and I'll introduce you."

She led Reg to where Braeden stood cooling his heels. "Mr. Parker, I would like to introduce our chef, Reginald Worthington. Mr. Worthington has graciously agreed to tour you about the grounds." She smiled smugly and met Braeden's quizzical stare with great pleasure. She could see in his expression that he hadn't planned on this turn of events.

"Mr. Worthington, I'm pleased to meet you. I will be the hotel manager here at Casa Grande."

"Ah, Mr. Parker, it is an honor," Reg said, giving a slight bow. "Miss Taylor's schedule is already overburdened, and I offered to assist her in this matter. I hope you do not mind."

Braeden shook his head. "Of course, the company of a beautiful young woman is hard to pass by, but I shall enjoy getting a chance to better know you, Mr. Worthington."

"Likewise, Mr. Parker."

Rachel watched them go off together, and for the life of her she couldn't understand the disappointment that crept into her heart. *I should feel relieved,* she thought. But she didn't. Instead, she felt divided. The future and the past had just collided, and now she was hard-pressed to know which direction to take.

Chapter 6

Esmeralda hated old age. She hated feeling less capable of doing the things she had to do. She detested looking in the mirror to see yet another wrinkle mar her once beautiful skin. And she loathed knowing that death was not far away.

Dying had never frightened her, and it certainly wasn't an issue of eternity and what would happen in the afterlife—it was more the inconvenience of it all. She had great plans for the future and aspired to do it all properly and in full control. Dying would definitely put a halt to those plans.

It was both troublesome and a blessing to be classified as old. Troublesome because your body no longer cooperated with you as it did in youth, and people often considered it necessary to shield you from shocking events and scandalous thoughts. But being old could also be a blessing. People recognized that you had come this far by knowing something more than the count of chickens in the hen house. You were generally respected and often deferred to. But then there was that whole pesky issue of death. As far as Esmeralda could see, the only good thing about dying was the idea of joining her beloved Hezekiah. He had been gone for five years now and it seemed like an eternity.

Hezekiah had known her better than anyone. He had shared his hopes and dreams with her, and in turn they had become her own hopes and dreams. Now that he was gone, she was a lonely old woman, although she would never have allowed anyone to know that fact. Instead, she created a façade of strength and dignity that set her apart from others.

The Needlemeier mansion, a two-story native stone Queen Anne house, stood as an oddity against the adobe and clapboard buildings of Morita. Until Casa Grande had been erected in its wealthy beaux arts eclectic styling, Esmeralda's home had commanded the attention of everyone in the community. Now, standing in the shadow of Casa Grande, Esmeralda wondered if she'd made a mistake allowing the resort to be built so close to her own home. There was no doubt that Casa Grande was beautiful—she wouldn't have had it any other way—but having it steal away the attention her home had otherwise enjoyed was a bit like being passed over at the dance for a more beautiful belle.

Staring down at the collection of letters on her desk, Esmeralda sorted through the replies to her advertisements. She had taken up the cause of her dear husband's dream and had worked to create a town that would flourish and grow with the ages. Hezekiah had wanted to be remembered for something, and Morita embodied that memorial. Now, with Esmeralda hard-pressed to let go of his desires, Morita was slowly but surely taking shape.

It hadn't been easy to convince investors to consider the small whistle-stop as a possible location for development. After all, Albuquerque wasn't that far away. It wasn't until she had convinced the Santa Fe and Fred Harvey to come to Morita with the idea of creating a resort hotel that Esmeralda had found any real portion of success. She had spent a fortune cultivating acres of gardens and creating bridges over the hot springs and falls. She'd given up equally large amounts of money to support the development of a proper town and to entice businesses to fill the buildings once completed. Her fortune was completely tied up in Morita, and now more than ever she intended to see it succeed.

Some said she was a bit touched in the head. She had no family except for her uppity niece, Ivy Brooks. But she was working to create a legacy that perhaps no one but those left behind could appreciate. She felt her emotions stir. The years had left a void inside her that couldn't be denied. Sometimes the loneliness of carrying on Hezekiah's dream herself was more than she could bear.

Stiffening her resolve, Esmeralda refused to allow her feelings merit. She would simply give her attention to the job at hand. There was no sense in allowing her heartbreak to interfere with that which demanded completion.

Picking up an envelope, Esmeralda considered the reply of a Baltimore storekeeper. He stated that he would be happy to take her up on the offer of free rent for the first six months and to consider signing papers pledging himself to a full five years of service in Morita. He went on to list the type of store he'd owned in Baltimore, and Esmeralda placed his letter in the stack of acceptable businesses.

The next letter had been penned by a banker who offered to bring his knowledge to the West. He wrote in a most condescending manner, saying that while he understood the desire to strengthen the town economically and to bring in business, he believed Esmeralda's methods to be a bit addlepated. His letter went immediately into the trash. Esmeralda would brook no criticism of her plan.

An interruption to her day came as it always did at two-thirty every Tuesday afternoon. Lettie Johnson, the plump and rather plain-faced pastor's wife, was led into the parlor where Esmeralda formally received her company. Lettie called this her Christian visitation and, as the pastor's wife, considered it a solemn duty. Esmeralda called it her Tuesday gossip session and would have refused the woman altogether had she not always brought with her valuable information related to the attitudes and current thoughts of the townsfolk.

"Good afternoon, Mrs. Needlemeier," Lettie said, removing her simple brown bonnet. "My, but it's a beautiful day out there. Have you managed to take a walk today?"

"No," Esmeralda said, tapping her cane upon the hardwood floor as she moved to take her position in a red velvet chair. "I've been much too busy with the affairs of the town."

"Mr. Johnson tells me we're going to elect a mayor," Lettie said, her full face breaking into a grin. "Word has it that there are several who would qualify for such a position of importance. I wonder whom you might consider acceptable for such a position."

Esmeralda hated the woman's prying, knowing that her utmost concern was to find out whether her husband would receive the backing and support of the town's matriarch.

"I don't suppose I've had much time to think about it," Esmeralda stated rather severely. "Politics has its place, but there are matters of far greater concern."

Lettie nodded, her expression showing her disappointment. "I suppose so."

Esmeralda refused to be goaded. "The affairs of the new resort have kept me quite consumed. Have you managed to take a tour of the grounds?"

"No," Lettie replied. "We do plan to attend the festivities, however. I'm quite looking forward to it, and I even received my husband's permission to make myself a new dress. Won't that be wonderful!"

"I suppose all of the women of the church sewing circle shall consume their days with fashioning new creations to show off at the grand opening of Casa Grande," Esmeralda replied dryly. She could imagine the insufferable ninnies running about in their homespun gowns, each boasting the smartness of the other's design. They would all be put to shame by the dignitaries' wives who would come with their collection of Worth gowns and expensive jewelry.

Lettie giggled as though she were a young girl instead of a woman quickly approaching her fifties. "We're having a sewing circle tomorrow morning, and you would certainly be welcome to attend."

"I hardly think so," Esmeralda replied, looking down her nose at the woman. She had worked hard to establish a position of aloofness and reserve. Sometimes it served her well, and other times the loneliness it caused consumed her. However, sewing circles were hardly the type of socializing Esmeralda would bend to attend. Instead, she looked forward to the class of clientele that would be drawn to Casa Grande. The resort was expensive, and that in and of itself would help to keep the riffraff out. And given the diversity of Morita, Esmeralda was a firm believer in keeping society properly divided.

"Well, you'd be welcome just the same," Lettie continued. "We all think it's just wonderful the way Morita is coming to life. I walked down Main Street yesterday and thought I'd bust a button when I saw the new apothecary. You know how I suffer with my headaches and that strange little pain I get in my back. It'll be nice to have remedies so close at hand."

Esmeralda harrumphed this breech of etiquette. Lettie would have discussed her physical ailments with total strangers if given a chance. But instead of rebuking, Esmeralda picked up a bell to ring for tea. "I'm certain the town will continue to grow and meet the additional needs of its citizens," she finally replied. "Ah, here is Eliza with our tea."

Esmeralda hired only a few workers for her home. She cherished her privacy, and a large house staff would hardly fit with this need. Servants tended to put their noses where they oughtn't. With only a few trusted people—a cook, a butler, and a housemaid—Esmeralda was more certain of keeping them under control.

The young, dark-headed woman poured their tea and offered a selection of cakes before replacing the tray on the cart and bobbing a curtsy. Esmeralda waved her off before sipping the lightly creamed tea.

"I presume Mr. Johnson is busy at work on the church budget," Esmeralda said as she placed her cup and saucer on a nearby table.

Lettie took a bite of her rich dessert, spilling powdered sugar on the front of her brown dress. She laughed and nodded, working to brush off the crumbs. "That he is," she managed to say in between chewing. She didn't appear to notice that her manners were atrocious. "He's real excited about the improvements you want to make. Just imagine, real pews in the church! Those benches have been so uncomfortable that it's hard to concentrate."

Esmeralda rolled her eyes, grateful that Lettie's attention was focused on the dessert tray. "Would you care for another?"

Lettie grinned. "Well, I shouldn't, but you know you have the best cook in town. Perhaps you should have her start up a bakery. I'll bet folks would come from miles around."

Esmeralda nodded. "I'll keep that in mind. Please help yourself."

Lettie did so, as Esmeralda knew she would. She could hardly abide the woman's manners, but there was something about these Tuesday afternoon visits that Esmeralda refused to let go of. Perhaps it was because Lettie was one of the few to come calling. Esmeralda ranked herself clearly above the other women in the community, and she could hardly expect them to worship at the heels of their matriarch and include her in daily activities.

"So what else do you have planned for Morita?" Lettie asked.

Knowing the woman to be unable to keep a secret, Esmeralda smiled stiffly. She had long since learned that this was the easiest way to get information out and about the town. "We are to have a new dentist and another dry goods store," she told the woman. "We have a new saloon, which of course I was not a bit happy about, but it is on property that did not belong to me. I suppose they shall make a rowdy time for themselves," Esmeralda relayed, "but with them positioned near the river, it is my hope that they will not be a problem to proper society."

Lettie laughed. "Saloons and soiled doves seem to be a natural fact of life for towns out here. Why, the mining town we left in Colorado had twenty saloons in a four-block setting. We didn't even have a school or proper church building, but those saloons were never empty."

Esmeralda nodded, knowing that the woman spoke the truth. Until the Santa Fe had agreed to purchase her land for Casa Grande resort, she could easily say that the saloon was probably the most productive business in her town.

"Speaking of saloons," Lettie said, leaning forward, "did you hear that Mrs. Mills' husband was locked up again?" She didn't wait for Esmeralda to respond. "He shot a hole in the floor of the Mad House Saloon and threatened the bartender when he refused to pour Mr. Mills another drink. The poor woman was beside herself when she learned the news. It practically broke her heart. You know they have five children and barely make ends meet with his profits from the mercantile.

Not only that, she's going to have another baby, and I figure it was this that sent Mr. Mills to the saloon."

"Another child is far from what they need," Esmeralda admitted.

"Well, they aren't the only ones making additions to the town," Lettie replied. "We have at least three women in the congregation who will give birth next year. Of course, I can't mention them by name, but one of them just married two weeks ago. I'd imagine we'll see that baby arriving just a little sooner than the date on their marriage license would indicate proper."

Esmeralda nodded and listened as the woman continued to chatter about the matters of the townsfolk. One child had a broken arm, another had nearly drowned in the river but was saved by a kindly passerby. The town marshal believed he would seek out a deputy, and the butcher was to have fresh lamb available on the day after tomorrow.

Eventually the conversation lagged, and as it did, Esmeralda followed routine and glanced up at the ornate mantel clock. "My, but the afternoon is getting away from us."

"Oh, indeed," Lettie replied, wiping her mouth with her linen napkin. "I still have several calls to make so I mustn't tarry here. I do wish you would reconsider the sewing circle. We would be pleased to have you join us." She brushed off her crumbs, mindless of where they fell, and placed her teacup on the serving cart. "It's always so nice to chat with you."

Esmeralda walked her to the door, ignoring the way Lettie gaped at the furnishings of the house.

"You simply must take me on a tour of the house when I have more time," Lettie said.

This, too, was a part of the routine. Lettie always pushed

for an invitation to see beyond the front parlor, and Esmeralda always managed to put her off with a simple, "We shall see." Lettie never seemed to understand that she had once again overstepped the bounds of propriety. Nor did she worry overmuch about what Esmeralda thought. She seemed quite happy just to make her rounds and visit—sharing tidbits of information Esmeralda might otherwise never hear. Lettie Johnson was better than any town newspaper.

"Give my regards to the pastor," Esmeralda told the woman as she pulled on her bonnet.

"I will do that. See you Sunday," Lettie replied, taking herself down the stone steps. "Oh, and don't forget there's to be a potluck dinner after church. I sure hope you'll come."

"I seriously doubt that I will," Esmeralda replied. She offered neither explanation nor excuse, and Lettie didn't press for one.

Esmeralda sighed in relief after the woman had gone, but even as she closed the door, she realized the sensation of emptiness that flooded the house. It was bad enough that Ivy had chosen to stay on at the resort. She had thought to bring the girl home and still allow her to maintain her ludicrous idea of waiting tables for the Harvey House, but that failed to work out.

She remembered their fierce argument when Ivy had learned of Esmeralda's decision to remain in Morita. It hadn't been a pretty sight because Ivy had felt certain they would return to her own native St. Louis or maybe even Chicago. But when Esmeralda had announced the coming of the resort and her decision to help Morita flourish, Ivy had been livid.

The girl had even refused to speak to her for days, but because she was underage, there was little she could do. Esmeralda was in charge, and without her approval, Ivy had little or no funds with which to make a move. She had hoped to guide the child into understanding how one could easily invest money and, if done properly, see a nice return for their efforts. But Ivy couldn't care less. She wanted nothing more than a wealthy husband and a home of her own.

Esmeralda looked up the long staircase to the second floor. Ivy's empty room stood just to the left of the top of the landing. The door was closed, reserved for that time when Ivy should choose to come home. Esmeralda didn't waste time worrying about when that might be. The child was stubborn and headstrong. Her willful nature had destroyed much of her life, and though Esmeralda had tried to mold her into a responsible adult, Ivy missed the mark in many ways.

Walking back to the parlor, Esmeralda stared at an oil painting of her now departed brother, Carl. "I fear I've failed you. Ivy is hardly the child you would have taken pride in." She drew a heavy breath and realized the futility of talking to the image. She was totally on her own in the matter of trying to rear Ivy in a responsible manner. That the child had no moral values and no interest in godly matters was alarming enough. But that she put her own aspirations and desires ahead of everyone else's, even to the point of hurting those around her, was too much for Esmeralda to comprehend. Perhaps it was better to give her over to Rachel Taylor and the Harvey system. At least that redheaded manager seemed not to be intimidated by Ivy's cunning and conniving ways.

"Perhaps this will help the child to change," Esmeralda muttered to herself, having little faith in the thought.

Chapter 7

After immersing himself in his new duties for over a week, Braeden realized the job of managing Casa Grande was going to entail a great deal more than he'd originally understood. He was not only in charge of keeping the hotel books and records, arranging for the supplies and staff, and seeing to the reservations for special events, but he was also responsible for bringing in entertainers, scheduling resort appearances, and continuing to improve the grounds. Dealing with entertainment, he quickly learned, was guaranteed to be enough to drive him positively insane.

Making his way back from the telegraph office at the depot, he felt only a moderate amount of relief from the two telegrams in his pocket. Both confirmed acceptance of performances for future dates, one by a well-known acting troupe and another by a renowned European opera singer who would divert from Denver to join them in Casa Grande on the twenty-first of October. He supposed he should feel happy about the news, but he found he couldn't take pleasure in the matter when his thoughts were consumed with Rachel.

A mountain breeze blew across the valley, causing Braeden to raise his head. The dry warmth of the air felt good against his skin. The past few days had been unseasonably warm, and in spite of the modern convenience of electric lights and fans, Braeden knew Casa Grande would be rather stifling by midday. He speculated that once they were actually up and running with guests, most folks would take afternoon naps or spend quiet moments in the shaded gardens. For himself, he knew there would be more than enough work to occupy him through the heat of the day and didn't relish the idea at all. Chicago could have its own blistering summers, but generally they were mild and easily tolerated. He had no idea what to expect from New Mexico. Nor did he know what to expect from Rachel.

The walk from the depot to the resort wasn't all that far, but Braeden slowed his approach to the two-story hotel when his thoughts rested on Rachel. She'd been avoiding him as if he were the Grim Reaper. Many times he'd seen her in the dining room and had thought to approach her, only to have her duck out through the kitchen and into the private parlor for the Harvey Girls. Men were simply not allowed in that portion of the hotel, and infringing upon this rule would mean instantaneous dismissal. Braeden had little desire to be fired, but he had an overwhelming need to set the record clear with the only woman he'd ever really cared for.

He smiled, thinking of the months to come and how closely they would be expected to work together. Already there were a number of staff meetings scheduled, and he would have the opportunity to co-head the meetings with Rachel at his side. It promised to be entertaining, if not advantageous to his situation—if he played his cards right.

He paused on the bridge that spanned Morita Falls. Fed by the abundant hot springs and two other streams, the falls cascaded in a series of steps, dancing over rocky passages and splaying out in a churning pool some twenty feet below. Someone had thoughtfully placed park benches in the grassy area at the bottom of the falls for scenic enjoyment. No doubt it would also make for a lovely romantic interlude.

The picturesque scene drew him to reflect on how he might woo Rachel into agreeing to give their love a second chance. Moonlight, waterfalls, and the flowery gardens just might create the needed atmosphere. The hardest part would be setting the stage that would put them together in such a place. If Rachel had her way, she would never again be alone in his company.

Sighing, he turned away from the enchanting little falls and made his way up the drive and past the white marble fountain to Casa Grande. On his desk he had a stack of original inventory sheets to compare to the inventory recently taken by his housekeeper, and there was no telling how long it would actually take to reconcile the two. With this business in mind, he raced up the steps and plowed through the doorway just as Rachel was exiting the hotel.

He had to take hold of her arms to keep from knocking her to the ground, but the look on her face was his reason for maintaining his hold. She was surprised, to say the least, but there was a longing in her eyes that matched the emotion in his heart. She trembled at his touch, and Braeden felt encouraged by the fact that he was the reason for her reaction. *She must have feelings for me; otherwise this wouldn't affect her at all.*

"Rachel," he whispered, refusing to call her anything else.

For a moment, neither one of them moved. Braeden was afraid to move for fear of what might happen afterward. No doubt she would rush off and hide herself away from him, and that was the last thing he wanted.

"I have to . . ." she tried to speak, then stopped.

She appeared to be battling within herself, and Braeden was even more certain her feelings for him hadn't died. What could he do to help her realize that they could overlook the past and move forward?

"I've tried several times to talk to you," Braeden finally offered.

"I've been busy," she replied.

Gently, he rubbed her upper arms with his thumbs. "Too busy for a simple conversation?"

Rachel's resistance returned and she stiffened. "With you, there is never a simple conversation. Now, if you'll excuse me, I have business to attend to at the depot."

Braeden dropped his hold, seeing the hostility return to her expression. "You'll have to talk to me sooner or later."

Rachel smiled rather snidely. "I think you underestimate me, Mr. Parker."

"You can't avoid me forever."

"Watch me," she replied and hurried past him and down the steps.

Braeden said nothing more. It was hard to let her go, but he had no desire to force her to remain, only to have an argument. Instead, he returned to his office and buried himself in paper work. He felt more frustration now than in the six years since they'd separated. He tried to pray, but in truth his frustration extended to God. Why would God bring them back together if humiliation and anguish were to be Braeden's only reward?

Finding no consolation in thought, prayer, or duty, Braeden finally gave up on his work. Glancing at his watch, he saw that two hours had passed since he'd encountered Rachel. Was time to be forever gauged by his last moment with her?

Slamming his ledger closed, Braeden realized he could just as easily mope over lunch. Hotel staff were allowed to take part in the Harvey dining room and were, in fact, an intricate part of the preparations. All of the girls had received their month-long training in Topeka, and most of the girls had worked for months elsewhere on the line, but Casa Grande was a new layout for everyone, and it was imperative that the operation run smoothly. Especially once they were dealing with hundreds of guests.

Grabbing his suit coat of worsted navy blue, Braeden made his way to the dining room. He had a chance of seeing Rachel here, but it was a slim one. She often saw him coming and would quickly exit to busy herself elsewhere. But sometimes he managed to catch her in the act of instructing one or more of the girls, and even watching her from afar made his meal more enjoyable.

Braeden slipped into the coat, hating the added burden as the day warmed considerably. Fred Harvey kept a hard, fast rule that all men dining in his restaurants would wear suit coats, and staff members for the resort were no different. Stopping at the door, Braeden could see that the black-and-white-clad girls were already bustling around the room, and in the corner Rachel spoke intently with two of the waitresses.

Smiling to himself, Braeden took a seat at one of the empty tables and watched as Rachel continued her instruction. She intrigued him as she always had—partly because she didn't see herself as pretty and therefore it only seemed to add to her beauty, and partly because she was an extremely intelligent yet tenderhearted woman. She had a way about her that bespoke of her confidence, but in managing this group of girls, he saw an almost motherly side to her.

He could see, however, that this moment appeared to present a confrontation of wills. The petite blonde on her left appeared anything but gracious in receiving direction. He could tell by the stance she took and the tilt of her chin that she was in complete disagreement with Rachel. The girl on Rachel's right seemed far more interested in what the blonde had to say, and Braeden instantly felt sorry for Rachel.

As if she could feel his gaze upon her, Rachel glanced up. She stiffened notably and squared her shoulders as if preparing herself to do battle. She refocused her attention on the job at hand, but it wasn't another minute before the blonde was pointing out that Braeden was going unserved.

Rachel nodded and instructed both girls to follow her to the table. Fixing her gaze somewhere above Braeden's head, she said, "Welcome to the Harvey House."

"Thank you," Braeden replied, trying hard to keep a straight face. "I see today I will have three lovely ladies to wait upon me."

"We're in training," the blonde replied with a flirtatious smile. "Miss Taylor says I need to improve my serving skills in order to better please everyone."

"Hmm, that is a lofty task," Braeden said, lifting his gaze to Rachel.

"The degree of difficulty depends on the customer," Rachel replied curtly.

"But we have only the nicest customers," the blonde interjected.

"There will be times, however," Rachel said, turning her full attention on the young women, "when the customers will not be so nice. You must be prepared to deal with them in an open, friendly manner. That does not mean, Miss Brooks, that you mistake acting in a flirtatious manner for a courteous one."

"I hardly see that the girl did anything wrong," Braeden said, undermining Rachel's instructions.

She turned to glare at him. "No doubt you see her actions as acceptable, but Mr. Harvey sets the rules in this house, and he expects his girls to act in a dignified manner."

"I'm sure even Mr. Harvey enjoys the smile of a beautiful young woman. Miss Brooks, is it?" he asked, knowing he was infuriating Rachel further. Something inside him couldn't resist agitating her in this manner. Perhaps if he continued, she would take him aside and speak to him about his actions, and then he could force her to listen to him.

"Yes," Ivy said, beaming him another smile. She lowered her lashes coyly and added, "I'm glad someone can appreciate my charm."

"You are here to serve meals," Rachel countered while the other girl giggled. The blonde seemed unmoved.

Braeden thought they made a most unlikely trio and grinned. "Yes, serve me a meal, I'm nigh on to starving." He grabbed the oversized napkin and snapped it out.

Rachel frowned and looked at Ivy. "Your service should be pleasant and friendly, but not improperly so."

"I haven't been given friendly or pleasant service by you, Miss Taylor," Braeden interjected. "I wonder, is the rule only for your girls or must you follow it as well?" The Harvey Girls giggled while Rachel turned crimson.

Through clenched teeth she managed to say, "Forgive me."

"Now, there is an admirable suggestion. Forgive me," Braeden said thoughtfully. "Forgiveness is an important aspect of a happy life. Wouldn't you agree, Miss Taylor?"

"Mr. Parker, we haven't time to dally here. What would you like to drink with your meal?" Rachel questioned sternly.

"First, I want that friendly service," he answered. "I think this is the perfect opportunity to show your young ladies here how to interact when you feel less than friendly."

Braeden watched the curious expressions of the two waitresses while Rachel seemed to deliberate within herself as to how to continue.

"There will always be days when you feel less than friendly, and there will always be irritating people who make you want to act less than cordial," Rachel finally said.

"Yes," Braeden added, "but everyone deserves kindness and consideration."

"Sometimes that is true," Rachel replied, seeming to forget the girls. "But sometimes people act in a way that causes you to feel less inclined to put yourself in harm's way."

"Sometimes people are simply misjudged—misunderstood," Braeden answered flatly. He looked hard into Rachel's eyes. "Sometimes people don't bother to get all the facts."

"I take the word of those I trust, and that trust allows me to believe in them regardless of circumstances."

"Oh, and what would it take to build this trust?"

Rachel paled. "We're getting off the subject."

"We've never quite been on the subject," Braeden retorted rather sarcastically. "Not unless Mr. Harvey has somehow included the subtleties of how to deal with your customers' painful past experiences and disappointments."

"Only if it interferes with the future."

"Mr. Harvey's future or yours?" Braeden asked seriously.

For just a moment, Braeden saw a flash of something akin to sorrow pass through Rachel's eyes. She quickly recovered, however, and smiled.

"Mr. Braeden likes coffee with his meals," she said, then turning to the Harvey Girls, she added, "I'll let you continue to serve him while I attend to other matters."

Braeden watched her walk away, wishing he could go after her or at least call to her and force her to deal with the issues between them. No matter what happened, he had to find a way to get her to open up to him.

I still love you, Rachel, he thought. *I love you more now than I did then. If only you would listen to reason—forget the past— forget the lies that destroyed us.*

"So where did you live before coming to Casa Grande, Mr. Parker?" Ivy Brooks asked, smiling sweetly.

Braeden looked up to see her face, wishing it were Rachel instead. "I hail from Chicago originally," he replied. "But Morita is now my home."

"Surely you don't intend to stay on here forever?" Ivy questioned.

"It all depends," Braeden replied.

"On what?"

"If there's something worth staying for."

Ivy watched as Braeden finished the last of his coffee and bid Faith good-bye. Faith giggled all the way back to where Ivy stood. Her eyes fairly shone in admiration.

"That man is so handsome," Faith whispered.

Ivy nodded. "Yes, he is."

"Miss Taylor doesn't seem to like him much," Faith continued, "and I don't know why. He was perfectly charming the entire time we waited on him. And I thought him especially gallant when he admonished us to pay him no mind and to heed Miss Taylor at all times."

"Heed Miss Taylor, indeed. I'd rather heed a rattlesnake. There's something going on between those two," Ivy replied. "It's more than the simple fact that they knew each other before now. I'd bet my best petticoat that there is some reason why Miss Taylor treats him the way she does. And," Ivy said with a smug smile, "when I find out what it is, I'll use it to my advantage."

Chapter 8

"Rachel, are you receiving visitors?"

Rachel looked up from her desk and a smile immediately came to her lips. "Simone! Come in."

The exotic-looking Simone O'Donnell entered the room attired in a very comfortable calico afternoon dress. The coral-colored flowers set against the cream background complemented Simone's lightly tanned skin and black hair. Rachel envied the simplicity of her beauty.

"I've always heard that expectant mothers are radiant, but you are fairly glowing," Rachel declared. "Close that door and we shall retire to my living quarters and make ourselves more comfortable. That way no one will be inclined to interrupt us."

Simone did as she was instructed and joined Rachel in her private suite. "This is lovely," Simone said upon seeing Rachel's small sitting room.

"Yes, Fred Harvey has been most generous with me. I have all the privacy in the world back here."

"I should say so."

Rachel gave her a short tour. "I have my bedroom set up on this side in order to buffer myself from the noise of the lobby. It's a snug fit, as you see, but by putting the dresser at the end of the bed, I'm able to give the bedroom a little bit of separation from the sitting room."

"This is a wonderful quilt," Simone commented, running her hand along the top of the bed.

"I purchased it from the ladies' sewing circle at the church. They call the pattern Crown of Thorns, and I think it is absolutely marvelous. However, Reginald calls it English Wedding Ring."

"Reginald? Who's that?" Simone questioned, her perfectly arched brow raising ever so slightly.

Rachel laughed. "He's the chef for Casa Grande."

"And he's seen your bedroom?"

Rachel felt her face grow hot. "Certainly not. He caught me walking home from the church sale. As I came in through the back door, he saw me and commented on the quilt. That's all."

"But you must be good friends. I mean, I've never heard you refer to any man, save my Jeffery, by his first name."

Rachel bit at her lower lip. She had hoped for a quiet moment to share her heart in regards to Braeden. "Well, Reginald insisted, and I didn't see any harm in it. I mean, you remember how I felt about maintaining a closeness among staff members when we were back in Topeka."

"Of course I do," Simone replied, watching Rachel very carefully, "but you seem awfully preoccupied, and Jeffery told me there was a man here at the hotel who was upsetting you. Someone from your past."

Rachel nodded. "Come sit with me and I'll explain." She moved away from the bed to her sitting area and offered Simone one of the two high-backed, thickly cushioned chairs. Once they were seated, she continued. "Jeffery was right about there being a man from my past here at the hotel. But it isn't Reginald. The man is Braeden Parker. He's the manager for the hotel."

"I see," Simone replied with a grin. "And is he the reason

you suddenly seem so nervous and pale?"

Rachel laughed, but not with her usual enthusiasm. "No, that's caused from trying to straighten out my girls and make certain they work in perfect order."

Simone smiled. "I should be here with you."

"Yes, you should. How dare you go and get pregnant on your wedding night?" Rachel teased. "Have you seen the doctor yet?"

"I have. He says that I am the picture of health. Of course, he hasn't seen me in the morning with my head bent over the washbasin."

"Have you been terribly sick?"

"No, not really," Simone replied. "I'm fine so long as no one mentions food before eleven-thirty. Poor Jeffery. He's had to start taking his morning meal down at the café or up here. I can't even stand the smell of food cooking. But after the morning passes, I feel much better."

"I suppose that's why they call it morning sickness," Rachel commented.

"I think it's pretty normal," Simone answered, "but one of my neighbors informed me that she was never sick in the mornings but suffered terribly at night. So apparently there's nothing routine or regulated about having a baby."

Rachel nodded. "I would imagine each case is pretty much unique—like the babies involved." She reached out and took hold of Simone's hand. "I'm so very happy for you, Simone—and for Jeffery too. I know you'll be a wonderful mother." She felt the words stick in her throat as tears filled her eyes. She dropped Simone's hand and looked away.

"What is it, Rachel?" It was now Simone's turn to voice concern. She reached for Rachel's hand and squeezed it gently. "Please tell me. Jeffery said you are hardly yourself, and I can see that now for myself."

Rachel forced her emotions under control. "It all has to do with Braeden Parker." She looked up at Simone and tried to smile. "We . . . that is to say, I . . . oh, I don't know what to say." Rachel shook her head in exasperation. Simone was her dearest friend, and if she should be able to speak to anyone about this mess, it should be her.

"You two were once very close?" Simone questioned.

Rachel nodded.

"You loved him?"

Again Rachel nodded, fighting back tears.

"You're still in love with him?"

Simone's words hit Rachel like a slap in the face. Rachel had argued over and over with herself about her feelings. She knew she would never love anyone save Braeden, but she had tried desperately to convince herself that she was no longer "in love" with him.

She looked up and met Simone's compassionate expression. That was her undoing. With a sob, Rachel answered, "Yes."

"Is he married?" Simone questioned quietly.

"No." Rachel pulled a handkerchief from her deep apron pocket. "No, it's nothing like that."

"Then what is it?"

"We were once engaged," Rachel said with a heavy sigh. "I broke off the engagement because of something someone told me. Something that condemned Braeden as being unfaithful to me."

"And were the allegations true?"

"I thought they were, but now I'm not so sure." It was the first time Rachel had ever admitted her doubts on the matter. "I took the word of my mother and her friends. They told me Braeden was seeing someone else. My mother was well-known for having knowledge of the neighborhood and those around her. It seemed logical to believe them—especially her . . . because . . . well, I'm not a beautiful woman and I had no fortune to speak of. Braeden had plenty of money and a good job. He was well liked and dashingly handsome. I knew it was a wonder that he would even look at me."

"Rachel, you are a lovely woman. You have a beautiful face and your figure, well, I've heard the girls comment on wishing they were so well proportioned."

Rachel sniffed and smiled. "My hips are too wide and my bosom equally full."

"Yes, but your waist is small. You have the perfect hour-glass figure."

"You're sweet to say so, but even if I could take pride in my looks, it wouldn't change the past. I had no confidence in anything about myself then. I was the daughter of a railroad worker. After he died, we were even poorer and my mother had to seek financial support by running a boardinghouse. I'd only managed to meet Braeden because we attended the same church."

"Ah, so he's a believer?"

"Yes," Rachel admitted. "Or he was. I haven't talked to him lately about his feelings on the matter."

"Have you talked to him about any of his other feelings?" Simone asked seriously.

"No, I can't. Every time he's near me, I know I can't speak to him about anything important. I've hidden behind a façade of anger and snobbery, and I hate myself more each time I walk away and leave the matter unresolved."

"So tell him this."

Laughing, Rachel dabbed her eyes. "You make it sound so simple."

"Why does it have to be hard? You obviously still care for this man. He isn't married, and you will be working closely together under the same roof. I'd say this isn't likely to be a situation that will go unquestioned for long."

"I know you're right. I've seen him go out of his way to talk to me."

"What happened?"

"I went out of my way not to be talked to," Rachel replied with a hint of a grin. "I just keep thinking that I'll accidently open my mouth and out will pour all manner of thought that I've kept buried and would like to keep hidden for good. I mean, what if I suddenly declare my feelings and he laughs at me? What if he despises me for my weakness?"

Simone shook her head and let go of Rachel's hand. Easing back into her chair, she crossed her arms. "You must stop this nonsense of worrying 'what if?' and talk to him. Take him aside on the pretense of business and force him to listen to what you have to say. Just be honest. If he won't listen to you, then you will have at least tried."

"I'm afraid it isn't Braeden who refuses to listen. It's me. I suppose I'm just as afraid of what he might say."

"Like what?"

"Like it was a good idea for us to part company and how he's glad we never married. I could just see myself baring my heart, then having to watch as he devours it."

Simone nodded. "Or you can say nothing and always wonder."

Silence filled the room for several moments as the two women simply looked at each other. Rachel wished the answer were that easy, but she knew deep inside that the entire matter of Braeden Parker was anything but.

"I let hearsay destroy my life. Even knowing what the Bible says about avoiding idle talk, I allowed it to influence my choices in life. I refused to trust my heart on the matter because I was young and figured my naïveté had led me to this place. I never gave Braeden a chance to defend himself because I'd always known my mother to be right about the things going on around us." Rachel sighed. "I don't know if we can go back to what we had."

"Then don't," Simone replied matter-of-factly. "Go forward to something better."

"I just don't know." Rachel felt overwhelmed and frightened by the feelings raging within her. One minute she was convinced that Simone was right and she was ready to march across the lobby and plant herself in Braeden's office and tell him everything. The next minute she was certain that as soon as she admitted to having feelings for him, Braeden would mock her and cause her further pain.

"A wise woman once told me that God does nothing by chance. He has a perfect order for everything. Do you still stand by that philosophy, or was that just a flowery speech for my benefit?"

"I still believe that," Rachel finally admitted.

"Then God must have brought you two together for a reason. And if not for love, then for reconciliation," Simone said softly. "Either way, you win."

"But if he doesn't return my feelings—"

"You'll be in no worse a state than you are right now."

"But he'll know how I feel."

"So your pride gets a little singed," Simone replied. "At least you'll know, and you'll have this matter behind you. Either way, I'm figuring that God is big enough for the job."

Rachel considered Simone's words long after she'd gone. She had very nearly convinced herself that leveling with Braeden was the right thing to do when Reginald approached, declaring that it was time to finish interviewing the last of the kitchen staff.

"I have two men who should do nicely for the baking," he told her. "And there's a local boy, Tomas Sanchez, who is in desperate need of employment. I thought he might work out well as a general errand boy and stocker. He's only sixteen, but he's now the man of his family."

Rachel thought of the awesome responsibility. "Are there many in his family?"

"I should say so. He has eight brothers and sisters, a sickly mother, and an ancient grandmother. He's the only one old enough to seek employment."

"Give him the job," Rachel quickly agreed and dabbed at her forehead. The afternoon heat was quite taxing, making everyone irritable.

"Would you rather I take responsibility for hiring the bakers? That is to say, I see no reason you should have to add to your labors when they will be under my direct supervision."

Rachel smiled. Reginald was always looking for ways to ease her burden. "That would be wonderful, Reginald."

"Call me Reg. Reginald always sounds so formal. You Americans are good about putting aside formalities and ceremony—let it be so between us."

"All right, Reg," Rachel replied and smiled. "As hot as it is, I'm not about to argue with you or anyone else."

"September is said to be a cooler month. I believe we shall enjoy an enchanting Indian summer, with less severity in temperature."

"Who told you this?" she questioned, knowing that Reg was as foreign to this part of the country as she was.

"Mrs. Needlemeier. The woman is a vast source of information. She informed me where I might find fresh mint. Her gardener planted an abundance, and she has given me leave to harvest it whenever I have need."

Rachel smiled. "Nothing seems to escape Mrs. Needlemeier's attention."

"She has a bevy of other herbs in her private garden and has also made these available to the Harvey House. I told her we could pay, but she said that was nonsense and shooed me away."

Rachel could well imagine the scene. She dabbed her forehead again and silently wished she could go lie down and cool off as many of her girls were doing. Reg must have sensed her exhaustion because in the next moment, he turned her away from the kitchen.

"I am perfectly capable of handling this job. You go rest. You are very much like our beloved Queen Victoria. Her majesty is well-known for her hard work. You are like her in that way and in many others," Reginald said, guiding Rachel gently to the door of the Harvey Girls' parlor. "I will bid you good-afternoon and leave you to rest. I wouldn't want anything to happen to one so lovely and delicate as you, Rachel."

Rachel thought his concern to be quite refreshing. She wondered why Braeden couldn't respond to her in such a tender way. It seemed that whenever they met up, he was always sarcastic and forceful, and Rachel, angry and scared.

"Thank you, Reg," she finally said, noticing that he seemed to be awaiting her decision. "I think I will go rest for a little while. I'm sure to be a new person once the sun goes down."

"That's the spirit," Reg replied. "Then off with you, and I will return to my duties."

Rachel nodded and left him there in the kitchen. The parlor was empty as she moved through it to the adjoining hall. She smiled to think of Reg comparing her to Queen Victoria. Rachel had once seen a picture of the woman in a newspaper. It was her golden jubilee or some other sort of celebration. The woman was not at all a pleasant-looking sort, but instead wore her authority in her very expression. She could certainly not be called a beauty, although Rachel recalled having heard that in her youth she had been quite lovely.

"But youth fades," Rachel sighed, bringing her hand to her cheek, as if feeling her own face wrinkle and wither. "Time is passing by quickly for me. It won't be that many years before I'm thirty, and then my life will be half over and I'll still have nothing more to show for it than this."

She looked down the hallway of doors and polished wood floors and sighed. For all her responsibility and the admiration of her superiors, it would never compensate for the lack of love and family in her life. For although she loved her job and even loved her girls, at least most of them, they would never fill the need inside her nor satisfy her hunger for marriage and children.

"If you have a purpose, Lord," she said, glancing upward, "I certainly pray you reveal it soon. Otherwise I shall end up as old and wrinkled as Queen Victoria, without the country and family to show for it."

Chapter 9

Set amidst an arched grotto, the hot springs at Casa Grande generated an invigorating flow of warm mineral waters that made it a particularly welcome attraction. Even in the heat of summer, the hot springs were sought out by the staff of Casa Grande for entertainment and restoration. With her work completed, Rachel thought a dip in the springs would be just the thing to help her sleep better.

She donned a bathing suit supplied by the hotel and laughed at the shortness of the skirt. It barely came to the middle of her stocking-and-bloomer-covered legs. The top, with short, fitted sleeves, buttoned up the middle to her neck. Rachel had never worn anything so daring and still had trouble believing it acceptable to be seen in such a condition—especially without a corset. She pulled on her robe, took up a book of poems and a towel, and steadied her nerves. The hour was well past the time when most of the staff went to the pool, so she kept her confidence and hoped she might be the only one there. She had no desire to share small talk with any of the girls—most were considerably younger and chattered away about the handsome men they'd known or had seen. Such talk was boring at best, and at worst it depressed Rachel.

It wasn't for a lack of understanding, because Rachel knew what it was to daydream about such things. But the pain it stirred deep inside made her miserable, and therefore it seemed senseless to occupy herself with such idle conversation. Besides, she was their supervisor. A motherly, matronly figure who told them what to do and when. And although she enjoyed a closeness with the girls, Rachel knew it didn't compare to the camaraderie that they shared with one another as peers. They might come to her with their problems, hoping for solutions and an understanding ear, but they were not likely to share their dreams or invite her to partake in their entertainment.

At least there was Simone, and that was a great comfort to Rachel. Perhaps God had perfectly interceded on Rachel's behalf by having Simone be unable to work at Casa Grande. Now they could just be friends and not worry after the incidentals of running a business.

Rachel slipped out the back door and made her way around the side of the resort to where a stone walkway led to a lighted path to the pools. Once the guests actually arrived at Casa Grande, Rachel would wait to change her clothes at the bathhouses that extended off the stone grotto, but for now it was far more convenient to do things this way. She hummed as she made her way in the darkness. Somehow it helped her feel less self-conscious about her appearance. She tried to believe what Simone had told her about having a fine figure, but it was difficult at best. Rachel had always believed that beauty came from within a person, and right now she didn't feel at all beautiful.

A frown came to her face. *No, I feel hard and frustrated. I have so much misery inside of me, it would be difficult for anything lovely to coexist.*

Opening the wrought-iron gate at the grotto's central arch, Rachel felt a small sigh escape her as she found the main pool completely deserted. She put her book and robe aside and hurried to get into the pool before anyone else could appear. At least the water afforded her a bit of coverage.

The warmth penetrated her aching muscles and brought a smile to her face. Her feet hurt from the long hours she'd spent working, and her neck and shoulder muscles seemed to be bound in cords that refused to relax. For a moment she floated lazily on her back and tried to concentrate on nothing but the starry sky overhead. It was a little more difficult to see the stars because of the soft glow coming from electric light posts, but they were there. This was the reason she chose the main pool rather than the more secluded women's bathing pool. The latter had a lattice-styled wall connecting with the rose stone arches to completely surround the bathing area. Overhead, another series of vine-covered lattices helped to shield the harshness of the sun. The lattice allowed the mountain breezes to blow through, while shielding the women from view. It was a lovely setting, but you couldn't gaze upward into the night skies and see the diamond-like sprinkling of stars. Here, so near the mountains in the dry, crisp air, the stars often looked close enough to touch. Even now the skies spread out like a masterpiece unlike anything Rachel had ever seen. Reaching her hand to the sky, Rachel pretended she could touch the stars. The idea made her smile. When she was a little girl, her father had often put her on his shoulders so she could "reach" the sky. She liked to imagine that even now, as she reached upward, her beloved papa was reaching down to touch her from heaven.

Feeling her body begin to relax, Rachel rolled over on her stomach and dove under the water. She felt the rush of warmth hit her face. What a marvelous sensation. It caused her nose to tingle and tickle as she pushed toward the bottom of the pool. She continued to dive underwater for several moments, desiring only to stay there forever and let the water continue to drain away her miseries. But soon she found herself short of breath and forced herself to return to the surface. As her face emerged above the water, Rachel instantly became aware of a presence. Smoothing her wet hair out of her face, Rachel gazed up to find Braeden quietly watching her.

"You shouldn't come here by yourself," he said, leaning back casually against the stone entry arch. "Don't you know it's dangerous to swim alone?"

Rachel felt her pulse quicken. "It's not proper for you to be here. Leave at once!"

"I've as much a right to come for a swim as do you," he answered with a grin. "After all, this is the common pool for both men and women."

Rachel realized that she would have to do something. She couldn't just remain in the pool and allow Braeden to join her. It simply wouldn't be proper for them to swim together—alone. Knowing that she would have to expose herself to his view, she very calmly swam over to the stone steps and climbed out of the pool. She quickly toweled off and pulled on her robe without another word. What she had hoped would be a quiet, leisurely swim and a chance to read a few pages of poetry under the twinkling stars quickly faded into a confrontation.

"Have your swim, Mr. Parker. I wouldn't dream of interfering. However, I see that you, too, are very much alone. Are you not worried about such evils?"

"But I'm not alone," he replied softly. "For you are here."

Rachel shook her head, then squeezed out the water from her long, curly hair. "But I shall not linger."

She tried not to notice the look of disappointment on his face, nor how marvelous he looked in the dim lamplight. He stood fully clothed but more casual than she was used to seeing him. His shirt, usually buttoned and secured with a necktie, was daringly open, while his sleeves were turned up. She glanced around him and noticed there was no sign of a suit coat anywhere.

"You hardly look ready for a swim," she finally managed.

"It doesn't take that much time to disrobe," he said, grinning.

Rachel felt her cheeks grow warm. "I shall bid you good-evening and give you over to your own preparations."

"Rachel, don't go."

She ignored him and turned to walk away, but he called after her in such a pleading tone that she had to stop.

"Please."

The richness of his voice and the desperation in that simple word forced her to turn back around. She looked at him for a moment, unable to find words to berate him with for delaying her departure. His sandy hair fell forward across his brow, leaving her with a strong desire to push it back into place. But it was the intensity and pleading of his stare that fixed her to the spot. How could she not stay? How could she not remember the time they'd shared so long ago? She could almost remember what it was like to be in his arms—to laugh at his stories—to tremble at his spoken words of love.

"Rachel, I know you've been avoiding me," he said softly. "I know it was a shock to see me turn up here after so many years. But now that it's happened, now that we're both here, couldn't we at least discuss the matter?"

"I don't know," she answered plainly. Trepidation coursed through her like white-hot fire.

"Why?" he asked, taking a couple of steps toward her.

Rachel clutched the lapel of her robe. "I don't think it would be wise."

"Again, I must ask—why?"

Rachel swallowed hard. "There's no sense in dredging up the past."

"In our case, I would beg to differ. Our past has never been resolved. You never allowed me a chance to defend myself, and I'm asking for that chance now."

Rachel considered his words for a moment. She supposed it was only fair to allow the man to speak his mind after six years. It was true enough that she'd denied him any real chance to counter her accusations. But if she let him talk now, she might have to face her fears. Fears that suggested she had been wrong six years ago and that by her own hand she had ended any chance she had for happiness.

"All I'm asking is that you give me a chance to speak," Braeden said, stopping directly in front of her.

Rachel nodded. "Very well. Speak."

"Thank you. I know you're afraid of what I have to say, but I honestly think it will be better for both of us in the long run."

She had no idea how that could possibly be the case, but she nodded and tried to steel herself inside for whatever declaration was to come.

"You never let me defend myself six years ago. You refused my proposal based on the inaccuracies you'd been told, and you never allowed yourself to trust in me. I suppose our love was rather immature to have to weather such an intense storm, but I believed in you and I thought you believed in me."

She said nothing. How could she? It was so hard to admit that she had given up her trust in him with a few well-intended words of warning.

"I was at the hotel that day, as your mother's friends revealed. I was even in the company of a beautiful young woman, and yes, I was headed up the grand staircase with my arm around her. But she wasn't my mistress or my new lady love. She was, however, the daughter of a dear friend whom I was scheduled to meet that afternoon at the hotel. She had just given me the news of her impending wedding and . . ." He paused, seeming to search for the right words. "I told her of our own plans—of the ring I'd just purchased for you. We were congratulating each other, and she was accompanying me to meet her father."

Rachel felt the blood drain from her head. Hadn't she already presumed it to be something innocent and misunderstood? Hadn't she already condemned herself for allowing hearsay to be the final word on a matter of such importance? But she had loved her mother dearly and had been confident that her mother would never do anything to harm her. Even given Elvira Taylor's penchant toward gossip, Rachel couldn't believe her mother would ever pass judgment on something so important without anything more than the supposition of her friends.

Braeden reached out to touch her cheek. "I did nothing wrong. I couldn't have betrayed you."

Rachel found it impossible to admit that she knew of his innocence. She could hardly stand the thought of what she'd done. She had lost six years of happiness with the only man whom she would ever love. And perhaps she had lost future years, as well, for why should he find any reason to believe in her now?

She bit nervously at her lip and looked away. "So how have you been all these years? Did you . . . that is to say . . . you said you never married?"

When he didn't answer her right away, Rachel forced herself to look back at him. His expression seemed pained, and he appeared to be considering her words with great thought.

"No, I didn't marry," he finally replied, as if deciding she deserved an answer after all.

"Oh," she said, trying desperately to sound neutral on the matter.

He smiled ever so slightly. "Don't you want to know why?"

Rachel did indeed want to know the answer to that question, but she wasn't about to ask it. "I suppose," she said slowly, "that is a rather private matter. It's really none of my business."

Braeden took hold of her hand. "It is very much your business, Rachel. I never married because I have loved only one woman." He paused and looked deep into her eyes. "And that woman is you. It's always been you. It will always be only you."

Rachel felt her knees begin to tremble. Shaking from head to toe, she pulled away and walked to the archway. She couldn't think. Her mind flooded with the wonder of the declaration he'd just made, but she couldn't force herself to form a coherent thought.

"Rachel, you must believe me," Braeden said, coming up behind her.

"Yoo-hoo!" The voice of Ivy Brooks carried lyrically on the night air.

Rachel felt herself tense. It didn't look good to be seen here alone with Braeden, much less to have him standing so close to her.

"Oh, there you are, Mr. Parker," Ivy declared.

Rachel whirled on her heel. Ivy approached them wearing a scandalously short bathing suit with bloomers but no stockings.

"I received your note," Ivy fairly purred the words as she batted her eyelashes.

Her sultry words and scandalous apparel were enough to cause Rachel to believe the worst. Had it all been a lie? A carefully plotted and contrived scene for her benefit? Had Braeden decided to hurt her as badly as she'd hurt him by pretending to still care? Then, once she gave in to her feelings for him, he'd have Ivy appear poolside at just the right moment to plunge the knife into her dream of reconciliation?

She shuddered and moved past Braeden and Ivy and headed up the walkway. *I have to get away from here,* she thought. No matter what the real reason was for Ivy's appearance, Rachel felt extremely vulnerable. *I can't believe I almost admitted my love for him.* The image of him laughing in her face caused tears to come to Rachel's eyes. Simone might have thought injured pride was a nominal price to pay, but at this moment Rachel felt it unbearable.

"Rachel, wait!" Braeden called after her while Ivy's lyrical laughter filled the night air. "Rachel, it's not what you think!"

It pained her to think he might have duped her. The thought of him setting her up in order to crush her once and for all was enough to cause tears to wet her cheeks. Just then she remembered her towel and book. Only it wasn't her book—it belonged to the resort, and she couldn't just leave it outside exposed to the elements. She would have to stop and retrieve it, but that meant going back and dealing with Braeden and Ivy.

She stopped midstep and realized that she had to go back for more reasons than the book and towel. If she allowed them to drive her away, she would never have any control over Ivy and she'd never, ever be able to face Braeden again. She wiped her face and drew a deep breath. *God, give me the strength to face them.*

Slowly she marched back to the pool just as Ivy let out a shriek while Braeden wrapped his arms around her. Rachel stopped for a moment and watched them. She tried to make herself believe that it didn't affect her. That it meant nothing.

But in truth, it cut her to the core.

Braeden's gaze locked with hers. "She lost her footing," he tried to explain, setting Ivy upright on the walk.

"A girl could certainly lose a great many things around you, Mr. Parker," Ivy said seductively before glancing over her shoulder at Rachel and adding, "Her heart for one."

"I forgot my book and towel," Rachel stated very calmly. Her façade of strength was back in place, and she refused to allow either of them to know the true emotion of her heart. She gingerly moved across the now wet stones, retrieved her book, and made her way back to the open archway. "Do not forget your curfew, Miss Brooks," she stated stiffly.

She looked briefly at Braeden, saw his expression of pleading, but refused to say anything more. She felt overwhelmed by confusion and anguish. There was nothing she could say.

Blinded by tears, Rachel made her way back to her quarters. She clutched the book to her damp robe as though it could somehow offer her strength to deal with the pain inside her. She wanted to believe Braeden's words—believe that he still loved her. But why should he? After the way she had acted, why should he care?

Once inside her room, she quickly changed her clothes, then fell across her bed, sobbing. *I've ruined it all now. He'll never want to see me again. He'll believe me unworthy of his trust, and perhaps he is right. I am so fickle and silly. How could I have acted like that?*

Such thoughts only made her cry harder. All of her life she had only been made to feel special by two people. One was Braeden, the other was her father. Now both were lost to her.

Her words tainted with pain and regret, she looked up and asked, "God, what have I done? Why did I act like such a child?"

Chapter 10

"Well, as I see it," Rachel said, beginning the meeting, "we're right on schedule. There are some minor problems, but I feel confident we can deal with these issues before the grand opening." She watched as Braeden eased back in his desk chair, grateful that the management meeting had been held in his office instead of hers. This way, when all was said and done, she could quickly exit before anything became too personal.

"I've simply had marvelous luck obtaining help from the locals," Reg declared. "Fresh produce, fish, lamb—not to mention spices and herbs."

Rachel looked to Reg with a smile. He created the perfect buffer between her and Braeden. There could be no talk of the past with Reginald Worthington situated neatly between them. Rachel felt no small amount of relief in realizing this benefit. She would simply stay close to Reg in all matters pertaining to the dining room, and when she exited the company of her girls, she would do so through the private parlor and hallway. That way, she wouldn't allow herself to be caught unaware of Braeden's presence. Furthermore, she would insist that Reg be present at every management meeting. He was, after all, in charge of managing the kitchen, and she had already delegated a great deal of responsibility to the man. He should, by all rights, be included in their meetings.

"I have a problem with my inventory," Braeden said,

glancing over the papers in his hand to meet Rachel's gaze. "The originals do not match the tallies made by my house-keeper and her staff."

"We have the same problem," Rachel declared. "Reginald—" She felt her face grow hot as she corrected herself. "That is to say, Mr. Worthington has taken an inventory of our supplies, as well, and they do not match my original paper work."

Braeden put the papers down. "What do you suppose it means?"

Rachel shrugged. "Why must it mean anything? I would imagine the manifest listing of what was originally shipped here was inaccurate."

"Seems unlikely that they would be so remiss in their inventory," Braeden countered. "After all, the Santa Fe is suffering from some poor investments, and they are no doubt counting their pennies carefully as they bring this new resort to life."

"But people make mistakes," Rachel said softly. She realized he might believe her words to hold a double meaning and quickly moved her attention to Reg. "Have you been able to figure anything out from our inventory?"

"Personally, I believe it to be a simple case of miscounting," Reginald replied. "I presumed the mistake to be my own, but I had Tomas redo the count and he came up with the same thing. There are various articles missing: silver services, pots and pans, utensils, linens, napkins, even food. With such a wide variety of articles in dispute, it seems unlikely that it would be a mere case of thievery."

"Why?" Braeden asked seriously.

Reg ran his fingers along his pencil-thin moustache. "An intelligent thief would have purloined only those articles of value. The silver services, for instance. Our inventory counts show a discrepancy of two; however, neither of those services were of the highest quality. The very best of our silver has been untouched."

"Perhaps the thief is untrained as to the value of silver."

Rachel listened as the two men reasoned the situation. Finally she interjected a question. "What exactly are you missing, Mr. Parker?"

Braeden allowed his gaze to linger on her for a moment before picking his papers back up. "Many of the bed linens are off count. There are soap dishes, books, lounging chairs, towels, and bathing suits," he said, glancing back up. "Along with a variety of other odds and ends."

"None of which sound like the kind of thing to make a thief rich," Rachel replied.

Braeden shrugged. "I don't know. It depends on what the thief is looking to gain. Money or possessions. You might well have a very poor thief who is simply supplying his family with needed linens and table service."

"Linens obviously marked for the Harvey Company?"

"A lot of folks wouldn't care about such a thing."

"I still believe it's possible the inventory sheets were simply wrong," Rachel replied. "After all, we're still receiving supplies daily from the trains. Perhaps some of the goods are still en route."

"I suppose it's possible," Braeden finally conceded. "However, I'd like to call the town marshal in on the matter."

"I hardly think that's necessary," Rachel said sternly. "It would make us look incompetent. No, I suggest we wait and see what happens as we go. Let us do an inventory daily and see if anything else turns up missing."

"Daily? I don't have time for daily inventories. Not if I'm going to have this resort ready for a grand opening in little more than a week."

"Then assign someone to help you," Rachel replied impatiently. "I've done that very thing with Reginald, and it's working out very nicely. Put your housekeeper in charge of the matter. That is, if you trust her." She knew her words were cutting, but she didn't care. The tension in the room grew stronger and even Reginald was starting to look uncomfortable. Rachel grimaced and tried hard not to let her emotions control her actions.

"I trust her," Braeden said, staring hard at Rachel. "She's proven herself to be worthy of my faith."

His eyes narrowed and seemed to deepen in hue. To Rachel they were the most beautiful shade of blue she'd ever known. Why did he have to be so handsome? Why couldn't she just forget what they had shared and leave the past well enough alone?

"I . . . ah . . . quite agree with Rachel," Reginald said hesitantly. Obviously he didn't really want to get in the middle of their affair.

At the usage of her given name, Braeden visibly clenched his teeth together. The ticking in his cheek told Rachel he was quite irritated at this new-found friendship she shared with the resort's chef. It bothered her to have him angry, but at the same time it infuriated her to think he would perhaps consider her undeserving of friends.

"Thank you, Reginald," she replied, feeling only the tiniest bit of comfort to have him take her side in the matter. "If the inventory continues to disappear, then perhaps we could call in the law."

Braeden shrugged. "Have it your way."

"Good, now moving on to other business," Rachel said, trying hard not to notice his agitation. "I plan to appoint Gwen Carson as head waitress. She will be in charge of everything whenever I am off duty or otherwise occupied. Gwen has just over three years with the Harvey system, and I find her to be the best candidate for the job. However, there is a slight problem."

"What kind of problem?" Braeden questioned.

"Esmeralda Needlemeier."

"Ah," he replied, nodding.

"The old woman is quite a fearsome creature, if I do say so," Reg offered.

"Still, the railroad and Mr. Harvey have asked us to treat her with the utmost of respect," Braeden interjected. "She owns over half the town, and what she doesn't own, she seems to have little trouble controlling. She could easily make life for us here at Casa Grande most difficult if we don't allow her a say in some of the issues."

"Well, this is one decision I cannot heed her advice or desires on," Rachel replied. "She expects for me to put Ivy Brooks in the position of head waitress, but the request is completely out of line. Ivy has barely made it through her training and has no experience, at least not in being a Harvey Girl." She knew her words sounded sarcastic, but she didn't care.

Braeden took her words for what they were, a reminder of that evening by the pool. "I wonder if Miss Carson knows how to trust people and not jump to conclusions?"

"She appears very level-headed," Rachel answered, tensing at his words. She'd known better than to goad him that way, but the truth of the matter was that Ivy was inexperienced and unacceptable as head waitress. And before Braeden could further cause her pain and suggest she appoint Ivy to the head waitress job, Rachel wanted to dismiss the idea once and for all.

Trying hard to ignore the scowl on Braeden's face, Rachel continued. "Gwen Carson is the most reliable person I have on staff. She is always willing to do additional jobs when need demands, and she never complains about the extra work. There isn't an aspect of the job she doesn't know, and we get along very nicely."

"I should speak to her and learn her secrets," Braeden muttered.

Rachel ignored him and looked away to Reg. "You've worked with her. I presume you have some thought on this matter."

"I believe she would make an excellent leader for her peers," Reginald replied. "She seems quite willing to follow orders and to adhere to the suggestions of her superiors."

"Then it's settled." Rachel gave him a broad smile.

"I didn't know you needed our approval in order to make the decision," Braeden said seriously.

"I didn't, Mr. Parker, but I wanted you to understand the situation. Mrs. Needlemeier will no doubt raise quite a ruckus. She may even feel as though I have slighted her on purpose—which is not the case. Miss Brooks is often insolent and uncooperative, and her attitude toward those she deems to be her inferiors is generally harsh and demeaning. With this spirit and clash of wills, I could not have promoted her to the position even if she had more experience than all of the girls put together. Mr. Harvey firmly believes that attitude is just as important as experience."

"I agree," Braeden replied. "A good attitude can get you through the worst of times. How one deals with bad times has much to do with what lies in the heart."

Rachel drew a deep breath and got to her feet. "The time is getting away from us. I must join my girls for a staff meeting in the dining room. I believe we've resolved all of our issues for the day." She tried to smile, but when she caught sight of Braeden's expression, she knew of at least one issue that had not been dealt with—maybe never would.

Why, God? Why can't I let this matter be? Why does my heart have to be so consumed? Help me to get beyond this, to live my life without this burden. She sought solace in her prayer but found nothing but unanswered questions.

Saying nothing more, Rachel made her way from Braeden's office. She couldn't help but think of Braeden's reaction to her obvious openness with Reginald Worthington. He appeared not only irritated by her first-name basis with the chef, but if she didn't know better, she'd have believed him jealous of the friendship they shared.

She smiled. Maybe it would do him good to be jealous of Reg. After all, he treated Rachel with more respect and tenderness than Braeden did these days. Not that she had allowed Braeden much leeway in that area.

The meeting with the girls passed quickly and without too much ado. Rachel saved the announcement of Gwen's promotion for the very last. She knew in some ways she had done this to save herself from having to deal with Ivy's negative response, but she also saved it in order to leave the meeting on a higher note than the one she'd had with Braeden and Reg.

"Most of you know that the position of head waitress is appointed based on several issues. The most important being length of service and your work record during that time period. Secondly, personality and interaction with your fellow workers is considered. Head waitress is hardly a popularity contest, but how you work and get along with others is an important consideration. Lastly, I consider the way you have worked with me. The head waitress will be my eyes and ears during times when I am away or otherwise occupied. She will need to be someone I can rely upon and feel open to discuss problems related to our dining room. However, I don't want anyone here getting the wrong idea. My choice for this position is not based on whether I like one young woman more than I like another."

She looked out to meet the expression on each girl's face before continuing. With the exception of Ivy and Faith, everyone seemed happy and content and eager to hear her announcement.

"So without further delay, I would like to present our new head waitress, Gwen Carson." Most of the girls clapped, including Faith, who seemed content just to be a part of the group when Ivy wasn't forcing her attentions elsewhere. Ivy quickly jabbed her in the ribs, however, putting a stop to her revelry.

Gwen joined Rachel at the front of the group and beamed a proud smile as Rachel shook her hand. "I shall come to rely heavily upon you, Gwen."

"Thank you, Rachel. I won't let you down."

Over the last few days she had allowed the girls to start calling her by her first name, although it was clearly understood that this was only to be done when there were no customers or officials present. Rachel dismissed the meeting and watched as everyone but Ivy and Faith hurried to surround Gwen and congratulate her. Rachel felt a small amount of satisfaction in seeing Gwen's joy. She'd made the right decision, there was no doubt about that, but she sighed heavily as she saw Ivy slip out the side door. No doubt she would get word to her aunt as soon as possible, and then Rachel would have to face the music.

Nearly an hour later, Rachel was still considering the arrival of Esmeralda Needlemeier when the old woman appeared at her door. Her pinched expression made her intent quite clear.

"Miss Taylor, I believe a mistake has been made," Esmeralda said, tapping her cane loudly on the floor.

"Won't you have a chair," Rachel offered graciously.

Esmeralda tilted her chin slightly and took a seat. "I suppose you know why I've come."

"Yes. Ivy told you that I've appointed Gwen Carson as head waitress for the dining room."

"I thought we had an understanding that my niece was to receive that position."

"No, you had that understanding. I am under the instructions of Fred Harvey, however, and his understanding is considerably different."

"Miss Taylor, your Mr. Harvey and the Santa Fe Railroad assured me that I would have their utmost consideration in matters related to Morita and this resort hotel."

"And so you have. I considered your request for Ivy," Rachel admitted, even though she'd not considered it very seriously. "She is hardly qualified when compared to Miss Carson's experience. I personally trained Miss Carson in Topeka and have continued to receive letters from her since she was sent to Emporia to work for the Harvey dining room there. She was quickly promoted and attained the position of head waitress in little over a year. So not only does she have experience as a Harvey employee, she has already performed the duties of a head waitress. She is well versed in the rules and regulations, which your niece seems wont to ignore, and she is well liked by most of the girls on my staff."

"I see there will be no convincing you to change your mind," Esmeralda stated severely. "I suppose I shall have to take the matter up with the officials of your railroad."

Rachel felt frustrated by the woman's inability or refusal to see the reason behind her decision. "Mrs. Needlemeier, are you a Christian woman?"

The black-draped woman gasped. "I should say so! What kind of question is that?"

"I ask about your faith in order to ascertain if we value the same things. I seek my direction in prayer and God's guidance. If you held no value for that, then I would be wasting my breath in trying to justify my choice. But since you are a God-fearing woman, I can speak to you as a sister in the Lord."

Mrs. Needlemeier harrumphed at this thought but said nothing. She leaned both hands on her silver-capped cane and awaited Rachel's explanation.

"I prayed about the choice I made," Rachel began. "I prayed about coming to Casa Grande and I prayed about the girls I picked for my staff. Ivy was not one I would have chosen, primarily because a resort of this size and expectation needs to have staff members who are already well trained. Secondly, I have never cared for situations where people with money caused other people—good, faithful, hard-working people—to suffer loss because they were unable to compete with the money others used to buy themselves into a position.

"Your niece would certainly not be at this resort had I had my say in the matter. Not only because she is young but because she is totally new and inexperienced and the pressures that will come to her here are hardly fair to put upon a new employee. Also, there is the matter that this resort is looked upon as a privileged place of employment. Many requests for transfer were received for this house, but of course, only twenty-five could be accepted. To allow Ivy to take one of those positions, as well as Faith Bradford, the granddaughter of one of the board members, kept others who were more deserving from being allowed to serve here." She paused, surprised that the old woman hadn't seen the need to interject her opinion on the matter. Grateful to find Esmeralda listening intently, Rachel continued.

"I prayed about each one of these girls, asking God to

111

direct me in working with them. I continue to pray for each of them. I also asked for divine direction on choosing a head waitress. What few people know is that up until a couple of weeks ago, my head waitress was to be Mrs. Jeffery O'Donnell. She and I had worked together in Topeka, and I have come to consider her a good friend. However, she is expecting her first child and Mr. O'Donnell has requested she not work. That caused me to look elsewhere for a head waitress. After much prayer and contemplation, Gwen Carson seemed the most fitting. In fact, it would have been hard to explain choosing Simone O'Donnell over Gwen, as the latter has at least two years of service over Simone. So there you have it. I felt certain God had led me to make the choice of Gwen Carson. I would ask that you pray about it and see if God doesn't give you the same peace of mind on the matter. Rather than making this an issue of our wills, I propose it be given over to God for *His* supreme will on the matter."

Esmeralda rose to her feet. "You make a logical argument and a wonderful speech. I suppose, given your reasoning, it makes sense to appoint this Carson woman to the position of head waitress. However, I'm used to getting what I want."

Rachel stood and smiled. "I assure you, my choice was not made in order to deny you. You are an intelligent business-woman; your dealings with the Santa Fe and Harvey Company are proof of that. Your creation of Morita is another. I would hope you might see the logic of my choice in that light, if in no other."

Esmeralda tapped her cane to the door, then turned. "I am an intelligent woman, Miss Taylor. Intelligent enough to deal with your kind and any other who crosses my path. I will yield in this matter, but do not think to push me in any other. Regardless of your faith and religious convictions, God does not sit on the board of the Santa Fe, nor does He run the Harvey

Company, although there are those who would argue that point. I am God-fearing and a Christian, but I am also a businesswoman as you pointed out. Therefore, the decisions I make will be based on what will benefit my business, and my business is Morita and this resort—despite any thought you might have to the contrary. Good day!"

She left in the same stormy mood by which she had appeared, and when she had gone, Rachel fell back into her chair in a rather exhausted state of mind. The woman was simply more trying than any person Rachel had ever known. With a sigh, she picked up her paper work and tried to refocus her attention, but it was almost impossible. Between Ivy's conniving and hatred, Esmeralda's bossiness, and Braeden's presence, managing Casa Grande's dining room had ceased to be any fun. In fact, the stress of the whole operation was beginning to take its toll.

Then a frightening thought came to Rachel—one she tried very hard to ignore.

Perhaps she should resign her position and put in for a transfer elsewhere on the line.

Chapter 11

The night air was cool, almost chilly, as the shadowy figure slipped into Rachel Taylor's office. Quietly, the marauder closed the door, then lighted a candle. The dim amber light illuminated the office in an eerie manner, and this, coupled with the wind as it howled down from the mountains, set the stage for the covert scene. The wind would actually benefit the thief, throwing out noises and moanings as it whistled through the junipers, coyote willows, and jaboncillos to play itself out against the buildings of Casa Grande. That way, should some sound accidentally emanate from the scene of the crime, no one would give it a second thought. At least that was the plan.

Hot wax dripped down the edge of the candle, causing the thief to curse softly before tipping the candle in a different direction. It was always the little details that ruined great plans, and this plan needed very much to succeed. The job should be performed quickly, as well as quietly. Mistakes were not allowed.

Sliding Rachel's desk drawer out, the forager moved rapidly through the stack of papers until finally finding the one sought. Unfolding the bound copy, it was quickly scanned, deemed to be the necessary article, then refolded. The search continued until all of the drawers had been examined for content. Two other papers were confiscated, and finally the robbery was concluded.

The looter gave a momentary glance toward Rachel's bedroom. That door was securely closed—probably locked, but it didn't matter. Patience needed to be practiced. Patience and wisdom. There would be time to see to her later.

Blowing out the candle, the thief quietly opened the door and stared out into the dimly lit lobby. The front desk was deserted and would continue as such until the grand opening brought in tourists and other celebrating fools. Pulling the door closed without a single sound, the marauder slipped the candle into a pocket and hurried away into the night. The first act of deception had played itself out rather nicely, but part two now needed to be planned.

Yawning, Rachel opened the door and stepped into her office. Though dressed to Mr. Harvey's standards and fully groomed for the day, Rachel couldn't seem to shake her weariness. She would have loved nothing more than to have remained in bed, but she saw little sense in it. Her mind simply wouldn't let her rest. She couldn't stop worrying about all the new complications to her job at Casa Grande, and with each succeeding thought she desired nothing more than to run away and hide. But she had a job to do—at least for now. She could give serious consideration toward her future while continuing to maintain her post.

She reminded herself that it was important to ensure that her girls were at their stations and performing. It didn't matter that she'd slept fitfully through the night, dreaming of Braeden Parker's strong arms and Esmeralda's scowling expression. The work had to be done, and until she resigned her position, the work remained her responsibility.

She heard a commotion down the long hall outside her door. The girls tried to be quiet for the sake of those who had the day off or were serving on a different shift, but nevertheless, it was hard to keep things absolutely still. A gathering of twenty-five girls would never be known for silence, but rather brought to mind giggles, scuffles, and shrieks of dismay, excitement, or protest.

Shaking her head, Rachel went to her desk and opened one of the drawers. It was payday, and she needed to complete some work before Jeffery O'Donnell appeared with the payroll. But before she could so much as find her pencil, a knock sounded on the lobby door.

"Come in," she said, barely managing to stifle a yawn. She looked up and found Reginald peering in through the door. "Oh, good morning, Reg."

"Good morning, milady," he said, throwing back the door to give her a wide, sweeping bow. He looked up and smiled. "And how are we today?"

Rachel laughed. "*We* are tired."

"You are taking far too much upon those delicate shoulders," Reg said from the doorway. "Might I suggest a solution?"

Rachel shrugged. "If you think you have one."

He smiled, came into the office, and closed the door. "Tell me what seems most taxing at this point." He took a seat opposite her desk without waiting to be invited.

Rachel found his actions surprising but made no comment on that fact. "I suppose I'm worried about this inventory problem. Perhaps Mr. Parker was right in thinking that we should involve the local authorities."

"That's possible," Reg admitted. "However, I think your idea has merit."

"It's just that I was hoping this wasn't going to turn into an actual problem. I wanted to believe that the inventory sheets were simply out of order."

"And perhaps they are. You mustn't let it worry you,

Rachel. We will do as you suggested and consider the inventory from day to day."

"Yes, but that only adds more work and with the grand opening coming up so quickly, the last thing I needed was yet another job."

Reg nodded. "Let me offer my services, then. I could easily put Tomas on the job to oversee the inventory for the kitchen and food. Perhaps one of your girls could help to keep a tally of the linens."

"That's awfully kind of you to offer," Rachel said, feeling blessed to have such good help. "But won't that put you in a bind?"

"I don't imagine it would be any worse than any other task. The key is to delegate the problem to others whose schedules are not quite so pressed. If not me, then you could always put several of your girls to work on the matter."

"No, I think I would feel better having you take it over. I don't mind you having Tomas assist you, but I don't think it would be wise to share the girls on the task. They need to recognize my authority over them, and to put them into this situation would confuse that authority. You would have say over them working on the inventory, I would have say over them otherwise—and what would happen when the boundaries of one job crossed another? See my point?"

"Of course," Reg replied. "The wisdom of it speaks for itself. I certainly hope you aren't suggesting that I was seeking to usurp your position."

"Absolutely not," Rachel answered, shaking her head. "I wouldn't think that for a moment. I'm grateful for what you're offering."

"Good. I'll get right to it. Do you still have those inventory lists?"

Rachel nodded. "Yes, they're here in my drawer. I'll get

them to you after breakfast, but first I have to see to the payroll paper work." She paused and smiled. "I hope you know I truly appreciate your help."

Reg shared her smile and his brown eyes fairly twinkled. "I rather fancy the idea of rescuing a damsel in distress and playing the brave knight."

"Well, I don't know how much bravery is required to work on the inventory, but you are indeed rescuing me," Rachel teased. She liked the camaraderie she shared with Reg. It felt good not to have to worry about guarding her words and actions. Stifling another yawn, she looked at her watch. "I need to get going. I have to make sure everyone is at their stations, then I have to come back here and sort through inventories, food orders, and the payroll."

"I wonder if I might make one other suggestion."

Rachel nodded as she got to her feet. Reg instantly stood and his face seemed to sober a bit. "I'm worried that you are working too hard. Have you taken any time for a leisurely walk or a quiet moment at the pool?"

Rachel felt her face grow hot as she thought of the night Braeden had surprised her at the hot springs. "I've tried once or twice but haven't found it to afford me much in the way of restoration."

"Then why not take a walk with me after breakfast?" Reg questioned softly. He gave her such a sweet look of concern that Rachel couldn't help but be touched. "We could stroll down to the falls and perhaps just sit and talk. They have installed charming benches for just such occasions. I could tell you about England. You always seem to find that of interest. Perhaps the setting would lend itself to something even more special."

"I'm sure we would have a wonderful time," Rachel said, growing suddenly uncomfortable. It was clear that Reg had interests in her other than just friendship. "But I can't."

Reg nodded, seeming to understand, but the words he offered next shocked Rachel.

"Is it because you're still in love with that Parker fellow?"

"I beg your pardon?" Rachel stared intently at Reginald. Meeting his gaze, she was certain that he knew something more than she had ever offered.

"It's fairly obvious that you two share something more than the management of Casa Grande."

Rachel felt as though a band had tightened around her chest. "Why do you say that?"

"Rachel, you don't have to worry. I won't share your secret, although others can probably surmise what I have."

"I see."

Reg came to stand a little closer and his voice lowered to a whisper. "You don't have to talk about this if it makes you uncomfortable. I simply wondered if that was the reason you refused to walk with me or if I somehow repulsed you with such an idea."

Rachel shook her head. "You could never repulse me, Reg. I certainly wouldn't want you to take that idea. No, it's a great many things. We can be good friends, but even Mr. Harvey has rules about us becoming more than that."

"Rules are made to be broken," Reg countered.

"Not when you are trying to live by God's rules," Rachel replied. "As a Christian woman, I should seek His will and not my own, and His will would never be to go against my authority on such a matter as fraternizing with another employee."

"And you aren't just saying this to put me off?"

"Absolutely not," Rachel replied. "I'm glad for our friendship, Reg, but it cannot be something more than it is."

"Because of him."

Rachel bit her lip and looked away. She didn't feel close enough to Reg to explain her past with Braeden. And she certainly didn't want to discuss the present or even the future, as it seemed most unlikely that she could possibly hope to make sense out of either one.

Reg spoke before she could reply. "I understand you two knew each other prior to coming here to Casa Grande. Were you very close?"

Rachel looked back to Reg and nodded. "But I don't want to talk about it. The past is the past and I'd rather leave it behind me."

"That might prove difficult given Mr. Parker's very real existence in your future."

"Maybe," Rachel replied. "But I don't see any other way to deal with it."

"Well, then," Reg said, moving toward the door. "I shall excuse myself and get to work. The dawn is nearly upon us and I must oversee my staff." He opened the door and started to leave, but Rachel called to him.

"Reg," she said softly, "thank you for caring about me. I consider you a dear friend."

He gave her another bow, then with a mischievous smile replied, "Perhaps one day you will consider me something more."

He was gone before she could reply, but Rachel couldn't help feeling a mixture of emotions at his words. She didn't want to lead the man to believe her capable of something more when she knew her heart was forever bound to Braeden. She tried not to think of the night by the pool—of Braeden's words of love—but she couldn't help herself. She longed with all of her heart to believe them to be true. To imagine that Braeden had spent the last six years just as miserable as she had was not exactly comforting, but it did make her feel better. If he had refused to marry because of his love for her, then perhaps there was hope for them to rekindle their relationship.

But even as these thoughts filled her head, Rachel remembered the pompous attitude of Ivy Brooks and her part in that disastrous night by the pool. She had mentioned receiving Braeden's message, and he certainly hadn't disputed sending her one.

Just then Rachel glanced down and noticed something on her chair. Leaning closer to inspect it, she chipped at the ivory-colored substance and realized it was wax. Why would there be wax drippings on her chair? Studying the area around her desk, Rachel realized there were also wax drippings on the floor. Casa Grande boasted electric lighting in all of their advertisements, and while oil lamps and candles were available in case of crisis, there was no reason to use candles at this point. Unless, of course, someone had come into her office after the electricity had been shut down for the night, as was the routine in Morita.

The wax made a curious presentation to Rachel. Where had it come from? Someone with a lit candle would have had to have been in her office, and since the wax wasn't there the night before, she could only guess that someone had come into her office in the middle of the night. But for what purpose?

A feeling of uneasiness crept over her. If someone had been in her office, that meant they were capable of going through her desk and other properties. She immediately began looking around the room to see if anything was missing. Nothing appeared out of place.

Sitting down, she pulled open her drawers and gave a cursory glance at the contents. Nothing looked disturbed. But She startled as she touched the unmistakable hardened wax that edged the top of several sheets of paper. Someone had gone through this drawer. Shaking her head, she couldn't figure it out. Why would someone have come into her office and helped themselves to her desk? What were they looking for? The only paper work she had in this particular drawer dealt with the Harvey House staff, inventory, and other necessary papers. What could the thief have been after? Better yet, did they find what they were after?

The only thing she could do was wait until after she managed to get the girls operating in an orderly fashion. After that, she'd have to come back here and go piece by piece through the contents of her desk.

Rachel shuddered as she closed the drawer and looked around the room. Someone had intruded upon her, and it left her feeling frightened and wary. Not only that, but it added to the complexity of her already complicated life—and that was something Rachel didn't need.

Chapter 12

Braeden had taken all he was going to take. For nearly a week now, Rachel had managed to avoid him no matter how hard he tried to see her. He had given her a wide berth at first, realizing she appeared to be consumed by her emotions and doubts, but his patience had run out. With new determination he laid a plan and set out to see it through. He would talk to her and she would listen. Whether she liked it or not.

Rachel's routine was nearly the same every evening. She concluded her business in the dining room, and then, if she didn't spy Braeden waiting in the wings, she made her way through the lobby to her office. However, if she saw him, she would hurry through the kitchen and into the private Harvey Girl parlor where no men were allowed. From there, he could only presume that she took the long dormitory hall to her office, where she could lock him and the rest of the world out.

He knew she was hurting. Knew, too, that her fears were running her ragged. He had spoken in brief to Jeffery O'Donnell, finding it easy to confide parts of the past to this old friend of Rachel's. Jeffery had been sympathetic but also very protective. He had told Braeden, in a most determined manner, not to dally with Rachel's heart. But Braeden had assured him that wasn't what he had in mind. He cared deeply for Rachel, but she would have no part of him. He'd tried on many occasions to force her to talk to him, but she always managed to create a scene that would allow for little or no privacy. And now she had managed to completely avoid him. But no more.

Braeden figured that if he waited in the darkness near her office, he could jump out and take hold of her before she had time to run the other way. Then he would drag her back to his office, if need be, and force her to sit down and discuss this whole ugly matter with him. She wouldn't like it, but frankly, it didn't matter. Braeden didn't like what was happening between them now, and no one seemed to care how he felt.

The grandfather clock chimed nine as Braeden took his place in the darkness by her door. He wondered silently what he should say to her when she first came upon him. It wouldn't be an easy scene, but hopefully it would take place quickly and quietly. The last thing he wanted was for Rachel to call out for help from Reginald Worthington or one of her girls.

The minutes ticked by and Braeden shifted uneasily, hoping he hadn't misjudged her routine. Of course, given his position, he would have heard if she'd come into her office through the other door. So far there was only silence on the other side, and certainly no sign of light. He silently prayed that she would follow the normal course and come his way. He prayed, too, that God would give him the words to say when they finally came face-to-face.

The swishing of her skirts brought him instantly to attention. She would stop and close the dining room doors before making her way across the lobby. He had seen her do this for the last three nights and knew she had established the habit over her weeks at Casa Grande. She would reach into her pocket for the key to her office just about now.

Braeden tensed and drew a shallow breath. He hoped he wouldn't frighten her overmuch, so just as he heard her approach, Braeden stepped into the lobby.

"Good evening, Rachel," he said in a low, husky voice.

He watched her stiffen and glance quickly around her as if looking for a means of escape. Her expression was one of pure shock, nearly panic. She moved backward, and he could see that already she was making her way to the dining room doors.

"I want to talk to you," he said, taking three quick strides to where she stood.

"I don't want to talk to you," she countered, turning away.

With a sigh, Braeden reached out and took hold of her. "I don't care at this point what you want. You will hear me out." He dragged her, protesting, to his office, then forced her inside and closed the door behind them. "Now I want you to sit down in that chair," he said, pointing to an ornate wainscot chair. Harvey had elaborately decorated the house in antiques of many varieties. This particular piece was a favorite of Braeden's and dated from the mid–1700s.

He could see Rachel battling against her emotions as she backed away from him. "I don't think this is appropriate," she told him.

"Sit!" he demanded, hating to take such a harsh tone with her, yet knowing there was no other way to get her to listen.

Rachel nodded and backed into the chair. It seemed to swallow her up, only adding to the helplessness of her situation.

Braeden came to stand in front of her, planning only to remain close enough to keep her in the chair. Yet when he came to that point, he naturally followed his instincts and leaned over her, planting both hands on either arm rest. The action imprisoned her, leaving her totally at his mercy.

She looked first to each of his hands, then took a deep breath and looked into his eyes. "Why are you doing this?"

125

she barely managed to whisper.

Braeden had thought he would berate her for her childishness at the pool. He would tell her how silly she had acted all week and how ridiculous she was to go on mistrusting him. Then he would explain the past again and demand that she understand and accept his explanation. It all seemed reasonable and logical. But standing this close to her, Braeden couldn't help but feel the pulsating current that seemed to travel between them. He looked down into her oval face, a face so sweetly fixed in his memories, and all he wanted to do was kiss her full red lips.

"Rachel." The name came out more as a moan than a word as Braeden leaned closer to kiss her.

She didn't fight him, which eased Braeden's guilt for forcing himself upon her. And as his kissed deepened, Rachel seemed to match his enthusiasm by leaning into the kiss. Neither one touched the other, except by the joining of their lips. It was a perfect moment, Braeden thought, losing himself in the stillness of his office. How he had missed her! Six years and not a single word to ease his worried heart. Six years of love stored away for a chance that might never come.

He pulled away just a bit in order to speak of his love, but when he did he watched her squeeze her eyes shut and knew he'd pushed her too hard.

"I'm sorry," he whispered, straightening to stand before her. "I didn't mean to upset you."

"It's all right," she murmured, still refusing to open her eyes.

He thought he understood and watched her for a moment. Did she strive to block out his image, or rather, did she send her memories back in time to a place where she would have enjoyed his actions? Braeden smiled to himself knowing that she had enjoyed his kiss just now. She hadn't even tried to put a stop to his advances.

Pulling up another chair, he sighed and pushed back the errant hair that had fallen across his forehead. He waited until she had regained her composure and opened her eyes. Her expression betrayed her longing, and it was this that caused Braeden to press forward with his explanation.

"I had to see you. I had to make you talk to me, or at least to listen to me," he began. "I've been half crazy working so close to you, yet never being able to be near you—to touch you—talk to you."

She appeared surprised by his words, and Braeden knew instinctively that she was still harboring painful memories from the past.

"Rachel, Ivy Brooks means nothing to me. She's a conniving little child who is searching for a husband and a ticket out of Morita. I'm not that man. What you saw at the pool was pure coincidence and nothing more."

"But she said you'd sent her a note," Rachel murmured, confirming to Braeden where her heart was in the matter.

"I forwarded her a note from her aunt. I had gone to the depot to pick up some telegrams and ran into Mrs. Needlemeier. She gave me a note for Ivy and asked if I would be so kind as to deliver it."

"I see," Rachel said, clearly enlightened by this news.

"As for her being in my arms when you returned for your book, it was just as I tried to explain. Either honestly or dishonestly, Ivy slipped. Instinctively, I reached out to steady her. It was nothing more than this. I left the pool right after you did and thought to come talk to you, but I knew you would need to change out of your wet clothes and figured it would be better if I talked to you the next day. But you wouldn't allow me anywhere near you."

Tears formed in Rachel's green eyes. "I'm sorry," she

127

managed to say before allowing a tiny sob to escape. "This has been very hard on me."

"You aren't the only one," Braeden countered with a smile. But his smile quickly faded as he saw how tormented she was over the entire matter. "Tell me that you no longer love me, and I'll never bother you again," he said suddenly. He knew it was a risk—he wasn't at all sure he wanted to hear the answer but felt confident that the matter had to be discussed.

She looked at him in disbelief, trying hard to rein in her emotions. "What?"

He leaned forward, reaching out to take hold of her hand. "Tell me, Rachel. Tell me that you don't love me."

He could see her breathing quicken and watched as her expression contorted. She was fighting a battle within herself, and he couldn't help her. But her battle gave him the answer he needed and that gave him hope.

"I love you, Rachel. That has never changed. I've never stopped, even when you refused to believe in me. All I ask is that you admit what you're feeling for me. If I'm right, then we can move past this and reclaim our future together. If not, then I'll leave you alone. In fact, I'll leave Casa Grande. You only need to tell me that you no longer care."

A gasping sob broke from Rachel's throat as she pulled her hand away from his. "Don't do this. I can't . . . I . . ."

Braeden's heart was encouraged. She still loved him, of this he was certain. It gave him all the hope he needed to press her for the truth. "Why not, Rachel? Why can't you tell me that you don't love me?"

Rachel shook her head in misery, giving him no answer but her silence. She began to cry in earnest now. "I've been wrong about so many things, and I just don't trust my judgment where my emotions are concerned. You must see that I can't have my life so disorderly—so disturbed. I feel like I'm constantly running up one hill and down another in some form of endless race. I'm making no progress, but I have to keep running. It's wearing me out."

He opened his mouth to speak, but she was too quick for him. Releasing all the pressures of her life over the last few weeks, Rachel poured out her heart, edging close to hysteria as she did so.

"First I have to deal with the likes of Ivy and her aunt. Esmeralda Needlemeier has interfered in my decisions at nearly every turn. She criticizes my choices, my decisions, and my close observation of Mr. Harvey's instructions. She threatens to have me fired at least once a day, and she considers it her personal business to see me miserable. Then she saddles me with Ivy. Ivy comes along and wreaks havoc with my authority—questioning every order, commenting on every detail of instruction. She's young and beautiful and she knows it, so she works her wiles on every man who comes through the door—including you."

She drew a ragged breath and continued. "It's just too much. Can't you see? The pressure is too great and it's destroying me. You are here as a constant reminder of what I've lost, while Reginald pursues me in hopes of courtship and a future that I cannot give him. I can't go on like this!" She buried her face in her hands and cried in great heartbreaking sobs. "I can't."

Braeden felt momentarily overwhelmed. He had never seen anyone break down so thoroughly. Even when Rachel had bid him good-bye in Chicago, she had been rather stalwart. This time, however, was clearly a different case. It stunned him and left him totally confused as to how he might help. He certainly hadn't anticipated causing her this kind of misery.

Help me, Lord, he prayed as he edged forward on his chair. *I don't want to hurt her anymore. I only want to love her.*

Uncertain that it was the right thing to do, Braeden got to his feet and pulled Rachel up into his arms. She nearly collapsed against him, unable to fight him or to stop her tears. He let her cry, holding her tightly against him, feeling her tears wet the front of his shirt. Her entire body trembled from the force of pain and misery inside of her. Searching desperately for something to say, Braeden found he could only stand there, praying and waiting for her to release the anguish that seemed to consume her.

He lost track of time, knowing that it didn't matter. He would have stood there for years had it taken that long. If it meant that Rachel could leave off with the past and her doubts and give him a second chance at a happy future with her, Braeden would have waited forever. When her sobs seemed to quiet a bit and the trembling and great wracking heaves eased off, Braeden began stroking her hair. His fingers tangled into the rich auburn curls, pulling loose her hairpins. Her hair was soft and it smelled like lilacs and roses.

He loved her so much and he just couldn't lose her again. *Please, God, don't let me lose her.*

She finally quieted against him, her arms wrapped tightly around him, clinging to him as if he were some stronghold in the storm. Finally it seemed right to speak.

"I love you, Rachel. I have always loved you. You must trust me. You must believe in that love, for it will never die."

She pulled away just far enough to look up into his face. She seemed to study him, as if by observing his expression she could tell the truth of his words. He remained quite sober as her green eyes seemed to search him for answers.

"Esmeralda can't hurt you," he continued softly. "She's a lonely, domineering old woman who is used to having things done her way. She doesn't know how to deal with someone who stands her ground against her as you do. But she is not the one in charge of your position here, and Fred Harvey knows what an asset you are to his system. He won't let you go easily, and he certainly won't dismiss you at the grumblings of one old woman.

"And Ivy is nothing to me. She is a spoiled brat who seeks to cause problems. I wouldn't take her too seriously. She's just a child. She has no power over you, unless you give it to her. And as for Reginald Worthington, well . . . let's just say I'll deal with him."

Rachel sniffed and shook her head. "It's not your problem."

"But I want it to be my problem," Braeden countered. "I want it to be my problem because I want *you* to be my problem."

"He's done nothing wrong."

"Nothing but ask to court my lady," Braeden said with a grin. He reached up and touched her tear-stained cheeks with his index finger. "He can't have you, Rachel. You belong to me—just as I belong to you."

Because they were still in each other's arms, it seemed only natural that he kiss her again. He lowered his mouth to hers very slowly, giving her every chance to protest. He might have forced that first kiss, but not this one. This one he wanted to be a symbol of their life to come. He wanted it to be the first of many sweet, passionate kisses they would share by mutual desire.

Rachel closed her eyes, and he knew she wanted this kiss as much as he did. Gently, so as not to startle her, he pressed his lips to hers. He felt her embrace tighten, even as he held her closer to him. His heart rejoiced that he had found her again and that she cared for him. Although she'd not said the words, he knew she still loved him.

But without warning, Rachel pulled away, this time putting several feet of distance between them. "Mr. Harvey doesn't allow for dating between his employees. You mustn't . . . I mean . . . we mustn't—"

"Mustn't what? Love each other?" Braeden asked, stepping closer.

"No!" Rachel exclaimed. She held out her arm as if to ward him off. "You must understand. I have been quite strict with the girls and even with Reg. I told him it was not allowable for Mr. Harvey's employees to court. It's against the rules."

"So we break the rules."

She shook her head again. "That's what Reg said, but you know that isn't what God would want of us."

Braeden smiled. "I don't recall there's any law of Mr. Harvey's against being married to another employee. In fact, as I recall, there were several incidences of that at the Las Vegas resort where I took my training."

"Married?" Rachel questioned, her eyes growing wide with what Braeden could only surmise was a mixture of shock and fear.

"Rachel," he said softly, hoping to alleviate her fright, "would marriage to me be so bad?"

"Marriage?" She seemed stuck on variations of the word.

He smiled. "I don't wish to court you. I've already done that. I want to marry you and make you my wife forever. I don't want there to come another chance for you to slip away from me. Marry me."

"Marry you." She said it rather stoically, as if he'd asked for nothing more than her assistance in sending a telegram. She took a deep breath and let it out before answering. "Braeden, I think we both need to pray about this. We're acting on emotions and the turmoil of the moment. We can't think clearly under the circumstances."

"I'm thinking quite clearly," he said, taking a step toward her.

She shook her head and backed up to the door. "I can't."

He knew he couldn't continue to force the issue and nodded. "Very well. Then I suppose I must wait until that time when you can think this through and see it for the sensible remedy that I know it to be."

She appeared to relax a bit. "Thank you, Braeden." She opened the door but paused as if reconsidering what had just taken place. With the tiniest of smiles she said, "I seem to have made a mess of your shirt."

"No more so than I made of your hair," he offered with a grin. "I'd say we're even."

Her hand went to her hair, and she smiled as she pulled loose the last remaining pins. "I might as well let it all down."

"I've always liked it very much that way."

She shook her head. "You've never seen it this way, as far as I can recall."

His grin broadened. "I have in my dreams."

He watched as her ruddy complexion darkened to crimson in her embarrassment. He thought her the most beautiful woman in the world. "Good night, Rachel. Don't forget."

She looked at him quizzically. "Don't forget what?"

"That I love you." He barely whispered the words, but they seemed to echo loudly in the room. It seemed an inadequate representation of all that he felt for her, but he knew they were the words she would most understand.

She nodded but said nothing more, leaving him there to watch her leave. He went to the doorway and watched her cross the lobby to her own quarters. His arms ached to hold her again, and it was all he could do to keep from running after her. *I have to give her time,* he reasoned. *I have to be patient and steadfast and prove my love to her all over again, if that's what it takes to win her heart.*

Chapter 13

Seeing Braeden and Rachel greet each other rather amicably that morning at breakfast, Ivy Brooks could only imagine that they had resolved their differences and had agreed to be friends. Such a development didn't fit into Ivy's plans at all.

Finishing the last of her breakfast, Ivy considered how to spend her day off. She had planned to go to her aunt's house and spend a luxurious amount of time in a hot bath where not only would there be no line of giggling girls awaiting a turn, but she would have peace and quiet to think. However, seeing Rachel smile demurely at Braeden's comments caused Ivy to feel a bit riled. She had hoped they would go on being enemies. At least as long as it took to find out from her aunt Esmeralda who Braeden Parker was and what prospects he might afford her as a potential husband. She'd already overheard bits and pieces of information pertaining to his relationship with Rachel, including what she'd overheard that night at the pool.

"Wish I could spend the day with you," Faith said as she cleared away some of Ivy's dishes.

"I'm sure Rachel arranged to keep us separated," Ivy said snidely. "She claims to want us to act and relate as one happy family, but she certainly goes out of her way to see that we are kept from spending too much free time together."

Faith frowned. "I suppose that's true. I simply hadn't considered it."

Ivy nodded, knowing there was a great deal Faith had never bothered to consider. The girl was positively daft, and Ivy wondered quite seriously how she managed to remember how to breathe without someone standing by to instruct her.

Tossing her napkin atop the table, Ivy got to her feet. "Well, I must go and visit my auntie. She pines away for me, you know."

Faith nodded as if fully understanding this to be true. "At least you have somewhere nice to go."

"Don't fret, Faith. One day I shall take you to the mansion with me, and we shall have a lovely tea and you may try on my Worth gowns." Ivy threw this last temptation in to remind Faith just how far beneath Ivy's status she truly was. She might be the granddaughter of one of the Santa Fe board members, but she was still a simple girl from Kansas. Ivy, on the other hand, had been abroad, had shopped in the finest stores in New York, and was more than a little aware of the differences between her life and Faith's.

"Oh, that would be simply divine," Faith said, hugging the plates to her apron.

Just then Rachel walked by. "Miss Bradford, is that a stain I see on your apron?"

Faith looked down rather mortified. "I hadn't noticed."

"Well, now that you have, I would suggest you go change immediately. You know Mr. Harvey's rules."

"Yes, Rachel," Faith replied and hurried off to do as she was instructed.

Ivy looked at Rachel and smiled. "Well, I'm off to enjoy my day. I don't suppose that nice Mr. Parker also has the day off?"

Rachel frowned. "No, I don't suppose he does, and even if he did, you know Mr. Harvey's rules on that issue as well as rules about stained aprons."

Ivy laughed. "Rules are made for those who can otherwise not figure out how to govern themselves. I, Miss Taylor, am certainly not amongst that crowd. I can think for myself, and I can certainly structure my life accordingly. I'm very organized."

"Well, I would keep in mind the time, Miss Brooks," Rachel said, squaring her shoulders. "You were late returning on your last day off. I certainly wouldn't want to assign you extra duty in order to make up for that infraction of the *rules.*"

"Don't worry. I'll be back," Ivy said, giving Rachel what she knew would be her haughtiest stare. "So long as this job suits my needs, I'll be here."

She sauntered off toward the lobby, thoroughly enjoying the fact that she'd just made Rachel very uncomfortable. Ivy was one of the few people to stand her ground with the spinster and she enjoyed making it clear that she didn't need the position, but rather was entitled to it if she wanted it. Rachel might be a problem to her immediate plans, but Ivy decided it was a problem she'd soon take care of. The likes of Rachel Taylor was hardly an adversary worth fretting over.

Moving down the hall, Ivy exited the building out the side door. This door opened onto the wide, sweeping sun porch that lined the garden side of Casa Grande. Here guests could sit and study the parklike garden that stretched out for acres between Casa Grande and the Needlemeier estate. It was quite picturesque and said to be some of the loveliest country for miles around. But it could never be lovely enough to entice Ivy to want to stay. She hated Morita. Hated it more than any place else on earth.

She remembered coming here after the death of her parents. The house fire that had taken their lives had left her with little but borrowed clothes and bad memories.

Ivy frowned. Thinking of her parents pricked a spark of conscience that Ivy had long since refused to deal with. It had a way of making a person regret their mistakes, and Ivy had no time for such things. The past was the past and nothing would change it. The future, however, still held great possibilities . . . no thanks to her aunt or this pitiful town.

Ivy had hoped and prayed that Morita would be something exotic and wonderful. Instead, she found a desertlike town with a funny little hot springs oasis and a vast garden that her aunt likened to Eden. But other than this and a few minor business establishments, Morita was as desolate as St. Louis had been exciting.

Leaving the porch to venture along the stream, Ivy tried to take some pleasure in the series of tiny waterfalls. They traveled in rapid succession downward to the greater Morita Falls, allowing for the energy that provided some parts of the town with electricity. Aunt Esmeralda said very soon the entire town would have access to the power source, but it still wouldn't be enough for Ivy. It was hard to get excited about something that had once seemed rather commonplace in her life.

No, Ivy longed for the thrill of the uncommon. She longed to travel again as she had when she'd been a child. She wanted to see the world, at least more of the world than this little stop along the Santa Fe Railroad. Faith had chided her to be patient because after one year of service, Ivy would be entitled to a vacation and a free pass to go anywhere the Santa Fe Railroad went. Ivy thought the idea laughable. There was no destination on this wretched railroad that enticed her to travel. Unless, of course, she considered the possibility of Kansas City or Chicago. Both places would be accessible along the line. But even this idea held little interest. What Ivy really wanted was a wealthy husband—someone who could arrange for her travels and see to it that she never wanted for anything.

Smiling, she made her way across the small footbridge that connected the Casa Grande side of the gardens to the Needlemeier side. It was all open territory for the guests of Casa Grande. Her aunt had even offered to give her gardeners to the resort, and Mr. Harvey and the Santa Fe had eagerly accepted. They reasoned that if this team of workers knew how to create a garden in the middle of the arid, sandy soils of New Mexico, they were well worth any pay to keep on staff.

Of course, the Santa Fe officials had never had to spend a winter in Morita. When winter came, everything seemed rather dried up and dead in spite of the usually mild temperatures. But sometimes the snows came, and then the boredom of sitting in the middle of nowhere with nothing to do was almost maddening. But with or without snow, Morita was sheer misery to Ivy.

Aunt Esmeralda had tried to interest Ivy in everything from needlework to music lessons, but nothing appealed to her. Ivy had pleaded her case to go east, to live in a bigger city where she might truly benefit from the agenda it could offer. Her aunt was nearly convinced until the Santa Fe and Mr. Harvey had taken notice of her oasis. Of course, Ivy hadn't learned until recently that Esmeralda had been issuing a barrage of letters to those officials, enticing and urging their interest in the property. She had made all manner of promises, and with their purchase of the land, Ivy saw her dreams go up in smoke.

"I hate it here," she muttered, cursing the very ground that she walked on. "If I have my way, I won't spend another winter here."

The real trick was to figure out how she might make her

dreams come true. She needed a wealthy husband—someone who was already established in one of the eastern cities, or who had a mind to go there once Ivy assured him it was for the best. The grand opening celebration was sure to bring in dignitaries and wealthy investors, and Ivy figured to give them all a lengthy consideration before deciding her true course.

She passed her aunt's beloved roses and stopped to pick a particularly delightful pink blossom. The thorns pricked her finger as she ripped the stem away from the plant. *I'm like this flower,* she thought. *I, too, have my sting. Pluck me if you will, but it comes at a price.* She put her bleeding finger to her lips in order to ease the pain and smelled the sweetness of the rose at the same time. It was exactly as she saw herself. Lovely and sweet to the senses, but deadly and painful if taken the wrong way.

Humming to herself, she went into the house through the kitchen door, snagged one of the cook's cherry tarts, and tossed the rose to the housemaid as she came down the back stairs.

"Put this in water and leave it in my room, Liza."

The girl caught the rose, grimacing as the thorn stuck her thumb. "Yes, miss." She curtsied, and Ivy gave a nod as she left the kitchen.

Ivy nibbled at the tart and made her way through the house. She had planned to take a bath first and change out of her uniform into some of her lovely clothes, but she needed information, and that would only come from her aunt. Ivy was desperate to learn more about Braeden Parker, and if anyone would know his history, it would be Esmeralda Needlemeier.

"Aunt Esmeralda," Ivy said, going into her aunt's favorite sitting room. She could see the old woman was poring over her mail and telegrams. No doubt spending more of Ivy's inheritance trying to further populate the tiresome little town.

"Ivy," the woman said, glancing up momentarily. "I expected you to come home last night."

Ivy shrugged and took another bite of the tart. "I had things to take care of and it wasn't convenient. So what are you doing today?"

"Business as usual," Esmeralda replied. "I have the possibility of luring a New York seamstress here to Morita."

Ivy sunk casually to her favorite rococo-styled chair. This particular chair had been fashioned in Italy, and the arms had been inlaid with mother-of-pearl. The exotic design against the ornately carved walnut wood gave Ivy the feeling of being a queen on her throne. A fitting depiction, in Ivy's mind.

"And what would Morita do with a New York seamstress?" she asked, toying with the last bits of her treat.

"Casa Grande will attract a high class of clientele. A seamstress already well acquainted with the desires of such women will stand ready and able to meet any necessity they might have. Perhaps those staying for lengthy respites will find themselves in need of lightweight but fashionable clothing. A seamstress could provide this and make herself a reasonable living, while also serving the community. You yourself have complained about the quality of the local gowns."

"Yes, but a trip to Denver quickly rectified the situation. Others might find it just as easy to take the train north."

"Not if the goods are readily available. I plan to see that no one desires to leave for any reason. I will install all of the necessary businesses to make Morita a success. It's just as your uncle would have wanted it."

"Would he have wanted you to waste your money—money that is your only hope of survival for the future?" Ivy asked, seriously eyeing the old woman.

"I believe he would have," Esmeralda said. She put down the letter and met her niece's stare. "I suppose you believe it foolish. Youth cares very little for the concerns of making a mark on the world. Your uncle wanted to leave something behind that would cause men to remember his name. He had no son to carry his name, thus he determined to have something else."

"But Morita hardly bears his name," Ivy countered. "You should have at least called it Needlemeier."

"Rubbish. Your uncle liked the way the word sounded and used it accordingly."

Ivy shrugged, ate the last of the tart, and brushed the crumbs from her fingers. "Still, what if this venture refuses to pay out?"

"It will pay out. There's already good money attracted to this town."

"Truly?" Ivy questioned, taking immediate interest in the conversation.

"Yes," Esmeralda replied, nodding. "That rather tolerable Mr. O'Donnell hails from a wealthy Chicago family. I've heard it said they're worth millions. Then Mr. Parker, the hotel manager, has a considerable sum in his bank account, and as I'm told, it is only the tip of his worth."

"Honestly, Auntie, how do you manage to find these things out?"

Esmeralda smiled a tight, reserved little smile. "I ask questions, and I demand answers."

"And you did this in Mr. Parker's case?" The conversation was playing out exactly as Ivy had hoped it might.

"I completely investigate each of the businessmen who come to Morita."

"And Mr. Parker is wealthy?"

"Apparently he is very comfortable," Esmeralda replied. "He, too, comes from Chicago, where his family was heavily involved in banking, the stock market, and other manners of moneymaking. Mr. Parker attended college, chose the field of accounting, then found an interest in hotel management. For whatever reason, I can scarcely imagine. He is unmarried, his parents are now deceased, and he claims to have absolutely no regrets in coming to such a small town after living in the big city all of his life."

"Well, that could change," Ivy said, fingering the mother-of-pearl.

"I wouldn't count on it. Apparently there is some old friendship between him and your Miss Taylor. Of course, this comes to me clearly through the grapevine, but I wonder if it isn't enough of an attraction to keep him here."

"I doubt it," Ivy said, narrowing her eyes ever so slightly. "I have seen them nearly at each other's throats. I don't think they have the slightest liking for each other," she lied, even now wondering how difficult it would be to make this an absolute truth.

Esmeralda harrumphed this news and returned her attention to the letters before her. "I suppose time will tell."

Ivy nodded. "Yes, I suppose it will." Getting to her feet, Ivy could think of nothing more than a hot bath and time to consider all that she'd learned.

"I would imagine that with the changes and elegance provided by Casa Grande, you might well learn to content yourself with this small town of ours."

Ivy paused at the archway and laughed. "Don't imagine that too hard, Auntie. I hate this town as much as I ever have. I don't intend to live here one second longer than it takes me to find a rich husband who lives elsewhere." She could see the brief expression of hurt on her aunt's face. The woman covered it quickly, but it was enough to encourage Ivy to speak further.

"This town will never amount to anything. People will come, but inevitably they will go because there is nothing here to entice them to do otherwise. You can hardly believe that a cheap railroad resort, even one that brings in famous entertainers, could ever hope to hold the attention of the public for long. Once the people have come here and experienced it, what's left? Do you really suppose they would venture to this barren land solely to enjoy your hot springs and pitiful little town? Do you really imagine that the whispered promise of a New York seamstress will bring upper society running to Morita?" She laughed, knowing that she'd just cut her aunt's dream to ribbons.

"It will merely run its course as everything else does," Ivy said, turning on her heel before a satisfied smile crept across her face. *Live with that thought, old woman. You've forced me to live in this desert hole, but don't imagine that I will ever stay here.*

Hours later, Ivy emerged from her bath and wrapped a robe of pink lawn around her still-damp body. She sat herself down in the window seat and let the wind gently blow dry her waist-length blond hair. She knew her appeal to men and smiled to herself as she thought of the handsome Braeden Parker.

"So what if he has a past with Rachel Taylor," she murmured. "It hardly matters, considering the plans I have for him."

She stretched catlike and leaned back against the wall. She needed a plan in order to entice Braeden to see the benefits she could offer him. He had taken off too quickly the night of the mishap at the hot springs, or she might have allowed him to better understand how easy it would be to fall in love with her. But the real dilemma wouldn't be in getting Braeden Parker to lose his heart. No, Ivy had confidence enough in her ability to get her man. The greater problem would be how to convince him to leave Casa Grande and New Mexico and return to the big city.

Thinking on this, Ivy smiled to herself. "Of course, if Casa Grande's reputation were ruined, it might provide an answer. Say, if the guests were constantly taking ill from the food . . ."

The idea intrigued her. How difficult could it be to add a little something here or there to the already prepared meals? After all, it was her job to handle and serve that food. Who would know?

"It might take a bit of time," she reasoned aloud, "but it could be done. If people grow sick dining at the Harvey House Restaurant, they certainly won't be coming back to Casa Grande." Not only that, but by targeting this attack on the restaurant, she would also cause Rachel a tremendous amount of trouble.

She smiled smugly and lifted her chin in an arrogant manner. "If there are no customers for Casa Grande, there can hardly be a reason for Braeden Parker to remain here. And, of course, he would have to take his wife with him wherever he ventured. And that wife . . . will be me."

Chapter 14

"Reginald Worthington, may I introduce Mr. Marcus Smith of Topeka," Jeffery O'Donnell stated more than asked.

Reg looked up from his labor to create curried rack of lamb and smiled. "How do you do, Mr. Smith? I hope you'll forgive me if I fail to shake your hand."

Smith, a robust man with a thick mass of curly gray hair, nodded. "I completely understand, Mr. Worthington. I have heard great things about your cooking and couldn't resist coming here to sample some of the fine cuisine."

"Very good, sir. We shall offer only an abbreviated menu, but it shall be our very best efforts."

"Mr. Smith is here to make a final inspection of the resort on behalf of the Santa Fe board," Jeffery explained.

Reg nodded and listened as Smith immediately jumped in to explain his position. "I find that taking matters into my own hands often allows me to avoid those pesky complications that become destructive elements at later dates."

"I trust you've found no such complications here at Casa Grande," Reg said, putting the lamb aside. He gave a quick instruction to one of his assistants, then went to wash his hands.

"No, I am very pleased with what I've found," Smith replied. "Why don't you come join us in the dining room for a moment and tell us how you feel about the matters of the kitchen."

Reg hardly felt it necessary to sit about a table and discuss issues of his kitchen. He was very much under control, knew his job, and desired no outside interference. However, he knew what was expected of him and gave the briefest nod of his head.

"I shall be there momentarily," Reg told the men. "Allow me to put together a tray of refreshments."

"What a capital idea!" Smith said enthusiastically. He rubbed his stomach and grinned. "I could go for a bit of refreshment."

Reg nodded, figuring the man would go for much more than a "bit" of Casa Grande's delicacies. He pulled out a silver tray and instructed one of the baking assistants to arrange a selection of pastries and cakes, then ordered another man to bring him a pot of coffee. At just that moment, Gwen Carson appeared. She was in charge of the dining room for the evening meal, and while Reginald liked her well enough, she couldn't compete with the high esteem he held for Rachel.

"I understand there is to be some form of refreshment offered to the gentlemen in the dining room," she said, greeting Reg. "I thought maybe I could help. Would you like me to serve for you?"

Reg smiled. "I say, that would be quite the thing. Show Mr. Smith a bit of our Harvey charm before the evening meal!" He smiled at the soft-spoken girl. "The trays are being prepared even now. We shall await you in the dining room."

Gwen nodded and went to work while Reginald, seeing that everything was under control, exited the kitchen to join Smith and O'Donnell.

"We are to be served in Harvey fashion," he told the men. They looked up at him as if to question his empty hands and he smiled. "The head waitress herself shall look after us."

147

"Miss Carson is a very amiable person," Jeffery told Smith. "She was originally trained in Topeka and held a position of high regard at the Emporia House."

"I must say, Fred Harvey's idea sounded completely ludicrous to me. He never makes a profit, and in fact, he must be concerned by the Santa Fe losses. However, everywhere I go people talk of his fine food and service," Smith commented.

"I know," Jeffery replied. "It doesn't sound reasonable, but Harvey's restaurants are making the Santa Fe a prosperous rail line. Despite poor showings this year, profits continue to rise where passenger service is concerned, and the hotels and resorts should make even more money. So lavishing the guests with outrageous portions and gourmet cuisine at the dinner table hardly seems to keep Mr. Harvey from success. I believe Harvey's prosperity has crossed over to benefit the Santa Fe as well."

"Well, it won't be beneficial for long if those in power continue to make poor decisions," Smith countered.

"Whatever do you mean, sir?" Reginald questioned.

Just then Gwen appeared holding a silver serving tray. She quickly arranged cups and saucers, dessert plates, and silver before them, then placed the pot of coffee in the middle of the table. Without giving them any chance to comment, she returned to the kitchen and came back with a tray of delectable goodies.

"Oh my," Smith commented as she asked them to make choices. "Such decisions."

"Have no fear," Reginald said, seeing the heavy man lick his lips, "there are more awaiting us in the kitchen."

This seemed to satisfy Smith, who quickly pointed to two cream-filled pastries. Gwen served the men, poured coffee, then returned to the kitchen for cream and sugar.

"If you gentlemen need anything else, don't hesitate to let

me know. I'll be over there folding napkins," she told them and pointed to a small counter where even now another Harvey Girl was at work.

Smith nodded and quickly tore into the pastries with his fork. He sampled the éclair first, closing his eyes as the food met his lips. With a broad smile he exclaimed, "Simply superb!"

Reginald smiled at the man. "Thank you." He paused momentarily, worried that he might be overstepping his bounds with the next question. "You mentioned that there were poor decisions being made among your railroad officials."

"Indeed there are," Smith replied in between bites. "The Santa Fe is not as solvent as we would like. Unwise business decisions have proven harmful to the well-being of our industry."

"Is it truly all that bad?" Jeffery questioned.

"I believe it may prove to be so," said Smith, though he appeared far more concerned about his desserts. However, he quickly moved the focus of the conversation back to Reginald's kitchen.

"So how do you find this resort, Mr. Worthington? Is your kitchen everything you need it to be?"

"I'm quite pleased," Reginald replied. "The equipment is of the highest quality, and I am in want of nothing. I would venture that even Her Majesty in England does not have a finer kitchen."

Smith seemed to sober a bit and leaned toward Reginald, almost conspiratorially. "I'd venture to say the queen is missing out on the finest of cooking since you are here among the commoners of the United States." He laughed at this and slapped Reginald on the back.

Reg smiled, although he despised being handled so familiarly. Americans seemed to think nothing of touching each other at the slightest provocation. They slapped each other when they were happy, they punched each other when they were angry, they even hugged and kissed each other—sometimes quite publicly—whenever the mood struck them. It seemed even worse here in the West, where manners and decorum were often overlooked due to the rugged wilderness setting. And while Reg found this sometimes difficult to accept, he also found himself using the freedom to his advantage.

"If they intend it to be a successful investment," Smith said, sampling the coffee with a smile, "they will have to continue drawing the attention of eastern supporters."

Reg had no idea what Smith was talking about now, but neither did he really care. His mind drifted to thoughts of Rachel. She was one of the biggest reasons he could appreciate this American style of liberty. He had little trouble introducing ideas for sharing moments alone or private conversations.

"Mr. Worthington?"

Reg realized he'd apparently missed a question directed to him by Mr. Smith. "Forgive me, my mind was back on the rack of lamb," he lied.

"I merely suggested that towns such as Morita and Las Vegas pale in comparison to New York and Chicago, but that they also provide hidden surprises and new variations for the cuisine. In Las Vegas I had something called an enchilada. The chef used little pancakes called tortillas and stuffed them with chicken and cheese. He topped them with a spicy red sauce, and I tell you, I've not tasted anything like it in the rest of the country."

"Yes, Tomas, my errand boy, has shared several of his mother's recipes with me. I've experimented with some of them, but I cannot say that I would feel comfortable in introducing them to the menu."

Jeffery laughed. "I've had some great cooking here in Morita. Down near the depot and river there's a wonderful little café. I've had enchiladas. They're just as you've described."

They talked on of food and the grand opening of the resort, and when the conversation seemed to wane a bit and Jeffery heard Braeden Parker at the front desk, he excused himself. "Mr. Smith, I believe Mr. Parker has returned. I suggest we make a meeting with him and Miss Taylor while we have a chance."

"You go ahead and see to it, Mr. O'Donnell," Smith replied. "I shall indulge myself with one more of Mr. Worthington's delicacies."

Jeffery patted his midsection and nodded. "I think I'd better quit for now or I'll ruin my appetite for dinner."

Reginald looked up as Jeffery crossed the dining room. Then he glanced to where Gwen was instructing a couple of the girls on inspecting napkins and tablecloths for any sign of wear.

"It's good to finally have a face with the name," he said softly as Smith finished devouring his fourth pastry.

Smith's eyes brightened. "Do you still believe you can accomplish our goal?"

"I see no problem," Reginald replied. "I'm keeping my eyes open for all the right opportunities."

"Keep your ears open as well. There's no telling who might try to thwart our effort, and the plans for this resort absolutely must come together."

"I heartily agree. Especially in light of the money you are paying me," Reginald said, getting to his feet as Jeffery made his way back to their table. Braeden Parker was at his side and Reg immediately stiffened. This man was the only real obstacle that stood between himself and Rachel.

"Here's Mr. Parker," Jeffery announced. "He has time now for us to discuss resort matters." Jeffery glanced at his pocket watch and noted the time. "However, I can see that soon the dining room will afford us little in the way of peace and quiet. Why don't we take this meeting to your office, Mr. Parker."

Braeden smiled and Reg felt his distaste increase. He was much too confident in his position, his looks, and his entire demeanor. Reg figured him to be no more than five years his junior, yet if rumor held true, the man certainly didn't need his position at Casa Grande. He could walk away at any time and live off the money he had in the bank or the dividends paid him through stocks and bonds.

"If you'll come this way," Braeden said to Mr. Smith.

"I'll go find Miss Taylor," Jeffery offered.

"She is in her office," Reg said, reaching up to run his index finger against his thin moustache. "We've been working on the inventory. Trying to clear up those discrepancies. We certainly can't let that get out of hand."

Braeden's eyes narrowed a bit, and the action was not lost on Reg. "No," he agreed, "we don't want anything out of hand."

"Well, we appear to have it under control. Miss Taylor and I seem to work very well together."

"Yes, she's mentioned how hard you've pursued the matter."

Reg got the distinct impression Braeden was hardly talking about matters of inventory. Could Rachel have shared some mention of Reg's interest in her? It hardly seemed likely. She and Mr. Parker, although more amiable toward each other of late, were still at odds over their past . . . weren't they? He realized the matter was beginning to make him most uncomfortable.

"If you'll excuse me," Reg said with the briefest bow, "I must see to my lamb."

He then headed to the kitchen while the men laughed and discussed their dealings. He felt a twinge of anger and pushed it aside. There was nothing to be gained by losing his temper. He had a job to do here—several jobs. He needed to think clearly and focus himself entirely to ensure their success.

He inspected the cooking, chided the cook in charge of the breaded veal cutlets for having cut the pieces too thick, then moved on to taste the salad dressing being prepared by yet another.

But his mind was hardly on cooking. Reg couldn't forget the look in Braeden Parker's eyes. The man assumed him guilty of something, but of what? Reg had done nothing more than voice interest in Rachel, gently suggesting outings that would allow them to grow closer. Perhaps it was nothing more than jealousy, but if that were the case, why bother with the look or the words that seemed to hold a double meaning?

Rachel is all that I have ever wanted in a woman, full of life and joy—when she's not busy pining over that pompous fool. Reg wondered how he might convince Rachel that Braeden Parker was hardly worth her time and energy.

He picked up a sprig of parsley and studied it to ascertain the freshness of the piece. Satisfied, he replaced it on the plate and moved on. There had to be a way to create a wedge between Rachel and her Mr. Parker—a separation that would so completely divide them that there would be no hope of them ever coming back together. It would only be then that Reg would have a chance to win Rachel over.

He stirred a concoction on the stove and frowned. "Idiot! You've curdled it. Now start again and throw this mess out." The dark-skinned man cowered at Reg's anger but nodded obediently.

Finally satisfied that all was moving along as it should, Reg went back to working on the rack of lamb. "It shouldn't be that hard for an Englishman to overcome a dim-witted American," he muttered with some satisfaction. "After all, we've been at the game far longer than they have."

Chapter 15

With some of the dignitaries arriving early for the next day's celebration, Rachel began to feel a bit overwhelmed. Not only were there meals to oversee, but there were also last-minute changes in menus and other arrangements that were nonsensical and frustrating to her sense of order. The last thing she needed was any further interruption. But that was exactly what she got when Ivy Brooks demanded her attention.

"My ruby brooch is missing," she declared, coming into Rachel's office without an invitation.

"I see," Rachel replied, not even bothering to look up from her desk. "And what have I to do with the matter?"

"I want you to look for it. I believe one of the girls came into my room and stole it."

This caused Rachel to glance up. "Stole it? One of my girls? Ivy, I hardly think anyone would consider such a matter."

"Well, they've not only considered it—they've done it, and I demand that you find my brooch and jail the thief."

"Ivy, the resort opens tomorrow. There are already dignitaries here from Topeka and Chicago, and more are due to arrive tomorrow morning. Is it really necessary to cause this kind of disruption?"

"It's hardly my fault!" Ivy wailed. "I'm the one wronged here, and you act as though it were unimportant. The brooch was a gift on my fourteenth birthday from my dear departed mother and father. That piece means a great deal to me."

Rachel could see there would be no living with the girl until she acquiesced to find the pin. "Very well. Where did you last have it?"

"I had it in my dresser drawer. That is why I know it has been stolen. And since no man is allowed in our quarters, it must have been one of the Harvey Girls or you!"

Rachel stood and shook her head. "I have no need for your brooch. Now, tell me what it looks like."

Ivy described the pin as being in the shape of a butterfly with rubies dotting the wings and black onyx for the eyes. "And the entire body is gold," she added.

"All right. Let us go ask among the girls."

Rachel rounded up those who were still in the house. A few extra girls had been given the day off because the following day would require that everyone work around the clock. "Has anyone seen Ivy's brooch?" She described the piece for her girls, then stood back and watched as each one shook her head. She had presumed it would be just this way, but in order to pacify Ivy she had gone the extra mile.

"There you have it," she told the smug-faced girl.

"Surely that's not all you plan to do!" protested Ivy. "That brooch is quite valuable. Of course those ninnies are going to say they didn't take it. The thief could hardly admit to it."

"I didn't ask if they stole the brooch," Rachel reminded her. "I asked if they had seen it. There's a big difference between seeing something and stealing it. Isn't it possible you left the brooch at your aunt's house?"

"No, it isn't possible I left the brooch at my aunt's house," Ivy replied sarcastically. "It was here in my drawer. You may ask Faith if you don't believe me."

Rachel knew better than to take that route. "Very well.

What else would you suggest?"

"Search their rooms! I want that piece back, and I want the thief thrown into jail!"

"Ivy, if the brooch has been stolen, do you seriously think it would be left in plain view of anyone who might come along to find it?"

Ivy looked to be fairly seething by this time. Not that Rachel really cared, but she was getting weary of the game. She was supposed to have dinner with the O'Donnells that evening, and she wasn't about to let Ivy's madcap chase alter her plans.

"Everyone search your rooms and see if it is possible that Ivy merely dropped her brooch there by mistake." Rachel turned to Ivy after saying this and added, "I'm sure if the piece is located, the girls will tell you."

She started back to her office and had nearly reached the door when Ivy demanded she stop. "This is outrageous! You plan to bring in wealthy guests from all over the world, yet the brooch of one woman is not safe. I will tell everyone of this incident if you refuse to help me."

Rachel knew the reputation of Casa Grande was at stake. She had no desire for the girl to spread falsehoods and finally nodded. "Very well, Ivy. Let us conduct our search." Glancing at the gathering of girls, she spotted Gwen. "Gwen, I would like your assistance on the matter."

"But perhaps she stole the brooch," Ivy protested. "Remember, she did take Faith's hairbrush."

"I did not. I found it in the hallway," Gwen argued.

"Well, maybe you *found* my brooch there as well."

"Enough!" Rachel declared. "We shall search Gwen's room first, and when we clear her of any suspicion, then she will take this side of the hall and I will take the other."

This surprisingly seemed to satisfy Ivy and should have

been Rachel's first clue in the matter. They entered Gwen's room, the only one not shared with another worker. As head waitress, she was given this extra privilege of privacy.

"Gwen, please open your closet and drawers," Rachel instructed.

The young woman did as she was told while Rachel quickly went through each article. When she finally finished with the last drawer, she turned to the nightstand and bed. "Please pull down the covers, and Ivy, you stand on the other side with Gwen and help lift the mattress." Every possible nook was checked. Rachel wanted to leave nothing undisturbed. She'd not have Ivy coming back later to complain of a less than thorough job.

They found nothing under the mattress, but as Rachel replaced the pillow on the bed, something rolled out of the case and made the sound of a dull thud on the floor. Looking down, she discovered the pin.

As she picked it up, Rachel was heartsick to realize that Ivy had planted it there. Rachel's trust in Gwen was complete, but how could she prove that Ivy was to blame instead of Gwen?

"Is this your brooch?" Rachel questioned, knowing full well that it was.

"That's it! See, I told you it had been stolen. Gwen Carson, I hate you!" Ivy declared.

There was much murmuring from the gathering of Harvey Girls outside Gwen's door, and Rachel knew the matter was about to escalate into madness. Calmly she asked, "Gwen, did you take the pin?"

Gwen had tears in her eyes. "Honest, I didn't take it. I don't know how it got there."

"How convenient," Ivy replied snidely. "Of course the thief can't remember how it found its way there. I demand that you fire her immediately and call the marshal!"

"Calm yourself, Ivy," Rachel replied. "No one is getting fired or going to jail."

"She stole my pin. I want her punished."

"Your pin is safely returned to you and shows no mark of harm. Now, I suggest you all forget about this and prepare for the evening meal. Tonight's crowd will be the largest yet." Rachel looked at Gwen, who was silently sobbing into her apron. "Gwen, you need to change that apron and prepare for the evening. You will be in charge, as I will be out until late."

"You can't just leave her in charge. She's a—"

"Miss Brooks, I have very little patience left," Rachel stated firmly. "I believe this matter to be nothing more than a misunderstanding. Unless, of course, you wish for me to make more out of it." She eyed the girl sternly, hoping Ivy would realize her determination in settling the affair.

"Well, fine! It will be a pity, however, when things start disappearing in earnest around the hotel."

Rachel eyed Ivy seriously for a moment. She thought of all the missing articles in her inventory and wondered if that, too, was a part of Ivy's game. Glancing at her watch, she decided she could consider the matter in more depth at a later time.

"I want all of you to get to work," Rachel declared. "Right now!"

The girls scattered, seeming to sense Rachel's frustration and mounting anger. "Ivy," Rachel called as they made their way into the hall, "I want no more of this."

Ivy looked at her, feigning stunned concern. "Why, whatever do you mean?"

Rachel shook her head. "You know exactly what I mean. I won't have it, and that's my final word on the matter. From now on, if so much as a radish disappears, I'm coming to you first."

Ivy's eyes narrowed and her face contorted hatefully. "You'll pay for this. You'll see," she whispered loudly enough for only Rachel to hear.

"And then she stomped off to her room," Rachel told Jeffery and Simone, "and I readied myself for our visit. But other than that, the day was fine."

"It's too bad you can't fire Ivy Brooks," Simone said, getting up from the kitchen table. "Come sit with me in the front room. I'll see to this mess later, and Jeffery can go check on his new pride and joy."

"I thought that wasn't coming until March," Rachel said, eyeing Simone's still-flat stomach.

She laughed. "Oh, it's not the baby. It's a matched pair of carriage horses. They came in on the four-o'clock freight."

"Ah, I see. Well, then," she said, turning to Jeffery, "I quite understand."

"I won't be a moment," he said, kissing Simone on the head. "You ladies make yourselves comfortable."

Rachel nodded and followed Simone into the parlor. "I have quite a bit to tell you before he comes back."

"Oh?"

"Well, it's just that it's not exactly the kind of subject to share in a man's company."

Simone grinned and touched a hand to her ebony hair. "Hmm, I believe this must be a matter of the heart."

Rachel laughed. "Does it show that much?"

Simone nodded. "But then, you figured out my feelings for Jeffery long before I did. So tell me. Have you mended fences with the wonderful Mr. Parker?"

"I suppose I have, in a sense. I mean, he did ask me to marry him."

"What!" Simone exclaimed and clapped her hands. "Why,

that's wonderful! When is the happy day?"

"I don't know," Rachel said, sobering rather quickly. "I didn't say yes."

Simone shook her head. "I don't think I understand."

"I'm not sure I do either. I mean, he forced me into his office, made me listen to his speech about loving me, then I started crying because everything at Casa Grande seemed to be overwhelming me. The next thing I knew . . . well . . ." She felt her face grow hot. "Well, the next thing I knew, he was kissing me. And it was as if all the years melted away and we were back in Chicago—happy and engaged."

"But that's what you wanted, isn't it?"

"I don't know," Rachel said, giving a bit of a nervous laugh. "I thought I would never see him again, and even if I did, I presumed him lost to me. But this was the second time he assured me of his love. He chided me for not trusting him, begged me to put the past behind us—and when I reminded him that Harvey employees could not date, he proposed."

"Is that all?"

"He reminded me that plenty of people along the line enjoy both matrimony and Fred Harvey's employment."

Simone smiled again. "Rachel, I think you're finally getting your prayers answered. I mean, why fret over this turn of events? The man obviously adores you."

"Does he?" Rachel questioned. She twisted her hands together. "I don't mean to be such a doubting Thomas, but what if this is just some grandiose scheme to win me back, only to turn around and crush me for having betrayed him in the first place?"

Simone raised a brow and asked, "Does that speak to the character of the man you know?"

"But it's been six years since I felt I honestly knew Braeden, and even now, I see that apparently I didn't know him well at all. He explained away the incident that divided us, chided me for listening to whispered gossip, and has lamented my lack of faith in him. I don't know what to do. I want to trust him, but I'm so afraid."

"Why?"

The question seemed ridiculously simple, but the answer came at great price. "I suppose because I'm afraid of being hurt again. I'm afraid that he truly hates me and has played this like a hand of cards. Well . . . I just don't think I could take it."

"If it were true," Simone pressed, "and he merely wanted to punish you, what's the worst thing that could happen?"

"I think I would die."

Simone smiled. "We both know that isn't true. Your heart might break and you might decide to never again love another, but I doubt seriously you would die."

Rachel knew how silly it sounded, but at the same time she thought of how empty her life had been without Braeden. "It might not happen exactly that way, but—"

"But you'll never know if you don't at least give him a chance. You may well be passing up your last chance for happiness. You've prayed about this, right?"

"Not really," Rachel replied. "I mean, I prayed after we separated. I used to pray God would right the wrong between us and bring us back together, but I never believed it would happen."

"I can't believe *you*, Rachel Taylor—woman of faith—would say such a thing. You're the one who taught me the benefit of believing in miracles. You helped me to come to understand how important it is to have faith—especially when nothing seems possible. And furthermore, you taught me that no decision should be made without first considering it in prayer. Are you telling me now that you doubt

God's abilities in the matter?"

Rachel sighed. "I've never doubted God's abilities, but I've certainly doubted mine."

"Show me someone who hasn't."

"But in this case, Simone, I'm doubting not only myself. I'm doubting Braeden as well. And if I continue to doubt, I may ruin my only chance with him. I don't want to lose that."

"Then don't. From what you say, I must believe that he loves you. Why would the man waste his time in grandiose schemes, as you put it? Men hardly think that way in affairs of the heart. That sounds more like the reasoning of a woman."

"Truly? Do you really think so?"

"It doesn't sound like anything Jeffery would ever do. No, if Jeffery wanted to play that role, he would completely snub me. He'd have nothing to do with me. He certainly wouldn't open his heart to me—going out of his way to make sure I listened to him, pleading his case. Mr. Parker may be wounded by the past, but from what you are telling me, he sounds sincere in his desire to put it behind him."

"I hope you're right. I would really love to agree to his request," Rachel replied, feeling happiness at the mere thought of marriage to Braeden.

"I wouldn't fret anymore about this, Rachel. I think after tomorrow's grand opening, you'll be under far less pressure and you'll see for yourself if Braeden is sincere."

"Tomorrow is just the tip of the iceberg," Rachel said with the hint of a laugh. "There are so many other problems to consider that I can't begin to explain."

"Why not try me?"

Rachel looked at Simone in appreciation. "Ivy Brooks is causing me no end of grief."

"Jeffery told me that her aunt forced your hand in accepting Ivy at Casa Grande. Is that true?"

163

Rachel sighed. "Yes. It's a constant source of frustration, mainly because of how unfair it was to accept Ivy into a position that was considered to be a privileged assignment. Money bought her that position, and money is keeping her in place."

"The old woman bought your cooperation?" Simone asked in disbelief. "That doesn't sound like the Rachel Taylor who trained me to Mr. Harvey's rigorous regimen."

"No one has bought me," Rachel replied. "And that's more than half the problem. Esmeralda Needlemeier haunts my office every other day complaining about one thing or another, and Ivy tries her best to interfere in my life—even where Braeden is concerned. No, I have a feeling tomorrow will just be the beginning of many days of continual conflict and problems."

"Well, to bring back the subject of marrying Mr. Parker, think how much better it will be to spend your time with a husband at your side, rather than a mere managerial partner. It seems ideal to me. The man would be with you to offer strength and support."

They heard the back door open and close, and Rachel immediately put her finger to her lips. Simone nodded conspiratorially and grinned.

"Are they as you left them?" Simone questioned as Jeffery took his place at her side.

"Yes, and just as beautifully matched as two geldings could be. So what did you ladies discuss while I was gone?" Simone grinned broader, while Rachel's face flushed. "Ah," Jeffery continued, "I can see it must have been of an intimate nature. Did it have anything to do with Mr. Worthington?"

"Reginald?" Rachel asked rather surprised.

"Ah, so you are on a first-name basis."

Rachel rolled her eyes. "You know I do that with all of my

staff. At least when no one is around."

"Well, Reginald has asked me numerous questions about you and your past. It seems the man can't get enough information when it comes to you. I'd say he has more than a passing interest."

"He's very nice," Rachel admitted, "but that's all. He has asked me out to walk with him or to go riding, but I've always refused. I can't see trifling with him."

"Why would it have to be a trifling?" Jeffery asked.

Rachel looked to Simone for help, but her friend just shrugged her shoulders. Finally Rachel noticed the hour. "Oh my, it's nearly ten o'clock. I really should be getting back. I have a feeling four-thirty is going to come around mighty early. Are you sure I can't help you with the dishes, Simone?"

"Absolutely not," Simone replied. "I'll have them done before you even reach the front steps of Casa Grande."

The trio rose together, and after Rachel hugged Simone good-bye, Jeffery announced that he would walk Rachel back to Casa Grande. "I would take you in my carriage and show off my new horses, but since I've not yet had time to try them out—"

"And since we have scarcely half a mile to walk," Rachel interjected, "it hardly seems worth the trouble of hitching a team."

They walked through the night in a companionable silence. The gentle roar of Morita Falls made for lovely night music as they passed over the bridge. However, as they climbed up the carefully cultivated lawn and passed by the lighted fountain, Rachel noticed a light on in her office.

"That's odd," she said, turning to Jeffery. "Someone's turned on my light."

"Are you certain you didn't do it yourself and left it on

when you came to see us?" Jeffery questioned.

"No, I'm certain of it. Furthermore, I'm certain that I locked both doors to my office."

They climbed the front steps and as they reached the front door, they saw a dark form pass before Rachel's window. Jeffery frowned and put out a hand to stop her once they were inside the lobby. "You wait here and let me check this out."

Rachel nodded and waited while Jeffery went to the door. Her breathing quickened as she watched him calmly try the door handle, finding it locked. He gently eased the knob back into place, then quickly came back to Rachel as the glow of light disappeared under the door.

"The light just went off!" she exclaimed.

"Quick! Give me the key!"

She handed the key to Jeffery and watched as he raced back, no longer worried about being quiet. He unlocked the door and stepped into the darkened room.

"Who's there?" he called out.

Rachel bit her lip, wondering if she might at least give Jeffery the assistance of turning on the light. She tiptoed toward the room just as a loud crash sounded.

"Jeffery!"

Without concerning herself over what the consequences might be, Rachel raced into the room and turned on the light just as someone exited the other door, slamming it behind them.

"Jeffery? Is that you?" she called out, uncertain as to who it might have been if not Jeffery. But just as she came to the door, she found the moaning, crumpled body of Jeffery O'Donnell.

For a moment Rachel felt frozen in place. She could see that he was bleeding from a wound on the side of his head, but it all seemed surreal. By the time she opened the other door and glanced down the hallway, the intruder was gone.

"Rachel . . ." Jeffery barely whispered the word as he struggled to sit up.

"Don't move," she ordered, finally back in control. "You're bleeding."

"I'll be all . . . all . . ." He gasped and fell back against the floor.

"Dear Lord, help me," Rachel prayed, realizing that Jeffery was now unconscious.

Chapter 16

Knowing of nowhere else to turn, Rachel ran across the lobby and pounded on Braeden's office door. After several moments of knocking with no answer, she grew even more fearful. She was just about to give up hope when she thought of the entrance to his private quarters.

Maneuvering past the front desk, she turned to her right and made her way into the darkened shadows where Braeden's second door could be found. This door opened, she was told, into his private living quarters. If he were in bed, even asleep, he would surely awaken at the sound of her knocking.

"Please answer me, Braeden," she whispered as she pounded against the door.

It only took a couple of minutes before a very disheveled Braeden appeared. He was struggling to pull up his suspenders and tuck in his shirt with one hand while opening the door with the other, and Rachel couldn't help but be taken aback by the way he looked.

"Oh my," she said in a raspy voice.

At this, Braeden stopped fumbling with his clothes and looked up in surprise. "Rachel?" He reached back behind him to twist on the light. "What in the world are you doing here?" Then he grinned. "Come to give me an answer for my proposal?"

She shook her head. "I wish it were that simple. Look, something has happened in my office, and Jeffery O'Donnell is bleeding."

"What?"

"It's a long story," she said, trying to regather her wits. "Jeffery was walking me back from dinner at the O'Donnell house, and we saw a light on in my office. Then we saw the shadow of a figure pass in front of the window. No one should have been there, but Jeffery went to investigate and someone hit him over the head. I need your help, Braeden. He's bleeding and I have to get him to the doctor."

Without warning, Braeden pulled her into his room. Rachel tried to pull away, but his grip was too tight. "What are you doing?" she demanded. "I can't be in here. I can't be seen in your private rooms."

"I need my shoes," Braeden replied, now fully alert. "It would be foolhardy to leave you alone if there's some madman running around the place hitting people over the head. This will only take a second." He sat down on the edge of his bed and reached for his shoes.

Rachel felt her face grow fiery hot and quickly turned her back to him. There was something so intimate about seeing him there, sitting on the bed. She stared at the closed door and wondered how she'd managed to get herself into this mess. If anyone saw her coming from his room, her reputation would be in shreds.

"You can turn around," Braeden told her.

"That's all right," she managed to say. "I'll just stay right here."

She heard him chuckle and wondered why he thought the matter so funny, but there was little time to further consider it. Braeden came up from behind her and put his hands on her shoulders.

"If you won't move, we cannot open the door."

Rachel felt his warm breath upon her neck and shivered from the sensation. "We need to hurry," she reminded herself aloud. She reached out for the door handle just as Braeden did. His hand closed over the top of hers, causing Rachel to turn and look up into his face. "I'm sorry I had to bother you. I had no place else to turn."

"Reg wouldn't help you?" he asked with a mischievous grin.

"He never entered my mind," she replied flatly. And he hadn't. When the first sign of trouble had come upon them, she immediately thought of Braeden.

"Good. See that it stays that way," he said and opened the door.

They hurried across the lobby and found Jeffery regaining consciousness. "Jeffery, don't move," Rachel told him, kneeling down beside him. "I've brought Braeden to help, but you mustn't move."

Braeden moved Rachel's desk back in order to get closer to Jeffery. "O'Donnell, can you hear me?"

"Yes," Jeffery said. His head wobbled back and forth as he struggled to focus his eyes on Braeden.

"We need to get you to a doctor," Braeden declared. "Rachel, grab one of those linen napkins Mr. Harvey loves so much and wrap it around his head."

Rachel nodded and ran down the hall to the linen closet. She grabbed a handful of napkins and hurried back to her office. Just as she did, Gwen Carson's door opened.

"I heard the noise," the young woman said softly. "Is something wrong?"

"Yes!" Rachel exclaimed. "Mr. O'Donnell has been injured. Would you run and wake Tomas? He should be sleeping in the storage room. Send him to bring up a carriage from the stables. We'll have to drive Mr. O'Donnell back to town." Gwen nodded and, mindless of her robed attire, hurried down the hall to find Tomas.

"Here," Rachel said, coming into the office. She handed the linens over to Braeden. He quickly folded one into a thick bandage, then ripped another in strips and tied the bandage to Jeffery's head. "I had Gwen wake Tomas. He should be able to bring around a carriage."

"Good thinking," Braeden said, giving her a look of approval.

Rachel relished his gaze. He was proud of her actions, and his expression told her without a doubt that she had done the right thing.

Braeden helped Jeffery to his feet but had to fully support him. "Did you get a look at who did this?"

"No," Jeffery managed to say. "In fact, I don't remember anything but opening the door."

Braeden turned to Rachel. "What about you? Didn't you see anything?"

"No," Rachel answered, feeling a deep sense of disappointment. "I wish I could say that I had. I heard the crash, which undoubtedly was Jeffery falling, but when I came in and turned on the light, the other door was just slamming shut. When I opened it and looked down the hall, the intruder was already gone."

Braeden nodded. "Let's get Mr. O'Donnell outside. We can wait on the porch for Tomas, and maybe the cool night air will help clear the haze in his head."

Rachel followed behind the two men, feeling rather helpless in the matter. *Poor Jeffery,* she thought, then realized she would have to be the one to break the news to Simone. She only hoped the shock wouldn't hurt the baby.

"Rachel, you open the door," Braeden instructed.

She hurried to do his bidding, opening not one, but both of the entry doors. Braeden maneuvered Jeffery onto the porch and helped him to a chair, while Rachel closed up the hotel again.

"Where does the doctor live?" he asked Rachel.

"Just down the road," Rachel replied. "His house is actually across the street from Jeffery and Simone's house."

"And the O'Donnell house is the first one on the right after passing over the falls, correct?"

"Yes."

"All right. I'll get Mr. O'Donnell to the doctor and—"

"You aren't going alone. I'm going with you. Simone is a dear friend, and I need to be the one to tell her about her husband."

Braeden looked as though he might argue with her, then nodded. "Sounds reasonable."

Tomas then appeared with the buggy. It would be a tight squeeze, since he'd only thought to hitch the lightweight two-wheeler.

"Thank you, Tomas," Rachel said as the boy climbed down to help Braeden with Jeffery.

"You would like me to drive you, señor?" he asked.

"No," Braeden replied. "You go on back to bed. I'll see to putting the buggy away when we return."

"Sí."

"Rachel, you get in first. That way we can put Jeffery between us. If he passes out again, he can lean against you."

"All right." She climbed quickly into the carriage and scooted to the far side in order to give the men more room.

Braeden helped Jeffery up and followed behind in short order. Tomas handed him the reins and stepped back as Braeden urged the horse forward.

Jeffery moaned and leaned back against the seat, clutching

his head. Rachel felt instantly guilty for his misery. "I'm so sorry this happened, Jeffery. I blame myself."

"You didn't hit me," Jeffery muttered, even now trying to keep matters light.

Rachel smiled. He had become such a dear friend. "When we get to the doctor's house, I'll run across the street and get Simone."

"No, don't worry her," Jeffery replied.

"I'm not about to endure her wrath by not telling her that her husband has been hurt and is bleeding from a head wound in the doctor's office, while she sits in the parlor knitting."

Braeden laughed and Jeffery attempted to. "I suppose you're right," he said, seeming a bit more alert. "She has a temper, you know."

"What woman doesn't?" chuckled Braeden.

They pulled up to the doctor's house, and Rachel was grateful to see the warm glow of lamplight in the window. She hurried ahead of the men and knocked on the door.

It took a few minutes, but soon a robe-clad man opened the door. "Yes, what's the emergency?"

Rachel knew the gray-headed Dr. Krier because his daughter Alice was one of her Harvey Girls. "Doctor, Jeffery O'Donnell was hit on the head tonight. He's bleeding pretty badly."

The doctor looked past her to where Braeden was helping Jeffery down from the buggy. "Bring him in. I'll get some more light, and we'll see how bad it is."

Rachel nodded. "Thank you." She stood back to allow Braeden to bring Jeffery into the house.

"Come on back here," Dr. Krier called.

They entered his office, where he instructed Braeden to lay Jeffery down on the table. Rachel decided now would be the best time to go for Simone. "I'll be back in a minute," she told Jeffery and gave his hand a squeeze.

She was nearly to the door when, to her surprise, Braeden caught her by the arm. "Wait up, there. You aren't going out alone."

"I'll be just fine. It's only a few steps," she protested.

"Yes, and it was only a locked office that brought Jeffery a head injury. I'm going with you."

The look of determination on his face told Rachel that Braeden would do just as he said. And actually, she found herself grateful that he cared so much. "All right," she replied.

Rachel hesitated at the O'Donnells' door, not wanting to tell Simone what had happened. But as it was, Simone took the news very well, immediately grabbing up her shawl and heading out the door.

"I knew something was wrong," she told Rachel as they hurried back to the doctor's office. "I just had this feeling."

"He doesn't look all that bad," Braeden told her.

Simone looked up at him as they entered the doctor's home. "Thank you for being there, Mr. Parker. I've heard such nice things about you."

"Oh?" he said quizzically. "I wonder from whom."

Rachel bit her lip as her cheeks flamed. She could feel the heat even though the night air was chilly. But Simone saved her from any further embarrassment.

"Why, from my husband, of course."

Braeden grinned and looked at Rachel. "Of course."

Simone walked into the doctor's office without any apparent fear of what she had to face. Rachel admired her strength because she herself had been trembling ever since finding Jeffery. Braeden must have sensed this, as well, for he put his arm around her and pulled her close.

"Jeffery O'Donnell, I suppose you are getting me back for all the worry I've caused you," Simone stated as she went to her husband's side.

"Mrs. O'Donnell, good to see you," the doctor said. He sat at the head of the table threading a needle.

"Yes, Mrs. O'Donnell," Jeffery said with a lopsided grin, "good to see you."

"I'm gonna have to stitch your husband up," the doctor said, turning his attention to Simone. "It's not all that bad, and once I'm done he'll be nearly good as new. However, he's lost a good bit of blood."

Simone paled a bit at the final statement, and Rachel knew it stemmed from Simone's painful memory—one that included Simone hitting an attacker over the head and believing herself to have killed the man because of all the blood.

"Head wounds do that," the doctor continued. "Funny thing, though, usually they aren't all that bad, even when they bleed like they are. It'll make him light-headed, though. You'll need to keep him in bed for the next few hours." Simone nodded but said nothing. The doctor finished preparing the needle, then looked back up at Simone. "Why don't you all wait out there. I'll call you when it's done."

"I want to be with my husband," Simone insisted.

Rachel stepped away from Braeden and put her arm around Simone. "Don't you think it would be better, given your condition? We'll be right here if Jeffery needs you."

Jeffery nodded. "Go. I can't cooperate with the doc if I'm all worried about you passing out on the floor."

Simone reluctantly let go of his hand. "Very well."

She let Rachel lead her into the front room and sat down with a sigh on Doc's very worn sofa. "I don't suppose it would do any good for me to have argued."

Rachel laughed. "Not in this case."

175

"Why in the world did this happen?" Simone questioned, looking to her friend for answers.

"I don't know," Rachel replied. "Strange things have been happening at the resort. There were some discrepancies in the inventory, and we're pretty sure someone is stealing from the storage rooms. The dining room things seem to be safe now that we have Tomas sleeping in the back room, but Braeden is still losing things from time to time. Then not long ago I found wax on the floor in my office—"

"You what?" Braeden interrupted.

"I found wax on the chair and on the floor," Rachel said, knowing he would be furious that she had kept it from him. "And there were some correspondences missing from my desk." She looked up, feeling rather sheepish about the whole matter. "I meant to tell you."

"I should hope so," Braeden replied, his brow knitting together as he considered this news. "What correspondences?"

"Honestly, it didn't seem like anything important. They were just letters related to the . . . inventory."

"And that didn't seem important?" he asked.

"Well, not as important as the fact that the original inventory list was also missing. I thought Reg had come to get it, but he hasn't seen it either. I sent Tomas with a telegram to Topeka, in hopes of having them send me another list."

"And when do you suppose you were going to get around to telling me about this?" Braeden questioned, crossing his arms and leaning back in the chair opposite her.

Simone laughed. "You two make such a funny couple. I think you're perfect for each other."

Rachel turned to stare at her in absolute horror. "Simone!"

"Mrs. O'Donnell, I couldn't have put it better," Braeden replied.

"Thank you, but if you are to marry my best friend, then you must call me Simone."

"Simone!" Rachel declared again. Now Braeden would not only know that she had discussed everything with her friend, but he had Simone's blessing as well.

"Oh, stop being such a ninny," Simone said, patting Rachel's knee. "I could tell the man loved you from the moment I opened the door. Look at the way he's so attentive to you, the way he worries after you, the possessive way he treats you. For goodness' sake, Rachel, it doesn't take a genius to figure out what's going on."

"Rachel's only put off because it *is* taking her a while to figure out what's going on," Braeden countered with a grin.

"I suppose we women can be that way," Simone replied. "Jeffery says there's a lot of times when I don't know what's good for me."

Braeden nodded as if in complete agreement.

Rachel wanted to get up and run. To be cornered by two of the people who meant more to her than anyone else was almost more than she could stand. Simone seemed to understand, however, and took hold of Rachel's hand.

"Please don't hate me for what I've said. You know how I am about speaking my mind. It's just that when I saw how he looked at you, I was certain of his feelings for you." Then turning to Braeden, Simone added, "However, Mr. Parker, you are not to take advantage of my outburst."

"I will adhere to your request, only if you acquiesce to call me Braeden."

She nodded and craned her neck in the direction of the doctor's office. "I wonder what's taking so long. I've always teased Jeffery about being hardheaded—I guess now I have proof. The doctor probably can't get the needle through his thick skull."

Rachel secretly wished the doctor would hurry up, too, so she could make her way back to Casa Grande and be rid the scrutiny of her good friend. But then a troubling thought came to mind: She'd be making that trip back with Braeden, and what had seemed like such a short distance when walking with Jeffery now loomed ahead of her like a cross-country journey.

"Mrs. O'Donnell, you may come back in," the doctor called out.

Simone jumped to her feet and hurried past, leaving Rachel and Braeden alone.

"So you've been talking about me behind my back, eh?" Braeden questioned.

Rachel swallowed hard. "She's my friend. I come to her for advice."

"And will you heed her thoughts on the matter?"

"I don't know," she whispered, forcing herself to meet Braeden's eyes.

"I like her very much," he said with a grin. "She seems quite sensible."

"I suppose, but—"

"Rachel," Simone said, coming into the room with her arm around Jeffery's waist, "would you mind lending me Braeden just long enough to get Jeffery settled at home?"

Braeden was already at Jeffery's side, much to the other man's protest. "I'm fine," Jeffery said. "I'm not as light-headed as before."

"That's great," Braeden replied. "Then clearer thinking shall prevail and you won't mind the assistance."

"Ah, a man of logic," Simone said with a nod. "Just the one to get this pigheaded husband of mine into bed without an argument."

It barely took ten minutes to get Jeffery settled in. Simone hurried Rachel off, reminding her that the grand opening would take place in the morning whether Rachel had any sleep or not.

"But what if you need help in the night?" Rachel questioned. "I could stay here with you." The thought had just dawned on her, and Rachel realized it would allow her to forego the ride back to Casa Grande with Braeden.

"Nonsense. The doctor lives just across the street. I could probably raise the window and yell for him," Simone said, patting her arm. "Just go. I'm sure Jeffery will be up on his feet in time for the celebration."

Rachel nodded and walked onto the front porch with Simone. Braeden stood waiting for her at the bottom of the steps.

"Take good care of her, Braeden," Simone said smiling. "She's very important to me."

"Me too," Braeden replied. "Do let me know if there's anything else I can do for you or Mr. O'Donnell."

"I will," Simone promised. "Oh, and thank you for what you've already done. I'm sure things would have been much worse if you hadn't been there to help."

Rachel made her way down the steps and nervously allowed Braeden to help her into the carriage. She slid to the far edge of the seat and looked away when Braeden gave her a curious look. Instead of saying anything, however, he slid up against her, trapping her between himself and the edge of seat. The contact was electrifying.

"Braeden," she whispered. She could feel the warmth of his body generating heat to her own. She wanted to tell him that he should move away but couldn't bring herself to say the words. There was great comfort in his closeness. "Thank you for your help," she finally managed to say.

"You're quite welcome. I would have been grieved had you turned to someone else."

Rachel opened her mouth to speak, then closed it tight. Her heart was in turmoil over the gamut of emotions within her.

"Are you cold?" he asked.

Shaking her head, Rachel replied, "No, why do you ask?"

"You're trembling. I can feel you shaking from head to toe."

"Oh," Rachel said, feeling her face flush. She was grateful for the dim moonlight, hoping her embarrassment was less evident in the shadows of night.

He chuckled, however, leaving her little doubt that he knew the real reason for her quaking body. They drove in silence to the resort, and Braeden happily handed the buggy back over to Tomas when the boy appeared.

"I know, señor, you say to go to bed, that you take care of the buggy—but I could no sleep. Is Mr. O'Donnell all right?"

"He's fine, Tomas. Thank you for waiting up. I need to help Miss Taylor with cleaning up her office, so I appreciate you taking the responsibility for the buggy." The boy beamed at this compliment and jumped onto the buggy seat.

"Come along, Rachel, and tell me about the wax you found and the missing papers and why you tremble every time I touch you." He pulled her close and smiled. "Let's start with the last part first."

Rachel stiffened in his arms, but Braeden moved her up the stairs and inside to her office before she could even protest. Someone had thoughtfully left an oil lamp blazing cheerily since the electricity had been shut down at ten.

"I told you everything I know," she finally managed to say. "Someone apparently broke into my office one night. I don't think it's really all that important."

He pulled her into an embrace and shook his head. "That's to be decided. It still doesn't explain why you won't be honest with me—with yourself."

Giggles were heard from the girls' dormitory hall. Rachel glanced over her shoulder to find Ivy and Faith watching the scene. Instantly, Rachel pushed Braeden away and turned to meet the girls head on.

"What are you doing up at this hour?" she questioned, taking the upper hand.

"We might ask the same thing," Ivy said, toying with the ribbon on her robe. She looked seductively at Braeden and smiled. "I don't suppose you're having a meeting over the resort at this time of night."

"Mr. O'Donnell was injured in here earlier," Rachel announced. "He was hit over the head by someone who had broken into my office. We've just come from the doctor's office, and Mr. Parker has come to help me get things back in order."

"Things look just fine to me," Ivy said, her gaze never leaving Braeden.

Rachel glanced down at the floor and noticed that the blood had indeed been cleaned up. "Gwen must have done that. How thoughtful." She looked up at the girls. "Well, then, since you know what's going on, you may go back to bed."

The girls smiled at each other, then turned to leave. Rachel heard them giggling, but she didn't care. She was just surprised to have Ivy leave without a fight. Braeden was already repositioning her desk when Rachel bent down to put the iron doorstop back in place against the wall. But as she picked it up, her hand touched the wet stickiness on the backside. She looked at her hand and saw it stained with blood. Jeffery's blood. A small gasp escaped her and she dropped the doorstop in fright.

"What is it?" Braeden questioned, but he quickly saw the cause of her alarm. Taking out his own handkerchief, he wiped the blood from her hand. "It's all right, Rachel. That's probably what the thief used to hit O'Donnell."

"Yes," she replied. "I'm sure you're right." She was trembling again and couldn't stop, only this time it wasn't Braeden's nearness that caused her to quake. She kept thinking of how Jeffery could have been killed. How would she have ever explained such a thing to Simone?

Braeden pulled her close. "It's all over now. It's all right."

"But it could have been so much worse."

"But it wasn't. God had it all under control."

Rachel pulled away and frowned. "If God had it under control, then why does Jeffery now have six stitches in his head?"

Braeden shrugged. "I don't suppose to have all the answers, but you have to trust God to know what He's doing, Rachel. Trust is very important."

"Trust is hard."

"Yes, it is," Braeden replied. "No one knows that better than I do. Trust is believing God is still in control, even when the woman you love walks away. Trust is believing that God can clear your name of wrongdoing, even when everyone around you believes falsely against you."

"Oh, Braeden," she said, realizing the depths to which she had wronged him. It only served to add to her guilt. "I'm so sorry."

He put a finger to her lips. "I wasn't looking for an apology. I only wanted you to know that after questioning God and wondering why in the world He would allow bad things to happen to good people, I came to realize that it isn't important that I have the answers—it's only important that I trust Him."

She looked into his blue eyes and lost her heart all over again. Trust was the key. She knew it as well as she knew anything, but she also knew that letting go and trusting made her very vulnerable. And that frightened her more than anything.

Braeden was nearly back to his own quarters when Gwen Carson called out to him from the dining room doors. Surprised to find the normally shy young woman calling to him, Braeden stopped immediately and went to see what was wrong.

"You're keeping mighty late hours, Miss Carson."

"I know," she said, glancing over her shoulder as if afraid someone might see her. "But I had to tell you something, and I couldn't do it with Miss Taylor around."

Braeden narrowed his eyes. "What is it?"

"I cleaned up the office—"

"Yes, I saw that. It was a kind act of responsibility."

"I didn't tell you about it in order to receive praise. It's just that . . . well . . . there was something else."

"I don't understand, Miss Carson. What is it you're trying to say?" He could see that she was extremely nervous, and instantly his mind began to conjure all manner of thought. Had she seen something? Had the thief returned? "Please tell me what's the matter."

Gwen nodded. "I cleaned up the blood, then I tried to move Rachel's desk back, but it was too heavy. So I thought if I opened the drawers, I could take them out and lighten up the weight."

She faltered, and Braeden could see that she was clearly shaken. "Go on," he urged.

"I opened the largest of the drawers . . . and . . . and . . . inside it . . . well, inside it was a snake."

"A snake?" Braeden questioned. "How would a snake get inside a desk drawer?"

Gwen shook her head. "I don't know, but it was there and

I think somebody put it there to hurt Rachel."

Suddenly Braeden got a bad feeling about the entire matter. "What kind of snake was it?"

Gwen's eyes widened. "It was a rattler."

"What did you do about it?" Braeden was trying desperately to keep his emotions under control.

"I took it out of there."

He smiled at the shy girl. "You?"

"I've had to deal with snakes since we lived in a soddy when I was just a girl. They don't frighten me all that much, but this was different."

Braeden actually reached out and hugged the young woman. "You may well have saved Rachel's life. You should be commended."

"I figured I'd tell you because Miss Taylor might not think it was all that important. She tries hard to take care of herself, you know. She's a very proud woman."

He smiled. "Yes, I know. Look, you did the right thing in telling me. I believe you may well be right about someone trying to hurt Rachel. I'll need you to help me keep an eye on her. Can you do that for me?"

"I'll do whatever I can to keep her from harm. She's been a wonderful friend to me."

Braeden nodded. "Go to bed. Tomorrow is a big day and we'll all need our strength." She turned to go, then Braeden called again. "And thanks for what you did." He watched her until she disappeared into the kitchen. With a calm he didn't feel, Braeden closed the dining room doors and wondered silently how he was going to deal with this latest incident. It would appear, he thought, that this was no theft. This act was more along the lines of a threat, and Rachel was clearly the intended victim.

Chapter 17

Casa Grande appeared to be a tremendous success. From the first morning meal until the afternoon luncheon, elegantly dressed people flooded into the resort with no other purpose than to celebrate. Rachel was exhausted by the time the noon meal was finally served, and as customers sat around the tables enjoying their dessert, she finally took a moment to grab a glass of water for herself.

"You are working much too hard," Reg chided her. He seemed genuinely concerned, but he also seemed a little pre-occupied, even as he studied her.

"This day is much harder than the others will be," Rachel replied. "I'm not giving anything of myself that everyone else isn't giving."

"I suppose you didn't sleep well last night," he murmured. His expression seemed to almost dare her to deny it.

"Honestly, I'm fine."

"Still, you haven't even eaten."

"I had some breakfast," she protested.

"Here, at least have a bit of fruit," Reg encouraged.

"No, I have to get back on the floor. Ivy Brooks is giving me considerable grief, and I must oversee her constantly. She never listens to Gwen." Reg nodded, as if understanding completely.

Rachel handed Reg the glass, smiled, and squared her

shoulders. It was rather like going into battle, she thought. She came into the room just as Ivy's lyrical laughter filled the air. She stood at a table of well-dressed business associates for the Santa Fe. Smiling and batting her eyelashes, Ivy flirted outrageously with one particularly handsome man.

Gritting her teeth, Rachel went to the table and smiled. "Are you gentlemen finding everything to your liking?" she questioned.

Like children caught stealing cookies, the men looked nervously down at their plates, while Ivy sobered and turned on Rachel.

"I have everything under control here," she told Rachel sternly.

"That's wonderful," Rachel replied. "Then if you gentlemen have no other needs at the present, I must have a word with my employee."

They nodded, murmuring their understanding, but Ivy was hardly receptive. She was clearly angry that Rachel would dare disturb her plans. Rachel ignored the look on Ivy's face and instead stopped long enough before leaving the dining room floor to tell Gwen Carson that they were retiring for a few moments to the office.

Once inside the privacy of her quarters, Rachel closed the office door and turned to face Ivy's hostility.

"If someone else takes my tips because of this little escapade," Ivy declared, "I'll tell my aunt and see to it that justice is done."

Rachel folded her hands calmly and stared in silence at Ivy for a moment. She had hoped only to reduce her anger and get her emotions under control, but Ivy took it as some sort of threat and said so.

"If you are trying to intimidate me with that look, you might as well forget it."

"I'm not trying to intimidate," Rachel finally replied. "I brought you here for a long-overdue verbal warning. Fred Harvey has a strict policy regarding the actions of his girls and their service to customers. While some small portion of flirting is to be allowed and expected, outright wantonness is not to be tolerated. It is hard enough to get people to understand and believe that Harvey Girls are not an extension of the lewd women who serve at saloons. However, by your actions in there just now, I would say your charms would be better used at Big Clara's Cathouse down by the river."

"How dare you!" Ivy said, drawing up her full five-foot-four height. "I am the niece of this town's founder, and you have no right to talk to me like that."

"You are my employee. I decide, in spite of what you might otherwise believe, whether you stay or leave Casa Grande. I have given you more leeway than most, allowing for your stubborn willfulness even when I knew it was not the best thing for the welfare of our group. I allowed you to fashion your hair differently, spend nights away from the resort at your aunt's home, and have, in general, overlooked many of your offenses even while taking someone else to task for it. But no more. I sympathize with your plight in life. I am deeply sorry that your parents had to die so young, leaving you an orphan. However, I will not tolerate insolence. Nor will I allow for your lewd behavior on my dining room floor."

"What of your own lewd behavior?" Ivy questioned.

"And what behavior would you be speaking of?" Rachel questioned, knowing she was implying having found Braeden and Rachel alone in her office well after curfew hours.

"I think you know very well what I'm talking about."

"If you are referring to last night, then forget it," Rachel countered, her Irish temper beginning to flare. "Go look at the stitches on Mr. O'Donnell's head if you think to contradict me."

"Rules are rules. You said there was a ten-o'clock curfew for everyone. You said that no men were to be allowed in private quarters and assured us that no men would be allowed in your office after nine o'clock at night when the dining room would be formally closed and business concluded for the day."

"And all of those rules are still in effect," Rachel replied. "I don't have to explain myself to you, but in this case, I will. I took dinner with the O'Donnells, and when I returned, someone was in my office. I could see this because the thief was apparently not smart enough to think about leaving the light off while they came to steal what they would."

"How do you know it was a theft?" Ivy said smugly. "Maybe there was some other reason for someone to be in your office."

"There are no reasons for anyone to be in my office without my permission. The office was locked, which means someone had to find a way into it without notifying me for the key. But that aside, as Mr. O'Donnell attempted to catch the thief red-handed, he was, in fact, hit over the head."

"That might well be," Ivy said smoothly, "but it doesn't explain why you were in Braeden's room earlier in the evening." She laughed at the shocked expression on Rachel's face, "I can see you weren't prepared for me to know about that little escapade."

"I went for help."

Ivy laughed. "That's not what it looked like. Oh, and don't think for one minute that it's just my word against yours. I have witnesses."

"I can't believe this!" Rachel declared. "An innocent man is injured in my office, and you would condemn me for getting him help?"

Ivy crossed her arms and gave Rachel a look of bored indifference. "Rumors have a way of getting around, and the truth isn't always as clear as it should be."

Rachel felt as though a knife had been plunged into her heart. She knew full well the power of rumors. She had seen her own life destroyed by them, and now she feared they could destroy her once again.

"My reputation speaks for itself, Miss Brooks."

"Maybe so, but you still broke the rules. And what about dear Braeden's reputation?" she said, using his first name casually.

Rachel ignored the bait and shook her head. "I'm sure Mr. Parker's reputation is as easily defended as mine."

Ivy laughed. "Not when word gets out that he seduced me at the hot springs. You saw it yourself. He lured me there with a letter saying that he had to talk to me, then grabbed me in his arms at the first possible chance. I was helpless. Had you not returned for your book, who knows what might have happened?"

"Mr. Parker explained that entire situation," Rachel replied. Then, seeing the smug look of satisfaction on Ivy's face, she realized that she'd played right into her hand. Now Ivy knew in no uncertain terms that the event had bothered her enough to require an explanation after the fact.

"Of course he explained it," Ivy replied. "He wouldn't want his reputation compromised, now, would he?"

"This is ridiculous. We're wasting time."

"I quite agree," Ivy said as her eyes narrowed. "Now you will listen to me. Unless you leave me alone and stop badgering me about my actions, I shall have to go to the proper authorities and tell them of Mr. Parker's behavior."

Rachel swallowed hard. She couldn't have cared less for the threats to herself, but that Ivy would actually seek to hurt

Braeden in the process was more than she was willing to deal with. Still, she couldn't allow the girl free rein, and that in and of itself created quite a dilemma.

As if sensing Rachel's inability to decide what to do, Ivy uncrossed her arms and walked to the door. "It does make a sticky situation, does it not?" she said, turning to pause. "I mean, if you care about him the way you seem to, then you have to save his reputation from harm. My aunt would never hear of him remaining in charge of Casa Grande if she thought him capable of molesting an innocent young girl."

"You know he did nothing wrong," Rachel protested.

Ivy gave her an ugly smile. "You'd really like to believe that, wouldn't you?" With that, she opened the door and walked away, leaving Rachel to stare in dumbfounded silence. The girl had managed to strike at the very core of Rachel's fears and insecurities.

"What do I do with this one, Lord?" Rachel muttered. She went to her desk and took a seat. Her mind raced with thoughts of running after Ivy and firing her on the spot, but her heart bid her to be less reactionary. What if Ivy was able to get Braeden fired? What if she so ruined his reputation that he couldn't remain in Morita?

"Why can't things be simple?" she questioned, looking to the ceiling as she did on so many occasions. "Why must I continue with this thorn in my side?"

Outside her office, music could be heard as a full orchestra played in the ballroom down the hall. They were featuring a piece with plenty of rhythmic changes and brass fanfare. It was intended to draw people in from all over the resort, and Rachel had little trouble believing it would do just that. The orchestra was to perform at one-thirty for half an hour, then one of the dignitaries would speak to the group and make announcements for the afternoon and evening's events.

Rachel would normally have taken great joy in the celebration, but Ivy's threats, Jeffery's injury, and the violation of her office were all weighing heavy on her heart. Putting her head down on her desk, Rachel prayed for the strength to endure and for the protection of those she loved.

"I wondered where you had gone off to," Braeden said in a soft, low tone.

Rachel immediately came upright. He was leaning casually against the doorjamb, watching her quite intently. The expression on his face betrayed the feelings he held for her. It nearly took Rachel's breath away. "I was . . . well . . . I had to . . ." She stopped and shook her head. "Never mind."

"The crowds are gathering in the ballroom," he said, stepping into her office. "It should afford you a bit of rest. You look completely exhausted."

Rachel smiled. She gladly let the conversation take a turn from anything too personal. "I suppose I am, but there's nothing to be done about it. Have you seen Jeffery?"

"Yes, I talked with him and his lovely wife. He appears no worse for the wear."

She nodded. "Yes, he came to speak with me first thing. I'm so relieved he wasn't hurt more seriously."

"It could have been much worse." Braeden's expression grew very serious, and Rachel couldn't help but wonder why. "I want you to be very careful, Rachel. It might not even be a bad idea to have me look through your office and private quarters before you retire for the night."

Remembering Ivy's threat, Rachel shook her head. "That's hardly necessary, Braeden. I'm sure I'll manage just fine. I'll keep the doors locked."

"You kept the doors locked last night and it did little good."

She knew he was right, but her mind was hardly on that incident as he came nearer to where she sat. She could smell his

191

cologne, and it reminded her of being in his arms. She thought of Ivy and her threats and knew there was no end to the lengths she would go to protect Braeden.

She also thought of Ivy's words about Braeden luring her to the pool. It hurt to imagine that anything like that would ever happen, and she knew that she had to make a decision about trusting Braeden. Maybe trust had to be earned, but no doubt there would always be circumstances that would interfere with the process. In this case, trust would have to be a choice that she made. Either she trusted him or she didn't, and looking up at him now, seeing the love in his worried expression, Rachel knew that she must trust him.

She tried to smile as she got to her feet. "I must return to my girls. But I want you to know that I've thought a great deal about what you said regarding trust. Trusting God is something I've never questioned—not in earnest, anyway. God has always been very faithful, and I've never had a reason to doubt Him. I know trust is important for us as well. I'm sorry that I allowed my mother to so thoroughly ruin our plans. It wasn't my intention—it was just that I couldn't believe that the one person who loved me most in the world would do anything to make me unhappy. I'm still positive that she never meant to unduly hurt me. She actually liked you very much. Anyway, what I'm trying to say is that I know I have a difficult time trusting—you or anyone else. But because I expect trust, I know I must give it."

He took hold of her hand and caressed it very gently. "I know this comes hard to you. But I promise to be faithful and never give you any reason to doubt me again." He raised her hand to his lips and kissed it gently. "I love you, Rachel, and I want you to always trust me."

Rachel nodded and drew her strength from her prayers. "I do trust you, Braeden. I honestly do."

Chapter 18

Ivy stormed back to the nearly empty dining room, pausing only long enough to collect her tips from the now deserted table. The money was good, but not nearly as good as it might have been.

I'll show Rachel Taylor who she can and can't order around.

She pocketed the money, then, ignoring the other girls, made her way into the kitchen, where Reginald Worthington stood talking to one of his bakers.

The man clearly had a romantic interest in Rachel, although Ivy couldn't figure out why this should be. Rachel's auburn hair and hourglass figure might serve her well enough, but her face was plain and her personality left a great deal to be desired. But perhaps because of Reg's interest in Rachel, Ivy could enlist him as an ally.

"Mr. Worthington," she said rather sweetly, "I wonder if I might have a word with you." She batted her eyelashes and added, "Privately."

Reginald looked up rather surprised, but nodded. "Step into the storage room, Miss Brooks."

Ivy nodded and followed him to the large supply room, where a conveyor belt was laden with crates. Maneuvering around stacks of boxes, a plan began to formulate in Ivy's head. She wondered how she might figure out his response before committing herself to something underhanded. The last thing she needed was for Reginald Worthington to act the part of do-gooder and go blabbing her plans to Rachel.

"Mr. Worthington," she said as he turned with a questioning expression, "I know you are interested in Rachel Taylor."

"Miss Brooks, I hardly see that this discussion is appropriate."

"Just hear me out. I think I might be able to help you."

"Help me what?" Reg questioned, obviously confused.

"Help you get Rachel."

"I'm afraid I don't understand."

Ivy wanted to scream. The man was positively dim-witted. Would she have to draw him a picture? "I know you fancy yourself in love—or at least smitten—with Rachel Taylor. I can see it in your face every time she's around you." The man actually blushed, and it gave Ivy all the fuel she needed to continue. "I believe there's a way for you to get Rachel for yourself. And, if you don't mind a tiny bit of underhandedness in the process, I believe you could have her in such a position by tomorrow . . . probably even tonight."

Reginald only stared at her for a few moments, and Ivy had nearly figured the issue to be of no interest whatsoever when he stepped closer.

"I hardly believe we can discuss this properly here. Meet me in fifteen minutes down by the falls."

Ivy smiled. "I'll be there."

She continued smiling the entire time it took for her to reach the falls. She thought it a perfect plan to enlist Reginald's help. He would keep Rachel occupied while she went to work on Braeden Parker. It all seemed too simple.

She crossed the lawns and the road and made her way down a narrow path that led to the powerhouse. The waterwheel churned vigorously from the constant surging of the falls. She had no idea how this all related itself to providing the community with electricity, but she had to agree that it had made life in Morita more endurable.

Pausing at the first park bench, Ivy took a seat and glanced back at the resort. Beautifully clothed people made their way inside to hear the music. Ivy envied the women who wore lavish jewelry and incredible creations of taffeta and watered silk. And as if these outfits were not opulent enough, Ivy knew the ball gowns and opera dresses that would be worn in the evening would be feasts for the eyes.

Staring down at her own black skirt and white apron, Ivy knew she couldn't endure the humiliation of continuing along these lines. She had been born to wealth and affluence. How dare her aunt hide her away in Morita when she should be doing the grand tour of Europe and dining with royalty?

She thought of the resort again and of the festivities planned to entertain the wealthy. These were the peers she desired, but dressed as one of Fred Harvey's serving girls, Ivy knew she would never be accepted into their circles. She thought about retiring her position and returning to her aunt's house. Perhaps she would have better luck of it if she merely showed up at the festivities gowned in creations from Worth. Surely she could find a wealthy husband among the visitors to Casa Grande.

She shook her head, however, remembering her angry words with Rachel. No. She would have Braeden Parker for her husband. He might not be the wealthiest man who would grace the steps of Casa Grande, but he would be the one to give her the most satisfaction. Now, if she could just find a way to interrupt his duties during the Casa Grande celebration.

The entire event was planned in detail, and for the next three days the atmosphere would be that of a three-ringed circus. There were to be balls, opera singers, magicians, lec-

195

turers, and all manner of banquets and teas. She would be overworked and every moment of her time consumed, except for this evening. This evening, with a celebratory dance to be followed by a solo performance by a famed Denver soprano, Rachel had announced she would only need ten girls to remain on the floor. A huge buffet would be arranged for the dance, and other than keeping the table stocked with all sorts of delicious delicacies, the Harvey Girls would not be needed. Rachel chose her more experienced girls for the duty, and Ivy had been very angry about the circumstance—until now. Now she was more inclined to see the opportunity it afforded her.

She watched Casa Grande's chef make his way across the lawn as she had done only moments before. He was a tall, thin man—not at all bad looking, but he was English and Ivy found Englishmen to be so void of emotion and feeling that she had no interest in pursuing him to see whether he might make a suitable spouse. Besides, he seemed rather content to remain at Casa Grande.

He had shed his white chef's coat and hat and pulled on a brown coat that matched his trousers. Reginald Worthington could have just as easily been one of the dignitaries, Ivy thought. He was refined and well-mannered, but oh, so boring. Not to mention that he'd settled for a position that practically put him on the same level as her aunt's cooking woman.

"Yes, well, I suppose you know why I've come," Reginald said as though he thought himself to be rather witty.

Ivy nodded. "Do sit down. I need to know exactly what your thoughts are when it comes to Miss Taylor."

"I can hardly explain all of my thoughts," he told her plainly. He sat down rather stiffly and continued. "But if you are trying to inquire as to the length I will go to pursue Miss

Taylor, then I'm not opposed to a little, as you say, under-handedness."

Ivy smiled. "Good. Because some people can't see what's good for them. Take Rachel, for instance. She's been very hurt by Mr. Parker, and while this was in the past, I've no reason to believe it couldn't happen again." She looked at Reginald and waited a moment before continuing. She didn't want to spill out the information without being certain he wouldn't betray her.

"Pray continue, Miss Brooks. You have me quite in-trigued."

Ivy adjusted her skirts and folded her hands. "Mr. Parker has shown an interest in me, and I have a great affection for him. However, Miss Taylor is still under the belief that he cares for her. And while I believe Braeden wouldn't desire to see her hurt, he clearly has placed his heart elsewhere."

Reg gave a bit of a chuckle at this. "Miss Brooks, if we are to help one another, then I believe we should first and fore-most be honest. Mr. Parker is clearly smitten with Miss Taylor, as is she with him. If you would like to plot a way to divide them, then I am most assuredly your man. If you desire to sit here and spin fairy tales, then I am much too busy."

Ivy laughed out loud. "And here I thought I would have to pick and choose my phrasing with the utmost of care. Very well, Mr. Worthington, I propose to place a wedge of circum-stance and doubt between Rachel and Braeden. I want this to be something so powerful that not only will Rachel walk away from Braeden, but he will be forced to remain with me. I have something in mind, but I will need your help in order to make it work."

"By all means, please proceed." Reg's interest was evi-dent.

"From my own understanding of what I've overheard,

Braeden and Rachel were once engaged. There was some manner of betrayal, however, on the part of Braeden. I heard them talking one evening down by the hot springs. Apparently trust is very important to Rachel, and she feels that trusting Braeden will require a good deal of effort on her part. I believe that should she find that trust violated again, she would not hesitate to turn her back on him once and for all."

"Why do you feel so confident of this?"

"Because she was clearly upset by my actions that night. I pretended to be there at Braeden's request and she became pale as a ghost. She stormed off, forgetting her book and towel, which I spied about the same time I heard her re-approaching. I feigned a fall and ended up in Braeden's arms and the look on her face told me everything. He tried to explain, but she wouldn't hear it. If I can manage an even more damaging scene, I believe it will finally dissolve any affection she has for the man."

"And you have such a scene in mind?" Reginald questioned.

"I would hardly ask you here if I didn't," Ivy replied. But in truth, she hadn't really considered the matter in much detail. "I have tonight off and while the festivities are going on, I believe I could arrange for such a circumstance."

"But Parker will, no doubt, be tied up with activities at Casa Grande. It would take the notification of someone other than yourself to drag him away from his post. Rachel, too, will be obligated to the evening."

"Yes, but Rachel will be free after nine o'clock—I heard her say so. Maybe Braeden will also be free after that. Either way, I believe I can work out the details. However, what I will need from you is this. You must make certain that Rachel is occupied this evening. I can't very well make my plan work if she's in Braeden's company or if she follows him around all night."

"What do you really have in mind for me to do?"

"Well," Ivy said, suddenly getting a brilliant thought. "I will send Braeden a note from my aunt Esmeralda. The note will demand he come to the mansion at ten till nine. That way, even if he hoped to spend time with Rachel, she'll be obligated to stay at Casa Grande until nine."

"But won't your aunt be obviously occupied with the festivities? Surely Mr. Parker will see her there."

"Yes, she does plan to come to the dance, but I know for a fact she will not remain for the singing. My aunt has an aversion to remaining away from the house after nine in the evening. She believes it improper to take in too much night air and, being an old woman, she needs her rest. She plans to return when the dance concludes, and that's where you come in. I want you to be with Rachel when that dance concludes. Tell her you need to go over inventory. Tell her you saw someone in her office. Tell her anything, but just keep her occupied and with you."

"I'm quite certain I don't understand how this will resolve anything."

Ivy smiled as the plan took form in her mind. "I'll arrange to meet with my aunt at nine o'clock on the pretense that I will walk her back to the mansion. She'll come looking for me and when she doesn't find me, I'll have Faith inform Rachel that I left for the mansion some time ago. My aunt will be livid, and if I know her the way I think I do, she'll head home immediately. That's where you come in. You offer to walk her home, insisting that Rachel go along to chaperone or give you companionship or whatever. Just make sure she goes with you. The rest will be up to me."

"So you want for me to ensure that Rachel shows up at the

Needlemeier mansion at a few minutes after nine."

Purely amused by her own conniving, Ivy nodded. "Exactly."

"But how can I invite myself or Rachel in once we've walked your aunt home?"

"I'll have one of the servants helping me. Eliza will do anything for extra money. She can keep watch, and when she sees you approach the house, she can let me know. Then I'll start screaming, and you will play the gallant gentleman and insist that my aunt accept your help in the matter. Hopefully this will cause all three of you to come upon Braeden and me in the front parlor. I promise the scene will be most compromising."

"And this doesn't alarm you?" Reg questioned seriously. "It will not only be Mr. Parker's reputation that you place on the line."

"I know," Ivy said, undaunted. "And because my reputation is also at stake, Mr. Parker will have to do the honorable thing."

"And if he refuses?"

"He won't," Ivy stated firmly. "He won't or else he'll lose everything. I'll make such a scene that he'll be fired from Casa Grande and publicly humiliated. He won't want to lose his job, and he won't want to be thrown into jail for molesting a young woman." She nodded quite confidently and looked out to the picturesque scene of the waterfalls. "He'll have to sacrifice his freedom one way or another. Either by marrying me or by going to prison."

"You seem particularly confident that this can work," Reginald replied. He stood and jammed his hand into his coat pocket and retrieved a pipe. "I suppose it is my one chance to play the comforter to Rachel. Perhaps her gratitude at my being there in her hour of need will open her heart to something more permanent and intimate." He nodded as if seeing everything fall into place. "I shall do my part, Miss Brooks."

Ivy got to her feet. "I knew you would see it this way. I could tell you were positively daffy for Miss Taylor."

"She is a woman of exquisite beauty and spiritual depth. I enjoy our conversations greatly, and I cannot imagine wanting any other woman for my lifetime companion."

Ivy couldn't imagine feeling anything but loathing for the woman. "Then we shall strike this pact between us, and, Mr. Worthington, I have many resources available to me. Don't even think of crossing me in this matter. I would not at all be adverse to making your Rachel's life a very miserable existence."

"You needn't threaten me, Miss Brooks," Reginald said, lighting his pipe and taking short little draws of breath to ensure the tobacco caught. "I know full well about your scheming, and I wouldn't dream of interfering. A person might well find themselves the victim of . . . well, let's just say something deadly."

Ivy eyed him suspiciously. "What are you saying?"

Reginald shrugged. "I'd like it very much if you would arrange no further attempts on Miss Taylor's life."

Ivy grew nervous. "I'm sure I don't understand."

"And I'm sure you do," Reginald said, his eyes narrowing. "I know about the snake in Rachel's drawer."

Ivy felt the blood drain from her head. How could he possibly know about that?

"I can see by your expression that this was a turn you did not expect. Well, you see, I overheard you pay the man who put the snake in her office. I followed him to see what he was up to and saw him enter Miss Taylor's office. I know, too, that when Mr. O'Donnell surprised him he was forced to attack the man and then make a run for it. You hid him in your room and let him escape through your window. I know, because I was just outside, hidden by the shrubs, when he came from your room."

Ivy knew her mouth had dropped open in stunned amazement. She wanted to say something that would sound completely unconcerned, but nothing came to mind.

"I have no intention of telling anyone about it, unless you have plans to harm Rachel further—other than emotionally, that is."

Ivy knew she would have to go along with Reginald's demands. "I only wanted to scare her so that she would leave. I never intended for her to get hurt."

"Of course not," Reginald said, eyeing her contemptuously. "Just so we understand each other."

"I agree completely," Ivy replied, regaining a bit of her composure. "I want very much for this to work, and I wouldn't have come to you if I didn't believe you capable of being an asset to me."

"Very well, Miss Brooks. We shall strike out this evening to win the hands of those we esteem and, dare I say it, love?"

Ivy watched him walk away and felt a wash of uneasiness settle over her. This evening she would once and for all come between Rachel and Braeden. Whether it worked to her advantage and she was truly able to force his hand in marriage or not, she would at least ensure that Rachel would want nothing more to do with him—and that was a very satisfying thought. What troubled her was Reg's knowledge of her actions. The last thing she wanted was to be under his thumb. What if he blackmailed her? The thought caused her to shudder. Perhaps she would have to think of some way to control Mr. Worthington while she plotted against the woman he loved.

★ ★ ★ ★ ★

"Marshal Schmidt, I'm glad you could give me a moment of your time," Braeden said, ushering the older man into his office.

"Can't say that I've ever seen anything quite like this place. Lived in Kansas and Texas most of my life, and usually the town was small. That there music is mighty fine," he commented.

Braeden nodded. "I believe that's Mozart."

"He that fellow playing the piano?"

Braeden couldn't help but smile. "No. Mozart is the composer of the music. I'm not certain of the pianist's name."

"Well, it's right purty just the same. Makes a fellow a little sleepy, though."

"At least the heat has subsided," Braeden commented. "I find this cool weather much more to my liking."

"Weather's been acting funny here lately. Usually stays pretty warm clear into November. I don't mean hot like it has been, but real comfortable. The natives are saying there's signs of an early winter with plenty of rain between now and then."

Braeden nodded, growing bored with the idle chat. "Look, I've called you here for a reason. I need your help."

"Problems?"

Braeden nodded. "It appears so. We've been suffering from theft of materials since our arrival. My inventory is reduced by several items on a daily basis, and all of this took place well before the arrival of guests. Miss Taylor is also having problems, and . . ." He let his words trail off as he tried to decide whether to continue. Rachel hadn't wanted the law involved, but then, she didn't realize that someone had made an attempt on her life.

"And what?" Schmidt asked.

"May I tell you something in the strictest confidence?"

The man's eyes narrowed. "I'm no blabbermouth, if that's what you take me for."

"Not at all," Braeden replied. "It's just that this is such a delicate matter, I can scarcely figure out how to handle it by myself. But I wouldn't want word to get out about it."

The man seemed to understand and relaxed a bit. "It'll be just between you and me."

"Good. That's exactly how I want it to be for the time being," Braeden replied. "Last night someone broke into Miss Taylor's office here at the resort."

The man scratched his chin, then hooked his fingers in his dusty leather vest. "Yeah, I heard about that. Jeffery O'Donnell's sportin' stitches in his head."

"That's right. The thing is," Braeden continued, "it wasn't the first time someone broke into her office. I didn't know about it until last night, but apparently someone snooped around in her room some time back."

"You thinkin' the thief came back for something?" the man questioned, seeming to mull the matter over in his mind.

"I can't be sure what the real reason for the first break-in was. Some papers were taken, but nothing else. However, this break-in was different. This time the person clearly wanted to cause Miss Taylor harm."

"In what way?"

"They planted a rattlesnake in her desk drawer."

Marshal Schmidt's eyes widened at this. "Do tell?"

"It's true."

"Then shouldn't she be in here discussin' this matter as well?"

"She doesn't know about it," Braeden replied. "One of the

other girls found the snake there and, having had a great deal of experience in dealing with them, simply removed it before Miss Taylor found out about it."

"I see. Sounds like a good little woman to have around." He smiled before asking, "What's her name?"

"Gwen Carson. She's the head waitress in the dining room. She came to me with the information but didn't want to get Miss Taylor upset by it."

"How come she came to you?"

Braeden felt uncomfortable explaining his relationship to Rachel but realized quickly enough it didn't matter. "I suppose she came to me because I'm rather like a partner to Miss Taylor. She manages the restaurant, and I manage the rest of the hotel. But, besides that, I think Miss Carson knows I care very much about Rachel. We've known each other for a long time."

The man nodded. "So you don't want to let this get around in case Miss Taylor might hear it and be upset?"

"That, and I can't help but wonder if by keeping silent, the perpetrator won't show their hand by asking questions that could help them to learn what happened that night. Maybe they think the snake is still in the drawer. I mean, after all, there might not have been an opportunity for Miss Taylor to need anything out of that particular drawer."

"Hmm, I see what you mean. Well, what do you want me to do?"

"I suppose I'd like to have the place watched, at least from the outside. Someone is stealing from the establishment, and while I don't know why or where they are taking the goods, the tally is growing at an alarming rate. It's almost as if they want to get as much as they can right away because it won't be available to them later."

"I can set up some deputies to ride up this way on a regular basis. You want me to start that tonight?"

"I'd appreciate it. And like I said, I'd rather we don't say anything to Miss Taylor or anyone else for that matter."

"Sure thing, Mr. Parker."

Chapter 19

Rachel put the finishing touches on her hair before doing up the final buttons of her new green calico gown. She looked forward to Braeden's promise of a walk in the gardens and wanted to look her very best. The dining room had closed only moments before, and now, with most of the resort celebrators installed in the theatre room to listen to Miss Lucretia Collins sing various operatic selections, Rachel simply needed to wait for Braeden to come to her. She took up her shawl, closed her bedroom door, and locked it. This had become her routine, even if she planned to only be away from her rooms for a few minutes. It was hard to understand what the thief had been after, but Braeden had insisted she be meticulous in her actions.

Glancing across her office, she could recall the image of Jeffery crumpled and bleeding on the floor. She still shuddered every time she saw the doorstop, realizing how much worse the situation might have been.

Opening her lobby door, Rachel quickly checked to make certain the other office door was locked before sitting down to await Braeden.

"Miss Taylor?" a bellboy questioned as he peered into her office from the newly opened door.

"Yes?"

"Mr. Parker asked me to give you this note about a half

hour ago. I looked all over for you but couldn't find you until just now."

Rachel nodded and took the folded paper. She thought to thank the boy, but he left just as quickly as he'd come. She glanced at Braeden's handwriting, easily recognizing it from all of the love letters he'd written to her six years ago. She still had those letters, although she kept them tied together and hidden in the bottom of her dresser drawer. Perhaps someday soon she'd take them out and reacquaint herself with their earlier love for each other.

She frowned at the contents of the note as she read, "Mrs. Needlemeier has called me to an emergency meeting at her house. Sorry about our walk. I'll make it up to you. Braeden."

Rachel thought it rather queer. Mrs. Needlemeier had been very visibly in attendance at the opening dance, and while Rachel hadn't seen her during the last hour of the affair, she had figured Mrs. Needlemeier to be partaking of all the festivities.

"My dear Rachel, you are positively glowing," Reginald said from the still-open doorway.

Rachel quickly put the note into the top drawer of her desk. "Thank you, Reg. What can I do for you tonight? I thought you might be listening to Miss Collins' performance."

"I thought it might be best to discuss the inventory situation," he said, suddenly turning quite serious. "There are additional items missing, and I knew you would want to know right away."

Rachel shook her head. "But I thought everything was okay after you put Tomas in the storage room. This just doesn't make any sense. Who could be stealing all of this stuff—and why? And why would anyone want to ransack my office? Surely they know they will get caught. I mean, now I feel like I have to go along with Braeden's suggestion and call in the law."

Reg nodded. "It would probably be wise. Maybe after the grand-opening festivities are over with and things settle down, we could sit down with the marshal and explain everything we know to be true."

Rachel shook her head. "Sometimes it just overwhelms me."

Reg moved closer. "Rachel, let me take you away from here. We can go back to England, and I'll set you up like a queen. You know how much I care about you, and I do detest seeing you overworked and underappreciated."

His words stunned her, but Rachel forced herself to remain calm. She smiled. "I doubt Her Majesty Victoria would appreciate two queens in her country."

"Don't tease me, Rachel." He moved closer and reached out to take hold of her hand. "You know I've come to care a great deal about you."

"Reg, we hardly know each other. Besides, as you pointed out so nicely once before, my heart is otherwise engaged."

"But he doesn't deserve you. The scoundrel can't possibly appreciate—"

"Miss Taylor!" Esmeralda Needlemeier called from the doorway, causing Reg to jump back and drop his hold. She tapped her cane across the floor and, pushing past Reginald, came to a standstill directly in front of Rachel.

"Mrs. Needlemeier," Rachel said, getting to her feet in greeting. She had presumed the old woman to be in her emergency meeting with Braeden. Perhaps she had now decided that it was necessary for Rachel to attend as well. Maybe she knew something about the missing inventory or maybe Ivy had spilled the facts about seeing Rachel in Braeden's room and later in his arms. But Esmeralda's next words shattered that thought altogether.

"I have come to see my niece. She arranged to walk me home this evening and spend the night with me."

Rachel had no idea of this previous arrangement, and it irritated her greatly to think that Ivy had once again taken it upon herself to arrange affairs. "I gave Miss Brooks the evening off. I'm sorry, but I have no knowledge of her plans with you."

"Well, I can't seem to locate her," Esmeralda said sternly. "She told me she would be here, probably in her room. May I have admission to that room?"

"We can go together," Rachel suggested. "Her room is just outside this other door." She went quickly to the door and unlocked it. In the hallway, several girls moved back and forth from room to room, causing Rachel to glance over her shoulder. "Mr. Worthington, I made an agreement with my girls that there would be no men in my office after nine o'clock in the evening. I realize you were concerned about the inventory, but we can further discuss this in the lobby. Would you mind waiting there?"

"Of course not. My apologies." He gave a courteous bow and exited her office without another word.

"Come along, Mrs. Needlemeier," Rachel instructed. She entered the hall and knocked loudly upon Ivy's door.

Faith opened it and smiled. "Yes, Miss Taylor?"

"We've come to see Ivy. Her aunt is expecting her."

Faith looked past Rachel to the foreboding Mrs. Needlemeier and the smile faded from her face. Her brows knit together as she tried to explain. "Ivy went to the mansion earlier this evening. She said someone had asked her to meet them there."

"I know of no such arrangement," Esmeralda declared.

Faith shrugged and seemed to cower back a bit. "All I know is what she told me."

"When did she go?" Rachel questioned.

"Hmm . . . about seven-thirty, I think."

Rachel had a bad feeling about the entire matter. Braeden had made it clear that the Needlemeier mansion was his destination, but he had said that he was to meet Mrs. Needlemeier. Was it possible that it was a ruse to meet Ivy? Shaking her head as if the question had been asked aloud, Rachel reminded herself that she needed to trust Braeden. Ivy was the one who deserved little or no trust.

"I apologize for the inconvenience, Miss Taylor," Esmeralda announced, making her way back to the office without even bothering to verbally dismiss or thank Faith for the information.

Rachel followed her quickly out into the lobby. "I'm sorry, Mrs. Needlemeier."

"Is something wrong?" Reg asked, coming up to the two women as they emerged from Rachel's office.

"It would seem my niece is already gone ahead of me. I shall make my way home before the night air grows too cool."

"You mustn't walk alone," Reginald said in his refined British manner. "Perhaps you would allow me, and perhaps even Miss Taylor, to walk you home?"

Rachel had no real desire to accompany the older woman anywhere, but she realized Reg was only being kind and considerate.

"Do as you like," Esmeralda countered. "I'm capable of taking care of myself."

"No doubt that is true," Reg said, extending his arm, "but as a gentleman, I could not rest knowing you went unescorted."

Esmeralda nodded and took hold of his arm. "Then let us be on our way. I will find out more about this matter concerning my niece."

Rachel realized she was committed to accompany the two unless she wanted to appear uncaring about Mrs. Needlemeier. "I'll be right with you," she called after them. "I must attend to something first." She quickly went back to her office and locked her doors before catching up with Reg and Esmeralda as they maneuvered down the hall toward the sun porch exit. All she could think about was that perhaps she should say something about Braeden's appointment at the mansion.

"You didn't come in one of your carriages?" Rachel questioned as they walked along the porch. The golden glow of light made the decorated porch quite lovely. Perhaps people would mingle here in the evenings and take a rest while conversing of their days at Casa Grande.

"No need to take a carriage when the walk is so short. It does a body good to walk and take the air—but not this night air. There come all manner of illnesses from breathing too much night air," Esmeralda told them. "Hard on the heart, you know."

Rachel said nothing but walked in silence behind Reginald and Mrs. Needlemeier. She rather enjoyed the crisp night air and seriously doubted that any harm could come from breathing it. Just then a shiver ran through her. Her mother would say someone had just stepped on her grave, but Rachel knew better. This shiver was neither from the cold nor from superstitious sayings. This came from thoughts of what they would find at the Needlemeier mansion. *Please don't be there, Braeden. Please let this be nothing more than a misunderstanding.*

Colorful paper lanterns hung from the porch to the hot springs and along the garden footbridge. Rachel thought again of how she and Braeden had planned to walk out here alone. She had hoped to tell him that she loved him. . . . Her intuition, however, told her that things were not going well.

Somehow she knew that as much as she desired Braeden to be elsewhere, they would no doubt find him with Ivy in the Needlemeier house. She sighed, but no one heard her. She felt terribly alone, despite her company. If only she could be strolling here now with Braeden instead of her over-amorous chef and the cantankerous matriarch of Morita.

Ivy took one last drink of brandy and felt it course through her blood as she ran the brush through her long blond curls one final time. She smiled at her drunken appearance in the mirror. Hours before, she'd discarded her uniform, bathed in scented water, and redressed in a low-cut gown of lavender silk. She had chosen this gown specifically because of the front fasteners. She smiled again and nearly laughed at the lopsided way her mouth appeared. She had only been drunk on one other occasion, but that had been purely for the purpose of forgetting the past. This time she was intoxicated just enough to make a bold and rather daring plan come to life.

"Miss Ivy," Eliza called from the door, "Mr. Parker is waiting downstairs. He wouldn't take a drink, but I poured one like you said and left it on the tray."

Ivy smiled to herself. "Thank you, Liza. You'll find your money in the cookie jar."

"Thank you, miss." Ivy heard her hurry off down the hallway.

"My plans are coming together perfectly," she said and turned to walk to the door. She stumbled a bit and laughed at her condition.

She managed to make her way into the hall and maneuver down the stairway by keeping a hand on the wall. She'd had more to drink than she should have, but not so much that she couldn't see this matter through to completion. She had planned to simply give an illusion of drunkenness to her aunt, rather than the real thing, but once she started it was hard to stop. The brandy gave her false courage and helped her to forget the demons of her past.

She hiked up her skirt, then noticed that she'd forgotten her petticoat. Giggling, she continued down the steps, wondering to herself what else she might have forgotten. She had barely managed to make the final step when the hall clock sounded nine.

Drawing a deep breath, Ivy summoned her wits and threw open the sliding doors to the front parlor. Sure enough, there sat Braeden Parker—dashingly handsome and apparently stunned.

"Miss Brooks, are you quite all right?" he questioned, getting to his feet.

"I'm fine, Braeden darling," she said softly.

"I beg your pardon?"

"Oh, Braeden, you must know how I feel. I've been waiting so long to get a chance to tell you."

"I don't understand," Braeden replied, his expression confirming his confusion. "I'm supposed to meet your aunt here. There's some emergency business related to Casa Grande."

Ivy laughed. He looked so pathetic standing there. "I know you were expecting my aunt, but in truth, the note you received was sent by me." Her voice lowered. "I had to see you. You must understand."

The reality of the situation was beginning to dawn on Braeden, and Ivy realized she would have to make her case rather quickly or he might leave. Already he was eyeing the open door behind her.

She reached up and began unfastening her gown. "You must know how much I love you. I want to be with you, Braeden."

"Ivy, you're drunk and this is completely uncalled for."

"Please don't leave me," she said, urgently running to him. She threw her full weight against him and Braeden couldn't do anything but take hold of her arms. She hugged him even as he attempted to keep her from him. "We belong together, Braeden. It's our destiny."

Then, just as Ivy had arranged, Liza dropped a heavy metal pan against the stove, signaling that her aunt was approaching. Ivy had carefully seen to it that all the lights in the house were off, with exception to the front porch and the parlor, necessitating their arrival through the main entrance.

"What was that?" Braeden questioned.

"Oh, just my silly maid. Don't worry about her. Think about me. Think about us."

Braeden again pushed against her. "There is no us, Miss Brooks. I appreciate your flattery, but I am not at all inclined to reciprocate your feelings."

"But you must. I'm giving myself to you. Just you," Ivy said, desperate to make him see things her way. Her mind felt rather muddled, but she was sober enough to realize that there was little time to make her plan work. Without thought, she ripped away the final fasteners on her gown just as she heard the front door opening.

Screaming at the top of her lungs, she fell against Braeden as if suffering some sort of fit. He caught her, as she knew he would do. Now, if Mr. Worthington had done his part, Ivy Brooks would put on a better show than Casa Grande could ever hope for.

Chapter 20

The first thing Rachel heard as Reginald unlocked the front door of the Needlemeier mansion was Ivy's imploring cries for Braeden to leave her alone. It sent a despairing chill up her spine and nearly took her breath away. *So he did come here to meet her!*

Another scream tore at the silence, and Rachel wondered if she herself might faint. She didn't want to witness what she instinctively knew was to come. Esmeralda pushed past Reg, but without giving thought to what they were doing, Reg and Rachel followed her into the house. All three halted at the front parlor. As the only room in the house with the lights on, it seemed the proper place to stop.

What they found there, however, was anything but proper. Braeden had Ivy in his arms and was bending down to place her on the sofa. She beat her fists at his chest, moaning over and over one single word: "No."

As Braeden stood up, Rachel, as well as the others, could see that Ivy's bodice had been undone. Her chemise and corset were clearly visible from where the lavender silk fell away. Unable to hide her gasp of surprise, Rachel instantly drew Braeden's attention to her impropriety as Ivy tried to sit up, clutching her bodice.

"Mr. Parker, you have a great deal to explain," Esmeralda said in a low, calculated tone.

"I suppose you might think so," Braeden replied, "but this

isn't at all what it looks like."

"I don't want to hear lies," the old woman continued. "I've heard enough lies in my lifetime. You are clearly out of line here, and I want to know what is going on."

At this, Ivy managed to get to her feet and, still grasping her bodice, stumbled to where her aunt stood. "Oh, Auntie, it was terrible. He came here, he said, to see you. I thought it rather silly since you were at the celebration and everyone knew you'd be there." She swayed a bit on her feet. "I told him he could wait here for you, but then he asked for a drink —"

"That's a lie!" Braeden roared.

Ivy looked terribly frightened and backed up a step. "Well, it wasn't for him, as it turned out. He forced me to drink it. In fact, he forced me to drink a great deal. See for yourself. The glass and the brandy decanter are over there."

All four of them looked to where she pointed and sure enough there was a half-filled glass and a decanter with less than two inches of amber liquid still inside.

"That was nearly half full," Esmeralda declared, looking to Braeden for explanation.

"I had nothing to do with her drinking," he replied adamantly. "She came in here drunk and started throwing herself at me."

"Oh really, Mr. Parker? You come here knowing I won't be here, then expect me to believe it was all for decent purposes?"

"I don't care what you believe," Braeden replied, but his glance went to Rachel and his eyes seemed to plead with her to believe him innocent.

Rachel couldn't think clearly, much less determine who was telling the truth. She knew Ivy was prone to deception, but was Ivy capable of pulling off something like this?

"He made me drink," Ivy continued, "and then he became too friendly with me." She let loose a stream of tears. "I'm ruined," she declared, nearly causing Rachel to scream out loud in fear and frustration. She put her hand to her mouth, as if to stop any sound from coming forth, but her action caused Reg to move closer. His protective stance became more personal as he drew her to him supportively. For a moment, Rachel actually welcomed his touch.

Braeden scowled at this but turned his attention back to Ivy and her aunt. "She is hardly ruined. She did nothing but throw herself at me—and it failed. What you saw was my attempt to calm her down and get help. I was merely placing her upon the sofa in order to keep her from falling down. Look at her. She's swaying back and forth as if she were a flag in the wind."

"Liquor has that effect on a person, Mr. Parker," Esmeralda stated severely.

"He's ruined me, Auntie. He doesn't care now that he's done the deed. You have witnesses," Ivy said boldly.

"Whether she's ruined or not," Braeden replied, "has nothing to do with anything I've done or not done. She's angry because I've rejected her for another, and she means to see me pay for it."

"Oh, Braeden, you're just being mean. That's not at all what you told me earlier," Ivy sobbed. "You made me believe you cared. You said we'd always be together and that—"

"It hardly matters what was said earlier," Esmeralda declared. "What I really want to know from you, Mr. Parker, is whether I send for the marshal or the preacher."

Rachel could take no more. She turned on her heel and ran for the front door. She couldn't bear the look on Braeden's face, nor the smug gleam of satisfaction in Ivy's drunken expression. She hurried down the front steps of the mansion, catching the hem of her gown and nearly falling down the final two steps. She righted herself quickly, and as she raised her head, she saw the church just across the street. It seemed to beckon her forward. It offered her comfort and hope. But no doubt it was locked up tight and would afford her no refuge. And right now, in her deepest desperation, she didn't want to take the chance that someone would follow after her, allowing no means of escape. Especially if that someone turned out to be Braeden.

Without giving another thought to what she was doing, Rachel cut across the well-kept lawn of the Needlemeier estate and made her way deep into the gardens. There were quiet spots of refuge along the pathway, stone benches and wooden swings, any one of which could afford her privacy and silence. But Rachel needed something more than this. She needed solace. She needed to hear the voice of God speak comfort to her heart.

Moving deeper into the gardens, away from the hot springs and the laughter of lingering resort guests, Rachel found a secluded bench and sat down to weep. Here, far from the festive lighting of Casa Grande, the blackness seemed to enfold her like a mother's arms. The junipers and mesquites shielded her from the brunt of the chilling breeze, but the coolness of the night seemed unimportant compared to the icy foreboding that stabbed at her heart. Suddenly she felt more weary than she had ever felt in her life. It was all too much to deal with, and down deep in her heart, all she longed for was a long, silent sleep.

"Come unto me, all ye that labor and are heavy laden, and I will give you rest." She remembered the verse from Matthew. "I need that rest, Lord." She sighed and gazed into the trees.

For several moments she did nothing but draw strength from her surroundings. The heavy scent of juniper and pine assaulted her senses, and the canopy they formed made her feel rather secure and hidden from the world. A glorious aroma of flowering shrubs and meticulously tended flower beds blended with that of the trees, painting a picture in scents more wondrous than the human eye could imagine. But as lovely as this was, Rachel could hardly appreciate the majesty.

Her ear caught the melodious rippling of the hot spring as it flowed down a series of falls. The sound soothed her nerves and helped her to relax. Pulling her shawl tighter, Rachel leaned back against the bench.

"I'm so tired," she said aloud. "I'm tired of fighting against the feelings I have inside of me. Feelings of love for Braeden, anger toward Ivy, frustration with Mrs. Needlemeier, and confusion over Reginald. I'm tired of the whining and complaining of the girls on my staff and the sinister turn of our unknown thief. I'm just worn out from it all. I get up in the morning more tired than the night before, and when I do make it to bed, I toss and turn for hours. God, what's wrong with me? Why can't I seem to find rest and peace?"

She thought of her father, a railroad man in Chicago. He had died only the year before she'd left to join the Harvey House system. He had been everything to her. While her mother was absorbed in the goings-on of her neighbors, her father had taken time to talk to Rachel, share stories, and encourage her.

"I wish you wouldn't have died," she murmured, remembering his joyful smile. "I wish you were here now to advise me. You could always help me to see the brighter side of my circumstances."

Sighing, Rachel hugged her body. It was as much to comfort herself as to ward off the cold. "There seems to be so much going on in my life. So much that is out of my control. I thought I had faith enough to get through those times, but maybe I've only been fooling myself. I honestly thought nothing could move me. Maybe I've never understood faith."

Rachel remembered the scene at the mansion and felt hot tears course down her cheeks. The world seemed suddenly turned upside down, and with it she had been tossed to and fro like a lifeless doll. She had come to Morita with one expectation—to serve and make life more easy for the guests of the resort and, in the process, maybe find an easier way for herself. But her life here had resulted in stress and heartache.

Rachel continued to speak aloud, hoping the sound of her voice would help clear the confusion within her. "It seems I've always anticipated something better than what I found. I come to expect things a certain way—believe I understand them perfectly—and then something happens to destroy my way of thinking. Sometimes it's simply because I believed the words of someone who knew far less about a matter than they were willing to let on. I'd step out in faith that those words were true, only to find they were lies. I've wasted a great deal of time giving myself over to such matters—trusting people who did not deserve my trust."

But your trust should be fixed first in the Lord, a voice seemed to say.

How often had she heard her mother say that people often fail you? Hadn't those been her mother's words of comfort when she had gone home completely devastated after her confrontation with Braeden?

Of course, there were different ways of looking at trust, and with exception to the trust she placed in God, Rachel had been otherwise disappointed. *Maybe I expect too much,* she thought. *Maybe I expect a perfection that only exists in heaven. People will always be motivated by hundreds of different reasons, and it isn't my place to judge them.* She knew her own thoughts were wise counsel, but it was hard to find strength in them.

Feeling completely spent, her limbs leaden and useless, Rachel contemplated what she should do. Perhaps she would just doze here in the gardens and when she awoke in the morning, all of her problems would be resolved and the burdens would be lifted.

"In prayer you are responsible to let go of your burdens," she remembered Pastor Johnson preaching. *"Remember, God cannot take them—if you will not give them."* She smiled. It seemed to be very sound reasoning.

"This will not be easy," she said, remembering the events of the evening. Ivy was a meticulous liar; of this Rachel had no doubt. She had caught the girl conniving against Gwen and others, and it should come as no surprise that she would scheme to get back at Rachel through Braeden.

Haven't I heard her state that she's only looking for a husband of means and then she will leave Casa Grande? She felt a wash of peace come over her. She stated as a confirmation, "Braeden is innocent. He's merely a victim of her manipulation."

It seemed so right to believe this, and Rachel took a deep breath and sighed. "I give you this burden, Lord. I give you my sorrow, my worry, my fears, and my doubt. I give all of this to you, but I give something more as well." She paused and again looked upward. "I give you my trust, my hope, my faith, and my love. I know that you are able to take all of this madness and turn it into calm and peace. I will rest in you."

Just then voices sounded from somewhere beyond her refuge. Rachel perked up and looked around her in the darkness. Had Braeden come to find her? Or Reginald? She drew a deep breath and realized she would have to face them sooner or later. Reginald had been supportive and kind, and she appreciated the way he looked after her. And Braeden—Braeden deserved her support in this trial. He had suffered by her hand because of her choice to believe in gossip and hearsay. He shouldn't be punished now by the manipulated circumstances fashioned by Ivy's hand. And Rachel was certain that was all the matter amounted to.

Getting to her feet, Rachel picked her way through the brush and vegetation and was surprised to find herself standing not ten feet away from the empty bandstand. The massive structure had been positioned about twenty yards from the hot spring pools and was large enough to contain a full-sized band or orchestra. But the gazebo itself didn't hold her attention for long—rather, the activity at the base of the structure urged her curiosity. Two men had taken off a piece of the latticework and one was now crawling inside, under the bandstand, while the other handed him something. It seemed most peculiar, and Rachel couldn't help but move closer.

When she was nearly upon them, Rachel could see a wooden crate with articles taken from the resort. "What are you doing?" she questioned without thinking of her isolated position.

The nearest man turned around and grinned a gapped-tooth smile at her. "Buenos noches, señorita," he said, moving toward her.

Rachel backed up several steps, realizing her mistake. She thought to scream but the man was too quick for her. He was upon her in a flash, clapping a filthy hand over her mouth and dragging her backward toward the cover of darkness.

Chapter 21

Still reeling from the events of the last few minutes, Braeden stared in disbelief as Reginald Worthington rushed out of the Needlemeier mansion after Rachel. Esmeralda seemed not to notice the departures as she stood staring at him, as though she expected something—perhaps a confession. But there was nothing to confess.

Ivy teetered back and forth, seeming rather pleased with herself and the events that had just taken place. Braeden was then certain beyond all doubt that he'd been set up.

"Ivy, you are positively drunk on your feet," Esmeralda declared. She rang for the maid and when the young girl appeared, she seemed rather frightened.

"She can vouch for the fact that I didn't ask for a drink. She told me upon instruction she was to leave a drink on the serving tray," Braeden told the older woman.

Liza seemed to cower as Braeden stepped toward her. Esmeralda looked at the girl for a moment, then questioned, "Is that true? And if it is, exactly who instructed you to leave the drink on the tray?"

Liza glanced to Ivy, then lowered her head. "Mr. Parker told me to pour the drink."

"That's a lie," Braeden said, his voice low and accusing.

The girl raised her head and met his eyes. Braeden refused to go easy on her. She was clearly Ivy's accomplice, and he'd have no part of their games. Because of her and her mistress, he might have lost Rachel.

"Tell her the truth," Braeden stated in an even tone.

"Lizzz-a al-waysss tellsss-a truth," Ivy said, slurring her words badly. It was evident that the liquor had taken a progressive hold on the girl.

"Liza, take Miss Ivy upstairs to her room. Help her to prepare for bed and get some coffee on to boil." Esmeralda waited sternly while the housemaid scurried to Ivy's side.

"Braeden." Ivy murmured the name as she passed by him.

Braeden held his arms tightly to his sides, afraid that if he moved even an inch, he might throttle Ivy Brooks and force the truth from her own mouth. But once Ivy and Liza had gone from the room, Braeden shoved his hands in his pockets and turned to Esmeralda Needlemeier.

"I don't know what kind of game your niece is playing, but I assure you nothing improper took place here tonight—at least not improper on my part. I received a note telling me to meet you here for some emergency meeting. I thought it rather strange, but given the nature of your demands of late," he said in a terse manner, "I figured it was probably legitimate."

"I sent no such note," Esmeralda declared, unmoved by his insult.

"Well, someone did," Braeden replied, pulling the paper from his pocket. "I have it here. It appears to be on your stationery. You will note the scrolled initials *E N* in the center."

The old woman's face contorted. "Let me see that." She snatched the paper from his hand as he extended it to her.

Esmeralda studied the note for several moments, then folded it and held it tightly in her gloved hand. "What happened here tonight was witnessed by two of the resort employees. Tongues will wag, no doubt, and my niece's reputation will be ruined. Despite how this event came to pass, it would be the honorable thing for you to act the part of gentleman and marry the girl."

"It would be a false honor," Braeden countered. "I do not love your niece, neither do I feel at all inclined to spend my life with her. She is a manipulating liar. You know it and so do I. She staged this entire thing, and if she has to suffer the consequences of not getting her way in the matter, then that is her problem."

"If it is a matter of money . . ."

"It is hardly that, madam," Braeden said, feeling his anger build. "I will not pay the price for something I had no part in. I suggest you take your niece to task for this event, perhaps even send her to some proper finishing school where she might be taught decorum and manners. No doubt she'll just try this again with some other unsuspecting fool. Now, if you'll excuse me." He stormed out of the room, barely remembering to take his hat from the table in the hallway.

"Mr. Parker, this matter is far from being settled. I will speak to my niece, but if I am not convinced of her guilt in this situation, I will send the law to speak to you on my behalf," Esmeralda called out from behind him.

"Send anyone you choose, Mrs. Needlemeier," Braeden said, turning to address her face-to-face. "It will not make this any more my fault than it already is, neither will it force me to marry your unruly niece. I believe you know the truth in what I'm saying. I see it in your eyes. For whatever reason you choose to maintain this stance of believing me guilty, it will not change the facts of the matter—and you know that very well." He put his hat on his head and gave her a short bow. "Good night, Mrs. Needlemeier."

He left the stunned old woman speechless as he raced down the porch steps, driven by the notion that somewhere

Rachel was dwelling on the scene she'd just witnessed. And possibly, Reginald Worthington was offering her comfort in his arms.

Braeden slammed his fist into his hand and let out a growl of protest at this thought. The nerve of Worthington to act as Rachel's defender! Braeden had nearly knocked the man aside when he'd dared to put himself between Braeden and Rachel. As if she needed to be shielded—protected from Braeden. But when the man put his arm around Rachel, as though they were both very comfortable in such an action, Braeden had desired nothing more than to put his fist into Worthington's smug face.

He moved through the gardens and across the footbridge, knowing that if Rachel was sensible and thinking with marginal clarity, she would have made her way to the privacy of her quarters. At least he prayed that's where she might have gone. He desperately wanted to talk to her, to reassure her that he wasn't unfaithful to their love. He knew how very tender her heart was in this area, and he knew that her trust in him had cost her everything.

"It won't be her fault this time," he muttered aloud. "If she initially believes the scene staged this night, well, who could blame her?" He knew the evidence was very damaging. He could easily imagine how the entire setup had looked to Rachel.

Grinding his teeth together, Braeden stifled the urge to ring Ivy Brooks's neck. He could still see her seductive little smile as she toyed with the bodice of her gown. She had planned it out in meticulous order. She knew when her aunt would return, and she somehow seemed to know that Rachel would return with her.

He entered Casa Grande through the back entryway, grateful that most of the hotel guests were listening to the conclusion of Miss Collins' singing program. He passed by the theatre room, where the crowd was congregated, and heard the thunderous applause as the soprano hit her final note. Picking up speed, Braeden moved down the corridor, past the intersecting hallway and the entrances to the library and dining room. All was ominously silent.

Reaching Rachel's office, he called for her first, then knocked loudly on the door. There was no response. He repeated the process two more times before deciding to go outside to see if there was any light shining in the windows of her private quarters. But when the windows only yielded darkness, Braeden found himself at yet another dead end. Glancing around the front lawns, he wondered if perhaps she had taken herself to the pools or to a quiet place to think. The gardens were full of benches for just such a purpose, and Morita Falls boasted a scenic walking path with tables for picnic luncheons.

Moving out across the lawn to where the illuminated fountain glowed in the darkness, Braeden prayed to find her—prayed that she'd be unharmed and at peace with the events of the evening. If she could only find a way to hold on to her fragile trust in him, she would recognize that he had no feelings whatsoever for Ivy Brooks—at least not feelings that entailed any warmth.

He paused beside the fountain, his reflection in the water catching his eye. He looked hard and long at himself for several moments. His anger was evident, and his eyes were dark in their fury. Forcing himself to calm down, Braeden took a deep breath and tried to formulate a plan. He couldn't just run from one end of the grounds to the other without any real purpose in mind. He should make a mental list and meticulously search from one end of the estate to the other. Time was of the utmost importance. While the days were still pleasantly warm, the nights bore a chill that could easily strike one down with illness.

Staring back at Casa Grande, Braeden watched as upper floor lights came on to indicate that the resort guests were retiring for the evening. Soon the front lobby doors would be locked tight, and while Rachel had a key to the resort, Braeden was uncertain that it would be upon her person.

"I have to find her," he whispered. "Please, God, help me find her."

However, despite his avid search, Rachel was nowhere to be found. No one had seen her. No one had any idea where she had gone.

Finally, with the upper floor lights now winking off for the night, Braeden went into his office and closed the door. He needed to concentrate. Rachel had to be somewhere nearby. But where? He contemplated the matter for some time. Then, breaking Fred Harvey's most important rule, he took himself into the dining room, back through the kitchen, and into the private parlor and dormitory hallway of the Harvey Girls. Curfew was ten o'clock, and since the hour was nearly midnight, all of the girls should be safely locked in their rooms. With this in mind, Braeden felt some confidence that he'd not have to be further accused of molesting yet another Harvey employee. His reputation was already suffering, and with Fred Harvey's strict rules on propriety and honor, Braeden wondered if he'd even have a job once Esmeralda spoke out against him. After all, Harvey himself had arrived that evening by train to share in the celebration. He would no doubt preside over any dispute of such a grand nature. For the first time, Braeden realized he might lose his job or even find himself jailed. He shook his head. All of that was immaterial to finding Rachel.

He knew where Gwen Carson's room was and made his

way there as quietly as possible. Knocking lightly on the door, he continued to glance over his shoulder to make certain no one else had appeared in the hallway.

"Yes?" Gwen asked, opening the door wide. When she saw it was Braeden, she shrieked and pushed the door closed all but a couple of inches. "Mr. Parker, what in the world do you want? You aren't supposed to be here!"

"I know, Miss Carson, and I do apologize. It's just that Rachel is missing, and I wondered if you knew of some favorite place she might go."

Gwen opened the door a few more inches. "Rachel is missing? What do you mean?"

"It's a long story," Braeden replied in complete exasperation. "Something happened tonight that upset her. I need to find her and explain."

Completely taken in by this development, Gwen let the door fall open. "The only place I know she goes is the O'Donnell house. Mrs. O'Donnell is probably her best friend."

Braeden felt relief wash over him. "Of course! Why didn't I think of that! Thank you, Miss Carson."

He hurried back the way he'd come and ran out the front door of the lobby, mindless of the bellboy who stared at him in curiosity.

The O'Donnells lived just over the main bridge, and they were less than three blocks away from the Needlemeier mansion. It made perfect sense that Rachel would have gone there. Braeden knew of her love for Simone O'Donnell and of Jeffery's deep abiding friendship for the woman he'd worked with. Braeden felt a small amount of relief in believing her to be there. She would be safe, and Simone would calm her down and help her to see reason. At least he prayed she would.

But when he arrived, the small clapboard house was dark and it wasn't until then that he remembered Jeffery and Simone had been at the resort celebration. Knocking loudly, Braeden felt his anxiety mount. They were probably already in bed and completely exhausted from their evening. After all, Jeffery was still recovering from his incident from the night before. If Rachel would have come to them, they probably wouldn't have even been here. Now his mind tried to logically conclude where she might have gone upon finding the O'Donnell house empty.

While he contemplated this, the door opened and Jeffery stood looking in questionable silence at Braeden. Without waiting for him to speak, Braeden apologized. "I know it's late, but I'm looking for Rachel."

"Rachel's not at Casa Grande?" Jeffery asked, concern edging his tone.

"No," Braeden said with a sigh. "Look, something happened tonight. Something awful—and Rachel thinks the worst of me. I have to find her."

"Why don't you come in and explain while I get dressed. Then I can help you look for her."

Not knowing what else to do, Braeden nodded and followed Jeffery into the house just as Simone O'Donnell appeared. She had wrapped herself up in a dark blue dressing gown and was fussing with her hair as she came into the room.

"What's happened?" she asked. Her gaze rested on Braeden as though she were trying to read his mind. "It's Rachel, isn't it?"

"Yes," Braeden said. "She's missing."

"I'm going to get dressed and help him look for her," Jeffery stated, as though that would answer all of Simone's questions.

"I'll get dressed too," she said. "Maybe I can help."

"No, someone should stay in case Rachel comes here," Braeden replied.

"Why would Rachel come here?" Simone asked, eyeing him sternly.

Braeden swallowed hard and tried to think of a delicate way to explain. In exasperation he ran his hand through his sandy hair, then plunged it deep into his pocket. His nerves were getting the best of him. "I was called to meet Mrs. Needlemeier at her house this evening. Only it turns out she didn't send the note—her niece, Ivy Brooks, did the deed. Ivy, as you may well know, has been a thorn in Rachel's side since the beginning."

"I do know that much," Simone replied, her expression revealing nothing but calm and the reassurance that she wasn't jumping to conclusions.

To Braeden, she seemed to be weighing all the facts and not reacting at all in a condemning fashion. It gave him the courage to proceed. "Ivy arranged for a seduction scene. It seems she wants—or maybe even needs—a rich husband, and she picked me for her victim. When I came to the house, she was as drunk as anyone could be and proceeded to disrobe. Rachel came in at a most inopportune moment, to say the least."

"Why would Rachel be there?" asked Simone softly.

"That was exactly my thought," Braeden replied. "I mean, Mrs. Needlemeier coming in was no surprise at all. It is, after all, her home. But Rachel and Reginald Worthington had no reason to be there. It made me realize Ivy had set up the entire affair to come between Rachel and me." Braeden felt a tightness in his chest. He hated feeling so out of control—so hopeless. "Look, I know she's talked to you, but I don't know how much she's said. You know I love her, but this may well have destroyed any hope for our future, and I can't let that happen. Trust comes hard for her—at least where I'm involved."

"Rachel is a good woman," Jeffery replied, hopping into the room as he struggled to pull on his boots. "She doesn't seem the type to just jump to conclusions."

"She is a good woman," Braeden agreed, "but even good women have their limits."

"Where could she have gone?" The question came from Simone, as though no one else might have thought of it.

"I had hoped she'd come here, but then I realized the ordeal took place earlier in the evening when you both would have been at the celebration. Rachel might have thought to come here but most likely would have found the place deserted. From there, I have no idea what she would have done. Has she spoken to you of someplace special to her? Someplace she might go for safety or solace?"

"The church might be a logical choice," Simone replied.

"That's a good idea!" Braeden replied. "And it's just across the street from the Needlemeier mansion."

"Come on," Jeffery told him. "We can walk up there and check it out. If she's not there we might need to wait until morning to do a more thorough search. Maybe the extra time will allow her to calm down and think things through."

"Maybe," Braeden replied, but he didn't feel convinced. "But I can't bear to think of her spending the night outside. The chill could be harmful."

"Possibly," Jeffery agreed. "But we don't need to jump to conclusions. Maybe she's safely spending the night with someone else. Maybe she went to pray at the church and the pastor and his wife urged her to stay with them. If she was as upset as you think she might have been, she might not have been capable of reasonable thought. Maybe the pastor just took charge and let his wife put Rachel to bed in their guest room."

"Maybe," Braeden replied, hoping that Jeffery was right.

However, when Rachel could not be found at the church, the parsonage, or anywhere in between there and the O'Donnell home, Braeden felt the bottom fall out of his world. Hope eluded him as he reluctantly agreed to wait until morning to begin searching in earnest.

Simone touched his arm gently as Braeden turned to go back to Casa Grande. "Rachel will consider the situation, and I believe she will know the truth."

Braeden nodded in resignation. Maybe upon reflection, Rachel would realize his innocence. There was a chance it could work out that way, though Braeden feared it was slim.

"I'm sorry to have bothered you," Braeden finally said. "If she's still not back in the morning, I'll be heading out to search for her at first light."

"I'll be there," Jeffery replied.

"What about your head?" Simone questioned her husband. "You probably shouldn't be anywhere near a horse for another few days."

Jeffery lightly touched his wife's cheek, but his gaze went to Braeden. "I'll be there."

When Braeden returned to Casa Grande, it was two in the morning. With no sign of Rachel anywhere, Braeden's frustration and misery mounted. It was only then that it dawned on Braeden that he might question Reginald Worthington about where Rachel had gone. Perhaps Worthington held the key to the whole matter if she had confided in him.

Braeden tried not to think of Rachel finding solace in Worthington's arms. He couldn't dare to react illogically in this matter—too much was at risk. Instead, he would simply go upstairs and speak to Worthington and state his case, plain and simple. With this in mind, he had reached the third step on the grand staircase when the lobby door opened behind him and in walked the very man he was going in search of.

"Worthington!" Braeden called out, going back down the stairs. "Where's Rachel?"

"I have no idea, Mr. Parker. I've been searching for her ever since the fiasco earlier this evening." He paused, and the look of contempt on Worthington's face matched the feelings Braeden held in his own heart. "Besides, even if I knew where she was," he added, "I wouldn't tell you."

Braeden balled his hands into fists but stopped short of raising them to Worthington's face. "I did nothing wrong," he managed to say, his jaws clenched tight. "That whole scene was Ivy's concoction."

"I suppose you might see it that way, but I think it probably appears otherwise to Miss Taylor. Now, instead of standing around arguing about it, I suggest we put together some sort of search party. It'll be light in a couple of hours, and while I have to oversee the kitchens, I'm certain you can be spared from your post," Reginald replied rather snidely.

Braeden grabbed Worthington by his lapels, and with his face only inches away from the Englishman's, he whispered low and menacingly, "If you are lying to me, I'll personally see to it that you never work again."

"I say," the startled man replied, "you needn't take your anger out on me. You've brought these problems upon yourself."

Braeden thought long and hard about punching the man squarely in the nose but instead tossed him backward so that he lost his balance and landed on the floor. "Just remember, Worthington, Rachel is my concern and my problem—not yours. Leave her alone."

Worthington watched him for a moment before getting to

his feet and dusting off his trousers. "You, Mr. Parker, are a ruffian of the worst kind, and if Rachel so desires it, I will do my utmost to protect her from you. Good-bye."

Braeden watched him go, wondering when he'd ever felt this angry. There was nothing to be gained by losing his head, however. And as much as Braeden hated to yield to Worthington on any matter, this was one of those few times he would do exactly that. Dawn would arrive in a few hours, and when it did, Braeden needed to be ready.

He decided the first order of business would be a change of clothes. He was still wearing his best suit on behalf of the grand opening, and it would never do to go traipsing around the countryside dressed in such formal attire. Opening the door to his office, Braeden turned on the lights, grateful that because of the resort activities the electricity had been left on instead of shut down at ten as was the routine. But no sooner had the light illuminated the room than Braeden found himself staring dumbfounded at the scene. Someone had ransacked his office—and from the looks of it, they'd done a pretty thorough job.

Papers were strewn all over the floor, his chair overturned and left in the corner, and every drawer of his desk had been pulled out and emptied. It didn't make sense. He had nothing of value here. There were papers related to the hotel's management, inventory, purchase orders, and payroll information, but all of the important things like actual payroll money, storage room keys, and anything of value were locked up tight in the hotel safe. What could the intruder have been looking for?

He squatted down and began picking up the papers. They were hopelessly mingled and would take hours to sort through. Braeden stood amid the disarray, trying to imagine what it all meant. As he thought of the note given to him by

Ivy and of the scene she'd managed to set up, he couldn't help but wonder if she was also responsible for this mess. Then again, someone had broken into Rachel's office on more than one occasion. Perhaps whatever was searched for there was never found and the thief thought to find it in Braeden's office.

"It doesn't make sense," he said as he set his chair upright. Beneath the leather chair, Braeden's gaze fell upon a square piece of stationery. He picked it up and realized instantly that it was a program from the opera singer's performance. How had that managed to get into his office? Had the thief left it there? It seemed logical to think they might have. Shaking his head, Braeden felt a growing sense of frustration. It was like having all the pieces to a puzzle but being unable to figure out where they all went.

After beginning to clean his office, Braeden realized there was no time for putting the papers in order. It would have to wait until after he found Rachel. Rachel's safety was more important than anything else. He couldn't allow himself to be distracted.

Distracted.

The word seemed to echo in his head. Maybe he was meant to be distracted. Maybe the mess he'd found in his office was created to slow him down. But slow him down from what? Finding Rachel? The intruder couldn't have known about Ivy's arrangements—or could they? He thought of the evening's events and realized that Ivy could very well have had many accomplices. She had incorporated the help of her maid at the mansion—why not additional help from her Harvey friends or other staff members of Casa Grande? Perhaps she had promised them money or something else.

He ripped off his tie and threw it on the bed in the adjoining room. Changing into jeans and a more serviceable shirt and coat, Braeden tried to figure out what it all meant. He uttered a prayer for guidance but felt no nearer to the truth. He recalled a verse in the Bible about seeing things through a glass darkly and thought it perfectly depicted his feelings just now. The images were distorted and unclear — the answers evaded his reach.

"I don't know what's going on," he murmured as he took up his hat, "but I'm going to find out."

Chapter 22

As Ivy sobered up, the first thing she became aware of was her aunt's imposing glare. The old woman glowered at her in such a way that it would have given her a headache—had she not already had one from the effects of the liquor.

Still, the fact that she'd managed to pull off her charade from the night before made the pain worthwhile, as far as Ivy was concerned. She had sketchy memories in places where the brandy had overpowered her senses, but for the most part she remembered everything—especially the look on Rachel Taylor's face when she found Ivy and Braeden together.

"You needn't smile," Esmeralda declared in such a no-nonsense manner that Ivy couldn't help but wonder if there was something more than the events of the evening that disturbed her now.

"I'm sorry, but considering all that has happened, I believe I am entitled to think of this entire affair in the best of possible ways. If I had to be ruined by someone, it's at least beneficial that he was handsome and rich."

"Stop it now. Stop this nonsense and finish your coffee. I want you good and sober in order to discuss this matter properly," Esmeralda told her niece.

Ivy stared at her aunt for a moment, then shrugged and downed the contents of the delicate china cup. The strong, hot liquid scorched her throat as she gulped it down, but Ivy hardly felt the pain. Soon she would leave this hideous place and the painful memories it harbored. She was going to marry Braeden Parker and move back east and live in a fine house for the rest of her life. She'd already planned it all out in her mind.

Putting the cup back on the saucer, she looked to her aunt as if to invite her to speak. When Esmeralda only continued to frown, Ivy realized she'd have to be the one to start the conversation.

"I'm quite myself now," she told Esmeralda. "Although my head hurts and there are other parts of my body that feel rather misused. But I'm ready to discuss this matter, if that is what you desire." She'd play the part with sweetness and consideration, especially since she knew it would take her aunt's power in the community to force Braeden Parker to marry her.

"I'd like an explanation, Ivy." The words were matter-of-fact and issued without emotion.

"An explanation for last night?" Ivy questioned. "Don't you think that would better be asked of Mr. Parker?"

"No, I do not. Mr. Parker hardly seems the one to question when you were the one to plan the entire event."

"I don't understand. A man comes into our home, tries to—no, succeeds at molesting me, and you want my explanation?" Ivy questioned indignantly. She reached for the ties of her pale pink robe and tightened them for lack of something else to turn her attention to. She was going to have to play this very carefully. Apparently her aunt had reason to doubt the scene she'd witnessed. "I think you are being very hard on me," Ivy continued. "But then again, you always have been. You've always treated me poorly."

"That's not true, but neither is it relevant to this discussion," Esmeralda replied calmly. "I know that you wrote the note that brought Mr. Parker to this house."

Ivy's head snapped up at this declaration. "What in the world are you talking about? I wrote no such note."

"Oh no?" Esmeralda said, pulling the piece of paper from her pocket. "Then suppose you explain this. The writing is clearly yours, not mine as the note implies."

Ivy knew what the piece of paper was without having to look at it. But for the sake of her story, she took the offering and looked it over. "I didn't write this."

"Well, neither did I, and whoever did has a remarkable ability to forge your handwriting to perfection," Esmeralda said rather sarcastically.

Ivy shrugged and handed her back the note. "I'm not responsible for this."

"Say what you will," Esmeralda replied, shaking her head. "We both know the truth. What I don't understand is why you were so desperate for a husband that you felt you had to stoop to such levels. Why, there isn't a decent man in Morita who would have you now, and you certainly cannot believe that Mr. Parker will marry you simply because of that little charade."

"Charade!" Ivy said angrily. "The man completely destroys my reputation and you call it a charade? There were witnesses—or have you forgotten?"

"I haven't forgotten anything." Esmeralda carved out a pattern in the floor as she paced, appearing to consider what she might say next. "I haven't forgotten the request you had for me to seek you out after the ball. I haven't forgotten that you expected me to return home at precisely nine o'clock, and I haven't forgotten your hatred of Miss Rachel Taylor. And because of this," she said, halting in front of Ivy, "I believe I am absolutely correct in saying that you planned the entire ordeal in order to take your revenge on Miss Taylor

241

and force the issue of marriage with Mr. Parker."

Ivy regained her composure and bowed her head to appear devastated. "Then you are wrong. I may have been angry with Miss Taylor, but I do not hate her. I would never plan my own ruin in order to get back at her. You may accuse me of many things, Auntie, but pettiness has never been one of my flaws. Nor is stupidity. I wouldn't risk my future in order to have my own way for now."

Esmeralda sighed and began to pace again. "At fifteen, you came to me with no one else in the world to see you through. You had lost your mother and father and the only home you had ever known. You were a child then, your actions and attitudes excusable. However, I had hoped you would outgrow this selfishness. I had hoped that you had learned the painful cost of your conniving and would have chosen a better way."

"I don't understand you," Ivy said, looking up to meet her aunt's mournful expression. What was the old woman talking about now? Ivy could hardly stand to listen to her aunt's useless blather. There were plans to be laid. She needed to find Braeden and declare the need for an immediate wedding. Instead, she had to sit here and listen to her aunt go on and on about something Ivy had no understanding of. "What conniving and painful cost are you speaking of?" she finally asked in complete exasperation.

Esmeralda held a look of immense pain. "You know very well where your conniving has brought you. After all, it brought you here to live with me."

Ivy felt a chill run up her spine. Could her long-buried secrets be known? She shook her head in denial. "I came here to live with you because, as you pointed out, I had no one else."

"No, not after your plans had gone awry."

Ivy remained seated but her heart began a frantic pace and

her chest grew tight. "My plans? I don't know what you're talking about."

Esmeralda leaned against the cane and scowled. "I know you caused the fire, Ivy. I know it was your hand that took the lives of your parents—of my beloved brother, Carl. I've had reports from the insurance inspector and a statement from the one maid who survived a short time after the fire."

Ivy felt her skin tingle. There was an almost unexplainable stimulation in having the truth be voiced aloud. "It was an accident," she replied, her voice barely audible.

"No," Esmeralda countered, this time her voice taking on an angry edge. "You planned that fire, just as meticulously as you planned to have us find Mr. Parker in this house last night."

"How can you say that?" Ivy questioned in disbelief.

"You thought I would never find out about the fire. You thought it would be perceived as an innocent accident by a clumsy housemaid," Esmeralda said evenly. "You spilled an oil lamp and let the parlor catch fire, and you did it in the middle of the night so that the fire would be well out of control by the time anyone noticed. The only thing I don't understand is why? Why, when you had everything an only child could possibly desire, did you burn down your own house and take the lives of your parents?"

"You're crazy! You've gone completely mad," Ivy declared.

Esmeralda refused to back down. "Have I? There were times after the fire when I wondered if I might go mad. Times when, burdened with the memories of having lost Carl so shortly after losing Hezekiah, that I wanted to go mad." She paused. "Madness would have been merciful. Instead, I was forced to live a lie with you."

"You are crazy," Ivy said quite seriously. That unwelcome

feeling of her conscience was threatening to surface. She knew better than to admit to the truth, so she intended to force her aunt to question the facts she'd been given. "I loved my mother and father. I would never have done them harm. It sounds to me that the people in charge of investigating the fire simply didn't want to pay out on Papa's insurance. It was just an accident—nothing more."

"That's not what the fire itself proved. The inspector and the witness explained the deliberate actions taken by you on that night. You may call them liars, especially since the maid is now dead from her burns, but I've spent a fortune—actually, your fortune—to ensure that the facts of those events remain forever hidden from the record."

"What are you saying?"

"I'm saying that I had to buy the favor of the inspector. I couldn't see you put on trial for three murders. You are, after all . . . family." The word was said rather snidely, and Ivy knew her aunt's wrath was mounting. "Your housemaid saw what you had done. But she was too late to sound the alarm, and the fire spread much too quickly. The inspector found her dying words to be convincing enough, and he was set to prosecute you for your actions. That's when I interceded to convince him otherwise. When all was settled and the inheritance your father had left you had been established with me as your guardian and trust keeper, I found it necessary to use that money to ensure that you would never be blamed for the deaths and destruction." Her aunt smiled as Ivy's mouth dropped open. "You had no idea, did you?"

"You took my money? All of it?" Ivy asked in disbelief.

"Yes. All of it. You have nothing, Ivy. Nothing but your life and that which I give you."

Ivy could no longer contain her anger. She had always presumed upon a fortune that would add to that of her husband.

In fact, the only reason she really pushed to marry early was because her own fortune was out of her hands until the age of twenty-one, and she had hated the idea of waiting.

"You've left me without anything?" she questioned, getting to her feet. She fixed her gaze on the elderly woman and felt her anger rise. She stalked toward Esmeralda while the old woman stood her ground.

"You left yourself without means," said Esmeralda without feeling. "You took the lives of your parents and destroyed the future your father had built for you. You killed my only brother because of your senseless, childish ways."

"All right, old woman," Ivy said, realizing she had nothing left to lose. "I did start that fire, but it was an accident that they died. I would never have wanted them harmed. My father spoiled me and my mother doted upon me. Why would I set out to kill them?"

Esmeralda appeared to understand her rage and took a step backward. "Then why burn the house?"

Ivy laughed cynically. "Because I wanted a better house. Father wouldn't listen to me. He didn't listen to me that night, either. I told him not to go back inside. But mother had gone after some photographs. Father saw me safely outside and went after her." Ivy remembered the scene as if it were yesterday: the three-story house ablaze, the sounds of the roaring fire greedily consuming the frame, people yelling and crying for help. The entire thing was permanently frozen in her mind like a bizarre, nightmarish costume party. The pain of the memory she had neatly buried within her now seared her deadened emotions, as if she herself were being consumed by flames.

Ivy looked at her aunt and shook her head. "He should never have gone back inside. Neither of them should have gone inside. We were safe. We could have gone on, moved to a better home. Papa had insurance on the house—I know because I saw the policy."

"But the policy never paid out. Not for a deliberately set fire. Do you not yet understand, Ivy? They would have sent you to prison. It's just that simple."

"I don't believe you. No one will believe you. I was just a little girl, and all I wanted was a better house." She paused, feeling the weight of truth fall upon her shoulders. "I loved them."

As Ivy continued to advance toward her, Esmeralda glanced over her shoulder, appearing more and more nervous. She obviously felt threatened, and for this Ivy knew a sense of power. She purposefully kept her voice low, refusing to allow any of the servants to overhear them argue. But she made certain her expression left little doubt in Esmeralda's mind that Ivy couldn't allow her to ruin her plans.

"You loved them? You risked losing everything for a better house, and you excuse your actions by saying you loved them. You don't know what love is, Ivy."

Ivy paused, feeling momentarily confused in her memories. "Our neighborhood was becoming increasingly common," she said softly. "I told Father we needed a bigger, more affluent estate, but he wouldn't hear of moving. Mother loved our little house and couldn't bear to think of going elsewhere. So I took matters into my own hands. I decided the house had to go."

As Ivy focused on the form before her, she suddenly realized she would have to deal with her aunt, for the old woman would never understand her plight. She'd never see things her way, which meant she would never keep her mouth closed or cooperate with Ivy's plans. She continued. "I know how to eliminate obstacles in my life. The house was an obstacle, and it had to go," she said, shrugging nonchalantly. "Just as I've decided that you have to go. You can't be allowed to stand in my way." She watched the old woman pale and stumble back another few feet.

Advancing on her aunt, Ivy forced her backward again, smiling as the old woman teetered at the top of the staircase. "I will marry Braeden Parker, and you won't interfere. I may have forced his hand last night, but I didn't go to all that trouble just to let you expose me to ridicule."

"Ivy, you're mad," Esmeralda said softly.

"No, not really. Not when you consider that after you are dead, all of this and most of Morita will be mine. I know you arranged your will to leave it all to me. You told me so."

Esmeralda shook her head. "I told you that I'd left you what you deserved."

Ivy stopped in her tracks. "What are you saying?"

"I'm saying that I left everything to the support and promotion of Morita. And a moderate amount of money will be used to erect a monument to my dear husband."

"You've left me nothing?" Ivy said, her eyes narrowing. "Me, your only living relation?" Confusion set in and she felt her ability to reason slip away. What was happening to her— to her plans?

"You, who killed my brother and his wife, and now plot the same demise for me," Esmeralda said matter-of-factly. "You will have nothing. Not even this roof over your head. It all goes to the town."

"Fool!" Ivy said under her breath. "You fool!" She reached out to strike the old woman, but Esmeralda moved backward once again. Only this time she stepped beyond the top of the stairs. As she fell, Ivy watched in stunned silence, her mind refusing to put the pieces together. "No!" she cried, reaching out at the thin air. "Don't go!" In her mind she saw her father dashing back into the burning house. She closed her eyes and tried to force the images out of her mind. When she opened them again, Esmeralda lay at the foot of the stairs.

Realizing the noise would draw the servants, Ivy screamed at the top of her lungs.

"Someone help! Auntie has fallen down the stairs!"

Liza came running, along with the cook and the butler. They all came running from different directions of the house, but all three stopped abruptly at the crumpled form of their mistress. The aging butler knelt down beside Esmeralda's pale, still form. He shook his head and stood once again.

"I'm afraid she has expired."

Ivy saw all three servants look up to her as if she might offer some explanation. In an act of instinct, Ivy collapsed to the floor. Her aunt was dead, another accident that Ivy couldn't avoid responsibility in. Thinking of it would only cause her grief and frustration. She had to think of her plans—of her future, especially now that she knew the truth. Now that she was without funds.

She heard the rush of footsteps on the stairs and focused on her purpose. Her obstacles were slowly but surely being removed. They would believe her to be the grieving niece, totally devastated by her aunt's passing, and because she didn't stand to inherit a cent, no one would believe Ivy to have done anything out of line.

"Here, miss," Liza said, reaching her side first. She fanned Ivy's face with her hand and struggled to raise her to a sitting position. "It'll be all right. Let's get you back to bed."

Ivy moaned softly and let the trio assist her to her bed. She mumbled something about getting help before closing her eyes and falling back against her pillow.

"Best get the doctor for them both," Liza said.

"Madam is quite beyond the doctor's help," the butler replied, "but I'll send for him on behalf of Miss Ivy."

Ivy lay silent, with her eyes closed tight. This entire thing might just work out to her benefit after all. Braeden might even take pity upon her, but even if he didn't, she knew she could depend on Reginald for support in what had happened the night before. She'd simply tell everyone of Braeden's actions and explain that the shock had been so great upon her aunt that while they were going downstairs, the woman had simply succumbed to the news.

With any luck at all, she'd find herself in a wedding by nightfall. Now there remained only one question on Ivy's mind. *What should I wear for my marriage to Braeden?*

Chapter 23

Braeden noted the pink hues of dawn against the eastern skies. He had hoped to be off with a search party by first light, but since he couldn't locate the marshal, it seemed Braeden would simply have to put together his own group or go off by himself to look for Rachel. Neither choice would probably be anywhere nearly as productive as if he had professional help.

Remounting the horse he'd borrowed from Casa Grande's stables, Braeden made his way back to the resort. He couldn't help but think about the events of the past few days. Casa Grande had begun to hold promise for him, and now with Ivy's manipulation, he wondered if it could represent anything but frustration and regret. People would no doubt think of him differently now. They might even mistrust him and his motives, and that could do nothing but bring misery on everyone. Then, too, if Rachel remained at Casa Grande and refused to listen to his explanation or believe his innocence, he might as well load up and go back to Chicago. There just didn't seem to be any easy answer, and the future was hazy.

Tomas greeted him as he arrived at the stable. The boy looked worried, even fearful. "Have you found her yet, señor?"

"No," Braeden replied, dismounting. He tossed Tomas the reins. "I'll need your help, Tomas. You know the local people. Can you round up about five or six men to help me search the area for Rachel?"

"Sí, I can do this." Tomas appeared relieved to have something to do.

"I'll go inside and get some provisions. There's no telling how long we'll be at this." Braeden said the cautious words, but in his heart he prayed he was overexaggerating the situation. Rachel had probably taken herself to some quiet point of refuge. After all, he didn't know her so well as to predict her every move. Perhaps she had other friends in Morita besides the O'Donnells. It was possible that she had made the acquaintance of someone else and had sought comfort from them when Simone and Jeffery proved to be elsewhere.

He took the side delivery entrance into Casa Grande and made his way through the kitchen. He saw Reginald frown at his intrusion but remained silent. Out in the dining room there were at least twelve Harvey Girls busying themselves with the morning chores. Spying Gwen Carson, Braeden saw the concern in her eyes. She came to him, even as he made his way to her.

"Have you found Rachel?" she questioned.

"No. I suppose you've had no word from her either?"

Gwen shook her head. "Nothing. Ivy Brooks is missing as well."

Braeden frowned. "Ivy probably won't be in this morning. She was rather unwell last night, and if my guess is correct, she won't feel like putting in an appearance."

"Is that part of what happened to Rachel?" Gwen asked softly.

"Yes." Braeden hated to admit it, but there was no sense in denying the truth.

"Ivy hates Rachel. She'd do anything to see her leave Casa Grande."

"Yes, and had I not been sure of Ivy's whereabouts, I'd

wonder quite seriously if she knew anything about Rachel's disappearance."

"Did you talk to the marshal?" Gwen questioned.

By this time several of the girls had apparently overheard their conversation and had moved closer to learn the truth of what was going on. Braeden sighed. He might as well make some form of public announcement. "Ladies, if you'll join us for a moment, there's something I need to share."

The girls quickly left their stations and tasks and came to stand beside Gwen and Braeden. "Miss Taylor is missing," Braeden announced matter-of-factly. "She disappeared last night and no one has seen anything of her since. That is, not unless someone here knows something about it." The girls shook their heads, their expressions showing their surprise.

"I didn't think so," Braeden said, continuing. "I'm getting ready to ride out to search for her. In the meantime, Miss Carson is in charge of the dining room. I'd appreciate it if you would keep an eye open for Miss Taylor. If you think of anything that might explain where she could be, or if you overhear something that could help us in our search, then by all means, please come to Miss Carson and give her the information."

"Ivy Brooks is missing too," Faith declared. "She was supposed to be here by now, but she never showed up."

"I wouldn't count on Ivy to show up this morning," Braeden replied, barely keeping the sarcasm from his voice. "She was a bit preoccupied last night."

"Oh, Braeden darling!"

Ivy's voice sounded from behind him, causing Braeden to turn in disbelief. He found it unbelievable that she would show her face after such a wanton display the night before. Had she no shame—no shred of embarrassment for her actions?

All of the Harvey Girls were staring at Ivy in disbelief. She was dressed in her uniform, but her hair was down and rather disheveled from what appeared to have been an early morning walk. But even this wasn't as shocking as her approach to Braeden.

Ivy reached out to touch Braeden's arm. "Something awful has happened. Something so very terrible." She pouted and batted her blue eyes at him, appearing to will the tears that formed there.

Braeden frowned. "Yes, I know." He despised her touch and moved away a pace to separate from her.

"No," she practically wailed, grabbing him again. "You don't know."

Braeden shook her off and raised a brow in question. "Then suppose you tell us what's happened now?"

"Aunt Esmeralda is dead!" she said, tears spilling from her eyes to her cheeks.

Braeden thought her to be a most consummate actress. He doubted the truth in what she said, but even if it were true, Ivy certainly would shed no tears of loss. Not if her actions from the past few days were any indication. He thought her rather hardhearted and callous—too callous to care whether Esmeralda lived or died.

"If Mrs. Needlemeier is dead, then why are you here?" Braeden asked rather coolly. "Shouldn't you be home planning out the funeral? You certainly aren't expected to work so soon after losing a loved one."

Just as the words were out of his mouth, Mr. Smith and several other Santa Fe officials, including Fred Harvey himself, appeared in the doorway of the dining room. Their stunned expressions indicated that they had overheard the latter portion of the conversation.

"Mrs. Needlemeier is dead?" Smith and Harvey questioned at the same time.

"Oh yes!" Ivy declared. "It's simply awful. She couldn't take the shock."

"What shock was that?" Harvey questioned.

Ivy stunned them all by throwing herself into Braeden's arms. "She came home and found us together. I knew it was wrong, but Braeden was most persuasive. I simply couldn't resist his superior strength and ardor."

Braeden realized she had him exactly where she wanted him. The entire room seemed to turn in unison to him for explanation. "She's lying," he said, trying to pry Ivy from his body.

"No, she's not!" Reginald Worthington declared. Everyone turned to acknowledge his statement. Seeing he held a captive audience, he continued. "I witnessed the scene myself. A more shameful display of forced attention I have never seen. Your Mr. Parker apparently is quite the rogue. He arranged to meet Miss Brooks when he knew she would be alone and unprotected, and now he scorns her."

Smith eyed Braeden in contempt. "You dallied with this young lady and now deny it?"

"I deny the entire matter. This young *lady*, as you call her, set up a scene of seduction to rival them all." Braeden realized how preposterous it all sounded even as he spoke the words. Ivy stood looking wide-eyed and stunned, tears glistening against her pale cheeks. Even Gwen looked at him with a questioning expression that suggested disbelief. "It was entirely her doing, not mine. She has it in her mind that the Harvey establishment is her ticket to finding a wealthy husband. She knew I had no interest in her, but she pursued the matter with a vengeance."

"Is this true?" Fred Harvey asked Ivy, giving Braeden the briefest bit of hope that she would come to terms with his anger toward her and admit the truth.

Ivy sobbed. "No, it's not true. What woman of proper breeding would allow her reputation to be put into jeopardy in such a manner? After all, such events do bring about consequences."

Fred Harvey stepped forward, a scowl on his bearded face. "Young woman, are you telling me this man dishonored you?"

Ivy again reached for Braeden. "It wasn't all his fault. I should have known better—I did know better—but I've loved him since I first laid eyes upon him. But I knew about the rules, Mr. Harvey. I remembered meeting you in Topeka, and you said we weren't to date other Harvey employees." She dabbed her eyes most effectively and gave the slightest hint of a smile. "I know I dishonored my auntie, but Mr. Parker made me forget myself. I'm sorry, but my heart wouldn't listen."

Harvey and Smith both smiled. "It's understandable," Harvey replied. "But apparently now that this man has taken some sort of advantage of you, he seems reluctant to own up to his part in the matter."

"I had no part in the matter," Braeden declared angrily. This time he pushed Ivy away from him, nearly causing her to fall. Had a couple of the Harvey Girls not stepped forward to help Ivy regain her balance, she would have done just that.

"Oh, Braeden," Ivy said, tears streaming down her face. "Don't be like this. You know I love you, and I promise to be a good wife. I don't care what happened last night. I don't even care if I'm carrying your child right now." There were notable gasps from around the gathered audience. "I simply need you now more than ever. Auntie is dead and I'm all alone."

Smith moved forward. "Is this true? Mrs. Needlemeier is really dead?"

Ivy sobbed and brought the edge of her apron to her face. "Yes. We were discussing my behavior and the need for Mr. Parker to save my reputation and marry me when she succumbed to some sort of apoplexy and collapsed on the staircase."

"Then why are you here?" Braeden questioned. "Dressed for a day of work, no less."

"I couldn't bear to be there alone," Ivy said, meeting the sympathetic nods of Mr. Smith and Mr. Harvey. "I wanted to be with the one person I knew could offer me comfort. The man I love."

Braeden felt everyone turn their attention to him, as if he held the key to the entire puzzle. With a sense of animosity and irritation that he'd never known, Braeden shook his head. "I've had about all I'm going to stand of this. She's lying about there being anything between us," he said aloud, directing his gaze to Fred Harvey's doubtful expression. "She was jealous of the friendship I shared with Miss Taylor—a friendship developed long before I ever came to Casa Grande. I'm deeply ashamed to have fallen for such a manipulation, but in truth, I didn't know to what degree this young woman would stoop in order to eliminate her competition." Just then the thought of the rattlesnake came to mind. He frowned. The situation was beginning to clear, and he could see and understand more of what had once been clouded and obscured. "I think I'm starting to realize it now," he muttered.

Ivy once again moved to embrace him but stopped directly in front of him. "I'm not ashamed of my actions. I love you and no matter what, I'm not ashamed." She looked to Mr. Harvey. "I don't even mind bearing a child because of it. As long as it's *his* child."

"There is no child!" Braeden raged, unable to contain his

anger. "Because there was nothing more than your errant plan to seduce me." He reached out as if to shake her, then stopped and stepped away. "I wouldn't marry you if you were the last available woman on earth. You are corrupt and conniving and you may lie all you like, but it won't change the matter."

"I say," Reginald stated, stepping closer to Ivy, "I witnessed the entire matter. There seemed to be no error on Miss Brooks's part. She was intoxicated, but that, too, came at the forced will of Mr. Parker."

"She came to me drunk!" Braeden declared.

Reginald's brow furrowed ever so slightly. "He was carrying her, half clothed, to a fainting couch. It was quite clear what had taken place, and what would have continued to take place."

"Is this true?" Fred Harvey asked Braeden seriously.

"No," Braeden replied, gritting his teeth together. "It's not true. Miss Brooks staged the entire thing in order to force herself upon me. She knows my interest lies elsewhere. Now the real crisis of the morning is not whether or not Miss Brooks's reputation has been ruined. It's not even that Mrs. Needlemeier has passed on to her eternal reward. The problem is that Rachel Taylor is missing and has been ever since she witnessed Miss Brooks's little charade last night."

"Missing? What do you mean?" Harvey questioned.

"I mean, no one has seen her since she fled the Needlemeier mansion. Worthington, here, went after her, but he claims to have had no luck in discovering her whereabouts."

Reginald shrugged. "I tried to follow her, but she was apparently running. She was completely gone from sight when I came out of the mansion, but I can't say I blame her. Mr. Parker had made suggestive promises to her as well. I think it simply devastated her to know that she had been duped into believing him honorable."

Braeden scowled and seethed at the suggestion that he had led Rachel astray. Supposition and lies had destroyed his life six years ago, and he would not stand for it to happen again.

Fred Harvey rubbed his bearded face. "This appears to be quite a disturbing situation. However, we can discuss this at length in private. Right now it would seem the dining room should be readied for breakfast. Who's in charge?"

Gwen stepped forward. "I am, sir. I'm the head waitress, Miss Carson."

Harvey nodded. "Very well, Miss Carson, I suggest you get your girls to their stations and ready yourself for the day. Miss Brooks, I believe you should return home and see to your aunt's funeral arrangements, and Mr. Parker—"

"I'm going to look for Rachel," Braeden interjected. "Fire me if you must, but that's what I'm going to do."

He turned without waiting for any other word on the matter and stalked across the lobby feeling nothing but anger blended with fear. Fear for Rachel—fear for himself. There was an entire audience of people who appeared to believe every word Ivy Brooks said. He would either be forced to leave his position or encouraged to marry Ivy, and neither option was one he wanted. He wanted Rachel, and he wanted to continue at Casa Grande with her at his side.

Tomas waited in the stable yard with four other mounted men. They were all dark skinned and filthy looking, but Tomas had supplied them with Casa Grande horses, and they appeared quite willing to help with the search.

"Tomas, you know this land better than I do, so I'd like for you to stay with me and act as a guide. The rest of you spread out and see what you can find. Miss Taylor has dark red hair and she stands about as tall as Tomas. She might be injured, so if you find her, fire off your gun once and the rest of us will come to you. Do you understand?"

Tomas relayed the information in Spanish just to make certain no one misunderstood the situation. When the four men nodded, Braeden mounted his horse and headed toward the open valley behind the stables.

"Wait up!" a voice called out from behind them.

Braeden turned to find Jeffery O'Donnell coming up fast from First Street.

"Glad you could make it," Braeden stated, trying hard to give the man a welcoming smile.

Jeffery brought his horse to a halt, kicking up a cloud of dust. "I couldn't sleep anyway. I would have been here sooner, but I wanted to check in at the depot and make sure she hadn't caught a train out of Morita. No one there has seen anything of her. What about here? Still no word?"

"None. No one has seen anything of her since yesterday evening. I've looked all around Casa Grande, but she just isn't here. Now we're going to head out and explore the countryside around the resort. She could have wandered off, not paying any attention to where she was going. Maybe she got lost."

Jeffery nodded. "I don't know my way around here very well, but I'll do what I can."

"I'm going out with Tomas. Why don't you go with one of the other men? They're all familiar with the area."

Jeffery looked to the four riders and questioned the man who appeared to be the oldest in the bunch. "May I ride with you?"

"Sí," the man said without further acknowledgment.

"Then let's get to it," Braeden said. "Let's plan to meet back here around noon." They all nodded and headed off in different directions, while Braeden watched them go. He felt a squeezing tightness in his chest as his mind asked a hundred questions he couldn't answer. What if they didn't find her? What if she had somehow left the area altogether? What if . . .

"Help me to find her, Lord," Braeden finally prayed. He pushed aside his worry and urged the horse forward. "Keep her safe and don't let harm come to her. Let her know the truth about me and what happened. Let her trust the love she has for me—the love I have for her." The prayer was barely whispered aloud, but Braeden wanted to shout it to the skies. He wanted to plead over and over for the life of this woman— but he knew he had to keep an eye on the trail. He had to remain alert and concentrate on anything that might give him a sign to Rachel's whereabouts.

They rendezvoused at noon without anyone having seen any sign of Rachel, and hours later, with a storm brewing on the horizon and the temperature dropping from the breezes off the thunderstorm, Braeden was growing increasingly worried. He studied the landscape around him as Tomas tested an obscure little trail that led up into the foothills. The sandy soil seemed stark and lifeless. An occasional flash of life came in the form of a jackrabbit or mouse, but that was it. Even the skies overhead seemed unusually empty.

His throat felt parched from the long day on the dusty trail, and tipping up his canteen, he was alarmed to find it nearly empty. They would have to find water or return to town.

"No one has passed this way, señor," Tomas told Braeden as he led his horse back down to where Braeden rested.

"Is there water nearby?" he questioned. "My canteen is nearly dry."

"We could go back to the river," Tomas suggested.

"If we do that, we might as well go back to Casa Grande."

"That might be best, señor. The storm is still coming this

way, and it won't be long before we lose the light."

Braeden looked toward the mountains and then at the rapidly approaching weather. Reluctantly he nodded. "I know you're right, I just hate leaving her out here . . . wherever she is."

Tomas nodded, then turned his horse to head back in the direction they'd just come. "Maybe she's already gone back to Casa Grande."

Braeden tried to be encouraged by the thought but knew it was probably far from the truth. Rachel was gone—maybe forever. Braeden had never known anything that hurt so much as acknowledging this possibility.

Chapter 24

Ivy ignored Mr. Harvey's suggestion that she return home and instead took off to the room she shared with Faith and sequestered herself away to think. The turn of events over the last twenty-four hours left her rather breathless. And in light of her aunt's dying declaration that Ivy would be left penniless, Ivy knew she had to quickly secure herself in marriage to Braeden Parker.

The scene in the dining room had been an added bonus that Ivy had not counted on. She felt especially comforted by the fact that Fred Harvey himself seemed to completely believe her statements regarding Braeden. Surely she could count on the kindly man to force Braeden's hand. She could only hope that once faced with the idea of losing his job and his honorable name, he would succumb and marry her. *And why not?* Ivy reasoned. *It's not like I'm some pudgy farm girl with brown skin and freckles. I'm beautiful and cultured, and I would do him honor by becoming his wife.* She reclined on the bed and punched at her pillow.

"He doesn't have to know that I'm penniless," she said, stifling a yawn.

For several hours she slept, dreaming of life in a big city with a lovely house of her own and a bevy of servants to wait on her every need. She was exhausted from the night before—exhausted, too, from having to carefully consider her problem from every angle.

Faith appeared shortly after one o'clock, waking Ivy with her noisy movements around the room. After allowing the girl to change out of her uniform, Ivy ordered her to spend the day elsewhere and Faith quickly complied. There was no way Ivy wanted the addlebrained girl interfering with her plans. When Faith was present, Ivy found it hard to think with any clarity for all the questions the girl threw at her.

After Faith departed, Ivy got out of bed and began to systematically pace the room, pausing only long enough to grab up her hairbrush. Stroking her long blond hair, Ivy considered the gravity of her situation.

She grimaced as she thought of the scene in the dining room. It wasn't that it hadn't gone her way, because in truth it had seemed to leave everyone in a sympathetic mood toward her. Still, she saw the way Braeden looked at her. There was no compassion, no feeling except anger. He would fight her on this if it took everything in his power. And if she did manage to force him to the altar, he would despise her for the rest of her life, and maybe even punish her by remaining in Morita or moving them to some equally horrid little community.

Perhaps she could find a way to somehow sweeten the matter for him. Perhaps there was a way to entice him to see things in a new light, to make him see that this would be monetarily beneficial to him in the long run. But remembering her aunt's rejection, Ivy knew that wouldn't be possible. Then a thought came to mind. Maybe she could contact her aunt's lawyer. Perhaps she could work out an arrangement with him that would benefit them both if he would be willing to change the will. It could work! There wasn't anyone in the world who couldn't be bought. Hadn't her aunt taught her that by explaining her deal with the fire inspector?

She put down the hairbrush and went to her window. Directly outside her room were the stables. She'd be able to see and hear when Braeden returned, and when he did return, she would be waiting.

She'd force him to talk to her, to make plans for their future. If he didn't show up with Rachel, she might even lie and tell him that Rachel had returned only long enough to confront Ivy and relinquish any hold she had on Braeden. The thought held some intrigue for Ivy. Maybe she could talk Reg into helping her once again. Maybe with the knowledge that Rachel was gone for good, Braeden would give up holding out for her and marry Ivy.

But Ivy was smart enough to realize the empty promise of that thought and of all the others she'd had. Braeden would rot in jail before he married her. Especially now. Especially after her public humiliation of him.

Muttering a curse, Ivy dropped her hold on the curtain and moved back to sit on the bed. There had to be an answer to the problem, a way to fix the situation. Maybe she could force Braeden to marry her by enlisting the help of Fred Harvey. Perhaps Mr. Harvey could offer him a job elsewhere if he promised to treat Ivy with respect and love. She thought of the thin, well-dressed man and decided it was surely worth consideration. Fred Harvey seemed to run his affairs in a completely honorable manner. He would surely not desire a scandal for this, his newest of resorts. Perhaps Braeden, in turn, would value his job more than making Ivy pay for coming between him and Rachel.

The idea seemed plausible in Ivy's mind.

The wind picked up outside, causing Ivy to return to the window. Clouds were moving overhead, shadowing the land below. Ivy knew from her three years of living in Morita that this was a sure sign of a storm. Perhaps it would drive the searchers back sooner than expected. After all, it was now afternoon, and they wouldn't want to get caught out in the weather and the darkness.

I still have no set plan, she thought. *I must decide what is to be done in order to be prepared when he returns.*

She glanced at the clock. It wasn't yet two. Perhaps she should seek out Mr. Harvey and discuss the situation with him. She could better tell from his reaction how to handle Braeden when he returned.

Slipping out of her room, Ivy ignored the chattering girls in the parlor and quickly entered the kitchen. Seeing Reginald working at the far end, she decided to question him on the matter of Rachel before going to Fred Harvey. It was always possible that he would have a better idea how to carry out her plans. After all, he'd come through admirably for her the night before.

"Mr. Worthington," she spoke softly. "Might I have a moment of your time?"

Reg eyed her suspiciously for a moment, then nodded. "What is it?"

"I thought perhaps you could offer me some counsel."

"You've never seemed to need advice from anyone before now," Reg replied, rather disinterested.

"It would benefit us both if you would give me just a few moments of your time," Ivy insisted.

"And how do you suppose that?" he asked, finally stopping to give her his full attention.

"You seem more than a little interested in making a financial profit from your days at Casa Grande," Ivy stated, loudly enough so only Reg could hear. After having Reg explain his understanding of her involvement with the attempt on Rachel's life, Ivy had sent her own spies out to learn anything they could about Reg. It appeared he had more than one job at Casa Grande.

His expression never changed as he considered her words. "I'm sure I don't know what you mean, but if you are of a mind to seek my opinion—or as you say, counsel—then be my guest."

She smiled, feeling rather herself again as the control clearly passed to her hand. "I wondered that you were not out looking for Miss Taylor. After all, I know of your affection for her. Is this lack of interest because you already know of her whereabouts?" She hoped to completely throw him off base by suggesting something so out of line that he would forget her earlier words. She wasn't ready yet to tell him what she knew about his actions and hoped to use her knowledge as a final trump card should the occasion necessitate.

Reg remained stoic. "I wondered that you were not home mourning the loss of your aunt. Is it because you feel nothing in her passing? Unless, of course, what you feel is relief."

Ivy tried not to react to his piercing gaze. "That's nonsense. There's nothing I can do there. Aunt Esmeralda is in the hands of the mortician."

"So it is with Rachel. There is nothing I can do to aid her search. My job requires me here, and Mr. Parker seems completely capable."

"But you don't want *him* to find her, do you?" Ivy questioned quietly, glancing over her shoulder to make certain no one else overheard. "After all, if he finds her, he might well convince her that what she saw was completely my fault."

"Which, of course, it was," Reginald replied. He gave his sauce a quick stir, then moved down the line to where he had arranged several platters. This put even more distance between the conspirators and the other kitchen staff members.

"Look, all I want is for Braeden to return so that I can discuss this matter with him in private. I figure once we do that, he'll come around to seeing things my way."

Reg smiled. "Oh, you think so?"

"And you do not?" Ivy questioned.

Focusing on the filleted chicken breasts, Reg shrugged. "All things are possible, or so they say. I simply believe you have given Mr. Parker an even more urgent desire to solidify his relationship with Miss Taylor. He is a desperate man at this point. And, Miss Brooks, desperation makes men do what they ordinarily wouldn't even consider."

"You talk as one who knows," Ivy said, eyeing him suspiciously.

Reginald smiled patiently. "I know a great many things, as you are well aware. My suggestion to you is to bide your time and your tongue. In Rachel's absence there are bound to be opportunities to speak to Mr. Parker, and in doing so, perhaps you can win him over to your way of thinking."

Ivy nodded. "Maybe. If Rachel isn't around to interfere, maybe I can convince him to—"

"Settle for you?" Reg asked with a sly grin.

Ivy felt her face flush. "No one settles for me. I chose Mr. Parker, and he'll soon see the merit in my choice. Otherwise, he'll find himself unemployed with no hope of ever securing another job on the Santa Fe."

She stormed off through the kitchen and out across the dining room, ignoring the soft comments of condolences people offered. Her only thought was to formulate a plan before Braeden returned from his search.

The wind picked up, blowing bits of sand and grit, stinging Braeden's eyes. He'd managed to pull up the bandana from his neck and tie it around his face, but it did little to help shield his eyes.

"We go back," Tomas shouted above the wind. Lightning

flashed in the distance, followed by a rumbling of thunder that unnerved the horses. As they danced around and pawed at the earth, Tomas added, "Storms here very bad."

Braeden realized his search was hopeless. "All right, let's go."

Frustration and misery coursed through his body. He felt as though he were deserting Rachel by returning to the resort. She was out there somewhere. But where? Urging their horses to pick up speed, Braeden couldn't help but issue another prayer for her safety. He felt so completely helpless, and the misery of it all left him defeated and drained of energy.

Back at the resort, Tomas took the horses and led them to the stable just as the first drops of rain started to fall.

"Braeden!" Jeffery called out as he came from the stable leading his horse. "I wondered if you'd make it back before the storm hit. Any luck?"

"No," Braeden replied, shaking his head. "You?"

"Nothing. No tracks—no sign of anyone having passed through in days."

"Same for us," Braeden said, his heart overwhelmed with grief. "I wish I knew where she was. I'm afraid for her."

Jeffery patted him on the back. "We'll have to keep praying. Look, I need to get home before this storm gets ugly. I'll ride over again tomorrow morning and we can try some different places."

"Thanks for your help. By the way," Braeden said, remembering Jeffery's injury, "how's the head?"

Jeffery shrugged. "Feels like I have an army marching through it, but I'd endure worse if it meant getting Rachel back safely. She's a good friend." He mounted his horse and secured the reins. "At this point, we have no choice but to wait it out. I know it would be foolish to say don't worry, because I know that this will be on my mind until it's settled.

Still, try to get some rest. You look worse than I feel."

Braeden nodded, not at all enthused by the idea. He waited to go inside until Jeffery had left. With slow, heavy steps he mounted the stairs to Casa Grande, turned, then stared out past the fountain and circular drive, down across the lawn to the falls and powerhouse. Although he couldn't see the falls from where he stood, he could hear them and see the fine mist that rose up. The rain began coming down lightly at first, gradually increasing until he could scarcely see past the fountain. Lightning pierced the sky with light and thunder shook the ground as the storm came closer.

"Rachel, where are you!" Braeden yelled out against the fury of the storm. And even though the wind blew the rain up across the porch, drenching Braeden in the process, he felt a grave reluctance to go inside. It was as if by doing so, he was somehow further separating himself from Rachel.

Ivy watched as Braeden came wearily through the lobby door. Because he'd grown dusty from his ride, muddy rivulets were streaming down the side of his face and down his neck and arms. Still, he was handsome. He took off his hat and shook the water from it, then moved across the lobby to the front desk. Ivy watched him speak momentarily to the clerk, but the man only shook his head. *No doubt he's asking about her,* Ivy thought. Moving quietly from her vantage point just inside the empty dining room, Ivy waited until Braeden slipped behind the front desk to go into his office. He closed the door and Ivy hurried to approach the clerk.

"Mr. Worthington asked if you could come quickly to the kitchen. He only needs your help for a moment, and I'll watch the front desk while you're away," she told the man. She needed to get rid of him in order to gain entry into Braeden's office without interference.

The man looked at her for a moment. "What does he want with me?"

"He needs your help moving something. It'll just take a minute."

The man sighed and nodded. "Very well." He raised the gate to the front desk, then eyed Ivy rather sternly. "If someone needs help, just keep them here until I get back."

She smiled and nodded. "I promise I won't do anything more."

He left his post and crossed the lobby to the dining room, while Ivy waited until he was out of sight before entering Braeden's office. She slipped inside quickly and closed the door just as Braeden came into his office from the bedroom. He was drying his hair with a towel and hadn't even seen that it was Ivy before issuing an angry retort.

"Don't you know how to knock, Wilson?"

"I do know how to knock, but I figured you wouldn't let me in if you knew it was me," Ivy replied softly.

Braeden drew the towel away from his head. "Well, you're right on that account. Now get out!"

"No." Ivy took a seat and stared at him intently. "We need to talk."

"There's nothing to be said," Braeden said, his voice low.

Ivy could see the anger flash in his eyes. His jaw clamped tight and his expression grew gradually more threatening. "Just hear me out and then I'll leave. You could certainly do that much. After all, I want to explain a few things."

"You've explained quite enough. Your lies this morning have probably cost me my job—not that it matters anymore. What does matter is Rachel. You've driven her away from safety and into harm's way. That's all I care about."

"If Rachel cared about you the way you claim to care about her, she'd be here defending you. Instead, she's taken off to who knows where," Ivy said defiantly. "I don't think she cares as much as you'd like to believe. She saw the scene in my parlor and believed what her heart told her to be true. If she loved you, she would believe in you. And if she believed in you, she'd be here now."

Braeden let the towel fall around his neck as he leaned over to place both hands on his desk. "I don't want to discuss this with you."

"Well, I think you'd better reconsider," Ivy replied. She twirled a strand of hair and smiled. "There are worse things than losing employment with Mr. Harvey. This decision could affect the rest of your life."

"You can't threaten me, Ivy," Braeden answered angrily. "You've already driven away the only thing I care about. But mark my words. I will find her."

"You don't need her. She doesn't love you."

"Oh, and you do, I suppose?"

"No, not yet," Ivy admitted.

"I think that's the only truth I've ever heard come out of your mouth."

"You are handsome, however. With a pleasant face to look at and a comfortable amount of money to live on, I could learn to love anyone. What *is* important is that I want you. You represent freedom from this miserable hole of a town."

"How can I possibly represent that to you?" Braeden questioned in surprise.

"Because after we are married I want to move east to St. Louis." She suddenly remembered her aunt's words about the fire inspector knowing she'd started the fatal fire that killed her parents. "No, not St. Louis. Chicago. Or New York. I want a big house and beautiful things and lavish clothes. You can give me all of that. My aunt said you are wealthy and—"

Braeden began to laugh. He sat down at his desk and shook his head. "You are quite insane, Ivy. I will never marry you. Go have your talk with Fred Harvey. Talk to the president of the United States. It won't change a thing. You are right; I have enough money to live comfortably without this job. My father was a wise investor and his investments continue to pay off. I chose to continue working because I enjoy the challenge of using my mind for something more than sitting around the house or going on grand tours of Europe. I chose this particular job because I knew Rachel was here." He eyed her distastefully and shook his head. "You are nothing to me. You will never be anything more than the adversary you have set yourself up to be."

"But why not?" Ivy asked, suddenly sounding very much like a little girl. "I'm a beautiful woman. Far more beautiful than Rachel Taylor. I have grace and charm and know how to conduct myself in proper circles."

"And you're a liar," Braeden replied. "An unfeeling deceiver who acts without remorse for the hideous things you've done. Believe me, Ivy, your looks could never hold a candle to Rachel's beauty. Not only is she beautiful in appearance, but her heart is pure and good and that makes her even more lovely.

"You, however, are selfish and self-motivated. You choose the path that will give you the most satisfaction. There is nothing of goodness in you. The woman I marry will love God and will seek to conduct herself in a Christian manner for all of her days. Rachel is that woman. Not some devious little harlot who has no remorse for her actions."

Ivy took a sharp breath, taken aback. She thought of her parents and the servants who perished in the fire. She thought of her aunt's crumpled form at the bottom of the stairs. She even thought for the briefest moment of Rachel's stunned and pain-filled expression. It wasn't that she had set out to inflict pain . . . not really. She simply wanted what was important to her. No one could possibly understand that she'd never intended for anyone to die in the fire. Neither would they believe her if she said she was sorry. And she was sorry. At least where her parents were concerned.

"I've done what I had to do," Ivy finally said. "You don't belong with someone like Rachel. She's much too common and plain. I can be much more to you. I can attend church as you wish, and I can be the docile wife you desire. In the years to come, you'll see that this was the wisest thing and you'll thank me for saving you."

"In the years to come, I will look back on this time as my darkest hours—those hours spent without Rachel." Braeden narrowed his eyes. "I don't suppose you have any idea of her whereabouts."

Ivy smiled. "If I did, do you think I would ruin all that I've planned and tell you?"

Braeden clenched his teeth and a rumble from deep in his throat sounded very much like a suppressed growl. Ivy refused to be concerned by it, however.

"We can marry tomorrow," she said firmly. "I'll talk to the preacher after I leave here."

Slamming his fists down on the desk, Braeden raged. "I won't marry you tomorrow or any day. I don't love you, Miss Brooks. I love Rachel Taylor. You are nothing to me but trouble. You have deeply wounded the woman I love, and while I shall forgive you, I won't ever forget."

Deeply shaken, Ivy fought hard to remain stoic. "You will learn to love me. I'm beautiful, and I'm sure we will find ways to—"

"Your outward appearance may be pleasing, but inside you are frightfully hideous," Braeden interrupted. "Marriage is about more than physical attraction. It's about commit-ment."

"We could be committed to each other."

"Maybe you could be committed to an asylum," Braeden said sarcastically.

"I'll ruin you if you refuse me."

Braeden shook his head. "Don't you understand? Without Rachel, none of this matters. Ruin me. Take my job. Turn them all against me. It doesn't matter, because *you* don't matter. Not to me, anyway."

Ivy suddenly realized he meant what he said. He found her abhorrent. No one had ever treated her in such a manner. She felt sick inside, unable to shake off the sense of dread. If she couldn't have him by choice, she'd take him by force. She could do this. She only had to think her plans through in a clear and concise manner. "You'll be condemned," she mut-tered.

"Not by those who matter. Not by Rachel, and not by God."

"You're already condemned by Rachel," Ivy retorted. She had to make him see the truth of the situation. "As for God, who knows what He thinks?"

"He hates lies," Braeden countered.

Ivy shook her head. "He understands why I did what I did."

"Yes, you're right. He does. He knows your motives and He knows exactly why and what you have done," Braeden re-plied ominously.

Ivy got to her feet, feeling rather unnerved by Braeden's certainty regarding God. "Don't think to threaten me, Braeden Parker. Everyone in that dining room this morning perceives you as a ruthless molester of helpless young women. If you don't marry me, you'll be stripped of everything, including your reputation and self-worth."

Braeden smiled and seemed to calm in the wake of their harshly spoken words. "You can't destroy my self-worth, Miss Brooks. God has given me a sense of self-worth through His love for me. I find my identity in Him—not in this place, this job."

"I thought you found all of that through Miss Taylor," Ivy said snidely. She was confused by his calm and thought feverishly for something more to say. She was losing him—losing her chance for a new start.

"Rachel gives from her heart. She loves me and I love her," Braeden replied. "But even if Rachel were gone for good, I would still find my hope and my future in God. That's something you can't understand, Miss Brooks. And it's something I can't explain. So go say what you will. Tell all the lies you think will serve your cause. But you won't win me over, and you won't be my consolation in Rachel's absence."

Braeden got up and walked around his desk. Ivy felt threatened by the action, even though he was much calmer than when she'd first come into his office. She backed up a step, but still he came forward.

"I want you out of my office. Now."

She backed up to the door and shook her head. "You don't know what you're saying. You don't know what might happen. What has already happened."

Braeden eyed her seriously. "If you know something about Rachel, you'd better tell me."

Ivy realized the power she could hold and felt a bit of her confidence return. "You weren't the only man to love Rachel," she said, standing her ground. "Rachel will seek protection and safety with someone she can trust. After what happened last night, you can't possibly believe that she would come to you."

"Where is she, Ivy?" he asked, moving in even closer.

Ivy felt excitement course through her body. She held the answers and now controlled the outcome. Even though she'd have to lie, she could weave a web of deceit that would permanently put an end to Braeden's illusions that Rachel loved him.

"I'm not the one to ask," she finally told him. "Rachel's been spending a great deal of time with Mr. Worthington, as you probably already know. She finds solace with him—comfort and maybe even that love you speak of so freely. Reg is really a wonderful man, and he is fiercely protective of Rachel. You can't deny the way he watched over her last night, and he left right after she did."

Ivy toyed with the doorknob. "If Rachel wanted you to know where she was, Braeden, she would have told you by now. She hasn't left Morita; she's merely taking refuge where you cannot harm her."

Turning the knob, Ivy was surprised when Braeden's hand slammed down on top of hers. "I mean it, Ivy. If you know where she is, tell me." He pressed down hard on her hand as if to emphasize the threat.

Ivy refused to be frightened, however. "Half-truths and rumors destroyed your lives long ago. I heard her telling this to Reg," she lied, for in fact she had overheard Rachel explaining the matter to Braeden. "So take this as you like," Ivy said, opening the door in spite of the pressure to her hand. "Rachel won't be turning to you this time around. She has someone else who is only too happy to fill in where you left off. If you don't believe me, just ask Reginald how he feels about Rachel."

She smiled and walked through the door, coming face-to-face with a very put-out Mr. Wilson. Turning, she saw the discomfort in Braeden's expression and couldn't help but play on his fears. "Oh, and you might also ask him why he's not been overly worried or eager to go chasing about the countryside looking for Rachel. Seems to me that, given his feelings for her, if he thought she were really missing he'd move heaven and earth to find her." She saw the look in Braeden's eyes and knew she'd hit her mark. Striving to drive in the final blow, she shrugged nonchalantly. "I've no doubt she's safe, Braeden. Reg wouldn't let harm come to her."

Chapter 25

The next morning Reginald had just completed explaining to his staff the process for stripping the meat from a lobster shell when a bleary-eyed Braeden Parker came into the kitchen. In spite of his exhaustion, he looked like a man with a determined purpose, and Reg had little doubt he was there to confront him about Rachel.

"You must collect all of the meat from the shells," Reg told his assistants. "But leave the brain for later. We will mix that with soft butter and add to the mixture later. Be very careful, as we will need every bit of lobster we can lay our hands on." The shipment of fresh lobsters had been shorted by thirty of the little beasts, and Reginald knew he would have to perform a minor miracle to make the food stretch for the huge banquet and party planned that night. Tonight would be the final celebration of the grand opening, and besides the banquet, there were refreshments for the formal ball that was to be given later that night.

"Mr. Worthington, I would like a moment of your time," Braeden said, coming to stand directly in front of the chef.

Reginald looked up and nodded. "Very well. Shall we go to the storage room or perhaps your office?"

"Given that the dining room is already full to capacity," Braeden began, "I suggest we stay here or step outside. I really don't want to have to walk through that crowd again."

"As you wish," Reginald replied. "Since the morning temperatures are rather cool, let us move to the storage room, where we might have less interference."

Braeden followed after him, and Reginald couldn't help but wonder how he would handle the big man if he decided to turn loose with a bout of temper. If Parker chose to use his fists instead of his mouth, Reg knew he'd be in trouble. Still, Parker seemed capable of controlling his anger—at least up until now. Perhaps he was worried over nothing.

But upon meeting Braeden's harsh glare, Reg wondered if he'd done something very stupid by isolating himself with Casa Grande's co-manager. Backing up against the delivery conveyor, Reg felt his pulse quicken. The man's eyes positively burned with a fire that suggested he would stop at nothing—nothing at all, in order to learn the truth.

"I want some answers and I want them now," Braeden said in a no-nonsense sort of fashion.

"I will tell you whatever I can," Reg replied calmly.

"Do you know where Rachel is?"

Reg raised a questioning brow. "Why would you ask me that? I already spoke to you on the matter the other night. I'm the one who suggested a search party."

"I'm asking you because Ivy Brooks implied that you are hiding Rachel away from me, that Rachel sought her solace with you, and that my searches will prove futile."

Reg smiled. So that conniving little idiot had put Parker on him, after all. She'd implied to know things about Reg's activities at Casa Grande, and while he had no idea what she actually knew, he wasn't about to allow her the upper hand. "Parker, I care a great deal about Rachel, but Ivy Brooks means her nothing but harm. She would tell you anything in order to get you on her side. She set her sights on winning you over, and Rachel was an interference in her plans. Knowing

Ivy even as little as I do, I realize she would do or say whatever she had to in order to eliminate her competition."

"What is your point?"

"I'm saying that Ivy has the ability to accomplish pretty much whatever she wants. As you guessed, she planned that little seduction scene at the Needlemeier mansion. She told me her plans."

"She told you the truth and you lied? You let everyone out there believe me to have harmed her—destroyed her reputation. Why?"

"Because I love Rachel," he replied simply. "And I knew so long as Rachel was deceived into believing you deserved her love, she would go on believing in you and loving you."

"Why, I ought to—"

"Tut, tut, Mr. Parker," Reg said, pressing hard against the rollers on the conveyor belt as Braeden advanced. "If you refuse to contain your temper, I will not continue to explain."

Braeden's face contorted in anger, but he held back and nodded. "Then explain."

Reg nodded. "Ivy told me of her desire to have you for her husband, and given the fact that I wanted very much for Rachel to think of me as a prospect for her lifelong mate, I agreed to help her with her arrangement. But I also did it out of fear for Rachel."

"Fear for Rachel? I don't understand."

"Ivy will stop at no length to harm Rachel. If she can't scare her off and force Rachel to leave on her own accord, I feared Ivy might actually try to eliminate the dear woman."

"Why would you say that? Do you have reason to believe Ivy would do physical harm to Rachel?"

"Not only do I think she would, I know she would. I know about the rattlesnake." Braeden paled and Reg nodded. "That's right—the one Gwen told you about. Ivy planted it there. Well, not exactly Ivy. She paid to have it done and then hid the man in her room after he hit Mr. O'Donnell over the head. She simply slipped him out her window and no one was the wiser for her actions."

"No one but you," Braeden said flatly. "If you knew about this, why didn't you go to the proper authorities?"

Reginald smiled. "Because it gave me power over Miss Brooks. And, as you have witnessed her vengeance and her conniving ways, I believe you understand what it might mean to hold at least a marginal amount of influence over that young woman."

"That snake could have killed whomever opened the drawer," Braeden said angrily.

"Yes, but I knew it was somewhere in the office, and when you all left to help Mr. O'Donnell, I planned to take the matter into my own hands."

"Only you didn't have to because Gwen Carson handled the situation."

"Yes," Reg said, nodding. "Quite a woman there."

"Yes, she is quite a woman, and she wouldn't have deserved to have been bitten by that snake either. You should have come forward before it went that far."

"Until I saw the situation being arranged and followed the man, I had no real idea as to what he was about. But that aside, you must understand that I went along with Ivy for Rachel's sake. I couldn't have another attempt on her life. She's too precious. I think even you would have to admit that protecting her was far more important than worrying about your reputation. Ivy told me that if I didn't help her, she would see to it that Rachel suffered. I didn't want to see Rachel in further danger."

"But she may be in danger at this very minute," Braeden said, eyeing Reg suspiciously. "That is, unless you know otherwise. In which case, I demand to know the truth."

Reg crossed his arms and tried his best to appear completely at ease. "Mr. Parker, I do not trust you, neither do I like you. You epitomize that typical American male mentality of taking what you want and worrying about the consequences at a later time. If in fact you have to suffer those consequences at all. But my feelings are unimportant. I believe, however, that after spending time with me, Rachel has come to see the difference in how men of proper breeding conduct themselves. I believe she cherishes the more genteel nature she finds in me, and I doubt very much that she cares for you anymore. Especially given your indiscretions with Ivy Brooks."

"Did she tell you that?"

"She didn't have to say it with words—her face told me everything I needed to know. I believe it told you the truth as well. I saw the exchange between you two. You know she believes the worst. You know she believes you to have taken up a dalliance with Miss Brooks. And because her trust was fixed on such fragile ground with you, you must also realize that such a blow would surely destroy any remaining love she held for you."

Braeden took two steps forward and stopped directly in front of Reginald. "If you know where she is," he said in a low, menacing voice, "you'd be wise to tell me."

"I don't know where she is," Reginald replied. "I wish I did. I certainly wouldn't be here if I had the opportunity to take her away from this mess. I have abhorred this place from the moment I arrived and had very nearly made up my mind to go back to New York when I met Rachel. I only stayed because of her. I only stay now because of her."

Braeden shook his head. "She loves me. I know she still loves me."

"Then you are a fool, Mr. Parker." Reg moved to the side and slipped past Braeden while he appeared to contemplate that final statement. "Now, if you'll excuse me, I have a party to prepare for."

"If you love her so much, then why aren't you out there looking for her instead of sitting here planning for a party?" Braeden suddenly asked. "I think you know where she is, and because you know her to be safe and out of danger, you are merely going about your business."

Reg turned at the door. "Think what you like, Mr. Parker. But remember this, I am a man with connections. I needn't do my own dirty work when there are so many people desperate for a job. I might not be out looking for her, but that doesn't mean I haven't hired others to be doing just that. Just ask around. Ask Tomas. He went with you yesterday, but today he's already gone, working for me. He was, in fact, under my pay yesterday. So don't judge my appearance here to be a sign of indifference. I know I am hardly cut out for the physical demands of searching the wilderness for Rachel, but I would never stand by idly while she's missing."

With that, he left Parker to consider his words. It irritated him that the man would question him when it came to Rachel, but he quickly dismissed it. Even more irritating was Ivy Brooks. He couldn't help but wonder what she might mean to his plans. He had a job to do, and the last thing he needed was the interference of that child.

Still, by sharing what he knew with Braeden, he had turned the tables on Ivy Brooks. He had explained his participation in her little charade, and Braeden couldn't argue that he had been perfectly justified in the choices he'd made. Smiling to himself, Reg felt a deep sense of satisfaction. Now, if only he could convince Rachel that Braeden's loyalty lay elsewhere.

Reg waited an hour after Braeden had taken off to search for Rachel before getting down to business. He had watched Braeden load up his supplies, speak to Fred Harvey and the marshal, and then take his leave. One thing Reg had to say for the man, he was driven and he was persistent.

Making certain that the kitchen staff and Harvey Girls were busy with preparations for the noon meal, Reginald picked up a small box and headed out of the kitchen. He paused at the delivery entrance to make certain no one was observing him, then removed his white chef's coat and hat and donned his tweed jacket before making his way down the road.

Taking a seat on one of the park benches, Reg waited for several minutes before he opened the box and began nibbling at the brunch he'd packed for himself. He needed the quiet moments to better organize his ideas, and looking back up at Casa Grande, he knew his plans would have to come together soon. Smith was counting on him, and so far things had run in a smooth and orderly course. Reginald needed to ensure that nothing disturb their undertaking.

Movement down below on the lower portion of the falls' pathway caused Reg to sit up and take notice. He continued eating, pretending to be unconcerned with the approach of two dark-skinned natives.

"Señor," the first of the two men said as they approached the bench where Reg sat.

"Yes, how can I help you?"

"You are the cook, are you not?" the man questioned.

Reg stiffened. "I am the head chef of Casa Grande."

"Good," the man said, smiling. "Pablo said you would very much like some extra help."

Reg relaxed a bit and nodded. "I'm always looking for good help. Come see me later in the kitchen. Let's say around eight o'clock."

The men nodded and continued toward Casa Grande as if the conversation had never taken place. Smiling to himself, Reg felt a sense of accomplishment.

After half an hour of mental contemplation, Reg finally repacked the remaining food and made his way back to the kitchen. His mind was consumed with what he had to do tonight, for both the banquet and the initiation of his well-thought-out task. Yet he was also consumed with Rachel.

When night fell and there was still no sign of Parker, Reginald decided the time had arrived for him to make his move. After meeting the two men he'd spoken to earlier in the day, where he handed them a great deal of money and whispered instructions, he waited until both men slipped out of the room before doing likewise.

Now he felt a sense of elation and excitement. It wouldn't be much longer, he reasoned. He would soon be on a train bound for Chicago and then New York, and from there he would take a steamer home to England. And Rachel would be at his side.

He pulled on his coat and stepped outside. He cursed the electrical lighting, which added illumination from the various streetlights in front of Casa Grande. Complete darkness would have suited his purposes much better, but with a sigh he realized he would simply have to make do. He stole across the open lawn and let the shadows swallow him as he neared the falls. The gentle roar offered him comfort as he maneuvered down the narrow walk to the powerhouse. The noise, like the shadowy darkness, offered him more in the way of coverage, and Reg was no fool. He knew he needed to remain completely hidden throughout his mission. Smith stressed over and over that no one could know of the matter, and though Reginald had hired the two men to help him, he had no doubts that the men would not survive the ordeal once everything was in motion.

Quietly, he opened the powerhouse door and, with one last backward glance, slipped inside. The room was dimly illuminated from one single light in the corner. The power was generally shut off after a certain time of night, but with the grand opening and the long nightly celebrations, arrangements had been made to leave the power on throughout the night. The situation would either serve Reg's purpose or oppose it—he hadn't really decided which way it would be.

Moving to the back of the room, Reg picked his way through the maze of buzzing belts and humming machinery. He knew very little about power stations, but it was of no concern. Nothing mattered now—nothing but the success of accomplishing what Smith had sent him here to do.

Lifting a trapdoor, Reg gingerly made his way down the ladder. He reached up to his right and felt for the light cord. Finding it, he gave it a yank and light flooded the lower level of the powerhouse. Here the noise of the waterwheel and belts were marginally diminished, but not by much. He glanced around and found to his satisfaction that stacks of linens and silver were securely stored away for future sale. He smiled as he thought of the ingenious plan to sell off the most valuable pieces of Casa Grande. He thought of how he manipulated the inventory and how pleased Smith would be with his share of the money.

Hearing a noise, his smile broadened. The most valuable treasure of all awaited just around the final stack of crates. Rachel Taylor.

"I came to make sure you were all right," he said softly. She was bound and gagged and could in no way communicate with words, but her eyes flashed anger and fear that made him feel the need to explain.

"You are quite right to be put out with me," he said,

coming to sit beside the small cot where she lay. "I don't suppose you'll believe this, but I've done this for your own good. You have to understand. There is about to be a tragedy, and I don't want you anywhere near harm's way."

Her eyes widened and she muttered something from beneath the gag. Realizing that no one would ever hear her above the roar of the power station and the waterfalls, Reg pulled the cloth from her mouth and smiled. "Better?"

"I want you to let me go," she managed to say before a spell of coughing hit her. "Water, please," she pleaded.

Reg got up quickly and walked to where the Casa Grande goods were stacked. He pulled out one of the crates and searched until he found a small silver sugar bowl. It would have to do, he decided. He went to the far end of the station, to the place where the waterwheel was partially exposed and water splashed over the edges of the paddles. Carefully, so as not to get his arm caught by the wheel, he extended the bowl and collected the water for Rachel. It wasn't exactly cold, having come from the hot springs, but it had cooled considerably as it had blended with other streams that joined to form Morita Falls.

"Here," he said as he made his way back to her. He helped to lift her to a sitting position and held the bowl to her lips. "I'll bring you something to eat later."

Rachel drank the entire contents before pulling away to look Reg in the eye. "Why are you doing this to me? I trusted you and thought we were friends."

Reg felt the sting of her accusation. "I did what I did in order to protect you. You have to understand that. I know what Parker is and why he's done what he has. He sees Ivy as his ticket to wealth and power. He can run Morita and lack for nothing."

"I don't believe you. Braeden didn't do anything wrong.

I'm sure what we saw was all Ivy's doing. She thinks if she can convince her aunt that Braeden has dishonored her, Mrs. Needlemeier will force him to marry her. But that will never happen."

Reg shook his head and reached his hand up to gently touch Rachel's cheek. "You're wrong. They are already married."

"What?" Rachel asked, jerking away from his touch. "What are you saying?"

Her voice rang of desperation, and Reginald instantly felt sorry for having grieved her. "I say, I know this comes as a shock. But you have me. I won't allow Parker's actions to further hurt you."

"They're married?"

"Yes. In fact, they've already taken the train east."

"I don't believe you," Rachel said, recoiling against the wall. With her feet tied to the end of the cot and her arms tied behind her back, it was difficult to maneuver, but she was accomplishing the job nevertheless.

Reg shrugged. "I'm so sorry to be the one to give you bad news. I never wanted to see you hurt. I know you loved Parker, but I hope that with this turn of events, you might come in time to love me. I want to take care of you, Rachel. I want to take you away from this hurt and pain you've suffered because of Parker's indiscretion."

"That was Ivy's doing. I know it was." She sounded even more desperate, almost pleading.

Reg knew she wanted him to confirm her suspicions and because it caused her such pain, he decided to give her that much. "Yes, it was Ivy's plan. She told me all about it and enlisted my help."

"You?" Rachel said, shaking her head. "But why would you help her? I thought you were my friend."

"It was because of our friendship that I agreed to help her," he said softly. "I wanted to prove to you once and for all that Parker was not what he seemed. He didn't deserve your heart or your trust. Ivy told me she could help prove this to you by setting a scene where Parker would come to her and behave in a less than honorable way. She would get what she wanted, and I would get what I wanted."

"And what was it you wanted?" Rachel questioned, her expression still betraying her disbelief.

"I wanted you. I want you to love me," Reginald admitted.

"I can't love you, Reg," Rachel replied flatly. "I have loved Braeden for so long that I don't know how to love anyone else in that way. I had resigned myself to spend the rest of my life alone, and then he reappeared in my life. I'm sorry, but he has my heart and always will. Now, won't you please let me go? I promise not to tell anyone that you've been keeping me here. I just need to see him."

Reg leaned back against the beat-up chair on which he sat. He eyed her seriously for several moments and shook his head. "He's not there. I've already told you. They were married yesterday, and Mr. Harvey demanded they pack their things and go. You know his rules. The man was positively livid. Mr. Parker had no choice."

Rachel blanched and Reg realized he'd finally hit upon a truth she had no doubt of. "Ivy made a big scene yesterday morning. You don't know this, but her aunt is dead. She succumbed to the shock of seeing Ivy and Braeden together."

"No!" Rachel gasped.

"It's true," Reg replied. "Ivy showed up at the hotel and announced this. Mr. Smith and Mr. Harvey were both on hand to receive the news and, well . . . one thing led to another and the truth about the night before came pouring out. Ivy was distraught because of her aunt's death, and Braeden was sympathetic and concerned for her. I suppose no one thought much of the matter until she mentioned the possibility of being with child. That was when Braeden decided they should be married."

Tears came to Rachel's eyes as she shook her head. "I don't believe you, Reg. Why are you lying to me?"

"Listen," he said, reaching out to touch her again. She pulled away, but he didn't let it stop him. He wanted to feel the softness of her cheek, the silky curls of her hair. He wanted to breathe in the scent of her perfume. Without warning, he grabbed her and pulled her across the cot and into his arms. "I don't want you hurt," he murmured against her ear. He tightened his grip as she struggled against him. "I want to take care of you. I love you, Rachel."

"No," Rachel said, fighting his hold.

"Shhh," he whispered. "You must understand. There are things that will happen tonight. Things I can't explain. You must stay here and be safe, and when it is over I will come for you."

"No! Let me go! I won't go away with you. I won't!" she declared.

Reg frowned, realizing she might not be the grateful, fragile being that he had earlier presumed. He might have to resort to other means in order to get her out of Casa Grande without having to answer a lot of questions or deal with an unpleasant scene.

"I need your cooperation, Rachel. You know about the missing inventory now. But it's only a part of my scheme. If you hadn't found my men hiding the materials, you might not be here now. But since you are, I can better protect you from harm. In the long run, after we're in England and married, you'll understand that my love has kept you safe tonight."

Rachel became still in his arms. She looked up, shaking

her head. "Reg, you've gone mad. You mustn't think that you can steal me away like this. I won't go willingly, and how will you explain that? No minister will marry us without my permission, and I will never give it. You are a sick man and you need help."

"I assure you that I am quite sane," Reg said, thinking how pleasant it would be to kiss her lips. He had nearly convinced himself to do just that but decided against it. No, he would preserve her purity and innocence until they were married. It was only right.

Lowering her back onto the cot, he tossed aside the gag. "I don't suppose this much matters," he said, looking at the piece of cloth. "The machinery is loud enough to keep your screams from carrying, and if not that, then the waterwheel. Besides, in a few hours I'll be back to take you away and there will be enough commotion that no one will even remember that you're missing."

"Braeden will remember," she said, sniffing loudly as tears streamed from her eyes.

"He might remember you, but I doubt Ivy will allow him little more than his memories," Reg said. He pulled out his watch and got to his feet. "I have to go. There are plans to set in motion." He smiled down at her. "Don't be afraid, my beautiful Rachel. I'll come back for you."

He left her there crying. He felt horrible that he could not offer her comfort. She had called him mad, and maybe he was. The lure of money had driven him to do this job. And when it was all said and done, he would have enough money to retire quietly to England and reclaim the family holdings that had been sold to cover his mother's debts. He would spend a quiet life with Rachel, and maybe they would even have children. Little curly-headed children like their mother.

Stepping into the darkness of the night, Reg was nearly

knocked over by a powerful gust of wind. The air chilled him to the bone and made him pull his coat tighter. Crossing to the resort, he was nearly startled out of his wits when Tomas called his name.

"Señor Worthington," the boy said, coming quietly out of the shadows. "I have your money."

Reg smiled. The boy had been an excellent help in moving the stolen goods and selling them in Santa Fe and elsewhere. "You've done a good job by me, Tomas," Reginald said as he took the cash. He handed a portion over to the boy and added, "This is your share." He glanced upward toward the mountains as another gale whipped down and moaned through the trees, chilling them both. "It would probably be best if you slept at home tonight."

Tomas looked at him with a questioning expression. He opened his mouth as if to speak, then nodded and pocketed the money.

"It has been good to work with you, Tomas. Why don't you come into the kitchen and take what food you would like for your family?"

"Truly, señor?"

"We won't be needing it," Reg said flatly, slipping the money into his jacket pocket. He looked at the boy and smiled again. "We won't be needing any of it."

Chapter 26

Reg made his way upstairs to his room after the revelry of the ball died down. He was confident of his plans and in having had no contact with Braeden Parker since morning. Perhaps this entire matter would be easier than he'd previously thought.

Once inside his room, he pulled out his suitcases and began to pack. There was much to consider and much to remember. Tonight's plans would have to run in perfect order or innocent people would suffer, and while he had no problem in watching the guilty endure such trauma, he would have no part in creating undeserving victims.

He threw his clothes into the cases in a haphazard manner and went to retrieve his toiletry articles. Forcing himself to slow down and breathe deeply, Reg tried to pace his actions. There was no hurry, no need to rush. Everything would come about in its proper time. His superiors would be pleased and proud to have him as an associate, and he, in turn, would be rich.

As if conjuring up Mr. Smith with that thought, Reg opened the door to find the jittery man on the other side. "Is everything ready?" Smith tenuously questioned.

Reg smiled. "Of course it is. Did you doubt me?"

Smith took a hesitant step inside the room. He leaned against the open door and pulled out a handkerchief to wipe his sweaty forehead. "It's just so important that this matter be resolved. I have to have that money."

Nodding, Reg went to his suitcase and pulled out an envelope. "Here's your share of money from the sale of the stolen goods. I think you'll be rather pleased."

Smith nodded and moved forward to lessen the distance between them, without thinking to close the door behind him. Somewhere down the lighted corridor a door slammed, causing Smith to jump. Panic-stricken, he looked over his shoulder, then snatched the cash. "It will help, but it won't come near to being the hundreds of thousands I need."

"Well, then," Reg said, straightening up, "it will only be a matter of time until the insurance money comes through and you have all that you need. As for me, I plan to make my way to England immediately. You may forward my share there. I'll leave you my address."

Smith nodded. "You're that certain this is going to work?"

"I am very confident of the matter. I've kept everyone in the dark about this plan. Even the two men I hired to do some of the dirty work only know a small part. You'll see. This will come together in such perfect order that no one will be the wiser for it."

"How will you set the fire?" Smith asked softly.

"It's better you don't know all the details. You can't be condemned for what you don't know," Reg replied. "Oh, and here are those papers I took from Miss Taylor's office. Rather useless in their content, but they served the purpose of creating a minor distraction, just as ransacking Parker's office set that poor man off on a wild chase."

"I don't think it was the mess you made of his office that set him off on the chase," Smith replied. "He's bent on finding Miss Taylor, and I can't say I blame him. She seems like a very nice young woman. I only pray she remains unharmed."

Reginald frowned and retrieved the last of his clothing from the closet. "She is a wonderful woman—a woman whom I intend to make my wife."

"Your wife? But I thought her interest was in Parker."

"It was. But that is in the past. She loves me now and plans to share a life with me in England."

"I see. Then I suppose you know where she is," Smith said, wiping his forehead again. When Reginald refused to acknowledge this statement one way or another, Smith continued. "Well, after you burn this place to the ground, I don't much care *whom* you hitch yourself up with."

"Well, I do," Braeden said, casually leaning against the doorjamb. "I think the marshal here would probably care as well."

Marshal Schmidt came to stand in the middle of the doorway but said nothing. Braeden eyed Reg with a look that demanded the truth. Reg knew the man would not leave without answers to his questions.

"It seemed rather strange that you and Tomas should spend so much time pouring over inventory sheets when there was so much else necessary to ready this place for the grand opening," Braeden began. "It also seemed strange that Rachel's inventory stopped disappearing, at least according to your tallies, while mine continued to show discrepancies."

He walked toward Smith and Worthington, appearing for all the world as though they were about to discuss the weather. "Of course, Tomas was really rather good at giving us the slip on more than one occasion. Weren't you, Tomas?" he called out, and the boy sheepishly appeared to stand beside the marshal.

"You see," Braeden continued, watching Reg carefully, "Tomas has just given us a full confession. He explained how you approached him to help you steal valuable articles from

Casa Grande and how he's used the money to help his family. Tomas had a very honorable reason for his thievery, but I wonder what your reason might have been, Mr. Worthington."

Reg shrugged and nervously twisted his hands. "The boy is lying, and you don't frighten me with your bullying ways."

"The boy isn't lying. I just heard more than a simple confession of stealing silver from your little conversation with Smith. You plan to destroy Casa Grande. I suppose the one question I have for you both is why?"

Smith seemed to understand that the matter needed to be taken quickly into hand. "Look here, Parker, you seem like a reasonable man, and while I don't know the marshal here, I would imagine he's intelligent enough to realize when something can benefit him."

Parker exchanged glances with the marshal and smiled. "He's a very intelligent man. He managed to lead us here tonight."

Smith bit his lip and nodded. "Yes, well, then you will understand when I explain the dilemma the railroad finds itself in. The Santa Fe has made some poor investments and, in the course of this last year, has suffered a financial setback. Their investment in Casa Grande alone has cost them hundreds of thousands of dollars."

"So how does it figure that you would benefit from destroying the resort? I thought the Santa Fe and Harvey Company were hoping this would be their best joint effort to date," Braeden said seriously.

Smith nodded. "They do. However, I've found a way to make it pay off in much quicker order. Fire insurance will more than cover the expense put into this place and leave money in addition to those expenses."

"Fire insurance? You figure to burn the place down and

collect on the insurance?" the marshal asked after taking a wooden toothpick from his mouth. He looked for all intents and purposes to be rather bored with the entire affair.

"Yes," Smith said flatly. "The idea to sell off the inventory was Worthington's idea, but I went along with it. It wasn't like the stuff would be useful to anyone after the fire. Worthington pointed out that we could take what we wanted and sell it off. No matter how much we received for the articles, it would still be a profit to both of us."

Smith moved closer to the men. "Look, I can make it worthwhile to both of you. I will control that insurance money when it comes in. Tonight is perfect for burning the place down because there's a storm brewing off in the distance, and once it hits here, we can plead a lightning strike or the wind knocking over a lantern. Then the wind will whip up a fury and hopefully—"

"Threaten the life of every man, woman, and child in residence," Braeden said sarcastically. "You really haven't thought this through, Smith. Are you ready to be a murderer as well as a wealthy man?"

"I don't stand to be wealthy from this," Smith replied. "There are some matters that have made this situation necessary. The money will help to keep me out of trouble in Topeka. You can't possibly understand."

"Try me."

Smith took a deep breath and blew it out. As he did that, thunder rumbled off in the distance. "We're losing time. The storm is moving in fast."

"The way I figure it," Braeden said, "you have all the time in the world to explain. You'll have even more time in your jail cell."

"You needn't threaten us, Parker. We know what we're doing," Reginald replied. Parker could threaten and rage all he wanted, but Reg held the winning card. He would have things his way. He would be the top man for once in his life. "We have a plan, and we mean to carry through with that plan. It's out of your hands, and frankly, it's out of my hands."

"What do you mean?" Braeden asked, his eyes narrowing.

"I mean that soon this place will be in a full blaze. You can't prove anything; it's your word against ours. And while Tomas may have told you a great deal, he'll quickly side with us when he sees that the welfare of his family depends upon it. Your reputation is ruined here, and Mr. Smith and Mr. Harvey are the best of friends. So in spite of your bringing in the marshal, I doubt seriously anyone will listen to your tale of intrigue. They'll remember your rejection of the woman you ruined—of her desire to marry you in spite of your actions. You are known now to be a liar, and frankly, I doubt anyone will give much consideration to what you have to say."

"Marshal, surely you could use the extra money?" Smith said in a questioning tone.

The man grinned. "I reckon I can always use a little extra money."

Smith nodded. "Then you'll help us?"

The marshal shook his head. "Nope. I didn't say that."

"But . . . I thought from what you said about being able to use the extra money," Smith countered, "that you were agreeing to go along with our plan. I know that if you will help us, Tomas will be happy to go back to keeping his mouth shut on the matter and rejoin our effort."

"Tomas isn't going to rejoin you," Braeden said, his voice dropping to a near whisper. "And you can't buy the marshal, so what do you propose to do now?"

"Gentlemen," Smith interjected, "we needn't argue

amongst ourselves. I can make your silence quite worthwhile. I'm prepared to offer both you and the marshal two thousand dollars in order to simply escort Tomas to jail and forget everything else. I'm sure that by the time you remove the boy and process him for his crimes, that the destruction of this fine resort will already be well underway. So what do you say? Two thousand dollars is a lot of money to turn your back on."

Braeden smiled, but it was a hard, unfeeling smile. Reg felt the hairs on the back of his neck prickle at the cool, unemotional expression on the man's face. "I have more than enough money to see to my needs, Mr. Smith. I hardly need your blood money."

"It's not blood money, Mr. Parker. No one has to be injured. We'll sound the alarm well in advance and everyone should make it to safety before the fire gets out of control." Smith stepped forward, his face pale, his skin sweaty. "I need this money, Mr. Parker. I'm afraid I did something rather foolish and gambled a good deal of money away. It wasn't even mine, but rather money the Santa Fe entrusted me with. If I can successfully obtain the Santa Fe share of the hotel insurance, which of course has to be shared with Mr. Harvey, I can manage things a bit longer. At least until I'm able to make back the money I borrowed."

"Stole, don't you mean?" questioned Braeden.

Reg saw a brilliant flash of lightning and smiled. The thought of the storm made him feel as if everything would be all right. He hadn't dared to hope they would be fortunate enough to have a lightning storm in the area, but now it seemed as if the destruction of Casa Grande was preordained.

If only they could force Parker to cooperate. They were too close now to lose everything they'd worked for. If Parker and the marshal wouldn't agree, Reg would have little trouble in seeing them both killed. And with Parker dead, there would be no further obstacle to Rachel's love. At this thought, Reg chuckled, causing all heads to turn toward him.

"What's so funny, Mr. Worthington?" Braeden questioned.

"You are," Reg said with a smile. "You stand here worrying about your precious hotel, when Rachel is still far from your reach. But it isn't important because she's within my care and that is all that matters. I shall take her to England with me, and we will live rather happily there. I would imagine she might mourn you for a time, but only in the sense of regretting her naïveté."

Braeden practically flew at him, grabbing Reginald by his coat. "Tell me where she is!" he demanded.

Reg thought it all rather amusing. It seemed ironic that he would be standing here in Parker's grip, while Smith begged the man to come in on their scheme. The marshal just stood there not saying a word, while Tomas trembled in the doorway, too frightened to run away and too unnerved to speak. To Reg it seemed like a poorly acted stage play. The final act, perhaps. The scene just before the ultimate climax, where all the pertinent players were gathered and the truth was finally told. He laughed out loud even as Parker shook him hard enough to rattle his teeth.

"Where is Rachel?"

"She's safe," Reg replied, still laughing. "She's with me and she's safe."

Outside, the wind picked up and lightning once again flashed to pierce the pitch-black darkness of the night. Braeden dropped his hold on Reg and turned to the marshal. "We need to get this trio over to your jail. I don't know what they have planned, but I'm determined to bring it to a halt. I'll—"

"Just a minute, Parker," the marshal cut in, tilting his head in the air. "I smell smoke."

Braeden looked at Reginald, as did Smith. But it was Smith who spoke. "Is this your work?"

Reg tried to rationalize what they were asking, for his mind had already drifted to thoughts of Rachel Taylor in his arms. The storm outside and affairs of the hotel no longer seemed important. He looked up with a blank stare. "I've done nothing. The fire will start at two."

Braeden looked at his watch. "That's hours away."

"Maybe lightning did strike," the marshal said, moving toward the door. "Whatever the reason, I smell smoke."

Braeden moved to follow the marshal into the hallway when the lights flickered and then went off. "What's going on?" he muttered.

"Storm must have blown the lines down," the marshal called out. He struck a match against the wall and looked to Braeden for help. "You have any candles or maybe a kerosene lamp?"

"We have them downstairs, but if there is a fire, we've no time to be running all over the place. Tomas, you go downstairs and get us a couple of lamps out of the storage room. If you cooperate with us now, maybe the marshal can see to reducing the charges against you." Tomas looked at Braeden hopefully before tearing off in the direction of the stairs.

The match burned out and the marshal quickly lit another one. "You take the west side and I'll take the east," he told Braeden. "We'll get the folks to safety and then figure out what to do with these two."

"It's too soon," Reg muttered over and over. He could smell the smoke now and felt his heart racing out of control. His plans had been altered and someone had taken matters into their own hands.

Pushing his way into the hall, Reginald was unprepared when Braeden slammed him against the wall, growling low and refusing to release him even as he struggled. "Tell me where she is!" Parker demanded.

Reg shook his head. "She's mine. She doesn't love you anymore. I told her you'd left with Ivy. I told her you were already married. She never wants to see you again." Reg laughed at the look on Braeden's face. Doubt mingled with fear as Braeden realized the potential such statements could have had on the already defeated Rachel.

"Señor Parker!" Tomas called as he brought the lamps. "There is a fire downstairs in the theatre. The stage curtains are already burning."

"That's under the west side rooms," the marshal called. "Come on, Parker, we have to get these people to safety."

Braeden glared at Reginald with contempt, then slowly eased his grip on Reg's shirt. Without a word, he turned and ran after the marshal.

What followed next was like a macabre carnival. People poured from every corner of the second floor. Some were already in their bedclothes, others struggled to dress as they made their way to the stairs. A few of the older women sobbed fearfully, while some were in hysterics. Children, frantic in the wake of their disturbed sleep, seemed to sense the urgency and fear of their parents. This caused them to begin crying as they clung tightly to hands, arms, or even legs. Whatever they could manage to hold on to became their lifeline.

Reg stood rather dumbfounded for several moments as people streamed by him, pushing and shoving, all trying to reach the stairs first. He wondered if the fire would be a success, and even though he wasn't responsible for the blaze, he knew he had completed his duty and could go back home.

Thinking only of leaving the hotel and retrieving Rachel, Reg systematically returned to his room, took up his luggage, and made his way to join the hysterical crowd.

Braeden choked on the thick black smoke. Because the hotel lobby was open to the second floor, smoke had no trouble pouring down the hallways and up into the second story. He took out his bandana and tied it around his nose and mouth, but it did little good. Pounding on each chamber door until someone came to answer it, Braeden felt light-headed from the lack of oxygen. He had to get the people to safety, but his mind kept going over and over the words Worthington had just told him.

"She doesn't love you anymore. I told her you'd left with Ivy. I told her you were already married. She never wants to see you again."

Braeden shook his head. He wouldn't believe it was true. God wouldn't let it be true.

Chapter 27

Braeden could barely make out the image of Reginald Worthington as he moved toward the staircase. Without thought to anyone else or even his own safety, Braeden pushed through the crowd and grabbed the chef by the back of his coat. Turning him around rather quickly, Braeden drew on every bit of his self-control to keep from hitting the man.

"You're coming with me, Worthington," he said angrily. Dragging Reg down the stairs with him, Braeden was surprised when Tomas appeared at the bottom. "You come with me as well," he told the boy, and Tomas nodded and followed Braeden outside.

Half dragging, half pushing, Braeden forced Worthington to the stables and instructed Tomas to get him a length of rope. "I don't want to worry about either one of you while I'm trying to ensure the safety of our guests," he said. Tying Reg and Tomas together, then securing them to one of the stall posts, Braeden left them and returned to the hotel.

Acrid smoke was now drifting from the open door, and as Braeden entered the lobby, he felt the air thicken and sting his nose and throat. Pulling his bandana close around his mouth, Braeden made his way upstairs to double-check for any guest who might not have found their way downstairs. He grabbed a lamp someone had thought to leave at the top of the stairs and hurriedly passed in and out of every room.

Relief washed over him when he found the second floor completely deserted.

Making his way to the back stairs, Braeden felt a rush of panic. The staircase was engulfed in flames. The fire greedily ate at everything in its path, the carpet on the stairway appearing to be a favorite meal. Realizing he couldn't use the stairs for his escape, Braeden hurried back down the long, carpeted eastern corridor. The fire seemed to have started on the west side, which would suffer the most damage. He could only pray that the east side would remain intact long enough for his escape. Running now to rid his lungs of the caustic fumes, Braeden nearly fell headlong into the figure of a woman. He took hold of her arms and started to comment on getting her to safety when the glow of the fire behind him made it easy to see her features.

"Ivy?" He pushed her toward the stairs, hoping to remove them both out of harm's way. "You need to get out of here. The whole place is about to go up."

"Oh, Braeden, you mustn't be mad at me," she said sweetly. She clung to his arm and didn't seem to notice that he had nearly lifted her off the stairs as he took them two at a time.

"I don't have time to worry about being mad at you," he said, grimacing as they hit the ground floor. "Look, you go on outside, I need to search the place and make certain no one else is inside." He pushed her toward the open front doors.

"No! You can't go back inside," she protested. "My mother did that. My father too. You don't understand. I did what I had to do."

Braeden shook his head and took the one remaining lamp on the front registry desk. "What are you talking about?"

"My parents died," Ivy said in absolute anguish. "I didn't mean for them to die." She wrapped her arms around

Braeden's and pulled. "You believe me, don't you? Auntie didn't believe me, but it's true." She pulled at his arm. "You have to come with me. You'll die if you don't."

"People will die if they're still inside," Braeden told her. "I'm going to make a quick check."

"No one's in there. I saw them all leave. I only came back inside to find you. You are free now. Casa Grande won't keep us from marrying. There will be nothing here for you, and you can take me with you to Chicago."

"You're insane, Ivy," he said, trying to push her away. The lamp nearly fell from his hands as she fought him.

"I had to do it. I know it was wrong, but by destroying this place, you would have no other reason to stay."

He stopped at this, and in spite of the building smoke and growing fire, Braeden simply stared at her for a moment. "You set this fire." It was a statement more than a question, and when Ivy nodded, he felt the overwhelming urge to slap her. He didn't, however. "Get out of here, Ivy. I can't help you now."

"I know about fires," she said, refusing to drop her hold on his arm. "My parents died in a fire. They shouldn't have—I didn't mean for them to, but they went back inside. You have to come outside with me." She actually managed to drag him a few steps toward the front door.

"Are you saying you set the fire that killed your parents?" he asked, almost horrified to know the answer. He coughed as his lungs fought to exhale the smoke. They couldn't remain in the resort for much longer.

She nodded, then threw him a pleading look. "Aunt Esmeralda didn't understand, but she's dead now. She can't hurt me. The secret is safe with us."

Braeden's mind reeled from the information. Then a sickening thought came to his mind. Esmeralda had died from a fall down the stairs. He knew because he'd asked. The doctor had been uncertain if the old woman had suffered some sort of seizure prior to the fall but had promised to do a posthumous examination.

For a moment, the smoke seemed to lessen and Braeden actually thought perhaps the fire was playing itself out. But as the wind blew in from the open door, he realized the reason. Ivy pulled at his arm.

"We have to hurry, look behind you!"

Looking down the hall, Braeden saw the unmistakable glow of flames. Casa Grande would soon lay in ashes.

Realizing there was no more time to waste, he pushed Ivy toward the door, acting as if they were both going to exit the lobby. As soon as Ivy crossed the threshold, however, Braeden ripped away from her hold and marched back into the hotel, heading straight for the dining room. He'd just entered the silent room when Ivy caught up with him.

"No, Braeden!" she screamed, coming after him in a fierce lunge.

Unprepared for this, Braeden dropped the lamp, spilling the kerosene. Flames leapt across the wooden floor. With their exit to the lobby cut off, Braeden pulled Ivy into the dining room just as a woman's screams sounded.

"We'll have to go out the side exit," he told Ivy. He would have just as soon left her to suffer on her own, but he couldn't do such an abominable thing with a clear conscience. God would deal with Ivy Brooks. It wasn't up to Braeden to mete out her punishment.

The scream came again, and this time Braeden was certain it came from the kitchen. Pushing Ivy forward, they entered the kitchen and nearly fell back from the heat of the fire. Apparently the flames had crossed over from the theatre and ignited the back of the kitchen—at least from what Braeden surmised.

"Help me!" a woman cried out.

Braeden made out the figure of Gwen Carson. She was stuck in a small alcove of the kitchen. Directly behind her and in front of her the flames engulfed the walls, counters, and everything else in its wake.

"Gwen, you'll have to jump through the fire."

"I can't!" she screamed. "I can't. I fell, and I think my leg is broken."

Ivy stood mesmerized as Braeden pulled off his coat. "Get out of here, Ivy. I can't help you both at the same time."

Still she refused to move, but Braeden was more concerned for Gwen. Pulling his coat over his head, Braeden made a mad run at the growing wall of flames. Ivy screamed from somewhere across the fiery wall, but he was unharmed as he came face-to-face with Gwen.

He assessed the situation quickly as a huge piece of the back wall gave way. Looking through the flames to where Ivy stood, Braeden was mortified to see that the fire had managed to surround her and cut off her escape. There wasn't much time left. They were all going to die if he didn't think of something fast.

The heat from the fire made his skin tingle and the air rapidly grew much too hot to breathe. *God help me,* he prayed, frantic to think of some way to help them survive the situation. Just then he remembered the storage room. There was a conveyance of rollers to slide goods into the room from the delivery platform window. That receiving window would be their means of escape!

"Ivy, you'll have to come this way. I'm going to get Gwen into the storage room. We can escape through the window."

"No! Don't leave me!" Ivy screamed.

Braeden had already lifted Gwen into his arms. "You'll have to do this on your own, Ivy. I'll be back in a minute." He

heard her screaming his name over and over, and in spite of
all the trouble she had caused him, he felt a horrible sense of
inadequacy in leaving her there. Surely she would muster her
courage and come after them, he thought. She wouldn't just
stand there and let the fire take her without a fight.

Gwen was sobbing softly in his arms as Braeden moved
through the storage area. The fire behind them created
enough light to see through the smoky shadows—but just
barely. "We're almost there," he told her, pushing past crates
and bags of flour.

Placing Gwen on the rollers, he admonished her to hold
tight. "I'm going to get that window open," he said, maneuvering to unfasten the wooden latches. The window was more
of a door, for all practical purposes, with a heavy wooden gate
that swung wide to expose the room for delivery.

Braeden had it open in a matter of seconds. "Just ease your
weight down the rollers," he told Gwen. "Get yourself outside while I go back for Ivy. Can you do that?"

Gwen nodded, seeming to regain control of her senses.
"I'll do it, Mr. Parker. You go ahead."

Braeden left his coat by the window and maneuvered back
through the storage room. There was no sign of Ivy, but he
heard her screams through the roar of the blaze. He'd no
sooner made it to the kitchen when a huge piece of ceiling
gave way and crashed down before him to block off any hope
of going after Ivy. Sparks flashed up and pieces of debris
landed on his left forearm, burning his shirt. He quickly
smothered the flaming sleeve, then struggled again to see
where Ivy was.

"Ivy! This is the only way out!"

Her screams echoed in his ears, then fell silent as another
piece of wall gave way.

He felt sickened at the thought of her dying in the very fire she'd set. It might be poetic justice or proper revenge for all that she had done, but he would never have wished it upon her.

It wasn't until he made his way back to the receiving window, grabbed up his coat, and followed Gwen outside, that Braeden had time to think of Rachel.

Dear God, please keep her from harm. I have no idea where Worthington has put her, but I can only pray it's far from this resort. He again lifted Gwen in his arms. Lightning flashed in the distance, and Braeden felt only a small amount of relief to see that the storm was bypassing them. The rain might actually have put out the flames.

Yet instead of a welcome rain, the downdraft of the thunderstorm served instead to tear apart the delicate electrical lines and to stir up the flames that consumed Casa Grande. Seeing the destruction before him, Braeden wondered silently if the fire would be contained to the resort. After all, there were plenty of other buildings close enough to catch fire, and if they did, it might well spread to the entire town.

Looking down at the woman he carried, Braeden quickly realized Gwen had fainted. She must have suffered great terror at having been trapped by the blaze. He couldn't imagine what had happened to put her in that position, nor how she might have broken her leg. Carrying her away from the building and back around to the front of the resort, Braeden came upon a shocking sight. Half-dressed hotel guests of every age and size stood staring in dumbfounded silence as Casa Grande burned. Mothers tried to comfort children while the men went to help try to control the flames. No one even seemed to notice the storm in the distance or the wind. They were completely mesmerized by the conflagration before them.

A small gathering of volunteer fire fighters were present

with their two-horse pump and tank. It wouldn't begin to put a dent in the fire, nor would the bucket brigade lined up between the stream and the resort. The fire was hopelessly out of control.

Searching for a place to take Gwen, Braeden noticed Dr. Krier was already attending several people by the fountain. Someone had thoughtfully brought several lanterns and blankets to aid him in the process, and several of the townswomen were helping him deal with the injured. Braeden moved through the people to take Gwen to where the doctor worked.

"She may have a broken leg," he told Dr. Krier as the man's expression silently inquired.

"I don't know if she's received any burns," Braeden continued as Gwen moaned softly, "but she's definitely in pain."

"I'll see to her," Krier replied. "Are there any others? Anyone else inside?"

Braeden felt bile in his throat and pushed it down. "Ivy Brooks was trapped in the kitchen. I couldn't get to her."

The doctor nodded and turned his attention to Gwen just as someone shouted that sparks had apparently set the stables on fire. Braeden quickly remembered Worthington and Tomas and made a mad dash, along with several of Casa Grande's stable hands, for the building. If they were to die, it would be his fault for tying them there without hope of escape.

He found them just where he'd left them. Tomas was wide-eyed and fearful, but Worthington seemed to have slipped into his own world. He was muttering something about a ship and wondering what time they would dock.

"I have to move you," Braeden said, quickly mastering the knots he'd tied. "The wind has carried sparks to the stable. I wouldn't be surprised if the whole town burned down!"

He yanked them to their feet and pushed them toward the

door. "If I had time, I'd just move you on to the jail, but there are still others to consider."

"You have no right to keep me here," Worthington said in a strangely calm manner. "My ship is awaiting my arrival."

Braeden knew the man was either losing his mind or the shock of the fire had confused him. Either way, he didn't care. He only wanted to know where Rachel was, and if he had to beat it out of the man, he would get his answer.

Chapter 28

"It's too soon," Reg muttered over and over. He asked Braeden for the time, but before Braeden could respond he continued ranting. "I didn't have time to see to everything. It's too soon. I didn't do it."

Braeden directed him, along with Tomas, toward the bridge at Morita Falls. He thought this to be as safe a place as any to position the men. Here he could secure them to the structure and keep them out of harm's way, and then he would be free to go in search of Rachel.

"The power station," Reg said and muttered the phrase over and over. He looked at the sad little building beside the falls, the waterwheel still churning. "Mine . . . the power station."

"What is he talking about?" Braeden questioned Tomas.

"I don't know, señor. He's been talking loco ever since you tied us up."

Braeden reached the bridge and pushed Worthington back against the railing. "Where is Rachel? You must tell me now."

Reg looked at him with a blank stare. "It's all mine," he said. "All mine."

Braeden shook him. "Look, Worthington, I'm giving you just one chance to tell me the truth. That fire is going to destroy everything in its path. You have to tell me where Rachel is so that I can keep her from dying in the fire."

"I will miss my ship," Reg firmly stated as if his senses had suddenly returned to him. Then he began mumbling. "Water . . . the fire . . . power station."

"What's with the power station?" Braeden questioned, looking at Tomas. "Is there something that interests him?"

Tomas nodded. "We put some of the stolen goods there. He had me choose three places. We put some of the stuff under the bandstand. Then some of it went to the power station and some to a cave down below the falls."

Braeden began to think about the things Reg had said. It didn't make sense, but what did was that Reginald Worthington knew where Rachel was. He had put her somewhere. Somewhere for safekeeping—just like the stolen goods.

"Tomas, do you think it's possible that Mr. Worthington took Rachel to one of those places? I mean, were the areas big enough to hide a woman and keep her from being discovered?"

"Sí," Tomas replied. "The bandstand is not very big, but the power station has much room underground and the cave is far away and very big."

Braeden felt the first bit of encouragement. "Where is the cave? I'll check it out."

"The cave is that way," Tomas pointed down the side of the stream, "But, señor, I can find it in the dark. You can trust me. I promise I no run away. I may be a thief, but I would not do anything to hurt Miss Taylor. She was very good to me. Please let me help you."

Braeden nodded and began untying the boy. "You go to the cave and I'll take the powerhouse. How do I get to this underground room?"

"There is a trapdoor on the far side. A ladder will take you down there."

"All right. You go to the cave and if Rachel is there, bring her back. If she's hurt, stay with her, and I'll come looking for you. Do you understand?"

"Sí," Tomas replied and took off running down the path that ran parallel to the powerhouse. It took only a moment for the boy to disappear from sight.

Braeden took one last glance at Reg, who seemed completely enthralled with the fire. Turning back around to face Casa Grande, Braeden could see that the entire front section of the hotel had flames fanning out from every window. He looked quickly to the stables, which were now also engulfed in the blaze.

"The pool house and sheds are on fire!" someone shouted. "Looks like the wind might carry it to the entire town."

This caused shrieks of alarm and sent a rush of people toward the bridge. Braeden backed up as the townspeople hurried back to their own homes to save what they could and be prepared to fight the fire as it spread through the town.

"The powerhouse is on fire!" the station manager yelled, running up from the path.

This announcement sent a rippling shock through Braeden. If Rachel was there, she was now in serious peril. He left Reg tied to the bridge and pushed his way through the onslaught of townsfolk.

He opened the door to the station, grateful that the electricity still illuminated the small building. Not seeing any visible signs of fire, Braeden took no chance on the manager having been given over to a case of nerves. He moved quickly to the back of the room, searching through the mechanisms of belts, pulleys, gears, and machinery.

"It has to be here!" he said aloud.

Growing more and more frantic as the smell of smoke seemed to permeate everything around him, Braeden ripped at any object in his way and thrust it aside. Finally he spied the trapdoor and threw it open. He started down the ladder, then felt the tickle of something against his face. Reaching up to swat aside what he presumed to be a cobweb, Braeden's hand fell on the light cord. He pulled at it, silently thanking God when light flooded the room.

He jumped the final few rungs just as Rachel's cries reached his ears.

"Help me! Please get me out of here!"

"I'm here, Rachel!" he called, searching through the maze of goods and stored materials to find her tied to a small cot. Seeing her there, so pale and frightened, Braeden lost no time in working the ropes.

"I knew you would come for me," she said softly, her face taking on an expression of relief. "I knew you hadn't gone away as Reg told me."

"No," Braeden answered, freeing her feet. "I would never leave you."

"I know that now," she said.

He looked deep into her eyes. "You finally trust me, don't you?"

She nodded. "I will always trust you."

He pulled her up off the bed and turned her around to untie her hands. "Look, Casa Grande is burning to the ground, and this powerhouse is on fire. We have to hurry or we might not make it."

She gripped him tightly. "I love you, Braeden. I've never stopped."

He smiled and pressed a quick kiss upon her lips. "I know that. Why do you think I came here in the first place? Once I knew you were here, my only thought was of winning you back. But right now we have to get out of this building."

He pushed her ahead of him and maneuvered them back

to the ladder. He worried that Rachel might not have the strength after her ordeal to climb the rungs, but she surprised him by hiking her skirts and scurrying up them in no time at all. He followed behind, anxious to be out in the open and away from what was no doubt about to become another inferno.

He had no sooner emerged through the trapdoor when he noticed that Rachel had come to a dead stop. He found himself following her gaze to where the entire west wall seemed to instantly burst into flames.

"Come on!" he yelled, dragging her with him to the front door.

They burst out into the cool, damp air and raced up the path away from the station house. Panting for breath and fearful of what could have happened, Rachel collapsed into Braeden's arms, weeping softly and clinging to him as though she might well perish if she let go.

"Shh, it's all right now," he told her. "You're safe."

"I was so afraid. I kept thinking that Reg was actually going to get away with taking me to England. He said we would be married and that I . . ."

Braeden pulled her away and shook his head. "You don't have to talk about it. It's not important. He can't hurt you anymore."

"Where is he?" she asked, glancing over her shoulder and seeing Casa Grande for the first time. "Did he get out of the fire?"

"Yes," Braeden assured her. "I have him tied to the Morita Falls bridge."

"You do? But why?"

"It's a long, long story, one that I will tell you some long winter's night when we are curled up in front of a fireplace instead of a burning hotel. Suffice it to say, the man will be going to jail for more than kidnapping you."

Rachel shook her head and watched the resort scene in fascination. "All of that money—all that potential. And now it's gone, just that quick." She turned back to Braeden. "I don't understand. What happened? I thought I heard thunder. Did lightning strike the hotel?"

"No," Braeden replied, pulling her close and walking her farther away from the power station, which by now was completely ablaze. "Ivy Brooks set the fire, although Reg had plans to do the same. It's part of that long story, and it has to do with fire insurance money and some swindle that Worthington managed to get in the middle of."

"He told me you were already married to Ivy. He said that Mrs. Needlemeier was dead and that Ivy needed you and you complied."

Braeden rubbed her shoulder, letting his touch trail down her arms until he took hold of her hands. "But you didn't believe him."

"No," Rachel replied.

"Not even after what you witnessed at the Needlemeier mansion?"

Rachel gave him the briefest smile. "I knew it was all Ivy. I knew it even when I ran from the house. Still, I couldn't bear what had happened. Then after I calmed down, I realized that you needed my support, my trust. I knew you were not to blame, and I vowed not to let the circumstances destroy our love."

"But you never came back. I suppose Worthington caught up with you."

"No, actually, I found some men working to put stolen goods under the bandstand. I confronted them," she said, smiling sheepishly. "I realize now that was incredibly foolish."

He chuckled. "To say the least."

"Anyway, they gagged and carried me down here to the power station. They tied me up and, I figured, left me to die. Next thing I know, Reg appears. I hoped he was there to rescue me, but he quickly made it clear that he had other plans. He . . . he . . ." she shuddered and lowered her gaze to the ground.

Braeden lifted her chin gently. "It doesn't matter anymore what he did to you. No matter what he did. Do you understand?"

Rachel's expression instantly changed, but before she could speak, cries rose up from the crowd.

"The Needlemeier mansion is on fire!"

"So's the school!"

"We should go see what we can do to help," Braeden said, pulling Rachel with him. "I doubt there's anything anyone can do, but it's worth a try."

"What about Jeffery and Simone? What about my girls? Are they safe?" she asked, holding tightly to his arm as they joined the mass of resort guests.

"They're all safe, as far as I know," Braeden replied. "I pulled Gwen from the fire myself. She may have a broken leg and some burns, but I think she'll be fine." He paused, then answered flatly, "Ivy didn't make it."

"Oh," Rachel said and nodded. Her sense of purpose seemed to be resurfacing. "You do what you must. I should see to my girls and make sure they are safe."

Braeden refused to let her go. "I'll help you. We'll move them down the road, and if Jeffery and Simone's place is safe from the fire, maybe they can stay there until we see what else there is to do."

"Dr. Krier probably needs help," Rachel said, letting Braeden lead the way. "My girls and I could help with those needs."

"I think most everyone got out safely," Braeden told her, "but I'm sure the good doctor could always use a spare set of hands."

They came to the pallet where Gwen lay. She was conscious now and the pain that filled her eyes caused Braeden and Rachel to exchange a glance of worry.

"Gwen, I'm so glad you're safe," Rachel said, kneeling down beside the younger woman.

"Mr. Parker saved my life. I was trapped by the fire. He tried to save Ivy, but she wouldn't come with us."

"He saved my life too," Rachel told her. "Has the doctor taken care of you?"

Gwen nodded. "He says that my leg doesn't look to be broken, just badly sprained. I have to stay off of it, but otherwise I'll be fine."

"No burns?" Rachel asked softly.

"No," Gwen answered. "Mr. Parker got to me in time. He couldn't save Ivy," she repeated as if it was necessary to make certain Rachel understood. "She wouldn't listen to him. She wouldn't come with us. It's not Mr. Parker's fault."

Rachel nodded. "I know. Look, we're going to get the girls rounded up and moved down to the O'Donnell house. That is, if the fire isn't headed that direction." She straightened and looked at Braeden. "Can we get a carriage to transport the injured?"

"I'll see to it," Braeden replied, proud of Rachel's ability to forget her own ordeal in order to help her girls. "You stay here and I'll talk to the doctor."

Rachel watched Braeden disappear into the crowd before kneeling back down beside Gwen. "I'm going to see to the others, but I'll be right back. We'll not leave you here, so don't be afraid that we'll forget you." Gwen smiled weakly and nodded.

Rachel spied a couple of the girls standing not five feet away. Calling to them, she instructed them to find the other Harvey Girls and bring them to her. The girls seemed relieved for something to do and quickly set out to fulfill Rachel's request. Within a few moments twenty-three girls stood in front of Rachel. Some were dressed in their uniforms, others were wrapped in their robes. All of them wore expressions of fear and confusion.

"We're going to help Dr. Krier with any wounded, and if he doesn't need our help, then we'll set up in the depot and try to offer whatever assistance we can to the townspeople." One by one the girls nodded. This information seemed to give them new purpose. "Gwen has been injured and cannot walk. Mr. Parker has gone for a carriage and to speak with the doctor. I'm sure we'll have our hands full, and I'll require each of you to do your duty as if you were serving Mr. Harvey himself."

"That won't be necessary," a voice sounded from behind Rachel.

She turned and smiled to find Fred Harvey standing there, dressed impeccably as usual. "Hello, Mr. Harvey, I was just rounding my girls up to offer community assistance."

"An admirable idea and one I wholeheartedly support. There are supplies at the depot and more due in with the morning freight. If the fire doesn't destroy it, we should be in good order."

Rachel nodded and looked past him toward town. "Do you suppose the fire will spread that far?"

"I have no way of knowing. With the direction of the wind, we may find it contained to the southern part of town. And if the storm would move out or die down altogether, then the wind might ease as well. Only time will tell."

She nodded and caught sight of Casa Grande. "Such a waste."

"Yes, indeed," Harvey replied. "But it could have been much worse. The loss of life appears minimal and instead of hundreds being burned, we have only a handful of injuries. It seems Mr. Parker and the marshal were able to spread the alarm quickly and efficiently."

"It's so sad to see the dream die," Rachel said, meeting his compassionate gaze.

"The dreams never die so long as the dreamer still lives," Harvey said, smiling. "We will dream another dream and rebuild, or we'll go elsewhere. It's not the end of anything, just a postponement."

She admired his positive spirit and decided then and there that if Mr. Harvey, who had so much time and energy devoted to Casa Grande, could face the disaster with a hopeful attitude, she could certainly do no less.

Turning from the man, she rallied her girls. "You've all heard what Mr. Harvey just said. We have a job to do, and a Harvey Girl must always be prepared to serve the public with a smile and an encouraging word. Let us be to our tasks."

Chapter 29

The rains finally came, but they were too late to save most of Morita. The southern portions of town, including the church, the school, many businesses, and even the fire department, all fell victim to the blaze. The depot remained intact, as did several other buildings that were quickly converted into temporary housing for the resort guests. Those who were left in their bed-clothes were found something to wear, and before the morning train moved in from Lamy, near Santa Fe, and farther up the line, a telegraphed plea went out from Fred Harvey. Informing the telegraph operator in Lamy and Albuquerque that the resort had burned down, he asked for extra blankets, clothes, and anything else that might help aid the residents of Morita.

With the morning freight came a substantial amount of food and other goods, and only a few hours later a special Santa Fe passenger service was brought in to move the victims of the resort fire to Albuquerque, where they could recover from their shock before moving on to other destinations.

Rachel took up residence with Simone and Jeffery while her girls were disbursed, at Fred Harvey's discretion, throughout the town. Braeden took his leave of Rachel once he'd seen her safely to the O'Donnells, since he needed to deliver Reginald Worthington and Tomas to the marshal. Rachel understood, but she hated to see him go. She had worried about ever seeing him again when Reg had refused to free her. Now she didn't worry about whether or not he'd come back, but rather, how things would be for them now that this tragedy had taken place in their lives.

"You are awfully deep in thought," Simone said, coming into the front room.

Rachel stood at the window, staring out at the only part of town that remained. "I can't help but wonder about my future."

"I know what you mean," Simone replied. "I don't know what we'll do. I mean, Jeffery still has his job with the Santa Fe, but there may be no need for someone of his caliber to remain here in Morita. Especially if Mr. Harvey and the railroad decide against rebuilding."

"Is that what they're thinking?" Rachel questioned, moving away from the window with a slight limp.

"I think the doctor should look at your leg," Simone stated. "In fact, I insist. Now, are you going to make me drag you over there or do I need to run Jeffery down and get his help?"

"I just twisted it," Rachel said. "Reg had me tied by the ankles. I tried to get free and during the process I made matters worse. I didn't even notice it until after all of the excitement died down, so it can't be all that bad."

"Nevertheless, you aren't a doctor and neither am I. Dr. Krier is just across the street, so let's have you hobble over there and have him look at it."

Rachel looked at her friend and laughed at the look of sheer determination on her face. "All right. I'll go see the doctor, but you needn't accompany me. You have to take care of yourself and that baby. Whether or not we have a job to go back to in Morita or a place to live, you and Jeffery have a wonderful future to look forward to." She hoped the words didn't sound envious. She couldn't have been happier for Simone, but at the same time, she couldn't help longing for her own life to come into proper order.

"Don't forget your shawl," Simone admonished. "It's very chilly this morning. Jeffery wonders if there won't be an early winter this year."

"Could be," Rachel said, retrieving a navy blue shawl her mother had crocheted for her. "If Braeden comes back . . ." she said, opening the door and glancing with a hopeful eye down the road.

"If Braeden comes back, I'll tell him what he wants to hear. That you finally went to the doctor and that he's invited to stay for lunch."

Rachel smiled. "Thank you, Simone. You're a good friend."

Half an hour later, Dr. Krier finally had a chance to look at Rachel's ankle. He gave her some ointment to help with the rope burns and advised her to stay off her feet for a day or two and keep her foot propped up. She came out of his examination office telling him that she would do what she could to rest, while reminding him that as the woman in charge of the Harvey Girls, she had certain responsibilities that needed to be attended to.

"She'll rest," Braeden said quite seriously.

Rachel looked up, surprised to see him standing near the front door. She smiled and felt a rush of warmth come to her cheeks as he winked at her and came to help her.

"I'll see to it that she goes to bed and stays there, if I have to sit on her."

Dr. Krier chuckled. "I'd hardly think that necessary, but then again, I don't know her as well as you obviously do."

"She's a stubborn one," Braeden said, reaching out to Rachel.

Rachel took hold of his arm and was surprised to see him grimace. "What's wrong?"

"It's nothing," he said.

"Oh really." She put more pressure on his arm and watched his face pale. "I don't believe this. You're hurt and you didn't even tell me."

"Come on in here," Dr. Krier instructed.

Braeden rolled his eyes. "I'll be fine. There are a great many more folks who need your treatments. I'm not that bad off."

Rachel put her hands on her hips. "Braeden Parker, do you mean to disobey the doctor's direct order?"

"It's just that—"

"It's just nothing," Rachel said, pushing him in the direction of the examination room. "You have no excuse that I want to hear. Now get in there."

Dr. Krier laughed at the confrontation between them while Braeden rolled his eyes and gave up the fight. He let Rachel hobble in behind him and help him take off his coat. Once this was done, Rachel could see for herself where the sleeve had been burned. Braeden tried not to grimace as he rolled up what was left of the sleeve, revealing a rather nasty-looking burn.

Shrugging, he smiled sheepishly at Rachel. "I didn't even know it was there until this morning."

Rachel nodded. "And you were worried about my ankle."

He grinned and lowered his voice. "From now on, I intend to worry about every part of you, Miss Taylor. Not just the ankles."

She felt her cheeks grow warm again. Looking away, Rachel hoped to regain a portion of her dignity by changing the subject. "So what will happen to Reg and Tomas?"

"The marshal's going to see about getting Tomas off easy. He figures the boy was easily persuaded given the crisis at—

hey, that hurts!" he declared, forgetting how his words might affect Rachel.

She hurried to his side. "Is it all that bad?"

Dr. Krier grunted and continued working. "It might not have been so troublesome if you'd taken care of it first thing. You've got all sorts of dirt and bits of cloth imbedded here. It's going to smart as I clean it out, but if I don't, it'll probably get infected."

"Do what you have to, Doc. I'll be a good patient," Braeden told him.

Rachel tried not to look worried as Dr. Krier continued working on the ugly wound. Braeden seemed to sense her concern and reached out to touch her hand.

"It'll be all right. You'll see."

She swallowed hard and nodded. "I know."

"Look, if you don't have the stomach for this, you can wait in the other room. I'll walk you back to the O'Donnells' when Doc finishes up."

"No, I'm fine. I guess I just keep thinking how much worse it could have been."

"It's amazing that more folks weren't killed in the blaze. That thing went up like kindling. It didn't even seem to matter that the exterior was made of brick," the doctor said as he finished picking at the oozing burn. He went to a cabinet and brought back a bottle of solution, which he promptly poured onto the wound.

Braeden's hand tightened painfully hard around Rachel's hand, but she refused to even so much as wince. He seemed to realize quickly what he was doing and, even though his face grew white and perspiration formed on his brow, he loosened his grip and apologized.

"Sorry. I wasn't expecting that."

"That's the worst of it," Dr. Krier said, replacing the

bottle in the cabinet and opening a drawer below. "I'll bandage it up and you can be on your way."

Rachel sighed with relief when the job was finally completed. Braeden asked about the bill, and it was only then that Rachel remembered she'd not paid the doctor either.

"I'll need the tally for mine as well," she told the doctor.

"I'll see to hers," Braeden replied. "She's my responsibility now."

The doctor raised a brow and leaned in close to Braeden. "So you've asked her to be your wife, eh?"

"Not yet, but I'm working on it. I would have probably taken care of the matter had you not waylaid me here."

Rachel looked at them both in disbelief. What was Braeden thinking, discussing their future in such a casual manner?

The doctor just laughed, told Braeden the total, and waited while he counted the money into his hand. Rachel stood speechless as Braeden pulled on his singed and sooty coat and escorted her to the door.

"Come along, Miss Taylor, there are some matters that we need to discuss." He looped his good arm around her waist and pulled her close. "Lean on me rather than putting your weight on that ankle."

"You tend to your arm, and I'll tend to my ankle," Rachel countered.

"I rather hoped you'd take care of my arm," he said as they stepped onto the front porch. "Along with the rest of me. And while you were doing that, I'd take care of you."

Rachel looked up at him rather hesitantly. "Are you sure that's what you want?"

He grew very serious. "I'm positive. What about you?"

Rachel felt her heart flutter. Marriage to Braeden Parker was what she'd dreamed of for over six years. Marriage, children, a life lived with love.

"Hey there, Braeden!" Marshal Schmidt called from the street.

Rachel felt a sense of frustration wash over her, but instead of showing it, she turned to greet the lawman with a smile.

"What's up, Larry?" Braeden questioned.

"Just thought you'd like to know I found Smith. He was hightailing it off to Albuquerque on horseback, but I caught up to him. Seems he doesn't know much about horses and managed to team himself up with an ornery critter that didn't cotton to the saddle."

"Probably got one of the carriage horses," Braeden said with a smile. "So what about the others?"

"I let Tomas go on his pledge to show up for the trial. I have your Englishman ranting and babbling on one side of the cell, while Smith is muttering and cursing on the other side. Guess if we're going to have this kind of activity, I'm going to have to build a bigger jail."

Braeden shook his head. "From the looks of this mess, I'm not so sure it'd be worth the effort."

"Yeah, I kind of figured that myself," the marshal said, glancing back over the town. "I might just be out of a job once everything is said and done." He seemed to consider this for a moment, then tipped his hat. "Well, just thought you'd like to know about Smith. I've had Mr. O'Donnell wire the necessary folks, and now it's just a matter of getting all the facts in place. Oh, and I talked with Miss Carson. She told me how you tried your best to save Miss Brooks. I don't think there'll be any problem with folks assuming otherwise."

Braeden nodded. "That's good news.

"I'll be seein' you around," Schmidt said, moving off in the direction of the depot.

"Do you suppose anyone would have actually thought you

capable of leaving Ivy in that fire?" Rachel asked.

Braeden shrugged. "Sometimes folks believe whatever they want to—whatever seems to fit their logic at the time. Facts don't always matter."

Rachel felt the full weight of his words. "Of course, you're right. I guess no one knows that better than I do, especially after what I did to you—to us."

Braeden held her close and maneuvered her down the steps. They walked in silence as they made their way back to the O'Donnell house. Pausing on the back steps, Braeden turned Rachel in his arms. "That's all in the past. I want us to start fresh. I want us to share a complete trust in each other, no matter what the circumstances."

Rachel nodded, losing herself in his steely blue eyes. "I want that too. I'm so sorry for the way I wronged you. I'm so sorry for the wasted years. I put myself into a self-imposed prison, then prayed to find a key to let myself out. I was very foolish, and I can only hope that you will forgive me."

Braeden raised her hands to his lips and kissed her fingers. "You could never do anything so bad that I would refuse to forgive you. I love you, Rachel. I always have and I always will. Nothing about the past matters anymore. Only the future. I want us to be together always, and I'm hoping you want the same thing."

Rachel's heart felt as though it might pound right through her chest. Touching his cheek gently, she saw all the longing in her soul reflected in his eyes. She drew a deep breath and opened her mouth to answer, when Braeden's proposal was interrupted for a second time.

"Braeden! Rachel!"

It was Jeffery O'Donnell, and Rachel could only sigh, letting her breath out in an anticlimactic way. "Hello, Jeffery," she said, wishing she could say good-bye instead.

"Jeffery," Braeden said, his voice edged with the slightest hint of irritation.

Jeffery looked at them both for a moment. "Am I interrupting?"

"Yes," Rachel replied quickly. "Yes, you are, Mr. O'Donnell, and I'd appreciate it if you would go inside and keep your wife company. I don't need her to come out here as well."

Jeffery seemed a bit taken aback by Rachel's instruction and Braeden just laughed.

Leaning over to Jeffery, Braeden whispered loudly enough for everyone to hear, "I've asked her a rather important question twice now, and if I don't get an answer the third time, I'm not going to ask again."

Jeffery couldn't contain his smile. "I see."

"So unless you want to be in very big trouble with me—and with Simone," Rachel stated flatly, "you'll do as I asked."

Just then the back door opened and Simone stared openmouthed at the trio. "What's going on?"

Jeffery pushed his way past Rachel and Braeden and opened the screen door. Taking Simone in hand he said, "I'll tell you later."

"But—" Simone protested as Jeffery pulled her inside and promptly closed the door behind them.

Rachel looked up at Braeden and met his amused expression. "Now, before any more interruptions come . . ." Inside the house Simone let out a shriek, causing them both to laugh out loud.

"Well, now you have to say yes," Braeden teased, pulling Rachel back into his arms. "No doubt Mrs. O'Donnell is already making plans."

She carefully tried to avoid hurting his arm and maneuvered to wrap her arms around Braeden's neck. "So you were going to ask me something for the third time."

He grinned. "Okay, but this is it."

She nodded. "Absolutely."

"Marry me, Rachel. Promise to love me forever, as I will love you."

She sighed and answered in a whisper, "I will marry you, Braeden Parker, and I will love you forever, with all my heart."

He lowered his mouth to hers, touching her lips gently. She felt his hands in her hair and thought that nothing had ever felt so right or so good. Melting against him, reveling in the very strength he emitted, Rachel felt as though she had finally come home. The passion she had buried within her for six long years surfaced in that kiss. She wanted nothing more in life than to marry Braeden Parker and be his wife. And she wanted it very soon because she had already wasted a good portion of her life running from the love she felt.

Pulling away, Braeden looked at her very seriously. "Can we get married soon? Like maybe even tomorrow?"

Rachel shook her head. "No, Mr. Parker. I will not marry you tomorrow." She laughed at the stunned look on his face. "Unless, of course, Pastor Johnson can't do the job today."

Braeden grinned from ear to ear. "You're supposed to be off of that ankle, but I'll hit the road and find Johnson, wherever he may be. And whether he has the time or not—I guarantee you, he'll marry us."

Rachel watched him jump over the side of the steps and hurry off in the direction of town. Smiling to herself she looked heavenward. "Thank you," she whispered. "Thank you for making my dreams come true, even in the wake of such devastation."

Opening the door, Rachel hobbled inside to find Jeffery

and Simone waiting rather impatiently.

"So what happened?" Simone asked, looking behind Rachel. "Where's Braeden?"

"I sent him away."

"You what?!" Jeffery and Simone questioned at once.

Rachel laughed. "You two are worse than a couple of mother hens. I sent him off to get the preacher. We're going to have a wedding."

"Now?" Simone questioned. "Here?"

"Well, seeing how the church burned down, and how I have no desire to get married at the saloon or the depot, or even Doc's house, I figured this would be the best place."

Simone instantly flew into action. "Well, come on, then. We have to get you ready. You'll need a dress and we have to fix your hair."

Rachel laughed and let Simone lead her away.

Epilogue

Two hours after their impromptu wedding beside Morita Falls, Rachel and Braeden found themselves in a private railroad car, courtesy of Fred Harvey.

"It seems the least I can do after all you've done for us, Miss Taylor—Mrs. Parker," Fred Harvey said as the conductor called the final "all aboard."

Rachel threw a small bouquet of wild flowers from the platform and laughed with joy as Gwen Carson, seated on the back of a two-wheeled cart, caught them.

The train gave a lurch forward and then another. The jerky movement caused Rachel to grab hold of the railing as Braeden took a possessive hold of her waist. They waved good-bye as the train pulled out of the station and headed north toward Lamy.

Rachel couldn't help but notice the blackened destruction of the town as they passed by. In the background she could barely make out the charred remains of Casa Grande. Shaking her head, she turned away from it and let Braeden draw her into their home on the rails.

"I'd say we made out pretty well, Mrs. Parker," Braeden declared, motioning to the room.

"It was kind of Mr. Harvey to offer us this car," she said, suddenly feeling very shy. It was the first time they had been alone, truly alone.

Sensing her change of mood, Braeden drew her into his arms. "You look absolutely terrified, Mrs. Parker. Our future isn't that bleak. We may be temporarily unemployed and without a home or wardrobe, but it could be much worse."

She shook her head. "Yes," she whispered, reaching her hand up to his face. "I could have lost you in the fire."

"Or I could have lost you to Worthington."

She laughed. "No. There was never a real chance of that. Once he had me, he didn't seem to know what he wanted to do with me anyway. He never even touched me."

Something akin to relief seemed to wash over Braeden's expression. "I'm so glad. I would have hated for him to have hurt you." He put his hand over hers and pressed both to his cheek.

The uneven rocking of the tracks seemed to ease with a rhythmic flow as the train moved up to full speed. Rachel reached up to pull Braeden's face closer to her own.

"He only inconvenienced me," Rachel said seriously. "But losing you would have devastated me."

"You'll never lose me, Rachel," Braeden said before his lips caressed her mouth.

The future held many questions for them, but their love was the one thing that Rachel knew she could count on. Never again would whispered lies come between them. She would turn to truth and trust, and she would count on God's direction for their happiness. A long-awaited and hoped-for happiness that had come like an unexpected gift.

As Braeden lifted her in his arms, Rachel buried her face against his neck and sighed contentedly. She remembered a verse in the Bible about perfect love casting out fear and thought it very true. God had given her a perfect love through

His Son, a love so sure and so complete that her spirit could never want for more. And then God blessed her with a perfect love in the form of a man named Braeden Parker.